Missing Pieces

THE JAMESONS OF COYOTE RIDGE
Hot Chocolate Wishes
Rough & Dirty

AUSTIN ARROWS
Rush
Kaufman

CLUB DESTINY
Conviction
Temptation
Addicted
Seduction
Infatuation
Captivated
Devotion
Perception
Entrusted
Adored
Distraction
Forevermore

DEAD HEAT RANCH
Boots Optional
Betting on Grace
Overnight Love
Jared *(a crossover novel)*

DEVIL'S BEND
Chasing Dreams
Vanishing Dreams

MISPLACED HALOS
Protected in Darkness
Salvation in Darkness
Bound in Darkness

Missing Pieces

Brantley Walker: Off the Books, 12

NICOLE EDWARDS

MISSING PIECES

Brantley Walker: Off the Books, 12

COVER DETAILS:

Image: © tevarak11 (159358902) | 123RF.com | *Design:* © Nicole Edwards Limited

INTERIOR DETAILS:

Formatting: Nicole Edwards Limited

ISBN: (ebook) 978-1-64418-106-5 | (paperback) 978-1-64418-107-2 | (audio) 978-1-64418-108-9

Missing Pieces Blurb:

Brantley Walker and Reese Tavoularis are plunging headfirst into the satisfying chaos of married life. Although their preference would be to sit on a beach enjoying umbrella drinks for a week, the honeymoon will have to wait. With Jessica James treating her hospital stay like an all-inclusive spa getaway—complete with bed rest and boredom—Brantley, Reese, Baz, and the rest of the team are bracing themselves for the inevitable twists and turns ahead.

Meanwhile, Atticus James shares not only the same last name as JJ but also the irritation that comes with monotony. He's spending his days sifting through partner applications, waiting for the day he'll see some of the action. Just when he thinks his excitement levels have hit rock bottom, Brantley hands him his first case assignment. Only he's not sure he wants it once he learns what it is. But if suffering is the name of the game, he can think of no better partner in misery and mayhem than Slade Elliott.

While Atticus and Slade are busy with their detective shenanigans, the rest of the team isn't just tuning in to their favorite podcast; they're about to dive headfirst into a live episode of *Havoc Your Way* when the podcast's host stops by. But Simon Jennings isn't there to sign autographs. He's dropping in with a case that veers dangerously close to home, blending the bizarre with the familiar, as he seeks their expertise to untangle a web that's both outside their skill set and uncomfortably personal.

This book is dedicated to the unexpected, the unpredictable.

Just when you think you've seen it all,
another twist awaits around the bend.

Dear reader,

If you're keeping up with the Walker universe and reading the books in the order outlined on my website, you'll want to keep in mind that this book takes place after *Violet,* in the Walkers of Coyote Ridge series. While it isn't necessary to read *Violet,* you do meet several new characters who appear in this book, some of them become an integral part of the task force.

Also, I should mention that the "something big" I promised was coming… Well, it's here.

Thanks for reading!

Nicole Edwards

Chapter One

"I'M SURE A LOT OF PEOPLE WOULD be fond of hospitals if they were all like this," Brantley Walker mused as he strolled down the long corridor toward the labor and delivery wing. Although he'd visited at least once a day for the past nine days, it still caught him off guard how nice this place was.

"Yeah?" Reese Tavoularis, the man Brantley had married nine short days ago, didn't sound convinced.

"Shit. If you could be taken care of in a place like this"—he gestured toward the nurse's station, which held two child-size vases of fresh flowers, giving the sterile white space some life—"Why wouldn't you?"

"You and I both know those flowers came from Wes."

Brantley had figured as much. It made sense that Wesley Buchanan, grandfather-to-be, would ply the nurses in this wing with gifts simply because he could. Rumor was he'd catered in breakfast, lunch, and dinner for the staff in this wing at least four times in the past week. The man was generous like that. Not to mention, fucking loaded.

As they neared the door to JJ's birthing suite, Brantley's shoulders tensed. "I really hope she's in a good mood."

"I'm sure she's not," Reese said with a smirk. "But she wouldn't be JJ otherwise."

True. These days, his best friend, Jessica James, a.k.a. JJ, wasn't known for her charming personality. He didn't fault her for it, really, but it also didn't make him look forward to these daily trips. Since he'd been through worse—in the Navy when he was buried under a building and nearly died—he opted to suck it up. She wouldn't be in this hospital forever.

Taking a deep breath in, Brantley rapped his knuckles on the door with his exhale. There was no response right away, so they waited. He was about to knock again when he heard JJ say, "Get your asses in here already."

Nope. No good mood today either.

Squaring his shoulders, he pressed the handle lever to open the door. He pushed it open slowly, revealing the enormous suite where JJ was riding out the last days of her pregnancy—however many there might be.

"Hey, Tesha," JJ greeted, smiling down at their canine partner. These days, Tesha went along for the ride anytime they left the house. "I'm so glad *you* could make it."

Brantley fought the urge to laugh but instead rolled his eyes. *Passive-aggressive much?*

"We brought you somethin'," he told his best friend.

There was a barely-there hint of a smile on her face as she eyed the takeout bag Reese was carrying.

"It's about time," JJ grumbled, a dark storm cloud in the otherwise soothing gray room.

"Good mornin' to you, too," Reese told her as he walked the forty miles from the door to the bed to give her the breakfast they'd picked up on their way in.

And fine, maybe forty miles was a bit of a stretch, but the space was enormous. Large enough to hold a king-size bed, a long, glossy white dresser mounted to the wall, a bathtub that would hold at least four people, two wall-mounted televisions, two nightstands (on wheels to get them out of the way if needed), as well as a sitting area that was about the size of their living room. Oh, and there was also a private bathroom that put Brantley's to shame.

At the moment, JJ was propped up in the big bed, half a dozen pillows keeping her in place, while the father-to-be, Sebastian Buchanan, a.k.a. Baz, was occupying the sitting area on the far side of the room, feet propped up, laptop resting on his thighs. Brantley got the feeling they didn't move much from where they were and probably wouldn't until the delivery.

"Do you share that thing with him?" Brantley asked, gesturing toward the bed and then over to Baz.

"Only when I have to." She flashed a smile.

Brantley had to wonder which was more comfortable: the bed or the chocolate-brown leather recliners? If it were him, he would likely choose the chairs since they were positioned to face a fifty-five-inch television currently playing a news channel with the volume all the way down.

Brantley jerked his chin at Baz. "Mornin'."

Baz's smile looked forced, but he managed a subtle chin jerk in response.

"He's in time out," JJ announced.

"Time out?" Brantley barked a laugh. "For what?"

"You want to tell them?" JJ asked, sounding far too much like Brantley's mother back when he'd been a wild and rambunctious kid and she spent most of her waking hours reprimanding him. No doubt he'd deserved it. He wasn't sure the same could be said for Baz, though.

Baz inhaled deeply, exhaled slowly. "Because I went to the gift shop and forgot to pick her up a package of the little chocolate donuts," he droned, his tone defeated.

"He got these," JJ said, lifting up a package of powdered donuts. The white ones that left a mess on your shirt and fingers when you tried to eat them.

"And those are bad, why?" Brantley was almost positive he'd seen JJ eating those little powdered circles before.

Her eyes narrowed, and he knew he'd said the wrong thing.

"Well, it's a good thing we got you these," Reese told her as he set the bag on the tray beside the bed.

"They're your favorite," Brantley noted.

She curled her lip, reaching for the bag. "No, my favorite is—" Her eyes popped wide. "Oh my God! These are—" Her gaze slammed into Reese. "How?"

Reese grinned. "I stopped by Batter & Bliss yesterday and asked Ramona if she'd make you a couple. She made 'em fresh this mornin'."

3

Tears rimmed JJ's lashes but didn't quite spill over as she stared lovingly at her breakfast. "Cronuts. And it's not even Saturday."

Brantley watched as JJ sniffled, wrapping the croissant-donut hybrid in a napkin as if it were some sort of rare delicacy.

In an effort to change the subject, Brantley wandered over to the large tub that sat in the corner of the room. It was shaped like a Jacuzzi, only there weren't any jets. Apparently, those were bad for pregnant women, which he'd learned the first time he made the mistake of asking about it.

"Get any use out of this thing yet?" He patted the edge of the tub, knowing what the answer was. If memory served, the tub was used for water births.

"No. And we won't if I have anything to say about it," JJ insisted.

Based on Baz's expression, that was a topic better left unexplored.

"Alrighty then." He looked around the room, trying to come up with something to say. He figured talking about the large, fully tiled bathroom with its shower built for forty would likely not go over any better than if he brought up the machines discreetly tucked away behind a curtain at the head of the bed. They were tracking things like heart rates and contractions, feeding the information directly to the nurses working out there with all those flowers.

JJ nibbled on her pastry. "What's on the agenda today?"

That was a loaded question if he'd ever heard one. But only because JJ's mood swings were strong enough to take a fully grown man out at the knees. He wasn't sure whether he should tell her the truth or shrug it off as though there wasn't much to do. Either way, she would likely blow a fuse or two.

Since it was inevitable, he opted for the truth.

"We're meeting with a coupla people."

With the cronut halfway to her mouth, JJ paused, her eyes narrowing, green sparks flickering in them.

"People?"

Brantley nodded.

"*People* people?"

He nodded again, wondering if those monitors she was hooked up to caused brain damage.

"What kinda people?"

"The human kind."

"For what?"

Confused, he said, "For what *what?*"

4

JJ's eyes narrowed again. "What are you meetin' them for?"

"Interviews," he blurted because he couldn't think of anything better.

Her gaze shifted across the room, landing on Baz briefly before swinging back and slamming into him. "Why didn't I know about this?"

Brantley looked at Reese, wishing marriage caused telepathy because at least then Reese would be able to answer his silent question: *What the hell is the correct answer to that?*

OH, SHIT.

Reese knew they were in trouble. Which, to be fair, wasn't really new. At least not since JJ was admitted to the hospital. He only wished he'd put some distance between himself and her before they revealed that tidbit of information.

"Uh-uh," JJ snapped when Reese attempted to take a step away from the bed. "Don't you dare."

He swore he heard Baz chuckling across the room, and he could only imagine the guy was thinking, *Better you than me.*

"Why are you meeting with more people? I thought you'd hired everyone already."

"We did," Brantley said.

JJ's eyes narrowed to slits.

Definitely not helping.

Brantley laughed. "Cool your jets, woman. We're just meetin' to talk. That's it."

Although her eyes remained pinned on Brantley, JJ relaxed a little. "About what?"

Reese stared at Brantley, wondering how he was going to talk his way out of this.

"To see if they'd be a good fit."

Okay. Not bad. Not exactly the truth, but not bad for a little white lie.

Granted, Reese didn't think it was a good idea to correct Brantley's statement. They were actually meeting with Simon Jennings and Archer Halligan, but only Archer was a potential hire. The conversation they'd have with Simon was what would likely set JJ off if she found out about it. But only because she would want to be in on it. And he honestly couldn't blame her since they usually kept her apprised of those things. Now that she was technically on leave, not to mention she was supposed to be resting and not stressing about work, they were tackling things without her input.

And yeah, now that he thought about it, that was likely one of the reasons for her bad mood.

"I promise, we won't talk about anything in depth unless you or Baz are there," Brantley said, attempting to defuse the situation.

"Promise?"

Reese grinned when Brantley canted his head to the side. "I said that already."

She puckered her lips in a pout. "I hate that I can't be there."

"You've got far more important things to worry about right now," Reese reminded her. "And since the task force can't run smoothly without you, we're as eager as you are for you to get back. But only after you and those babies are healthy."

JJ's expression softened, and a smile formed. She looked at Brantley. "How'd you get lucky enough to get this guy to marry you?"

"I can be persuasive," Brantley teased. "And now that we've got that cleared up, we're gonna have to get to HQ."

"I wish you could take me with you," JJ said, relaxing on the pillows. "I'm bored."

"Bored?" Reese asked. "You've got a laptop, an iPad, a Kindle, and a phone beside you. How can you *possibly* be bored?"

Before she could blast him for not understanding, Brantley spoke up.

"We might have some things for you to research later today or tomorrow. I'll be sure to send it your way."

Her eyes widened and glittered with hope. "You better."

Reese watched as Brantley walked around, coming to stand at the head of the bed.

He leaned over and kissed JJ on the forehead. "Be good to that guy over there in the corner. He's one of a kind."

JJ's eyes lit up when Brantley stood tall, her gaze sliding to Baz. "Don't I know it."

Reese started toward the door with Brantley beside him, glancing back at JJ when he said, "If you think of anything you need, holler at us. If we don't make it by tonight, we'll do our best to come back in the mornin'."

"Do we have to come back?" Brantley joked in a conspiratorial whisper.

"Hey! I heard that."

"Love you! Keep those babies cookin' a little longer," Brantley tossed back before urging Reese out the door with Tesha trotting at Reese's side.

Once in the hallway, Brantley laughed. "Is it me, or does she get grumpier with each passing day?"

"Can you blame her? She's cooped up in that room day and night."

"It was her choice."

"Only because she didn't want strangers traipsing through her house."

She'd had two choices: stay at the hospital in a fancy suite paid for by Wes Buchanan or go home and have a nurse—the aforementioned stranger—who would take care of everything she needed. Because of all she'd endured recently, JJ had opted for the hospital stay because she was uncomfortable with people she didn't know being in her house. But it wasn't like she was being held prisoner. She could leave the hospital if she absolutely wanted to—although it would be against medical advice.

A flash of memory had a cold chill snaking down his spine. Reese shook his head to dislodge the image, but it took root. An underground concrete cage with no way out. Endless days and nights. Extreme heat, bitter cold.

Brantley's voice jarred him back to the present. "It's only been nine days."

"You say that like you'd last five minutes in that bed."

"I would if you were naked and in it with me."

Realizing there was a nurse sitting at the desk, Reese felt his cheeks heat. She had a phone receiver to her ear and probably hadn't heard the comment, but still.

"The good news is," Brantley continued, "Dr. Tinder said the babies are doing okay."

True. For now. To keep them that way, JJ's doctor put her on bed rest until her due date, which was still four weeks away. While everyone was praying to whatever higher power they believed in, the fact was those babies could be born any minute now.

Half an hour later, as they were pulling out of the Whataburger drive-thru with their breakfast quickly cooling in a white and orange paper sack, Brantley glanced his way.

"How long do you think she'll last? I mean, really last? I'm sure she's dangerously close to leveling the hospital, and it hasn't even been two weeks."

Reese took a sip of his coffee, peered over. "I'm sure the walls will hold. Even against her wrath."

"You really think she'll make it four more weeks?"

Reese gave a quick shake of his head. "I'll give it till the end of the week."

"Before she blows a gasket? Or before the babies are born?"

"Babies."

Brantley cocked an eyebrow. "You care to wager on that?"

Reese huffed a laugh. "I am *not* wagerin' on JJ's health."

"Yeah, yeah."

As was the case for everyone close to JJ, Reese was hoping the twins would make it full term, but according to Baz, that wasn't likely to happen. The soon-to-be father had been reading up on this stuff and was now a walking encyclopedia of potential problems that could arise, none of which made for a good night's sleep, he was sure. Reese damn sure didn't envy the man.

"Regardless," Reese said as he lifted the lid on his coffee, "we've gotta get the baby shower done."

Brantley leaned back, resting one hand on the steering wheel. "You know I'm not gonna do it, right?"

Reese's smile was slow and knowing. "I know you don't *want* to do it."

As expected, Brantley flopped back against the seat, adamantly shaking his head. "Come on, Tavoularis. Can you honestly see me leadin' the charge on a baby shower?"

"You're her best friend. Plus, you led the charge for a team of Navy SEALs."

Brantley nodded enthusiastically. "Exactly. And that was gravy compared to puttin' together a party that won't piss JJ off."

Reese laughed, letting Brantley see the truth in his eyes.

"You're fuckin' with me, aren't you?"

"A little, yeah. Holly, Elana, and Becs are workin' with Baz's mom to get it all done."

"When is it?"

"They're tentatively plannin' for Friday. Provided JJ doesn't have the babies by then."

"And if she does?"

"They'll wait until she comes home."

Brantley sized him up. "And how long've you known that little nugget of information?"

A slight shrug was Reese's initial response, his attention shifting to Tesha, who was watching out the window, tongue lolling out of her mouth.

"Sometimes it's too easy, right, girl?"

Tesha peered back at him, and Reese would swear she was smiling.

"Since when?" Brantley repeated.

Because he knew Brantley wouldn't let it go until he knew, Reese answered. "Since about the time JJ begged me not to let you handle the baby shower preparations."

Brantley reached over the center console, his big hand shifting to Reese's thigh. "Anyone ever tell you payback's a bitch, Tavoularis?"

That wicked hand wandered higher, higher still until Brantley's fingertips brushed the denim covering Reese's quickly growing cock. As much as he would've liked the tease, Reese knew they had things they had to deal with first, so he put his hand on Brantley's and shifted it back a safe distance.

"That's what I hear. Right now, we just need to worry about what kinda trouble we can get into today."

"We already know what that trouble entails," Brantley said, flipping on his blinker as they neared the exit for Coyote Ridge. "A podcaster." Brantley glanced over at Reese. "I got it right that time, huh?"

"You did." Reese grinned. "But I'm more interested in talkin' to Archer Halligan."

"You want him to work for us that bad?"

He did. Having talked to Archer at length on Friday night, Reese was convinced the guy would be the perfect addition to an almost perfect team.

However, he opted to tone down his excitement, not wanting to come across too eager.

"It wouldn't hurt. Now that the chaos has settled—Z's words, not mine—he wants us to take on more cases. Which means more people."

"Your brother's crazy if he thinks the chaos has settled."

"Don't you dare jinx us," Reese grumbled.

Chapter Two

TWENTY MINUTES LATER, AFTER THEY'D GOTTEN HOME, dished up Tesha's breakfast, and polished off their own, Reese was walking toward the barn, aptly named HQ by JJ, with Brantley not far behind him.

"I don't know how much of an update we're gonna get." Reese pointed at the parking area. "Not too many people are here."

"You're underestimating Holly and Elana," Brantley stated as Reese keyed his passcode in to unlock the door. "It's like they know where everyone is every minute of every day."

"Everyone but you," Reese corrected. "No matter when I ask, no one ever knows where you are."

Brantley smirked, reaching to hold the door open. "I've trained 'em right."

Reese walked into the barn, greeted by the sight of a nearly empty space accompanied by a man's voice coming from the speakers overhead. He recognized the voice instantly, but before he could comment, Brantley was pointing toward the ceiling, looking around as though trying to find a disembodied head.

"What the hell is that?" Brantley asked.

"Sorry!" Holly squealed, fumbling with her mouse. "We like to listen when no one's here and it's quiet."

The man continued to speak, his voice clear and concise.

Reese looked around, noticing there was no one else in the room. "We?"

Holly pointed toward the loft while she focused on her computer screen. "Elana and I."

"You two like true crime?" Reese asked, watching her wiggle her mouse one more time before tapping the button.

The sound cut off as Holly nodded. "Yeah. I listen to a couple, but *Havoc Your Way* is my favorite. Simon's very thorough."

"Thorough with what?" Brantley asked. "Reading a book?"

"It's not a book," Reese told him.

Brantley's eyes snapped to his face, his forehead creased. "No? What is it then?"

Reese laughed. "Think back a second. Friday night. Moonshiners. Violet's boyfriend."

"That?" Brantley pointed at the ceiling. "That was a cast thing?"

"Podcast," Holly corrected. "*Havoc Your Way* with Simon Jennings."

Brantley's forehead creased. "The guy who's stoppin' by today?"

"That'd be the one," Reese confirmed.

"And he's not readin' from a book?" Brantley asked, looking genuinely curious.

"No. He's probably got notes," Holly said. "But he's an investigative journalist. He's looking into actual events that happened."

"You really do like that shit?" Brantley asked, still pointing upward, presumably toward the speakers from which the voice had come a moment ago.

"Simon's comin' here?" Holly asked, eyes wide, jaw flopping open.

"Yes, he is," Reese told Holly, then looked at Brantley. "It's not shit."

Reese didn't bother telling Brantley that he found the podcasts rather fascinating. And yes, he happened to be partial to *Havoc Your Way* because Simon Jennings was good at deciphering fact from fiction in the cases he tackled. He laid out his thoughts while still managing to keep the truth from being lost.

"You should try it," Holly told Brantley.

"Thanks, but no. Where's everyone?"

"Evan and Slade are lookin' into a lead for one of the cases they're workin'. Becs had a parent/teacher conference early. She'll be in as soon as that's done. Charlie's workin' from home this mornin'. She'll be in after her meeting with her mother's case worker. Jay, Darius, and Atticus went to pick up the desks Baz ordered. They should be back soon. And I haven't heard from Luca yet."

"He texted me a little while ago," Reese told her. "Said he's runnin' late, but he'll be here."

Brantley said, "Tell me there's coffee," at the same time Holly said, "Did you see JJ?"

She directed Brantley toward the small kitchen with a point of her finger, clearly understanding Brantley's priorities. After he passed, she turned her attention to him.

"We did, yes." Reese perched on the corner of Evan's desk, which was closest to the door. "She's doin' as good as can be expected."

Holly chuckled. "King of the understatement."

"He is that," Brantley called from the kitchen. "She's losin' her mind."

"Wouldn't you?" Holly shouted back. "She's been there for nine days."

"You'd think it was nine years," Brantley shot back.

"Technically, she chose to stay there," Reese reminded them.

"Only because she doesn't want a stranger in her house. I'm gonna go up there at lunch," Holly said, using her inside voice once again. "Baz wants to come in for a while. I figured I could update JJ and work from there this afternoon."

"We have any new hires comin' this week?" Brantley asked Holly when he returned, carrying two to-go cups of coffee.

"Thanks," Reese said as he took one.

"Baz and Darius decided they'd have 'em start next week. On Monday. Baz is worried he won't be here and doesn't want to overload Darius."

"He'll be fine," Brantley stated. "He's quiet but more than capable."

Reese was glad they had another week at least. He wasn't sure now was the right time to onboard a bunch of new people. Not without confusing them more than was necessary.

Nodding his understanding, Reese asked, "Anything hot come in?"

Holly shook her head. "We got a call from Corpus Christi PD. They said they're lookin' into a missing tourist and might need our help. They're stretched thin, and the woman's family is puttin' pressure on them to drop everything. Her dad's a government official. They didn't say who or what, but they're thinkin' they might get a ransom demand soon."

Reese nodded. Unfortunately, they'd seen a lot of those cases lately. Most of them occurred during the summer, when college students went to the beach. Due to the proximity to Mexico, they saw a lot of kidnappings for ransom because it was likely easy money for the cartels. But because people were willing to shell out the dough to get their loved ones back, the bad guys weren't seasonal.

"If they need us, just holler," Brantley told her. "In the meantime, I'll be in my office."

"Me, too," Reese told her. "If Simon and Archer show up here instead of the house, send 'em over there."

"Archer Halligan's comin' here?" Holly asked, her mouth falling open.

"Close your mouth, girl," Brantley joked. "He's not your type."

"And why not?"

Brantley looked at Reese and smirked before responding. "I'll let you figure it out when he gets here."

Reese stood, grinning at Holly's confusion. Rather than explain, he followed Brantley out of the barn and over to the house. As they were walking, the beeping sound signaling a large truck backing up could be heard.

"You know if we don't get in the house quick, they'll target us to help them unload those desks," Brantley mentioned as they headed for the back patio.

"Shit." Reese shook his head. "We really should help 'em."

"No. We really should let 'em earn their paycheck."

"I'm pretty sure movin' furniture is not in their job description."

"Their job description is anything I choose it to be."

Reese chuckled. It was only funny because it was true.

"You have any luck gettin' a hold of Travis?" he asked when they reached the back patio door.

"Tried. Multiple times. I didn't leave a message. Figure if he's curious and ready to talk, he'll call me back."

Reese wasn't so sure that was going to happen. Travis Walker was quite possibly the most stubborn human being who ever lived.

And Reese considered himself an expert on the subject since he was married to a Walker and knew firsthand how stubborn they all could be.

Atticus James planted his foot on the step and hefted himself up into the back of the large box truck to join his co-workers, Darius Frost and Jay Hernandez.

"Have you never moved a piece of furniture before?" Darius asked, shuffling over to one end of the desk.

Based on his tone, Atticus knew that *no* was the wrong answer. However, it was the truth in his case. Despite knowing he would only be ridiculed by admitting as much, he went for it anyway.

"As a matter of fact, no," he said, lending his help by grabbing the side of the desk.

His admission had Darius coming to a halt, causing Jay to slam into the rear end of the desk. Atticus's grip slipped, causing the desk to tilt at an odd angle before they wrangled it back to level.

And to think the loading ramp was only a few feet away.

Professionals they were not.

"A little warning would be nice," Jay said, recovering quickly as they shifted the desk into place over the motorized ramp so they could lower it to the ground. Thankfully, someone had thought ahead and rented a truck that would suit their purpose. Damn good thing they hadn't asked Atticus to do it because clearly, he would've fucked that shit up.

Jay stepped to the side to press the button. The motor whirred as the desk lowered to the ground.

Rather than wait, Atticus hopped down from the truck, watching Darius ride down with the large metal and wood monstrosity. What the hell was Baz thinking when he ordered these things? They were enormous. And ugly. And quite possibly relics.

Once on the ground, Atticus and Jay moved into place to assist again.

"You can't be serious," Darius said, his eyes locked on Atticus as he backed off the ramp. "Never?"

"Never."

"*Never?*"

"Tacking on more *nevers* isn't gonna change my answer, dude. It's not *that* unusual." Atticus looked between them. "Right?"

Jay chuckled. "Not if you're eight."

Atticus flipped him off without taking his hands off the desk, so the gesture was lost in the chaos. And that was exactly what this was. Fucking chaos.

When Darius asked him to come along for a ride to the office supply store, he had no idea they would be bringing back desks. Pens and paper, sure. He was all for taking a trip. It beat sitting inside with nothing to do. He'd met his quota of reviewing applications and backgrounds for people the team was looking to partner him up with. At this point, he was willing to work solo to avoid going down that rabbit hole again.

But this … *this* was bullshit.

The worst part was he hadn't even seen it coming. Not when the guys at the store loaded all four desks into the back of the moving truck Darius had rented. Not during the drive back to HQ. And not even after Darius parked. It wasn't until Darius and Jay shouted at him as he was heading for the barn that he realized they were expecting him to move this shit.

Life was easier when he was scrawny and weak. No one expected him to do anything then. Now that he'd bulked up and was working out religiously, they were expecting more from him.

"We just have to get them inside," Jay told them. "After that, someone else can move them."

"Is that all?" Getting them from the truck to the door was the hard part. "And why couldn't we back the truck up to the barn?"

Darius's dark brown eyes widened. "Uh…"

"Seriously?" Atticus barked a laugh. "And you think *I'm* the idiot?"

That got Jay laughing, which then spread through them all, cutting the tension somewhat.

It still didn't thrill Atticus to have to move furniture—that wasn't in the job description, thank you very much—but it helped. It would've been nice if they could've scheduled this when Slade and Evan were in the office. Or Brantley and Reese, even. Then again, he got the feeling those four were purposely keeping their distance simply so they didn't have to do this part of it.

An hour later, Atticus was sitting at his desk, his feet up, sipping water while Holly, Elana, and Jay attempted to come up with some sort of seating arrangement that would make sense. At one point, the barn had felt enormous, but as they continued to crowd it up with desks and fancy electronic equipment, it was losing some of its bulk. If it weren't for the height of the ceiling, it would've been claustrophobic. The walls felt like they were closing in as less and less square footage was available.

Good thing he spent most of his time in the field. Or he would once they had the partner situation taken care of. Maybe that would happen once JJ returned. Without her there, no one seemed to know what was going on. A bunch of ants running around aimlessly after someone kicked the anthill and dislodged their queen.

"Hey!"

Atticus shot up out of his chair, dropping the water bottle.

A giggle sounded from over his left shoulder, and he turned to see JJ's head filling one of the large screen televisions.

A string of curses wove through his brain, but thankfully for all involved, Atticus managed to keep them from tumbling out of his mouth.

"Did I scare you?" she asked, watching him from her computer screen.

Atticus skimmed the edge of the television to see where the camera was, but he didn't see one.

"It's built-in," JJ told him, clearly figuring out his objective.

"And you can just pop in whenever you want?" he shot back.

"Whenever. I. Want," she drawled, making it sound like a threat.

"Do I hear—JJ!" Holly squealed as she raced over to stand in front of the television. "You're here."

JJ smiled.

Atticus scooped up his water bottle and took a step back so the girls could do their girl thing. He made a mental note to shift his desk so that his back wasn't to that damn television.

Since no one was paying any attention to him, he slipped out the door, pulling his phone from his pocket as he did. He brought up the text group he had going with Slade Elliott and Carson Briggs, the two men he was in a pseudo-relationship with. Was that a thing? Pseudo-relationship? Or were they just fucking? He honestly didn't know. Regardless, they frequently used the text thread to chat about nothing of importance.

Atticus walked over to the picnic table that had shown up sometime last week. He wasn't sure who brought it, but he knew it wasn't Brantley or Reese because they'd been as surprised to see it as everyone else.

He took a seat on the tabletop, putting his feet on the bench as he skimmed through the last of the messages. They had to do with getting together for dinner. Which they'd done on Saturday. Kinda. The togetherness had happened. As had the dinner. Just not exactly at the same time. Atticus had eaten while Slade excused himself to work out in his home gym, and Carson sat on the couch and watched Atticus eat.

But they'd been under the same roof, so he figured it was progress.

Since Atticus was currently renting Slade's guest room and Carson lived across the street, they saw each other often. More so now that Carson and Slade had made up. Well, technically, he wasn't sure *made up* was the right way to describe it, but they were no longer avoiding one another. Atticus hadn't gotten them to sit down (together) for a meal as of yet, but that was next on his to-do list. Granted, he was stalling a little on that because he was still trying to wrap his head around dating two men at the same time while those two men were dating each other.

Okay, fine. The three of them were in a relationship. There. He acknowledged it.

But was *relationship* the right word?

They were having sex.

The three of them.

Together.

Sometimes.

Sometimes separately.

Not nearly as often as Atticus would like, but that was partially his fault. Trying to get Carson and Slade in the same room without snipping at each other wasn't an easy feat. Sure, all seemed right as rain when they were naked because no one had time to snip at anyone then. But Atticus wanted more than that. If he was going to give this a chance to work, he wanted to do it the right way. There were just too many ways for it to go wrong otherwise.

Which begged the question: *what was the right way to date two people while those two people dated each other?*

"Whatcha doin'?"

Atticus launched up, stumbling as his feet hit the ground. "What the fuck!"

Slade was laughing. "I thought you heard me comin'."

Atticus flattened his palm to his chest. "If y'all keep this shit up, I'm gonna have a heart attack." *Could a twenty-five-year-old be scared to death?*

"Y'all?" Slade looked around as though expecting to see someone.

"I thought you were working a case," Atticus told him, wanting to change the subject and get his heart rate back to normal.

"Got a text from Reese to come back."

Atticus wondered why Reese was summoning people. Did they have a case?

Slade bumped his shoulder. "Figured if it wasn't life or death, maybe we could grab lunch later."

Shoving his phone in his pocket, Atticus frowned at Slade. "We?"

"You and me."

Atticus wanted to ask him if they should invite Carson, but Slade seemed to be in a good mood, and he was learning that you did not throw wrenches into Slade's good moods. There weren't enough of them as of late. And Atticus knew part of the reason was that Slade thought he was second to Carson in Atticus's life.

It wasn't true.

Hell, he didn't want to place an order on either of them because it felt wrong for so many reasons. He enjoyed spending time with both of them. They had a good time, no matter what they were doing. And yeah, he was attracted to them equally. Maybe for different reasons, but the heat level was still the same. Slade and Carson were as different as night and day, and strangely enough, together, they did it for Atticus in a big way.

"I could do lunch," he admitted.

Slade's face lit up as though Atticus had just given him gold bars wrapped with diamonds. He'd honestly never had anyone react to him the way Slade and Carson were these days, so it was still a bit of a surprise.

Good, for sure, but a surprise, nonetheless.

JJ STARED AT THE SCREEN, SOAKING UP the sight of her team as they laughed and joked while she looked on. She could only imagine how creepy it was to have her face planted on a big screen mounted on the wall, but for the moment, she didn't care. Not since it meant she actually got to feel as though she was at HQ with all of them.

"Have you listened to the recent podcast?" Elana asked.

"I'm two behind," JJ admitted. "So no spoilers."

"You need to get caught up," Holly said, excitement weaving through her words. "Simon's comin' here."

"What? *Here?* As in"—JJ pointed toward the screen—"there?"

Holly nodded enthusiastically.

"When?"

"Today!"

JJ frowned. "Why don't I know about this? Who's he comin' to see?"

"It's *they*," Elana clarified. "Archer and Simon are comin' to talk to Brantley and Reese."

Those no-good, lying buttholes. She knew they'd purposely left out names because she would've insisted on being there. She *should* be there.

"What are they talkin' about?" she asked, desperate to know.

Elana looked at Holly, then back at JJ. "A job, I think."

"You think?"

"They were all there at Moonshiners on Fri—"

"All who?" JJ asked, feeling as though she was on another planet for all the details she was missing out on.

"Simon came to town to talk to Holt—they're friends. He met Violet—"

"They're dating. I know," JJ told her. "They were at the wedding."

"Engaged," Elana corrected, grinning.

"Seriously?" Jesus. It was like the world was spinning at a faster rate while she was cooped up in this damn hospital.

"Yep. And they're buyin' a house." Elana smiled sheepishly. "Archer's gonna move in with them."

JJ swirled her finger. "Are they like … um…"

Elana and Holly stared back at her, clearly waiting for her to finish the question. She wasn't sure how to.

"Are they … uh…" Then it hit her. "Are they like Trey and them?"

Frowning, the women looked at each other, then back at JJ.

JJ swirled her finger again. "The threesome thing."

"Ah." Elana grinned. "Nope. None of that goin' on. Archer's just a roommate. Paige, their other partner, might be lookin' at a house to buy, too."

"So how'd they get on Brantley and Reese's radar?"

"Violet introduced them on Friday night when we were all at Moonshiners. Now they're comin' here to talk more."

Hmm. JJ needed to have a conversation with her best friend because clearly, he wasn't giving her all the details. Was that on purpose? Because Brantley didn't want to burden her with undue stress? Or was he simply not thinking about her because she wasn't there?

Considering the emotional roller coaster that was pregnancy, JJ decided not to jump to conclusions. At least not while Elana and Holly were looking on.

"I'll try to catch up on the podcast tonight," she promised. It was about the only time she could get any peace and quiet. Which she needed if she was expected to pay attention to a podcast.

"Don't forget, I'll be up there in a coupla hours," Holly promised. "Want me to bring you anything?"

"I'm good." And she was. Despite her complaints, she had pretty much anything she could possibly need next to her bedside.

Although she hated to end the call, JJ said her goodbyes before hitting the button to cut the connection. She stared at the darkened screen with a frown.

"I miss them," she muttered.

"They miss you, too," Baz said from his recliner in the corner of her hospital room.

She looked over. For a brief moment, she'd forgotten he was there. If only she could forget it was a hospital room, perhaps she could relax a little. From the inside, with the exception of the monitor that was currently keeping track of her contractions—which she was having sporadically, despite her denial—the place had very little resemblance to a medical facility. It was spacious and bright. Not quite homey, but she'd give them credit for trying.

And yes, it was comfortable. More so than she expected when she agreed to stay there. It sure as shit beat having strangers traipsing in and out of her house. No way was she doing that. No way, no how.

So this was her concession.

"I think Brantley's holdin' out on me." She cut her gaze to Baz. "Did you know Simon Jennings was comin' to talk to them today?"

She studied him hard, waiting to see if he would lie.

"They mentioned they might have someone in mind for the open investigator position, but they didn't tell me who or when they'd be coming by."

"You and I both know Simon Jennings is not lookin' for a job."

Baz looked sincerely confused. "Do we?"

Dang it. The man was too honest for his own good. If he'd lied, then she'd have a reason to blast him with some of her pent-up frustration. Since he didn't, she needed to come up with a different tack.

Ah.

"Maybe I could get a day pass," she told Baz, offering up her best puppy dog eyes.

"Not gonna happen."

"You are no fun at all."

He chuckled, his gaze lingering on her as he set aside his iPad.

JJ had to admit Baz had been a good sport about it all. For the past nine days, ever since they brought her in, he'd been by her side almost every minute of every day. If she were him, she would've gone home every night to sleep in their bed, where it was possible to get decent rest. Here, with nurses coming in to check on her, it wasn't conducive to sleep, no matter how comfortable he claimed that recliner was, since no amount of coaxing on her part would get that man to sleep in a king-size hospital bed. His words.

Granted, the nurses didn't come in as often during the night as she imagined they would have if she'd been in active labor. As it was, she was having contractions, but they weren't severe, and they weren't regular. According to Dr. Tinder, keeping her in bed as much as possible was the key. Now that her cervix was beginning to dilate, she'd noticed the good doctor was getting a little more worried about the situation.

"You should go to HQ," JJ told Baz now. "Check on things."

"You just talked to them. Sounds to me like they've got it covered."

"They were lyin'," she told him.

"Were they?"

She shook her head at the same time she said, "Yes."

There was no reason for her to believe they were pretending that everything was fine. From what she'd seen with her own two eyes, no one was bustling around the office. Evan and Slade were the only ones actively working on a case. Well, that wasn't entirely true. Charlie and Jay were still looking into the social media scam, but despite their efforts, that one was slow going. Everyone else seemed to be preparing for the new hires coming on board next week.

"I'll swing by there when Holly gets here."

That was what he always said, although he inserted a variety of names into the sentence. For whatever reason, Baz didn't want to leave her alone. JJ didn't want to admit that she was grateful for that. While there were nurses and doctors all over this place, she still felt more comfortable when someone she knew was around.

That was likely a result of the traumatic events she'd endured this past year or so. Which was precisely why she didn't want strangers coming and going from her house. That was her sanctuary. No way was she letting a stranger inside and risking them coming back to do her harm. Been there, done that. The T-shirt didn't fit anymore.

"I think I should shower," she told Baz. "Before Holly gets here."

"I can help with that."

She flashed a coy smile. "Promise?"

"JJ…"

"What?"

"You heard what Dr. Tinder said. No sex."

Her eyebrows slammed down. Yeah. She'd heard that part. And she'd never despised a person as much as she despised him in that moment. Darn those doctors and their medical nonsense. No sex because it might cause her to go into labor at this point.

"What does he know?" she countered without heat.

Baz laughed, just as she hoped he would. It was the little things that kept her going, and this man's laughter was part of it. She hated that he felt he needed to stay at her side night and day. At the same time, she loved that he was there because she needed him now more than ever. JJ didn't want to admit it to anyone, but she was scared. Not so much about being kidnapped or any of that. Not anymore.

No, at the moment, the one fear she couldn't seem to tackle was becoming a mom. It both terrified and thrilled her at the same time.

Chapter Three

"HOLLY JUST TEXTED. SIMON AND ARCHER ARE here," Reese called from his second-floor office. "She saw 'em pull up, so she's walkin' them to the back door."

Brantley looked up from his computer, tilting his head to stretch his neck.

They'd both gotten right to work after they'd checked in with the team—or rather with Holly, since no one else had been around. It had become routine. Waking up, going for a run, back for a shower, then a quick trip to the hospital, followed by breakfast on the go. After that, they worked in their offices for an hour or so to give the team time to trickle in before heading over to HQ. At that point, the day became a whirlwind of research and interviews as they worked on the cold cases Baz had assigned them.

While Brantley wouldn't outwardly complain about their daily hospital visits, he would admit it was causing a minor interruption in their sweet little routine. On the days they went early, Brantley missed out on water fun first thing. Not exactly how he liked to start the day—being inside Reese was his new favorite place—but he was dealing with it since it was only temporary.

Brantley pushed back from his desk, figuring it would be more professional to greet their guests directly, considering their introductions had taken place at a bar. Not that there was anything wrong with that. Brantley considered himself a laidback kinda guy. No need for formalities in the workplace. Certainly not with the amount of stress they endured on a given day. But he would admit that making a good impression was in their best interest. From a business perspective, anyway.

"You want me to bring 'em up here?" Reese asked when he reached the doorway. "Or not," he tacked on with a smile.

Brantley smirked as he approached. "We can go downstairs. I could use some food."

"Seriously?" Reese looked at his watch. "You just had breakfast a coupla hours ago."

"I had coffee and a sausage biscuit. Not exactly breakfast of champions," Brantley corrected. "Plus, comin' up with all the ways I'm gonna make you cry out my name takes energy."

It was impossible to miss the blush that crept up Reese's neck. He loved that he did that so often. It was fucking adorable.

Reese's eyebrows lifted slowly. "And you expect me to make you a sandwich."

"Nope. I'll make it."

"Will you now?"

Brantley nodded, then gestured for Reese to precede him toward the stairs. "Of course. Then tonight, you can reward me for makin' the effort."

"Ah. And what does this reward entail?"

"Your mouth. My dick."

Reese huffed a laugh as they walked down. "And if *I* make your sandwich?"

"My dick. Your mouth."

Reese snorted. "Nice try."

"What? Tell me you don't enjoy it."

The soft hitch in Reese's breath was the only answer he needed.

Despite his teasing, Brantley already knew which way this would go. Reese would make him a sandwich because Brantley's attempt at cooking was usually subpar. Even with something as simple as a sandwich. His patience made it as far as yellow mustard, bologna, and two slices of bread. Reese, on the other hand, piled on the deli meats, fancy cheeses, and veggies and even added some of that fru-fru mustard shit. There was no comparison. This meant, at some point this afternoon, Brantley would show his gratitude for Reese's determination. He preferred to do it when Reese least expected it.

"I'm not sure I trust you to make anything in the kitchen," Reese said when they reached the main floor.

"There's one thing I'm good at makin' in the kitchen," Brantley said, reaching for Reese's arm and pulling him to a stop.

"A mess?"

Brantley huffed a laugh as he stepped in close, lowered his voice. "If you think makin' you come is makin' a mess, then yeah."

God, he loved the way Reese's whiskey-brown eyes glazed over.

"That won't be happenin', Navy boy," Reese said. "We've got company comin'."

"Fair enough." Brantley leaned in, tilted his head slightly. "You can make me a sandwich, and when the house is clear, I'll put my mouth on your dick. How does *that* sound?"

To stop Reese from arguing, Brantley jerked him tight against him before crushing his mouth to Reese's. He figured they had no more than ten, maybe fifteen seconds before their guests reached the house, which was just enough time for a quick fix to hold his addiction to this man at bay.

It took tremendous effort to refrain from touching Reese. In a perfect world, he would keep the man naked all the damn time, simply so he could indulge whenever he wanted. Unfortunately, life was not kind to his overactive libido, but he was learning to deal with it.

Mostly.

Brantley pulled back just as the knock sounded. A second later, the sliding glass door opened.

"We have company," Brantley said, holding Reese's glazed stare.

"Payback's a bitch," Reese whispered before pivoting on his heel and heading for the kitchen.

Yes, it was. And Brantley was looking forward to it.

He followed Reese, stopping at the kitchen island in an effort to conceal the evidence of what they'd been doing seconds ago. His dick was threatening to tear through his zipper, and no one needed to see that.

"And who is this?" Archer asked, his full attention on Tesha, who was alert and standing but not growling.

Brantley was silent, expecting Reese to do the greeting. Only he didn't.

"Tesha," Brantley told him. "She's our … I was gonna say partner, but I'm not sure that's the case. She's more like the boss. We relocated her from a bad existence and put her in charge of ours."

"Sounds like a win-win. Would it be all right to pet her?" he asked.

"Sure."

Archer approached slowly, stopping with a few feet between them. The giant of a man squatted down and held out one big hand. "Hey, girl. Name's Archer. I like animals, all kinds. Not so much ferrets, but that's a story for another time."

All eyes were on Archer and Tesha. It only took a second for Tesha to move closer. She sniffed Archer's hand before moving again and again until she rested her chin in Archer's palm. He moved slowly, rubbing her head with his thumb and gradually shifting his hand until he was scratching the top of her head.

Tesha, not usually so friendly with strangers, moved in until she was practically in his lap.

"You must be all right," Brantley joked.

"Yup. You and I will be besties soon enough," Archer told Tesha as he stood slowly, grinning from ear to ear.

"I'll be in the barn if you need me," Holly said, her eyes trailing over Archer Halligan like he was a lollipop and she was about to take a lick.

"We were about to make sandwiches," Brantley told them while Reese busied himself with dishes and ingredients, likely trying to hide the blush on his face. "Want something?"

"I'm good. Thanks," Simon said.

Archer grinned. "I won't say no to food."

"Sandwiches," Brantley stated. "With ham."

"Turkey and roast beef," Reese corrected.

"Sorry. Turkey and roast beef on white."

"Wheat," Reese announced.

Brantley grinned and winked at their guests before continuing. "Turkey and roast beef on wheat with Swiss and mayo."

"Cheddar and must—" Reese pulled his head out of the fridge. "You're fuckin' with me, aren't you?"

"A little bit, yeah." He turned back to Archer and Simon, pointing toward the stools on the other side of the island. "Have a seat. Somethin' to drink?"

"Water works for me." Archer nodded toward Simon. "He'll have the same, although he'll tell you he's good."

Brantley had only met Archer Halligan a few days ago, but he would admit he'd liked the guy instantly. He couldn't pinpoint exactly what it was about him, but he had a feeling the beast of a man would fit in well with the team.

"I am good," Simon countered. "Not everyone likes to raid the pantry wherever they go."

"It's a good way to get to know someone," Archer argued.

"It is not."

"You say not, I say is."

"How long've you two been married?" Brantley asked, interrupting the banter.

"Sorry about that. I asked him to be on his best behavior," Simon said with a smirk. "He's not, so it must be a day that ends in 'y'."

Reese snorted a laugh from behind him. "I've got one like that."

"Now that *that's* outta the way…" Brantley grinned. "I thought maybe we could talk briefly this mornin', then reconvene this afternoon when I can get Sebastian Buchanan—we call him Baz—here. We've recently promoted him. He handles caseloads and whatnot. Runs the office. Or he will once he's back from paternity leave. JJ's in the hospital—bed rest until the babies are born."

"So she *was* right?" Simon asked, grinning as he glanced at Archer. "JJ was havin' contractions at the wedding but was adamant she was not in labor."

Brantley laughed. "That's JJ. She's stubborn enough to hold off until she's ready. Or she likes to think she is."

Archer glanced between them. "So you're not in charge?"

"Technically," Reese drawled.

"Don't listen to him. We tried that whole thing with me runnin' the show," Brantley admitted. "I'm not a fan of bureaucracy and red tape. Workin' for Sniper 1 Security means there's a shit ton of that. I leave that shit to Baz and Reese. I prefer to work cases."

"I know the feelin'," Archer said. "I'll do what needs to be done, but I like to get my hands dirty."

Yeah, Brantley liked this guy.

Since Reese was still working on the sandwiches, Brantley opted to jump right into it.

"If you're still workin' on the…" He circled his finger in the air. "The thingy cast."

"Podcast," Reese corrected.

"Yeah. *That* thing. How much time would you have to dedicate to the task force?"

Archer looked at Simon, and a silent question passed between them. A second later, Simon nodded.

Archer met Brantley's gaze. "I think the question is, how much time will you need me on the task force?"

"We'd prefer someone full-time, but there's some leniency in there when we're not workin' an active case." Brantley looked at Simon. "Do you have an idea of how much time you'll need him on a weekly basis?"

"Depends on the story I'm workin' on. If I keep 'em local, I do a lot of the investigatin' myself when Archer's off doin' other things."

"What's local? Like state level?"

"I was thinkin' more along the lines of keepin' it closer to home for a while."

"Home being…?"

"Here. Coyote Ridge. We'll have a permanent address on October thirty-first."

Brantley looked at Archer. "And you?"

"Same. I'm movin' in with them."

"No roots, huh?"

"Temporary ones," Archer said with a smirk. "I'm hopin' to shift that to more permanent in the future."

That made Brantley feel a little better. It was difficult enough to find someone, but hiring them, getting them set up and through the onboarding process was a pain in the ass, regardless of who was responsible for doing it.

"In case you haven't noticed, I know nothin' about what you do," Brantley told them. "So I don't know what it entails. You have experience lookin' for missing people? Or workin' cold cases?"

"The majority of the stories I do are cold cases," Simon explained. "The cases vary. Robberies, fraud, missing persons, unsolved homicides."

"Do you get to choose? Or do your podcast bosses decide?"

Simon chuckled. "No boss, but I do have sponsors. I've been a stickler for deciding on my own. I'm an investigative journalist by trade, so I have an eye for a story when there is one."

Interesting. He looked at Archer. "What about you? You an investigative journalist, too?"

"No. Just an investigator."

"Ah. You have a gun permit?"

"I do."

"Know how to shoot?"

Archer's grin widened. "I've got a little experience."

Reese brought over a plate, handed it off to Archer. "He was a Marine scout sniper."

Brantley looked at Archer. "Once a Marine, always a Marine."

"*Oorah!*"

"Brantley was Navy," Reese noted. "SEAL. SpecOps."

"He says it like he's a civilian." Brantley laughed. "Reese was in the Air Force. He did two tours in Iraq. One in Afghanistan. POW."

"No shit." Archer stared at Reese. "Glad you made it back."

"You and me both," Reese muttered, clearly not wanting to discuss it.

"Thank you for your service," Simon said. "All of you."

"When'd you get out?" Archer asked, looking at Brantley once again.

"A coupla years ago. Forced retirement. Medical discharge."

"Do you miss it?" Archer asked.

Brantley cut his gaze to Reese. "Not as much as I used to. Thanks," he told Reese when he passed him a plate. He was about to explain how the task force worked, simply to get off the subject, when the back door slid open, and Baz appeared.

"Hey, man," Brantley greeted with a grin. "You look just like you did a few hours ago. Like shit."

Baz huffed a laugh. "Thanks."

"You're welcome. I thought you weren't comin' in until later."

"JJ kicked me out." Baz waved a hand to encompass the room. "I think she's lookin' for the dirt on this meeting."

Of course she was.

"How's she doin'?" Reese asked.

"She's good. My mom's with her now. Holly's headed up there." Baz nodded toward the two men sitting at the counter. "I tried to warn her she's gonna get an earful about these two." His gaze snapped up to Brantley's face. "Because apparently, her best friend is a lowdown, no good, secret-keeping asshole." He flashed a grin. "Her words."

Brantley could pretty much hear JJ calling him that. She meant it with love.

"But on a positive note, she misses you guys."

"We miss her, too," Reese said, then made the formal introductions.

"This JJ sounds like a badass," Archer stated.

"She is," Brantley, Reese, and Baz said at the same time.

While he ate his sandwich, Brantley watched the interactions. They'd been looking for another investigator for what felt like a damn long time. One who could partner with Atticus now that the newest member of their team was fully onboarded and certified. They'd looked at somewhere around fifty applicants. A couple had seemed like they would work, but not exactly fit.

Not until now.

Archer Halligan ... yeah, Brantley got the feeling this guy was going to pull his weight and then some.

Reese stood beside Brantley, listening as the conversation came to a lull.

"How about we walk over to the barn, and we'll show you around," Brantley suggested once he and Archer had downed their sandwiches.

Archer got to his feet. "Sounds like a plan." He peered down at Simon. "You comin'?"

Simon glanced at Reese. "I thought I'd stay here and talk if that's all right with you?"

"Sure. We'll hang back," Reese told Brantley, figuring they didn't need an entourage to do a tour of a barn anyway.

"Come on, Tesha," Archer called as they walked out the door. "You can lead the way."

"Looks like those two are gonna get along," Simon said when it was just the two of them. "He really does like animals. Violet's got cats, and Archer's excited about living in the same house with them."

"I think Archer's gonna fit nicely," Reese admitted.

"Me, too."

"You don't think his workin' for the task force is gonna be a problem for your podcast? You've only got one other person who helps, right?"

"Yeah. Paige."

Reese piled the empty plates in the sink and turned on the water. "If I recall correctly, she usually does most of your editing work, right?"

"You know a little about podcasts," Simon said with a grin.

"I listen to them," he said as he poured soap on a sponge. "Yours mostly. Long-time fan. I think your best work was the story you did on Casey Jenner."

Simon nodded. "The little girl who went missing when she was supposedly walkin' home from the mall."

"Yeah." Reese paused what he was doing and stared at him. "She'd been there with her foster brothers, right?"

"And her foster father," Simon's tone turned somber. "The man who was supposed to take care of her was the one who took her life."

Reese remembered it like he'd heard it only minutes ago. That was how good Simon was.

"You broke that case wide open. Hell, you solved it when the police had spent years findin' nothin'."

"Sometimes the cards fall the right way."

"If you're ever lookin' for an idea for a story, we've got quite a few cold cases we're workin' on. You could even solve a few if you'd like."

Simon grinned. "I might just take you up on that."

"We could make a place for you in the barn," Reese told him as he got back to scrubbing the plates. "We've got the room. Get you a desk."

Simon chuckled. "Are you offerin' me a job?"

That wasn't his intention, but he would admit, the idea had merit. "You've got the investigative skills."

"It would be a damn good change of pace," Simon mused. "Especially if I'm gonna lose Archer. Don't get me wrong. It'll be a hardship to lose him, but I know this is more his pace. He gets bored easily, and you've got so much more goin' on than I do."

"What about Paige? Will she be able to take up the slack?"

Simon shrugged one shoulder. "Paige is dealing with some stuff. She's hesitant to move here. Keeps waffling on her answer."

"What're you gonna do?"

"Probably cut her loose. She doesn't make decisions well. If I make it, she'll adapt. If and when she's ready to commit to coming down here, she can come back."

"Well, the offer stands. You can stop by anytime you want." Reese rinsed the dishes and placed them on the drying rack while Simon remained on the stool across from him. "Or you can always tap one of us for help if you get to a point when you're shorthanded. We've usually got some leeway."

"How big is the team, anyway?"

"With Archer, that gives us six active investigators, including me and Brantley," Reese told him. "We're in the process of creatin' another team of six. They'll work on cold cases and special projects. Jay and Charlie are in place now, and we've got four new hires comin' in the next coupla weeks. Plus, we've got two hackers, two analysts, one assistant, and Baz."

"That's quite a team."

"It's taken some time for us to figure out how to make it work. There's some travel involved, and we've got a couple of people who need to stick closer to home. I think we've finally found the sweet spot. As you can imagine, active cases require all hands on deck."

"That makes sense."

"But as glamorous as this job sounds, they need a break from time to time."

"I know now's probably not the time," Simon said, his tone hesitant. "But Holt said I should talk to you and Brantley about Meredith Prescott. I'm not sure if you're familiar with her or not."

"Holt mentioned her. Kylie and Jessie's mother." Reese grabbed a towel and dried his hands. "What about her?"

"Holt believes she witnessed somethin' that caused her to go into hiding."

Reese frowned. Although they'd attempted to talk to Holt, they hadn't gotten far on the topic. Claiming not to be one for gossip, Holt had urged them to talk to Travis to get the details. Since Travis had been avoiding them for some time now, they hadn't been able to get information from him. And now Simon was here, looking into whatever it was Holt had unearthed. Although he was on the fence as to whether pursuing this was a good idea, Reese decided to entertain the notion. Just for the basics, of course.

"What did she see?"

"If rumors are to be believed, she witnessed a mob hit when she lived in Dallas."

Reese set the towel down and stared at Simon. He wasn't sure he wanted to know where this was going, but that little niggle of warning at the base of his skull told him he already did.

"You've heard of the Southern Boy Mafia?" Simon asked.

Yep. That was what he feared Simon would say.

As was the case whenever someone mentioned the Adorites, guilt settled like a lead weight in Reese's stomach. His past relationship with Max's sister, Madison, had nearly cost Reese his life as well as his relationship with Brantley. To say it was a sore subject for him was an understatement.

"Yeah," he answered, and it was his turn to hesitate.

"Holt uncovered something that leads him to believe Meredith witnessed Max Adorite kill a man. He also thinks the FBI tried to strong-arm her into testifying, which is the reason for her disappearance."

Reese wasn't sure what to say to that.

"I've done a little digging, and while I think there's a correlation of some kind, I'm not exactly sure what she did or did not witness. With Travis's permission, I've decided to investigate it further. It'll be the topic of my next podcast series."

"Travis's permission? You talked to him about it?"

"I did. Briefly."

"Investigate what exactly? Her disappearance?"

"Yes. And the events surrounding it."

"Travis knows about this?"

Simon nodded. "I reached out to him shortly after I got to town. I make it a point to talk to the family before pursuing cases. Since my job often entails making their pain public, their opinions matter, although it doesn't always mean I'll back off."

"Does Travis support it?"

"More than I expected he would." Simon sighed. "He's seekin' something. Closure, maybe. I'm not sure this'll give it to him, but it might help."

Reese wasn't sure what additional closure anyone could give Travis. The woman who killed Kylie was dead. As for how tracking down Kylie's absentee mother would benefit anyone, he couldn't begin to guess.

"And if Meredith Prescott doesn't want to be found?" Reese asked.

"That's a risk I'm willin' to take considerin' the bigger picture."

"Which is?"

Simon paused, glanced down, then looked back up. "If Holt's right, there are people conspirin' against the Adorites. Powerful people. And I honestly think Meredith Prescott was caught up in it somehow. From what I've come up with, I'm not so sure it was by any fault of hers."

"So you don't think she witnessed a murder?"

"I honestly don't know at this point. I've been holdin' off because I wanted to talk to you and Brantley about it."

"We don't know Kylie's mother. Hell, I didn't realize she wasn't in the picture until Holt brought it up. I'm not sure what we have to contribute."

"You'd be surprised. Holt's theory deviates from the norm."

"In what way?"

"He believes there's a government conspiracy. He's leanin' toward the idea of a group of rogue agents out to take down the Southern Boy Mafia on their own."

Conspiracy? Rogue agents? This was quickly venturing out of their wheelhouse.

"Are you talkin' about a cabal?" Reese asked, unable to disguise his curiosity.

"Exactly. From what Holt's found so far, there are some questionable actions by the FBI. He thinks perhaps they're workin' outside official lines."

"To what end?"

Simon grinned. "That's the question everyone keeps askin'. One I don't have an answer for yet, but I think if I start pullin' on these threads, it's gonna come to light."

Reese thought back to the information they'd uncovered during their trip to New York. JJ had found some interesting connections between some of their former team members. Connections that didn't make sense. At least not on the surface, but when you looked at them through a bigger lens, there was a good chance they were connected to this theory of Holt's.

"Travis encouraged me to pursue this," Simon said. "And I'd like to utilize the skills and knowledge of your team to get answers. Unless you're opposed to the idea."

"No," he said quickly. Perhaps too quickly.

Simon chuckled. "It's addicting, isn't it?"

Reese stared at the man, unable to hide the smile that crept up. "The finding the answers part?" Reese huffed a laugh. "Yeah. Addicting is one word for it. I think there are definitely more questions than answers at the moment, but I honestly don't know how our help will benefit the story."

"Let's just say there are some connections that need to be fleshed out. Because you and Brantley are familiar with some of the key players, having you and your team look at it will help."

"If we do and nothin' comes of it, what then?"

"Then we quash it altogether."

Reese nodded. "How often does that happen?"

"In all the time I've been doing this…" Simon's gaze shot skyward as though he were thinking. A second later, he looked back at Reese. "Never."

"Never? Really?"

"Really. I wouldn't agree to look into something unless I thought there was something there. If we work together, perhaps we can give Travis and his family some answers. It may not be the closure he's lookin' for, but like I said, maybe it'll help."

Reese wasn't so sure anything would help, considering Travis and Gage had lost their wife. Their children had lost their mother. Only time would lessen the pain of that sort of loss. But maybe Simon was right. Perhaps there were answers that would give them a little bit of peace.

"Okay," Reese told Simon, meeting his stare. "Say I give you full access to the task force. What's the next step?"

"We need to plug in some of the missing pieces. The only way I know to do that is to map it out from beginning to end."

"And how do you propose we do that?"

Simon smiled. "Holt and I have already started. We just need your team to add what they already know. Then we can establish a baseline."

A baseline.

Sounded easy enough.

Which Reese figured meant it wouldn't be.

Chapter Four

ARCHER WAS IMPRESSED.

Admittedly, he hadn't been sure what to expect when he learned the task force worked out of an old barn. His imagination had run wild. Everything from a horror flick complete with sharpened tools dangling precariously from the ceiling to the picturesque T.A. Moulten Barn in Grand Teton National Park, noted to be the most photographed barn in America.

This was so not either of those. The exterior could probably use a little work, maybe a coat of paint, some nails. Then again, perhaps Brantley and Reese wanted it to look that way to keep people from creeping around it. Considering the high-tech gadgets inside, it made sense.

"What do you think?" Brantley prompted as Archer took it all in.

"When do I start?"

"If it's up to Reese? Yesterday."

Archer chuckled. "Looks to me like you've got a full house. You sure you've got room for one more?"

"They'll make room. Trust me."

A few affirmative murmurs sounded from the people spread throughout the space.

"Believe it or not, we could use ten more," Brantley explained. "We continue to take on more cases passed to us by local PDs. All of them cold. Some by months, others by years. The longer they sit, the more stressed I get knowin' we've gotten nowhere."

Archer could see how that would be stressful. "What about hot cases? How often do you take those?"

"Since we've come under the umbrella of Sniper 1 Security, we've got more resources, so it allows us to get more information faster. We're rarely the first point of contact when someone goes missing, but if we learn of a tender age child within three hundred miles of here, we dispatch a team immediately. All others, we handle case by case, depending on the circumstances surrounding it."

Archer nodded, letting that sink in.

Brantley cleared his throat, getting the attention of everyone in the room. Those who just realized there were others present chimed in with various greetings.

"Hey, boss."

"What brings you by?"

Brantley waited until the room settled, and all eyes shifted their way. "I'd like to introduce you to Archer Halligan."

A hush fell across the room.

"Hey." Archer looked from one face to the next, not sure if Brantley expected him to launch into some sort of verbal résumé.

No one responded, and he could see the curiosity beginning to burn brighter and hotter in the eyes staring back at him. Luckily, Brantley didn't put him on the spot, forcing him to resort back to his high school days when he was cast as the Stage Manager in *Our Town*. It had been a horrific ordeal, considering he never auditioned. It was then he learned he suffered from debilitating stage fright.

"Let's start with introductions." Brantley pointed toward the man closest to the door. "Archer, meet Evan Vaughn. He's a former police detective, originally in Florida, then with Round Rock PD for a beat. Next to him is his partner, Slade Elliott."

Pretending not to recognize the name, Archer nodded in greeting. So *that* was Spencer's brother?

"Slade's a former bounty hunter. Next, we have Atticus James, who shares the same former occupation as Slade," Brantley told him.

"That's not all he shares with Slade," someone muttered.

"Hey," Atticus said, propping a hip on one of the desks. "You comin' on board this train?"

"We haven't talked nuts and bolts yet," Brantley told him.

"I hope you do," Atticus said, holding his stare. "I'm tired up to my eyeballs of lookin' at applications."

Archer chuckled.

"Atticus is our newest team member," Brantley explained. "He was a bounty hunter we encountered when workin' a case up in Dallas."

Atticus smirked. "A glamorous job, I know. Why would I ever give it up? I'd probably still be doin' it, but"—Atticus patted his hip where his weapon rested—"the big guy took one look at me and thought it'd be best to arm me and send me out into the world."

"Don't worry," Brantley said. "We trained him to use it first."

"Mostly," Baz added with a smirk.

"That desk right there belongs to Holly Switzer," Brantley continued. "She's the one who walked you over. She came on as JJ's assistant but shifted into an analyst role. She's currently at the hospital keeping JJ company."

"She's gonna be so sad to've missed this," Evan said with a laugh.

Brantley didn't miss a beat. "But you probably remember the woman keepin' her chair warm. Elana Buckley."

"Hey, girl." Archer tipped his chin in greeting. "Nice to see you again."

"I love the podcast," she said breathlessly.

"I think Simon deserves all the accolades for that one. He's the brains. I'm the brawn."

Her gaze shifted downward, and Archer pretended not to notice the approval glittering in her eyes.

"Elana's technical title is JJ's assistant, but don't let that fool you. She handles pretty much anything these people throw her way. JJ, Elana, and Baz man the fort from up there."

Archer glanced up at the loft that covered the back half of the barn.

"This is Jay Hernandez," Brantley continued. "He works on special projects. He partners with Charlie Miller"—Brantley gestured toward an empty desk—"who's not here right now. She's takin' care of some personal business."

"Nice to meet you," Archer told Jay.

"Likewise."

"And the redhead back there ... that's Rebecca Richter. She goes by Becs. She's one of our analysts, and she's got some experience out in the field with us."

"Jack of all trades, huh?" Archer said with a smile.

"Somethin' like that," Becs replied with a small wave.

"That guy back there is Darius Frost," Brantley continued. "He's a former techie JJ pilfered from a corporate gig in Dallas. He's gonna be Baz's right hand, in charge of cold cases and special projects. We've hired four additional investigators to join Charlie and Jay on that team. They'll be comin' on board next week."

"Darius'll also be the go-to when I'm out on paternity leave," Baz noted.

The door opened, and all eyes shifted in that direction.

"And last but not least…"

A man walked in, looking as though he was about to kneel before a firing squad, eyes wide, eyebrows cocked. "What's up?"

"This is Luca Switzer," Brantley acknowledged. "Luca, meet Archer Halligan. Luca can navigate the internet almost as good as JJ."

"Better," Luca corrected, walking toward them. "Just don't tell her that. I'm lettin' her hold onto the title for a little while longer."

Archer shook his hand. "Didn't I hear another Switzer a minute ago?"

"That'd be my pain in the ass little sister," Luca stated, releasing his hand.

"She's hangin' with JJ," Brantley reminded.

Ah. Right.

Not that Archer would know who was who. The overwhelming number, combined with his horrific ability to put a name with a face, meant he would no doubt flounder at their second meeting, but he appreciated Brantley making an effort.

"I know they're not all here right now, but that's the team," Brantley said, turning to face him. "We've got flexible hours because the job's the job. When we're needed, it's all hands on deck. Otherwise, they take care of their business as they need to. As long as the work gets done, I don't have to put my boot in any asses."

"I take it one of these is your office?" Archer asked, gesturing toward the wall of glass.

"Reese and I work out of our offices at the house. Second floor. Reese'll tell you we moved over there to free up space, but that's a lie. We did it to hide from these people."

A chorus of laughter sounded.

"That's the conference room." Baz pointed toward the long, narrow room, which was currently dark. "Behind it is the kitchen. Nothin' fancy, but there's coffee. Behind that, the restroom."

"We're in the process of rearrangin' things," Elana said, standing tall. "We got some new desks in today."

"She says that like they haven't rearranged this place a few dozen times in the past month," Brantley said.

Atticus pointed at Brantley. "*Exactly*. And the desks … they're new to us. They're actually ancient."

Archer peered around, taking it all in again.

"So, when do you start?" Luca asked.

"He hasn't taken the job yet," Brantley responded before glancing at him again. "And I'm sure he's got plenty of questions."

"A few."

"Let's head back to the house, and we'll get you some answers."

"It was great to meet you all," Archer told the room.

The rest of the team echoed the sentiments. Everyone except for Slade, who glared at him as though he'd just set fire to his car. Hmm. He wondered what that was about.

"You think you could see yourself workin' here?" Brantley asked when they stepped outside.

Archer was nodding before he realized he was doing it. He couldn't explain what it was about this place or the people, but he liked it. Far more than he'd liked anything in a long, *long* time.

"Yeah," he said, smiling as he turned to Brantley. "I like the vibe."

"They're a great team. We've had some bumps in the road, but our closure rate is high. I can let you look at some case notes if you'd like to get an idea of how we do things."

"That would be great." Archer wouldn't mind checking out the workload or seeing how the other investigators handle their cases. It'd tell him whether or not he would fit in.

AFTER INTRODUCING ARCHER TO THE TEAM, THEY returned to the house to find Simon and Reese shaking hands.

"That was fast," Brantley said, watching both men. "Y'all hash it all out without us?"

"Not even close," Simon answered. "But I think it's best to meet up at Holt's apartment. It's where he's got all his research. Not to mention, this'll be a lengthy discussion, and it's clear you're both busy. I don't want to overstay my welcome." He flashed a grin. "Not yet, anyway."

"Spoken like a true journalist," Archer noted.

"Let me get your contact info," Brantley told Archer. "I'll get you access to some of our case notes. I think Becs has written up some process notes. I'll make sure you get those, too."

"Sure thing," he said, reaching for the pen Brantley produced.

While he jotted down his email address and phone number, Brantley noticed Reese's curious glance. He offered a subtle nod, letting him know all was good. At least for the moment.

When they left a few minutes later, Reese gave him a high-level of what he'd talked to Simon about. Meredith Prescott. Mob hit. Adorites. According to Simon, Travis was on board with the idea of Simon pursuing a story about Kylie's mother. As for what that actually entailed, he had no idea. Wasn't even sure Simon was clear on it.

"I guess we'll find out sooner or later. What do you say we get some work done?"

"I'm good with that."

Brantley headed upstairs to his office so he could dig through his email in search of a light at the end of that dark, ugly tunnel. And, like every time he tackled it, he got sucked in for an hour and a half and accomplished pretty much nothing. He absolutely detested email. Unfortunately, Sniper 1 Security thought it was the be-all-end-all of communication. The majority of the crap he got in his inbox ended up in the trash folder.

"Tesha's got training with Magnus," Reese announced as he strolled into Brantley's office.

"At the old place or new?"

"Old, but I'm gonna help Trey with a few things at the new place, so Magnus is meetin' us there."

"What time?"

"Three."

Brantley glanced at his watch: 14:39.

Twenty-one minutes and Reese only had to travel across the street to make his appointment, leaving Brantley some time to seduce him. Not quite enough time for a quickie, but plenty for…

Oh, yeah. Plenty of time for that.

"What's your plan for after?" he asked Reese as his body hummed with anticipation.

"If I can, I figured I'd swing by and talk to Holt. See if he'll give me more on this supposed conspiracy."

Brantley sat up straight, all amusement disappearing. "You really wanna go down that rabbit hole?"

Reese exhaled heavily. "I don't know yet. When I think about all that Travis's family's been through and how…" Reese cleared his throat. "How we played a role in that. Yeah. I wanna help. More than that, I want answers. I think Travis wants us to do it, too."

"Why hasn't he said something?" That was the part Brantley didn't understand. For some reason, Travis was avoiding them. Was that why? Because he blamed them for what happened?

"I think he's been holdin' off. The wedding and all."

Ah. That made sense, too. Kinda.

"Now that it's done," Reese continued, "and Simon's lookin' to dig in his heels, I think it's only a matter of time before Travis comes to us."

Brantley nodded. "And because Holt Callahan was the one who uncovered the link between Kylie's mother and Maximillian Adorite, you think that's a good place to start?"

"As good as any. Simon wants our input, and I'd like to understand what their angle is before we proceed," Reese said, as though Brantley wasn't completely in agreement. "I'd like to sit down with Holt and have him tell me exactly what he told Travis."

"You don't want me to come with you?"

Reese stood tall and grinned. "Someone's gotta hang back and handle the Monday call."

"Ah, hell." Brantley had completely forgotten about that damn call. Every Monday they chatted with Z, giving him an update on their cases. He usually managed to come up with an excuse and left Reese to chat with his brother. This was likely payback.

"You sure you don't wanna do that? *I* could take Tesha."

"Not a chance, Navy boy. I took the last three calls. You owe me."

"I can think of a dozen ways I can pay you back. All will take"— he looked at his watch—"less than fifteen minutes."

"So you marry a guy and suddenly he forgets all about the romance because he can *get it done in fifteen*." Reese sighed dramatically. "I shoulda known."

God, he loved this man. More so when he teased him.

"Fine. But I can't promise Atticus won't flirt with me while you're gone."

"Nice try." Reese walked toward him. "Let him flirt. That ring on your finger says you're mine for life."

Brantley rubbed his thumb on his wedding band—something he found himself doing often—as he leaned back in his chair. He smiled when Reese planted his hands on the arms of the chair and leaned forward until their lips nearly touched.

"For life," Reese repeated.

"Damn straight." Brantley tilted his head back, closing the gap between their mouths. He let Reese kiss him, knowing the man wouldn't walk away without branding him after a remark like that one.

Reese didn't disappoint, angling his head, his tongue stealing into Brantley's mouth.

It was all Brantley could do to keep from grabbing him and manhandling him over to the couch. What he wouldn't give to strip Reese naked and bury himself deep inside his warm, willing body. He thought for sure his lust would've dimmed by now, but it seemed that being married had only amplified his need. It didn't matter that he'd fucked Reese before they rolled out of bed that morning—a routine that was becoming one of the very best parts of his day—or that tonight, when they went to bed, he would no doubt find a way to seduce him again. He couldn't get enough.

Curious as to whether Reese's willpower was stronger than his, Brantley slipped his fingers into the waistband of Reese's jeans. He found the swollen head of Reese's cock, teasing the tip. It was enough to have Reese gasping into his mouth.

"Let me suck you," Brantley told him, snagging Reese's lower lip between his teeth.

"We've got things to do."

"Those can wait."

"You're procrastinating."

"I want to suck your cock. I wanna make you come down my throat."

Reese pulled back enough for Brantley to see the glitter in his golden eyes. He took that as a sign to proceed. Not breaking eye contact, he continued to fondle the head of Reese's cock with his fingertips while he quickly unbuttoned and unzipped his jeans.

"You know you wanna fuck my mouth," Brantley taunted, tugging Reese's boxer briefs down to free his beautiful dick.

Reese grunted, standing taller and planting one hand on Brantley's head. He was taking charge, something he'd done quite a bit these past few days. He was giving himself over to the desire that burned like wildfire whenever they were in the same room.

Brantley peered down, admiring Reese's cock, his mouth watering in anticipation.

"You sure you want this?" he asked, letting his breath fan over the swollen head.

"Brantley…"

He lapped the bead of pre-cum pooling at the tip, then licked around the crest.

Reese grunted again, his hand tightening on Brantley's head. "Put me in your mouth."

Unable to resist, he pressed a kiss to the tip, then wrapped his lips around the bulbous head, sliding lower, swirling his tongue around the velvet-smooth flesh, relishing the familiar taste of strong, healthy male.

"Oh, yeah," Reese rasped, his voice low and soft.

Brantley let Reese take control, pumping his hips, driving his cock into Brantley's mouth as those strong fingers pressed firmly into his scalp. He could do this all fucking day, surrendering to this man. His partner. His lover. His husband.

"Fuck yes, Brantley. God, that feels good."

He let the awe in Reese's voice drive him, sucking, licking. He took his time, not wanting to rush but eager to give him the pleasure he deserved. He knew Reese was getting close because he began ramming his dick in deeper, pushing into Brantley's throat. His groans echoed in the small office.

"Gonna come," Reese warned. "Oh, yeah. Suck. Hard."

Brantley did as requested, letting Reese use his mouth, fucking his face roughly. He felt the first pulse of warning and prepared himself to consume every last drop. Reese let out a garbled shout as cum splashed his tongue. Brantley swallowed it down, easing off Reese's dick slowly, disappointed that he had to stop.

"Jesus," Reese hissed, lovingly caressing Brantley's cheek. With a huff and a sigh, Reese released him as he stumbled back, righting his clothes as he gasped for air. Brantley leaned back in his chair and smiled.

"You good to walk out of here?" Brantley asked, laughing when Reese grabbed for the desk as he headed for the door.

"I'll get you back for that one later."

"Promise?"

Reese looked back over his shoulder, his eyes glittering and a sinful smile on his face. "Damn straight."

Brantley laughed as Reese echoed his words from earlier.

"Don't you dare miss that call!" Reese shouted as he disappeared into the hallway. "I'm takin' Tesha."

"Yeah, yeah, yeah," he muttered. And he would certainly let Z know exactly how ridiculous he thought the weekly calls were. Again.

Chapter Five

AFTER REESE LEFT, BRANTLEY TOOK A MINUTE to let his body settle down. The adrenaline that fueled him after that brief interlude was a nice rush, and he savored it while it lasted.

That and he preferred not to venture anywhere until his dick wasn't fighting with his zipper. He'd been in a perpetual state of arousal since pretty much the day he met Reese. He probably should've been used to it by now.

Once he could walk without discomfort, he made a detour to the bathroom for some mouthwash. He had some time before the call with Z, and sitting still until then was not going to work for him. He needed to move around.

When he walked into the barn a short time later, he found himself looking at a large screen image of his best friend grinning from her hospital bed, Holly at her side. Charlie, Elana, Luca, Evan, and Jay were standing in front of the television, talking over each other, laughing.

The door closed behind him. "I guess it's a good thing I keep comin' over here," Brantley said loudly. "Otherwise, y'all'd get nothin' done."

The laughter and conversation ceased. A moment later, the bodies shifted backward to reveal JJ stabbing a finger in his direction. "You and me ... we're gonna have words," she threatened, causing everyone to look back at him as they started to disperse, heading back to their desks and returning to work.

"How many words do you think I'm capable of havin' in a day?" Brantley asked as he moved closer to the television. "And why are you video conferencing when these people should be workin'?"

"They miss me."

"Yeah, we do," Charlie said.

"And I miss them," JJ said sweetly.

"Shouldn't you be resting?"

"I'm a multi-tasker, and so are they," JJ countered. "Are you and Reese comin' by tonight?"

He could see the hopeful look in her eyes. Brantley had made a point of visiting her every day in the hopes of keeping her calm. He knew JJ wasn't keen on sitting in the hospital when she would prefer to be anywhere else, so visiting was the least he could do if it meant she would get the rest the doctor insisted she needed.

"Twice in one day? That might be too much," he joked, tucking his hands in his pockets. "But if I do, should we bring you dinner?"

JJ looked to the left. "Is Baz there?"

"I'm here," he called from the loft.

"Do you want them to bring dinner?" JJ shouted, which was completely unnecessary since the volume was already maxed out.

"Or I could pick it up on my way back there," Baz said, sounding amused.

JJ's green gaze returned to Brantley. "That would be yes. Text me when y'all are headin' this way, and I'll tell you where and what."

"Got it. Until then, get some rest. You're only focus should be on cookin' those babies a little longer."

Her bottom lip puffed out. "Fine."

Brantley winked at her, and the call ended, the screen going black.

When he turned around, everyone was at their desks, working as though they'd been doing it all along.

Several hours later, Brantley was sitting in one of the leather recliners in JJ's hospital room, feet propped up, a plate of food in one hand, fork in the other.

"Why wouldn't he take the job?" JJ asked, seemingly worried that Archer Halligan wasn't going to accept the position when only a short time ago she was on Brantley's ass about issuing an offer without asking her first.

"No one said he won't," he told her.

"He hasn't yet."

"Correct," he said, not wanting to debate JJ on this.

"Have you called him?"

Brantley frowned. "No. Why would I? I talked to him this mornin'."

"I know. And now it's night."

"Evening," he corrected.

JJ sighed, her gaze darting to Baz. "The least you can do is support me on this."

His eyes widened, and not for the first time, Baz looked helpless. It was enough to make Brantley laugh.

"We'll follow up with Archer in the next day or two," Reese said, clearly trying to get Baz off the hook.

"If we don't hear from him first," Brantley added before she could reply. "But I'm pretty sure we will."

"Pretty sure?" JJ glanced from one face to the next. "Why only *pretty sure*? Did you not explain that we're the most successful task force in the state?"

Brantley huffed a laugh. "I left that part out."

"Why? It's true."

"In your mind, maybe," he teased, lifting his fork to silence her so he could continue. "Plus, he doesn't care about shit like that. He doesn't need to be persuaded. He just needs time to let it all sink in."

"He should spend a day with the team," she said, returning her attention to the plate in front of her, although he hadn't seen her take two bites since Baz uncovered her food.

"If he wants to do that, we'll arrange it," Reese said.

Brantley continued to eat, waiting for JJ to add something else. He made it three whole bites before she did.

"I deserve to meet him before you officially hire him."

He glanced at Reese.

"What?" JJ asked, her gaze narrowed on him. "What's that look for? I should be allowed to meet anyone you intend to hire *before* you hire them, should I not?"

"She kinda has a point," Reese muttered, not looking up from his food.

Yes, she did. Because JJ had played a pivotal role in their very first case—before they were the governor's task force—Brantley considered her a partner, not an employee. And yes, he agreed that any partner should have a say in the hiring process.

Brantley looked at JJ. "Call him."

"What?"

"Call him," he repeated. "Call him and tell him you'd like to interview him before he makes a decision."

She looked horrified. "I'm not gonna tell him that."

"Why not?"

"Because—" Her eyebrows dipped down. "Fine." She reached for her phone. "What's his number?"

Reese grabbed his phone before Brantley could, so he continued to eat while Reese rattled off the phone number, and JJ dialed.

All eyes shifted to JJ when she put the phone on speaker.

"Hello?"

"Is this Archer?"

"It is."

"This is JJ. Jessica James, I mean. With the task force."

"Hey, Jessica James," Archer crooned. "What can I do for you?"

The man oozed charm with every syllable. Brantley would give him that.

"Brantley and Reese told me you stopped by today."

JJ stared at the phone as though waiting for a response, but there wasn't one. And there still wasn't one.

Reese cleared his throat.

Archer said, "Oh, sorry. Was that a question?"

It was quite possible his best friend blushed, but Brantley couldn't be sure.

"No," she said, not making eye contact with anyone. "It wasn't. I was just ... uhmm..." Her forehead creased. "I wondered if you'd have a few minutes to talk to me."

"Of course," he said cheerfully. "What would you like to chat about?"

"Here," she stated. "In person."

"Here as in ... where?"

"I'm in the hospital."

Brantley fought the grin that threatened. It wasn't like JJ to be flustered, but she seemed to be at the moment.

"Just tell me which one, and I'll be there whenever you'd like me to," Archer stated.

"Now would be good," she said, her eyes lifting for the first time since the call began. "Will that work for you?"

"Yes, ma'am."

"Do not call me ma'am."

"Yes, sir."

JJ huffed a laugh. "Do not call me that either."

"Yes, JJ."

"That's better." She rattled off the name of the hospital and her room number. "We'll be waitin' for you."

"I'll head that way now."

The call ended, and JJ looked at him. "Are you happy now?"

He snorted a laugh. "Me? Why me?"

"Because you're the one who wants me to meet with him."

Brantley choked on air.

Before he could defend himself, Reese held up a hand, waving him off.

How the hell did this become *his* idea?

JJ FELT A LITTLE BIT SILLY FOR insisting on talking to Archer Halligan. In her defense, she was bored to tears and so ready to go home. The hospital people were incredibly nice—far nicer than she'd expected them to be—but she wanted her own bed and her own house and her office at HQ.

She didn't want to sit here all day like she was an invalid or something.

She also didn't want to be walking from one room to the next and have one of the peanuts plop out onto the ground.

So here she was, and here she would stay. The least her team could do was entertain her.

"How long do you think it'll take him to get here?" she asked, directing the question at Reese and Brantley.

"Depends on where he is."

"He's stayin' at the B and B," she told him.

"What if he's somewhere else?"

"What if he's not?' she countered, worrying that she might've interrupted Archer's evening.

"Then I guess it'll take fifteen or twenty minutes. If he was ready to walk out the door."

JJ considered that for a moment, staring at the three men in the room. She could tell they were all reluctant to say anything. She didn't blame them. She'd been working on her reasons for being irritated, and she'd come up with many in the short time she'd been there.

"What would you like to do until then?" she prompted, wishing one of them would speak.

No one answered.

"Okay. Someone give me the basics on Archer Halligan."

"Basics?" Brantley asked.

"Yes. How old is he? Where was he born? Is he married? Kids?"

Brantley was the one to answer. "He's twenty-nine, from Dallas, never married, no kids."

When he stopped, JJ waited for him to add something other than the specific things she had requested.

He didn't.

"Jeez. Do I have to do everything around here? Tell me more?"

"What else do you wanna know?"

"I don't know. Where did he work before he started working for Simon's podcast?"

"He was a Marine scout sniper."

"Armed services, okay. Anything else?"

"Not according to his resume."

"You have that?"

"No."

JJ huffed, glaring at Brantley. "How'm I supposed to make an informed decision if I don't know whether he's got skeletons in his closet?"

"I'm sure that'll be discovered on the background check that Z's runnin'," Reese stated, setting his empty food container aside.

"I thought you were waiting for him to take the job."

"We are. But we want to be prepared for when he comes on board."

"Why are you so sure he will?"

"Because he's bored."

Well, it was good to know she wasn't the only one.

JJ frowned at Reese. "He told you that?"

"Simon did."

Before she could launch into another question, the nurse walked in.

Jenny, one of the nicest nurses because she didn't overwhelm JJ with questions, glanced at the men in the room, then turned her full attention to JJ. She went through the motions, checking the monitors and the fluids they were pushing into her since Dr. Tinder said she was a little dehydrated. She was gentle when she checked JJ's pulse, and quiet as she slipped out of the room a few minutes after she came in.

While they waited for Archer to arrive, JJ considered taking a minute to make herself presentable, but decided she didn't care. Her hair was clipped up high on her head, and she was wearing an oversized T-shirt and shorts rather than the hospital gown. Since the team had witnessed her like this throughout the day when she video-conferenced with them, she figured it was good enough for a potential hire.

Speaking of...

Someone knocked lightly on the door.

"Come in," she called, relaxing against the pillows as the door opened and an enormous man appeared.

Jesus God. The man was ... well, the truth was, Archer Halligan was quite possibly the most gorgeous man in existence. Not that she intended to admit that aloud, but yeah, he was hot. And tall. And muscular. And he had a dimple. Make that two.

Did someone turn the air conditioner off?

Granted, he wasn't as sexy as Baz, but she also figured that was personal preference.

Not that she was comparing the two of them. She wasn't, but she couldn't overlook the similarities, such as the dark brown hair and the brilliant blue eyes. Archer's eyes were a tad more turquoise. Not quite as clear.

But that was pretty much where the similarities ended. Archer was bigger than Baz. Much bigger. Both in height and breadth. Hell, he was bigger than Brantley, and that was saying something. If there were a single ounce of fat on Archer, she would be surprised. Deductive reasoning told her he was at least six foot seven since he was taller than Reese, and everyone knew Reese was exactly six and a half feet tall.

So what if Archer Halligan was a beautiful man? She'd expected as much. He'd become somewhat of a celebrity once the podcast took off because people liked to talk about beautiful men. Because Simon Jennings was quite adept at avoiding cameras, people were determined to get photos of him. Since they couldn't, there were an awful lot of Archer's on the internet. She knew because she'd searched.

"Hi. I'm JJ. You know Reese, Brantley, and Baz."

Archer glanced at the men as he walked toward the bed. "Hey." He turned to look at her, holding out his hand. "It's a pleasure to meet you. It's my understanding you're the backbone of this organization, and they wouldn't exist without you."

JJ shook his hand. "Flattery doesn't work on me."

"We'll see about that." Archer smiled and ... Jesus God.

JJ watched as Archer turned, making his way over to where Tesha was asleep on the floor. He squatted down to greet her, talking softly. JJ was almost positive she heard Tesha purr. Dogs didn't purr, but there was a good chance they would for Archer Halligan.

He took his time before finally standing tall and turning toward her.

Flustered, she launched into the first question. "Why would you want to work for the task force when you've got a lucrative job working for Simon?"

He grinned. "Define lucrative."

"Are you hurtin' for money?"

"Not at the moment."

"Okay then. Why do you want to give that up for the task force?"

"I'm looking for something to fill my downtime."

"Because you have so much of it?"

"More than I'd like." He leaned against the dresser, crossing his legs at the ankles. "Simon does a lot of his own investigating. Plus, Paige has been looking to do more."

"Was this Simon's idea?"

"No. But he's not opposed to it, either."

"What if the podcast becomes a conflict of interest? Would you quit working for Simon altogether?"

He didn't appear the least bit fazed by her questions, and she liked that he wasn't.

"If it came down to it, I'd do what was in the best interest of everyone."

"That's not a yes."

He smirked. "You're right. It's not."

"Do you not like hypotheticals? Because this job requires quite a bit of that line of thinking."

His smile was warm. "I can't say I'm bothered by hypotheticals, no."

JJ stared at him for a moment, letting the silence linger, wondering whether or not he felt the need to fill it. When he didn't say anything and he didn't break eye contact, she smiled.

"Did Brantley warn you about me?"

He chuckled. "He might've mentioned the task force wouldn't succeed without you and that I should remember that if nothing else."

Damn it. A flood of tears rushed to her eyes. Her sinuses burned, but she fought the urge to let them fall.

Stupid pregnancy hormones.

She sniffled and managed a smile. "I like you, Archer Halligan."

"I like you, too, Jessica James."

Brantley was right to like this guy. Eventually, she would have to tell him that. One day. Maybe.

Chapter Six

As soon as Slade got home after work, he went straight to his bedroom to change. He stripped off his jeans and T-shirt and opted for a pair of workout shorts. He didn't bother with a shirt. It was too damn hot. Plus, he hated the restriction of clothing. The shorts were a necessity since he now had a roommate; otherwise, he probably would've gone without those, too.

After changing, he headed for the bathroom to wash his hands and face. He was kicking around the idea of making dinner, but stalling since he wasn't quite sure what to make. Or why he was bothering at all.

He couldn't stop thinking about Archer Halligan. More accurately, the fact that Atticus was going to be partnered up with him. How the fuck was Slade supposed to compete with that? Atticus would spend endless hours, possibly sometimes days, with the man. What would happen if they were attracted to each other?

Gripping his hair with both hands, Slade glared at his reflection. He couldn't do this again. He couldn't risk ruining a perfectly good … whatever it was he had with Atticus because he was insecure. It wasn't benefiting anyone for him to second-guess every single thing Atticus was doing, thinking, saying.

He took a deep breath and let it out slowly.

He was going to start over.

What was the saying? Fake it until you make it. Yeah. He could do that. He could pretend to feel confident about his … whatever it was he had with Atticus, until he actually did feel confident.

Frowning, Slade wondered whether it would help to define what this was with Atticus. And Carson. Couldn't forget Carson, although there were moments when Slade wished he could. Even after the night Carson apologized and admitted to having feelings for him, Slade was still hesitant to take the man at his word. Hindsight and all that.

"Slade!"

Ah, hell. Atticus was home, which meant he couldn't hide out in the bathroom any longer.

Fake it until you make it.

He took one more deep breath and a slow exhale as he turned to the door.

"In here!" he called as he came out of the bathroom, heading for the living room. "I was thinkin' maybe I could make dinner."

"I'm gonna work out first," Atticus shouted from the workout room.

That was interesting. And new. Atticus usually came home, flopped down on the couch, and stared at his phone for a good half hour before he did anything. Was there a reason? Was he hoping to impress someone? Someone who might be Archer Halligan.

No. Dammit. He would not let his insecurities get the best of him.

Fake it until you make it.

He could go for a workout. It was technically his rest day, but a few extra sets of bi's and tri's never hurt—

Slade came to an abrupt stop in the doorway of the workout room. "Oh, fuck."

Atticus was standing in front of the wall mirror, his shorts shoved down, his cock in his fist. From Slade's vantage point, he could see the shift of the muscles in his back as he stroked himself slowly.

And fuck if that didn't turn him on like nothing else. From the very first time he'd laid eyes on Atticus James, Slade had found himself intrigued. Inexplicably. He'd fought it for the longest time, but he couldn't anymore. He wanted this man in a way he'd never wanted anything in his life.

Not sure what to say or do, Slade stood there, staring unabashedly, admiring the man.

"Have a seat," Atticus said, gesturing toward the workout bench in the center of the room.

This was also new. Slade was usually the one making demands or simply taking control because he knew Atticus enjoyed the dominance.

Continuing to watch Atticus's fist move up and down the length of his cock, Slade went to the bench and took a seat.

"Lie back." Atticus turned to face him, his eyes sparking with heat.

Curious what the man had in mind, Slade scooted his ass to the end of the bench and reclined until he was flat on his back, knees wide, feet on the floor.

"Do you remember the first time we were together?" Atticus prompted.

"Yeah." Slade relived that moment damn near every day. They'd been in this room. On this bench.

"Remember what you said to me that night?"

"I said a lot of things." Not to mention, he *thought* a lot of things, some of which he didn't put a voice to and wasn't sure he should bring any of them up now.

Atticus stopped at the base of the bench, standing between Slade's spread knees.

"You said I looked good with your dick in my mouth."

Oh, yeah. He probably did say that.

His gaze slid down Atticus's torso, fixing on his cock one more time. Right now, Slade preferred to find out how good he looked with Atticus's dick in *his* mouth. He wanted to taste him, to feel the splash of his cum against the back of his throat when Atticus came apart.

"Let's see if you still think so."

Still think so? About what?

"Oh, shit." Slade gasped when Atticus tugged his shorts down, his cock bobbing thick and heavy once it was freed.

"Have I mentioned how gorgeous your cock is?" Atticus wrapped a fist around Slade's dick as he went to his knees.

Slade shook his head, unable to speak. He was focused on breathing, enjoying the tug of Atticus's hand.

"Well, it is." Atticus leaned forward, licking the tip.

Slade watched, unable to look away, as Atticus teased him with his tongue and lips. His soft hums sent vibrations straight to his balls. Somehow, he managed to remain where he was, hands tucked under his head to keep from reaching for the man. He was so lost in the sensation he didn't hear the sound of the front door right away.

"Atticus?"

Fuck. Carson was there.

"In here," Atticus said, curling his fingers around Slade's shaft. "Don't move."

Like he could.

"Shit," Carson muttered when he appeared in the doorway.

Atticus pointed a finger at Carson. "Stay right there."

Slade glanced at Carson and cocked an eyebrow. He noticed Carson was as surprised by Atticus's adamance as he was. Slade's attention jerked back to Atticus when the man sucked him deep into his mouth again.

Arching his back, Slade let the pleasure swim in his veins, ignoring the fact that Carson had interrupted a perfectly good moment between him and Atticus. But Slade wouldn't let it bother him. He would pretend that he was as thrilled with Carson's presence as Atticus was.

Fake it until you make it.

"This is an experiment," Atticus said when he released his cock.

"An experiment?" Carson sounded amused.

Atticus stroked Slade's throbbing dick as he spoke. "Yes. Since no one seems to know how to proceed, I've decided to experiment."

"On?" Slade asked, his voice rougher than he expected.

"Both of you."

Slade moaned as Atticus stroked.

Carson said, "How so?"

"We're gonna start by taking turns watching." Atticus took Slade's cock in his mouth again, bobbing up and down several times before pulling off.

"I take it I'm goin' first?"

Atticus glanced at Carson. "No."

Slade watched as Atticus crooked a finger at Carson.

"Pull out your dick."

"Bossy little thing, aren't you?"

"He is," Slade agreed, watching as Carson did as Atticus instructed, unbuttoning his jeans and lowering the zipper as he walked into the room.

Atticus continued to fist Slade's cock, stroking up and down while Carson shoved his jeans down, freeing his monster cock. The man was hard as steel. From watching Atticus sucking him?

Slade's cock pulsed when Atticus wrapped his fingers around the base of Carson's cock and began stroking them at the same time.

And there it was. A tsunami of jealousy slammed into him, causing his breath to hitch in his chest. Sure, there was something erotic about feeling Atticus's hand on his dick and watching as he did the same to Carson. But that green-eyed monster was a powerful beast, and no matter how much Slade tried to beat it back, it rarely worked.

Fully expecting Atticus to give Carson the same attention he'd already given him, Slade was surprised when Atticus leaned down and began sucking him again.

"Fuck," Slade hissed. He shifted his focus to the warmth and suction of Atticus's mouth. It was goddamn perfect. So what if Atticus was dividing his attention, giving some of it to Carson? This was enough. Right?

Too bad it didn't last nearly long enough.

"You liked that," Atticus said, peering up at Carson. "Watching me sucking him."

Carson nodded. "Yeah."

Of course he had. Carson had always gotten off watching Slade with other men. Why would this be any different? Well, aside from the fact that Carson had feelings for Atticus. Feelings he'd never had for Slade.

Damn it. He was regressing. There was no time for self-pity right now.

Fake it until you make it.

Slade held his breath when Atticus leaned in and kissed the head of Carson's dick, then dragged his tongue over the glistening tip before taking him into his mouth.

He probably shouldn't enjoy watching that nearly as much as he did, considering he hated the idea of it just as much. He wanted Atticus for himself. He was doing his damnedest to pretend otherwise, but deep down...

Atticus pulled off Carson, turned toward him. "You liked it, too."

Slade met his gaze and lied. "Maybe."

Atticus squeezed his dick firmly. "In case you didn't notice, I felt your cock throb in my hand."

Busted.

"Don't deny it," Atticus said, his tone firm.

"I didn't." He couldn't.

Atticus grinned, looking between them. "Let's continue the experiment, shall we?"

ATTICUS WASN'T SURE WHAT PROMPTED THIS EXPERIMENT. He'd been driving home from HQ, recalling the hatred he'd seen in Slade's eyes when the team was introduced to Archer.

He had no idea what Slade could possibly have against the man, but Atticus got the feeling it wasn't so much personal as it was jealousy over the fact that Atticus would be partnering with him. That seemed to be Slade's go-to response.

Since Atticus wanted to smooth the waters, he decided to do something to keep Slade's mind from wandering to ridiculous things. Something that didn't involve tiptoeing around or worrying about the man's insecurities.

Sex was the only thing that had come to mind.

Which was ultimately the problem, he figured. Sure, this was good. Really fucking good. But it wouldn't be enough to sustain them in the long run.

As much as Atticus enjoyed this—and there was no denying that he did—he wanted more. More of something that was seriously lacking between the three of them. For whatever reason, Slade couldn't get past his jealousy, and Carson was walking on eggshells, trying to make it right with Slade. And that left Atticus wishing that these two didn't have a rocky history.

Unfortunately, he couldn't change the past, so the only option was to enjoy the here and now, to pave the way for some pleasure in the future. Sex was always a good distraction with them and as far as he was concerned, it was a damn fine way to pass the time.

"Fuck, Atticus," Carson crooned. "You look good with my dick in your mouth."

Atticus definitely enjoyed the shit out of being with them both. Their dominance was almost enough to allow him to forget all the other stuff that was working against them.

"Keep suckin'," Carson ordered, palming the top of his head.

Atticus focused, working Slade's cock with his fist and sucking Carson's dick down deep. Now wasn't the time to think about what could've been with these two. It made more sense to enjoy what he could have.

And this ... yeah, this was about as good as it got.

CARSON WAS PRETTY SURE HE'D DIED AND gone to heaven.

He hadn't known what to expect when he got Atticus's text earlier, asking him to stop by. There'd been no hint as to what Atticus had in mind, but Carson could safely say he hadn't expected this to be on the menu.

Then he walked into this room and found Slade laid out on that bench, all those muscles primely displayed while Atticus kneeled between his legs, his lips wrapped around his cock. It was a scene right out of his fantasies. In fact, he'd had a dream very similar to this last night. Only Slade and Atticus had been sucking each other while Carson watched.

"Jesus. That mouth," Carson moaned when Atticus took him to the root.

He honestly couldn't say which he enjoyed more, watching Atticus suck Slade or having Atticus's mouth on him. Both were erotically intoxicating and salaciously satisfying.

Lucky for him, he didn't have to decide because Atticus was determined to make them both come at the same time. Carson helped by moving closer, covering Atticus's hand and stroking himself while Atticus devoured Slade's cock. He watched Slade, the way his muscular chest heaved, his washboard abs contracting with every labored breath. Every now and then, he would meet Slade's gaze, enjoying the way those dark eyes were glazed with arousal. Slade might not admit it, but he was enjoying it too.

And when Atticus shifted again, taking Carson into his mouth, he stared down at those perfect lips stretched wide around him. Carson fought the urge to fuck his face, to take control simply because he knew Atticus would've given it if he'd pushed. But this was Atticus's game, and he was more than willing to play.

"I can get off like this," Carson admitted when Atticus was once again bobbing up and down on Slade's cock. "Watching him suck you."

Slade hissed.

"Make him come, Atticus," Carson commanded, his hand still covering Atticus's as he jerked himself to the bobbing rhythm of Atticus's mouth.

"Oh, fuck," Slade growled roughly.

"Come down his throat, Slade," Carson groaned. "Let me watch."

Slade's hand shot up, grabbing Atticus's head and holding him in place as his hips lifted. "Fuck, yes. Oh … fuck … yes."

Carson held on long enough to watch Atticus swallow Slade down before he reached for Atticus's head so he could ram his cock between his lips. One thrust, two. On the third, he let go.

Atticus moaned, the vibration making Carson's eyes cross as his dick pulsed in his mouth. It was then he realized Atticus was jerking his dick roughly, coming right along with them both.

"I think I might like this experiment," Slade said, his chest heaving, body relaxed on the bench. God, the man had a truly beautiful body.

"Me, too," Carson admitted.

"Me, three," Atticus said, sucking in air. "But next time, I get to watch."

Carson looked at Slade. "It's cute that he thinks he's in charge."

"I know, right?" Slade's rumbling laugh eased something inside him.

Maybe there was hope for them yet.

Chapter Seven

Tuesday, September 27, 2022

REESE WOKE TO THE SOUND OF BRANTLEY'S phone buzzing on the nightstand. Before he could elbow him and tell him to answer, Brantley was groggily muttering, "Hello."

He couldn't make out what the person on the other end of the line was saying; however, he could tell they were female, and he detected some excitement in their voice.

"Calm down, JJ," Brantley said, his voice thick with sleep.

Maybe it wasn't excitement. Perhaps it was panic. Was it time? Was she in labor?

The questions were enough to rouse him out of sleep, making it impossible to drift off again.

She was rambling on, too quickly for Reese to make out. Not that he cared to eavesdrop. Provided it didn't mean he was expected to be out the door in ten seconds once Brantley disconnected.

"Let me talk to Baz," Brantley rasped, his voice low.

Reese rolled to his back and propped his arm over his eyes, wishing for a few more minutes of sleep. It was a pipe dream at this point, but he wasn't quite ready to get out of bed.

"Yes, I believe you. But I'd like to hear it from him."

Smiling into the darkness, Reese listened until a deeper voice sounded on the phone.

"Is she really in labor?"

Reese dropped his arm and turned his head to stare at Brantley, waiting for the answer he wouldn't be able to hear. The room was dark, but the light in the hallway—the one they kept on for Tesha—provided enough glow to see his silhouette.

"Well, that's good to know."

Since Brantley didn't sound panicked, he figured they had time yet. Which gave Reese an idea. He wasn't ready to get out of bed, but he definitely wouldn't be going back to sleep, so there was only one thing left to do.

Moving slowly, he tugged the blankets off and scooted down the bed.

He felt Brantley shift. A second later, the bedside lamp came on.

Brantley's eyes opened, following him as he said, "Did Dr. Tinder say when?"

Reese settled between Brantley's legs, smiling when Brantley shifted to make room. He peered up to see the man watching, one arm tucked underneath his head, the other holding his phone to his ear.

"Is there anything we need to do for y'all?" Brantley asked. "Want us to stop by the house? Grab anything?"

While Brantley continued to watch him, Reese used the softest touch to tease Brantley's cock until it was hard and thick. With their eyes locked, he leaned down and took him in his mouth.

Brantley's soft gasp made him smile despite the cock stretching his lips.

"Yeah. Okay. We'll … Sure, Baz. Keep us updated."

Expecting Brantley to hang up, Reese began sucking him deeper, gently massaging his balls.

"Yeah … uh … *fuck* … No. Sorry. I was … Yeah. All right. I'll wait for him to call, sure. Later."

Reese pulled off Brantley's cock and wrapped his fist around the thick shaft, stroking as he stared up the length of Brantley's body.

"Wait for who to call?" Reese asked.

The phone clattered when it hit the nightstand.

"Does it matter?"

Reese chuckled. No, it didn't. Not at the moment.

He stroked with both hands.

"You're just rackin' up all the payback points, aren't you, Tavoularis?"

"Figured you needed some motivation this mornin'."

"So your mouth found its way to my dick to incentivize me?"

Reese chuckled, then resumed the blowjob, enjoying the way Brantley's grunts and moans grew louder.

"You know how much I wanna come down your throat right now?"

Reese moaned, urging him to do exactly that.

"If I do, I'm still fuckin' you in the shower after our run."

Reese peered up at him, met Brantley's gaze, hoping he could see the anticipation those words gave him.

"You want that? You want me to bend you over in the shower and ram my dick deep inside you?"

Fuck. His cock thickened, pulsing.

"I need to feel you," Brantley continued, bowing his back as Reese took him deep in his throat. "Oh, fuck, that feels good."

Seeing all those rock-hard muscles flex and bunch as Brantley's body arched and writhed was all he needed to continue. He loved watching this man, no matter what he was doing. But seeing him come undone was his favorite.

"Ah, Reese … *fuck* … don't make me come yet. I need to be deep inside you, baby."

Yeah, he kinda needed that, too.

Unable to wait, Reese pulled off Brantley's cock and crawled up his body, draping himself over him.

"Now," Reese insisted, reaching for the lube bottle sitting on the nightstand. "Fuck me now."

Brantley's smirk was laced with mischief. "I think I wanna wait until after the run."

"Fuck you," Reese said without heat, straddling Brantley's thighs as he poured lube into his hand and slathered Brantley's dick with it.

Laughing, Brantley tucked both hands under his head, groaning as he pumped his hips. "I love it when you're hot for me."

Which was all the damn time, but Reese was able to hide his arousal better than Brantley. Then again, he happened to like that his husband made a point to let him know how much he wanted him.

"Ah, yeah," Brantley moaned as he fucked Reese's fist. "Keep doin' that."

If he didn't know better, Reese would think Brantley was about to come and leave him aching.

"Fuck me, Brantley," he pleaded, although he didn't let up, stroking Brantley's cock firmly.

"How do you want it?"

He didn't bother telling Brantley he would take whatever he wanted to give him. He knew better. Brantley wanted to know. He was a generous lover.

"Hard and deep."

"Well, that's a given." Brantley grinned. "Fast or slow?"

Reese considered it. "Fast."

Brantley grinned. "On your stomach."

He wasted no time, moving off Brantley and flopping onto the bed. Seconds later, Brantley was manhandling him into position, pulling him this way and that until Reese's knees were bent and splayed wide, his ass hanging off the edge of the bed while Brantley stood behind him. He gripped the comforter tightly as Brantley breached his anus with the thick head of his cock.

Reese sighed, breathing through the initial discomfort, then giving himself over to the pleasure as Brantley pushed in slowly, inch by thick inch. Oh, fuck yes. He forced himself to relax even more, accepting Brantley's cock. He loved this part. Feeling Brantley, becoming one with him. It was quite possibly the best feeling in the world.

He knew how much Brantley loved morning sex. Reese had never been big on it until Brantley. It had grown on him. He loved starting the day with Brantley fucking him into oblivion. Or vice versa. He usually had no preference, but there were moments like this when he wanted to be at Brantley's mercy.

"Fuck, baby, you're tight like this," Brantley moaned, gripping Reese's hips as he rocked deeper into him. "You feel so damn good. You still want hard and fast?"

"In a minute," Reese sighed, resting his head on the bed as Brantley pushed in and pulled out, slow and deep, caressing his prostate and making him see stars.

Brantley chuckled, his hands moving over Reese's back as he maintained a slow, delicious pace. It lasted only a few minutes before Reese was pushing back against him, urging him deeper. Brantley provided, driving into him until he was fucking him in earnest.

"Oh, fuck, yeah. Reese ... don't you come yet."

Reese grunted, not sure he could hold off.

Brantley slammed into him several more times before reaching around, his fingers curling around Reese's cock, the side of his index finger rubbing the extremely sensitive spot just beneath the head.

Reese hissed, the sensation more than he could handle as Brantley fucked him and stroked him at the same time.

"Oh, God, yes. That's it, Reese. You're close. Squeeze my cock. Now you can come, baby."

And he did, crying out Brantley's name as his orgasm seemed to go on forever. The best part was that Brantley was right there with him.

"WE THOUGHT FOR SURE WE'D BEAT YOU here," Violet Anderson said as she approached the table Archer had gotten when he arrived twenty minutes ago.

Archer smiled up at his friend's girl. "I'm an early riser."

"Not usually, he's not," Simon quipped as he sat in the booth once Violet got situated.

Simon knew him too well, but that didn't mean he couldn't argue his point. "Hey, I'm turnin' over a new leaf."

"New location, new leaf, huh?" Violet smiled and snagged a menu from the stack docked neatly on the table near the wall. She passed it to Simon, then looked back at him. "So when do you start the new gig?"

Archer grinned as he'd been doing ever since he left Brantley and Reese's house yesterday. He wasn't sure what it was about the prospect of working for this task force, but he was eager to get started.

"I haven't given them an answer yet."

"What?" She looked sincerely confused. "Why not? Do you not want it?"

Oh, he wanted it all right. More than he'd wanted anything in a long time.

"He tends to overthink big decisions," Simon said, still perusing the menu.

"I do not," he argued, though it was somewhat true. "I just want to get all the information I can before I decide."

"You like to be informed," Violet said with a grin. "Good to know. You're gonna take it, though, right?"

"It's somethin' I could see myself doing, yeah. The people are cool."

"Speaking of cool people. How'd it go with JJ?" Simon asked.

"Good."

"You met her?" Violet asked.

"She wanted to interview me."

Violet's eyes glittered with curiosity. "How'd that go?"

"Good. Real good." He'd actually enjoyed meeting the badass Jessica James. It gave him a better understanding of the woman who seemed to be the glue that kept the task force together.

"And it pays well?"

Better than Archer had been expecting. "It does."

"And you'd be good at it, right?"

Archer smirked because Violet was looking at Simon when she asked, evidently attempting to get him to participate in the conversation.

When he didn't respond, she elbowed him. "Right?"

Simon looked up, frowned. "Yeah, sure."

She huffed a laugh. "You don't even know what the question was."

"You said he'd be good at it." Simon smiled. "And to answer, I said, yeah, sure."

Violet rolled her eyes, still smiling. "Whatever." She looked at Archer. "Once you say yes, what happens?"

"The yes is pretty much a box to check. They've already started a background check. I figure once that checks out, they'll push to get my answer."

Violet looked at Simon, her tone serious. "Should we be worried?"

Simon smiled. "We should *always* be worried about him."

She continued as though Archer wasn't there. "That's what I thought. Maybe I can pass Reese a buck or two under the table to make any skeletons in his closet disappear."

Archer chuckled. "Honey, I can assure you, there are no skeletons in my closet. Not since I came out of it when I was twenty-two."

"And that was *how many* years ago?" Violet asked, clearly fishing. "One or ten, I forget."

"Somewhere right in the middle."

"He's on the last leg of his twenties," Simon said with a smirk.

"Twenty-nine? Really? You're just a young buck, aren't ya," Violet drawled, giggling as the waitress approached to take their order.

"Hey, girl," Archer greeted the waitress with a smile.

As was the case far more often than should be, the waitress giggled and blushed. Archer pretended not to notice, just as he always did.

He gestured for Violet to go first.

"Strawberry banana pancakes and orange juice."

When Simon peered over at him, Archer smiled. "Age before beauty, my friend."

He knew Simon was mentally flipping him off as he ordered up his egg whites and toast.

"And you, hun?"

"I'll take four eggs, scrambled. Six pieces of bacon, two sausage links, and some tomato juice if you've got it."

"Goin' light today, huh?" Violet teased.

"Don't wanna be too full when we meet up with Brantley and Reese later."

Archer glanced at the door when he heard the bells chime. He was hoping to see Spencer Elliott strolling in, but as had been the case since he arrived, he wasn't that lucky. He'd texted the man late last night, asking if he'd meet him for breakfast, but got no response. Nor did he have one when he woke up this morning.

"Y'all are meetin' up with them?" Violet asked Simon.

"If they've got time, we were gonna meet at the apartment," Simon told her. "I wanted to walk them through the information we have. Reese mentioned wantin' to talk to Holt. Since they didn't connect yesterday, I figured two birds, one stone."

"You're not goin' to talk to the mob boss today, are you?"

Archer watched the interaction between the two, keeping his smile on the inside. He had to admit, he'd never expected his friend to fall in love. Simon wasn't the sort to skirt relationships or anything, but he'd never seemed interested enough in one woman to settle down.

Until he met Violet.

If Archer were a betting man, he'd put every penny he had in the bank on them getting married sometime next year. Violet had been sporting the ring for a few days now, but they'd yet to decide on a date.

"We're not goin' to talk to Max," Simon told her. "I promise, when we do, you'll be the first to know."

"Technically, you'll probably be the third or fourth to know," Archer corrected.

"He can't go by himself," Violet said, staring at Archer.

"I'll make sure he doesn't."

The bells chimed again, drawing his attention toward the door.

"Are you expectin' someone?"

Archer's gaze cut back to Simon quickly. "No."

Violet sighed. "If you're lookin' for Spencer, he said he's got some early showings today."

Good to know. Didn't explain why the man was avoiding him, though.

An hour later, after they'd polished off the food on their plates, Archer parked his Harley in a spot on Main Street in downtown Coyote Ridge.

Simon and Violet were already there, talking softly in front of Shelf Help, the bookstore Violet owned, smiling like a couple of lovesick teenagers.

Archer took his time removing his helmet, securing it. By the time he climbed off his motorcycle, he thought for sure they'd be done making googly eyes at one another, but he was wrong.

He made his way to the sidewalk, doing his best not to look at them or invade their private moment. When they still weren't finished, he stood back, pretending he found the sidewalk fascinating while he waited for Simon and Violet to say their goodbyes. Seriously, that was how Simon had phrased it. As though the man wouldn't be lingering around the bookstore for most of the day anyway. He could stop in at any point and see the woman, so Archer saw no reason for lengthy goodbyes.

Clearly he was the only one.

"If you're not busy at lunch, I could grab somethin'. Bring it by," Simon told Violet as they inched closer to the door.

Yeah, okay. As fun as this was, he had no interest in watching the two of them make out. Archer shook his head and gestured toward the second floor. "While you two do the kissy-kissy thing, I'm headin' upstairs."

Neither of them looked his way.

Amused at how far gone Simon was, Archer headed down Main Street, past the barber shop, toward the narrow alley between the two buildings. He turned left, eyeing the metal staircase that would take him up to the second floor at the rear of the building.

He wasn't in a rush to get to the apartment. Mostly because he hadn't bothered to grab the key from Simon, which meant he couldn't get in. Despite Simon's promise to stop in at the hardware store to get another made, the man had yet to do so. He knew it had to do with the fact he was in love and distracted by all the hearts and flowers that were swimming around in his brain, and not because the task was difficult. After all, the hardware store was right next door to the bookstore. Easy, right? Then again, the guy was in love, and since Archer never had been, perhaps—

He stopped on the step that was second to the top.

Frowning, he looked toward the opposite end of the building, expecting to see someone on the exterior walkway, although he had no idea who he would see. There were four doors, but only two had people coming and going. The first was the office that Spencer rented for his real estate business. Since, according to Violet, he was currently taking care of early showings, he wouldn't be there. The second was a storage room that Violet used for her bookstore. The third was the converted apartment that Holt rented from Violet, and the fourth was also storage, from what he'd heard.

So, unless Paige was at door number three—which she wasn't because she was back in Dallas taking care of some things—then that meant someone was at the real estate office.

Was it Spencer? Or someone who worked for him? Were they supposed to be there?

Only one way to find out.

Archer continued up and walked a few feet to the door with the placard that read REAL ESTATE OFFICE. He got the feeling they didn't have many clients meet them there. He thought back to a few days ago when Simon and Violet wanted to see a house they were interested in. Spencer met them at the house. Made sense that they wouldn't need to office out of anything fancy.

Reaching up, he was about to knock when the door opened a fraction of an inch. An eyeball appeared as though scoping the area.

"Spencer?"

"Oh, shit."

Before the door could slam closed, Archer put his hand up to stop it.

"Shit, shit, shit," Spencer muttered, stepping back and spinning around.

"What the fuck, man?" Archer followed him inside, closing the door behind him.

He looked around, ensuring no one else was there, and was pleased to find they were alone. He took another minute to take it all in, to get to know Spencer just a little bit more by his surroundings.

When it became clear Spencer wasn't going to say anything, Archer turned to face him.

"So, did you lie to Violet? Or did Violet lie to me?" he prompted, wanting to know why Violet would tell him Spencer had clients to meet early this morning.

"I lied to her," Spencer grumbled, not meeting his eyes.

"Hey, look," Archer told him, holding up his hands and backing up. "If you're not interested, just say the word. I'll leave you alone. No questions asked."

Spencer looked up, frowned.

"I'm not an idiot," Archer continued. "I know when to back off."

"It's not that I'm not interested," Spencer said, his tone somewhat weak. "It's just…"

"No questions asked, remember?" Archer repeated as he turned to leave. "You don't need to come up with an excuse."

"Archer, wait," Spencer snapped as he turned the knob on the door.

Releasing it, Archer turned back, stared at the man, and felt that same warm buzz in his veins that he'd felt the first time he saw Spencer in Violet's bookstore. The guy looked professional but not starchy with his blue jeans and polo shirt, which featured the name of his real estate company. He wore his dark brown hair neatly combed, tapered on the sides and back. His light brown eyes were lined with thick lashes and held a hint of worry in them.

When Spencer didn't launch into anything, Archer leaned back against the door and waited.

He'd been told more than once that he was intimidating. He figured it mostly had to do with his size. Then again, having been a gangly teenager at one point, he'd been called worse than that.

Spencer took a deep breath and exhaled on a rush. "Look. I really don't want you to think you're obligated to … I don't know … date me."

Archer's eyebrows lifted. "Obligated?" That was a first.

"Yeah. You know." Spencer huffed and waved a hand. "Because I told you what I told you."

"That your brother's ex-wife raped you?" he asked, addressing it head-on because that was how Spencer had done it when they first talked about it the night Archer interjected when Jennifer Elliott, Slade's ex-wife, was giving Spencer a hard time at Moonshiners.

You don't like her much, do you?

Not even a little.

Ex-girlfriend?

My brother's ex-wife.

Oh.

Oh, what?

She just acted like she was … familiar.

She is.

Y'all have a thing before?

No. The bitch raped me.

Spencer tucked his hands into his pockets. "Yeah."

"And because of that, you think I'm *obligated?*"

"I think you *feel* obligated," Spencer corrected. "It's cool, though. I don't need your pity."

Archer frowned, his eyebrows lowering. "Pity?"

"Yeah."

"You said it happened ten years ago."

"It did."

Archer peered around briefly, then met Spencer's gaze. "I don't think what I'm feelin' is pity."

"Then what is it?"

"I'm impressed, for starters." Archer pushed away from the door, taking one step forward. "You've built somethin' for yourself, which tells me you're solid and smart. You've got a good reputation in town when it comes to buying houses, so that tells me you're dependable. Probably honest."

Spencer stood tall, eyes peeled wide. "The entire town thinks I'm a wife-stealin' himbo. And *I* made them think that. I don't think that qualifies me as honest."

Archer chuckled. "Self-preservation makes us do strange things sometimes." He closed the gap between them, lowering his voice. "I also think you're hot as fuck."

Spencer gasped.

Archer lifted his hand slowly, ensuring he wasn't reading more into this than he should. He cupped Spencer's jaw, placing his thumb just beneath his chin, tipping his head up. He skimmed the man's face, looking for a clue that he should retreat.

When he found none, he said, "Would I do this if I pitied you?"

He held Spencer's gaze as he lowered his head until their lips touched. When Spencer didn't pull away, Archer tilted his head to the side and covered Spencer's mouth, licking his way past those smooth, warm lips. Spencer's tongue met his, gentle at first, then more demanding. Archer's body hardened when Spencer's arms circled him, his hands fisting into his shirt, holding on as the kiss went nuclear.

Archer had wanted to do that since the night Spencer ended up in his room at the B&B. But that night, Archer was on his best behavior because Spencer was too drunk to make any logical choices about what he wanted.

It took effort, but Archer pulled back first, swiping his thumb over Spencer's lips before leaning back so he could meet his gaze.

"Jesus Christ," Spencer muttered, eyes glazed.

Archer grinned, not moving away. He wasn't sure he could. He had a steel bat in his pants and the damn thing was throbbing.

"Now that that's outta the way, what do you say we start over?"

Spencer chuckled. "Start over? As in, repeat that … kiss?"

"If you'd like, sure. I'm game." Archer chuckled. "But I was thinkin' maybe we could grab dinner, get to know each other a little."

Spencer nodded. "Tonight?"

"Tonight works."

"Okay."

"The diner good for you?"

Another nod from Spencer.

"All right then. Six o'clock?"

"I can do six."

"Spencer?"

"Hmm?"

"Do you want me to kiss you again? Because if you don't, you're gonna need to let go of my shirt."

Spencer tipped his head down, his hands falling to his sides. He took a step back as though surprised he'd been holding on, but then took a step forward and grabbed Archer, surprising him. Their lips crashed together, and this time, Archer didn't hold back. He turned, pinning Spencer against the wall. He paused, pulling back enough to look at Spencer.

"I do somethin' that you don't like, you tell me. Cool?"

Spencer smiled. "I'm not fragile."

"Good to know." Archer kissed him again, pressing in close, enjoying the way Spencer leaned into him. He wasn't a small man, but Archer definitely had some inches and pounds on him.

By the time he had the presence of mind to slow down, Archer was panting, his heart racing. He released Spencer as he took a step back, missing the warmth of his body instantly.

"I'm lookin' forward to dinner," Archer told him, walking backward toward the door.

"Me, too."

Archer smiled, memorizing that handsome face for a little longer before he turned and walked out of the small office.

He was still smiling when he strolled into the apartment to find Simon standing near the windows overlooking Walker Park.

As soon as he heard him, Simon turned. "Where'd you go?"

"I had a chat with Spencer."

Simon frowned. "I thought Violet said he was with clients."

"Yeah, well. He wasn't."

"Okay, then."

"So, what do you want me to get done here?" Archer asked, glancing around.

Simon gestured toward the bedroom, which was being used as a writing and research space. "I'd like to walk them through the details Holt acquired."

"Man, you should see the equipment they've got in that barn," Archer told him as they headed for the bedroom. "It's state of the art. And from what I can tell, mostly digital."

"Holt's old school."

Yes, it would appear he was. There were pictures and newspaper articles wallpapering the room. All of them printed somewhere, using paper, killing trees. Archer didn't mention that because Simon already knew how he felt about that shit.

"If they agree to take on this case, I think we should relocate this stuff," he suggested. "Or digitize it."

"I'm good with that."

"Maybe then it'll make some sorta sense." Archer's gaze snapped from one photo to the next, one article after another. There was so much information lining these walls, yet it didn't appear to be in any semblance of order. If he hadn't heard Holt talk about it, he wouldn't have even known it all revolved around one woman.

"It makes sense," Simon countered.

"If you know what you're lookin' for, yeah. But it doesn't tell a story."

Simon sighed. "That's the problem."

That was the first time Simon admitted that he wasn't quite sure what angle his friend was aiming for with this information. Simon had arrived in Coyote Ridge almost a month ago, yet they were no closer to determining how to approach it. Hell, Simon hadn't even laid out an action plan for him. And his friend was well aware that Archer planned his life around those things.

So, was it the hearts and unicorns swimming in Simon's brain that made the story blurry, or was there really nothing there worth looking into?

Whatever it was, Archer hoped they could figure it out soon.

Chapter Eight

AFTER THEIR MORNING RUN AND HIS SHOWER—which he took separately from Reese despite his pleading—Brantley left Reese to whatever he was doing in his office in order to check on the team, see if they needed anything.

"You wanna go to the barn, girl?" he asked Tesha when she didn't move from her spot on her bed. "I bet Holly's over there."

That was all it took to get her on her feet, racing out the door ahead of Brantley.

The walk across the yard took seconds, not minutes, as did keying in the passcode and waiting for the locks to disengage. When they did, he opened the door and stepped aside so Tesha could rush in, seeking the attention she got every time she came here.

To his surprise and approval, the scene before him was vastly different than the one he walked in on yesterday when JJ's head was on the big screen, and people were standing around talking over one another.

"Mornin'," he greeted.

"Hey, boss," Slade called.

"Morning," Evan said.

He was pretty sure the grunt came from Luca.

"Any news on JJ?" Holly asked, looking at him with a mixture of hope and worry in her eyes, even as she knelt to give Tesha love. "I tried callin' her, but she didn't answer."

"We didn't get by there this mornin', but I talked to Baz. The doctor's closely monitorin' her contractions, which are increasing," he explained. "As soon as I hear somethin', you'll hear somethin'."

"She in labor?" Slade asked, his forehead creased with confusion.

"She thinks she is. Like I said, the doctor's keepin' a close eye on her."

Holly gasped and clasped her hands together, fingertips touching her lips.

"Are we expectin' babies soon? Like today?" Luca asked.

Brantley exhaled. "According to Baz, Dr. Tinder said there's a good chance, yeah."

"That's not bad, right?" Holly questioned, a boatload of worry in her tone. "That puts her at thirty-six weeks."

"Let's keep our fingers crossed," he told her, wanting them to focus on what they needed to get done. If JJ's labor did progress, they would all want to head over to the hospital, which meant they needed to tackle everything they could as soon as they could. The last thing he wanted was to hear from Z that the team was behind on their reports. Paperwork was the absolute worst part of the job, but it was also important if they expected to justify their existence.

"Do we have a case, boss?" Slade asked.

"Nothin' hot. Let's keep our fingers crossed."

Brantley looked at his watch. It was only a little after eight, but it felt like he'd been up for an entire day already. That was JJ's fault since he'd gotten the call moments before his alarm would've gone off. His best friend had been just shy of panicked when she explained that her contractions weren't stopping.

Luckily, he had the presence of mind to get the real details from Baz before they jumped the gun and raced up to the hospital. The soon-to-be father had been much calmer, insisting Dr. Tinder was confident it would likely be several more hours before she progressed any further.

At that point, Reese had effectively taken Brantley's mind off everything.

Shaking off the thought, Brantley looked at Holly. "You hear anything more from Corpus Christi PD?"

"Not yet, no."

"Anything from Z?" Brantley asked Darius, who was officially filling in for Baz.

"I talked to him half an hour ago. Gave him an update on the goings-on here," Darius explained. "I updated him on JJ. I think he's planning to come down with RT when it's confirmed the babies are being pulled outta the oven." Darius smirked. "His words."

"Oven. Cook a little longer," Atticus mused. "Y'all freak me out sometimes."

Brantley laughed.

Charlie raised her hand. "I have a question."

"Elana, would you mind gettin' me some coffee?" Brantley asked JJ's assistant. If he'd known he would be over here this long, he would've brought some with him.

"On it," she said with a beaming grin.

Brantley turned his attention back to Charlie. "What's up?"

"Rumor has it you hired a new investigator yesterday."

"That doesn't sound like a question," he told her.

She flashed a beaming smile. "Who'd you hire?"

Before he could answer, Holly said, "Archer Halligan."

"She's in love," Luca said. "Too bad for you, he bats for the other team."

"He does not," Holly argued, her gaze shifting to Brantley.

"What?" he asked. "Because I'm gay, I'm in tune with his sexual preference?"

She blushed. "I didn't—"

"I'm kidding." He laughed. "Not that I give a shit one way or the other, but yeah, I think he prefers misters."

"Archer Halligan?" Charlie asked, her tone confused. "The investigator for *Havoc Your Way*?"

"One and the same," Brantley confirmed. "But for the record, he has not accepted the job."

Holly's eyebrows lifted. "But you offered it?"

"Yes. Reese and I think he'd be a good fit. We talked a little yesterday, and I plan to answer any of his questions when and if he calls."

"*If?* You don't think he's gonna take it?" Atticus asked.

"I didn't say that. I'm gonna leave the choice up to him. Once I hear from him—one way or the other—I'll let you know."

"If he does take it, when will he start?"

"ASAP." At least Brantley hoped that was the case. "If he accepts, we'll submit the paperwork. He can start once it's processed. He'll be partnering with Atticus."

Slade's head snapped up, as did Evan's. Holly was grinning like she'd just won the lottery. Darius nodded while Jay stared blankly at him.

"Archer *Halligan*?" Charlie repeated as though the past minute or two hadn't happened. "From *Havoc Your Way*?"

Brantley looked at Holly. "Should I be worried that she's repeatin' herself?"

Holly giggled. "She's had less time to get used to the idea. He's kinda a god among men for those of us who like the podcast."

"Yay, me," Atticus said facetiously.

Brantley noticed Evan was grinning like an idiot.

"What's so funny?"

"Nothing."

Brantley stared, waiting him out as he took the coffee mug Elana brought him. "Thanks."

"Welcome."

Evan laughed. "Sorry, boss. It's just…" He coughed to cover up another laugh. "It's nothing. I'm sure it'll be fine."

"Somethin' goin' on that I should know about?" Brantley directed the question at Evan, but his attention shifted to Slade when the man ducked his head. It wouldn't have been quite so obvious if Atticus hadn't turned away at the same time.

Great.

"You two got a thing?"

Holly giggled.

Then Elana did.

And last, Charlie.

Brantley looked at each of the women. "What's so funny?"

"Nothin', boss," Slade said, his tone rife with frustration.

Brantley studied him for a moment, then looked at Atticus. He'd heard whispers that the two of them had a thing, but he'd purposely ignored them. Since they weren't paired up, he didn't really care what they were doing.

Didn't mean he wasn't going to keep an eye on them.

BAZ SAT IN THE RECLINER ON THE far side of the room, his gaze locked on JJ. He was doing his best not to hover, but it wasn't easy. Every time she made a sound, he wanted to launch to his feet and get her whatever she needed.

The problem was, she didn't need anything.

At least that was what she'd told him—very loudly—the last time he asked if he could do anything for her.

So here he was, sitting on his ass, not taking it personally because the JJ he knew and loved was hanging by a thread, and rightfully so.

In the time he'd known the woman, he'd seen her go through so much. From waking up in a bloody bed and not knowing how she got there, to finding her ex-boyfriend's finger—only the digit, not the ex—in her living room, to learning her house and everything she owned had exploded, to being kidnapped by a couple of lunatics. There was no doubt the woman had been put through the wringer.

She could handle labor. Hell, she was the strongest woman he knew. JJ could handle anything.

But he wasn't sure he was as strong as she was. He was antsy and nervous and maybe a little eager. He was ready for the babies to be born, but at the same time, he didn't want them to be born too early. Dr. Tinder seemed optimistic, although he did warn them that there was a good chance they'd be moved to the NICU—neonatal intensive care unit—for a period of time. He assured them they would be in good hands.

According to what Baz had read on the internet, the babies should weigh somewhere around five pounds each and be close to eighteen inches long. Of course, Dr. Tinder informed them that it was a good rule of thumb, but there were other factors that played into that, so there were no guarantees.

Baz liked Dr. Tinder. He also trusted the man, which was why he was practically living in a hospital and sleeping in an uncomfortable chair just so he could keep JJ from getting up and moving around any more than she absolutely had to. It was also the reason he was still carrying around an engagement ring in his pocket; he feared asking her to marry him might cause more stress than was necessary.

A soft knock sounded on the door a second before it opened.

Baz breathed a sigh of relief when he saw his mother's face peering into the room.

"Come in," JJ said, smiling.

Julia Buchanan pushed open the door and walked in. His mother looked as regal as ever. The same could almost be said for his father, who was not far behind, though not many people could get away with calling Wes Buchanan regal even when the man was wearing a five-thousand-dollar suit. And he was rocking it as he always did, looking very much like the corporate CEO that he was.

"I heard my grandbabies might be comin' today," Jules told JJ, her voice soft and soothing as she went over to her.

"That's what Dr. Tinder's sayin'," JJ agreed, rubbing her belly gently. "It's also why they downgraded me to this bed."

JJ's pout was cute, but Baz suspected she didn't really care that they'd given her a regular bed—a necessity in the event the medical staff was needed—and carted off the king-size.

"Hey, ladybug," his father greeted JJ.

"Hi, Wes," she said, smiling as she always did.

Baz watched the interaction between the three of them. The way his parents doted on her. The way she looked up at them with so much love in her eyes. Since he was close to his mother and father, he was glad that they'd taken to her so well. Then again, this was JJ. He couldn't imagine anyone meeting her and not being completely infatuated. He had been. From the first time they were introduced.

"Want to get some coffee, kid?" his father asked him.

Baz looked at JJ.

"Go," she said. "If Dr. Tinder's right, you're gonna need it."

He walked over and kissed her on the forehead, then looked at his mother. "Text me if the doctor comes in."

"Of course. Now get."

Baz glanced at JJ one last time before reluctantly leaving the room. If it were up to him, he would've been glued to her side from now until the end of time. After the last harrowing ordeal—when she was kidnapped in broad daylight right in the heart of Coyote Ridge—he'd felt absolutely helpless and terrified he would never see her again, so he wasn't keen on being away from her. He figured that might wear off. One day. But that day wasn't today.

"You look tired, boy," Wes said as they walked the hall toward the cafeteria.

"The chair's not as comfortable as you might think," he admitted.

"You could sleep in the same bed with JJ."

He could, yes. That was within the rules. With that said, the idea of sleeping in the same bed and having people traipsing in and out was creepy as fuck.

"I'll pass."

"They told you they'd bring in a cot."

Yes, they had. And he probably should've taken them up on it, but it was weird enough sleeping in a chair in a giant hospital room that looked very little like a hospital room.

"Have the contractions increased?"

Baz shook his head. "Still consistently inconsistent. But her cervix is dilated."

"Well, I think today's a great birthday for my grandbabies."

Baz smiled.

"Did I mention Jules had me fix up one of the extra rooms so you've got a nursery when you come visit?"

"Dad, that's not necessary. You only live thirty minutes away."

"Maybe, but if it makes your mother happy…"

Baz didn't buy for a second that Wes had only done it for Jules. He was over the moon excited about a grandchild. Back when they first told him, the man had cried. When they'd told him they were having twins, he'd been speechless, and yes, he cried then, too.

Admittedly, it had been sweet to see the big, tough Wesley Buchanan reduced to weeping with happiness.

Not that he would tell his dad that.

"I thought for sure Brantley'd be here."

"He's a phone call away, Dad. I told them I'd call as soon as anything changed. And if I couldn't, you would."

They walked in silence to the cafeteria. Baz opted for coffee. It wasn't the worst he'd ever had, but it definitely wasn't great. When he went to pay, his father stepped in and took care of that.

"How are things with Mom?" he asked when they found a table away from the main aisle to the food section.

"What?"

Baz stopped pouring sugar into his coffee to look up at his father. "Mom? You? How are things?"

"Fine," he said, his attention shifting to the people milling about.

"Dad?"

"Hmm?"

"What's goin' on?"

"Nothing."

Baz frowned, setting the empty sugar packet down. He waited for his father to look his way.

"Dad," he said roughly, keeping his voice low. "Did you and Mom get back together?"

Holy shit. Was the guy blushing?

"Oh, my God."

"What?" Wes tried for innocent but failed epically.

"She's still married." Baz huffed. "Hell, so are you."

"Only formalities. You know I filed for divorce a few weeks ago," his father stated. "Your mother filed last week."

Baz wasn't sure how he felt about this. About any of it. Not his mother divorcing his stepfather. Not his father divorcing stepmom number five. And definitely not his mother and father possibly getting back together, although it made more sense than anything else. Anyone who knew them could see that Jules was the love of Wes's life and vice versa. They were soul mates, yet they'd somehow allowed life to get in the way. While they would both admit they were better friends than spouses, Baz wanted to believe they would work if they just put their minds to it.

"Does that mean y'all are gonna get married again?"

"Would it matter to you if we did?"

That was a good question. An easy one. With an easy answer. "No, Dad. If it meant you're both happy, you know I don't care."

"Well, I don't know what it might lead to, but for right now, we're enjoyin' one another's company. That's all."

Since Baz didn't want to think about how close they were getting, he decided to let the subject drop. But he made a mental note not to walk into his father's house without knocking first.

Chapter Nine

"Is it time?"

Brantley paused in Reese's office doorway. "Time for…?"

"JJ. Labor. Babies."

"No."

"Good."

Brantley stood in the doorway, watching the man who was nose-deep in his computer monitor. He hadn't looked up once. Not even to ask that random question.

"What're you workin' on?"

Reese gestured toward the screen.

Brantley mimicked his gesture, only he was asking him to continue. "And that is?"

Reese still didn't look up.

With a sigh to show he was completely put out, Brantley said, "Not even married two weeks, and you're already leavin' me to fend for myself for lunch."

Reese didn't look up, instead pointing at the screen. "How did we not know this?"

Indulging him, Brantley walked around behind the desk. "Not know what?"

"That Kylie's mother witnessed a murder."

"I thought we did know that."

"Not until Holt."

"Okay." Brantley would give him that. "You're sayin' we should've known?"

"Yes."

"Do we know Kylie's mother?" Brantley asked, confused as to why Reese sounded so adamant about that.

Reese's eyes had a glazed, far-off look to them when he finally peered up. "She allegedly saw Max Adorite kill a man."

"I'm sure a lot of people have witnessed Max Adorite kill a man. He's not exactly Mr. Rogers."

"She saw him."

Since it was clear Reese needed to get this information out, Brantley decided to indulge him. "Okay. Kylie's mother—whom we do not know—witnessed Max Adorite kill a man. When?"

"I don't know."

"Can you guesstimate? A decade, two?"

"At least two. Probably."

He recalled hearing something about Kylie's mother having left after Kylie's sister turned eighteen. He didn't know their exact ages, but he had to assume it was about that time.

"Was it when she up and left? After Jessie turned eighteen?"

Reese frowned. "So you did know?"

"About her witnessing a murder? No. But I've heard rumors about Kylie's parents."

Reese was staring at him as though he needed more to go on.

Figuring it was only fair to fill him in, Brantley explained. Or tried to. "Travis is my cousin. Small town. Trey mentioned it once. Back when Kylie showed up in town and everyone learned Travis was married to her. Rumor was, her mom left for greener pastures."

Reese's forehead held a crease of confusion when he looked back at the screen. "I'm not so sure it was by choice."

"Let me guess, this is the theory Holt's goin' on about?"

"I think so. But somethin' feels off about this information. It feels … planted. You would expect it to've been in all the reputable Dallas newspapers, but it wasn't. In fact, I can't find where any of the local media caught onto the story until long after it supposedly happened."

"So you *don't* think it's true?"

"I think it's sus."

"Sus?" Brantley frowned. "What the hell is *sus*?"

"You know. Suspicious."

"Then why the hell didn't you finish the word?"

Reese waved him off. "It's *suspicious*. But surely I'm not the only one who thinks so." Reese shook his head. "Regardless, I'm still not sure the angle Simon's playing."

Brantley waited, expecting some sort of explanation. What he got was more of Reese skimming the words on the screen.

"Well, I guess it's peanut butter and jelly then." Brantley squeezed Reese's shoulder but didn't get a response.

Damn it. He really didn't want peanut butter and jelly. He was hoping for Whataburger. Or maybe Chick-fil-A. Something with a little substance. And by substance, he meant grease.

"Do you know any FBI agents?" Reese mumbled.

Well, that was random. And more than a little worrisome since Reese was still eye-locked with the computer screen.

"Hey."

"Hmm?"

"Reese."

"Hmm?"

"Look at me."

It took a few seconds, but he finally did.

"Can we have lunch? We can go … somewhere. Maybe Chick-fil-A. You like their salads. And while we eat, you can share what you know so I can be on the same page when we meet with Simon and Holt."

Reese spun in his chair, and Brantley realized it was so that he could look at the clock. "Holy shit. It's lunchtime."

"Yeah. My stomach's been remindin' me for the past hour."

A second later, Reese was on his feet, leading the way out of his office, down the stairs, then straight out the front door.

Brantley remained in the house, whistling for Tesha. She came trotting toward him, ears perked.

"I think it's safe to say he's got somethin' on his mind," Brantley told her as he hooked her leash to her harness. "Come on, girl. If you're good, I'll sneak you some chicken nuggets."

"Sonuvabitch," Reese grumbled, hopping out of the truck as Brantley approached. "I'm sorry, girl."

Brantley chuckled as Reese took her leash and helped her into the truck, hugging her numerous times in order to make up for his oversight.

"Whatever's on your mind must be good," Brantley said as he started the truck. "Go on. Let's hear it."

"WHERE DO I EVEN START?" REESE ASKED as they were taking a seat at one of the empty tables near the enormous playground inside Chick-fil-A.

"Why don't you pretend I know nothin'," Brantley said. "Because I'm pretty sure I know nothin'."

Reese chuckled. "You know some of it."

"Again, pretend I don't."

While he ordered his thoughts, Reese popped the lid off his salad and added dressing. By the time he got it prepared, Brantley had already polished off his fries and was unwrapping the first of two chicken sandwiches.

"Holt's workin' on a book," he began. "It's based in a small town. He's usin' Coyote Ridge as a baseline."

"You get this information from Holt?"

"Actually, no. He's still mum. Doesn't want Travis thinkin' he's spreadin' rumors."

"Makes sense. Who's spillin' the beans, then? Simon?"

"Yeah."

"Gotcha. Keep goin'."

"In order to make the story authentic, Holt does a lot of research upfront."

"Which is how he started diggin' into other people's business," Brantley muttered.

Reese hadn't seen it that way, but now that Brantley mentioned it… "Fair enough. It was durin' his research that he came across an article about Kylie's death."

"He writes mysteries, doesn't he?"

"He does."

"Her death's not a mystery."

"It's not," Reese agreed. "Have you ever started lookin' at somethin' online and gone down a rabbit hole?"

"A literal one, no."

Reese tilted his head. "Come on. Be serious."

Brantley grinned and Reese felt that smile through his entire body. And fine, maybe he had been deep in thought ever since he talked to Simon yesterday morning. He'd been given a lot of information. More than he expected. But what surprised him most was how it all seemed to fit. Add that to the bits and pieces they'd acquired during their trip to New York—the stuff he'd asked JJ to hide from Brantley until *after* the wedding—and Reese couldn't deny that it had created far more questions than answers.

"Fine. Online. Research. Rabbit hole. Keep goin'," Brantly urged.

"According to Simon, Holt doesn't recall how he got there, but he came across an article about the Southern Boy Mafia. It referenced a witness who'd seen Max kill a man."

"And naturally, he'd think Kylie's mom."

"No."

Brantley frowned, lifting his head slowly. "When was this really? Max supposedly killin' someone? Twenty years? You said the information seemed like it was planted. Did they wait a while?"

"Simon doesn't have specific dates, but he does know it's not too much before Kylie's mother disappeared from their lives. He hasn't ordered it, and he's only started a brief outline. He wants us to take a look at everything Holt's acquired to get the details."

"Everything he's acquired?"

Reese exhaled. "Yeah. Apparently, he's rentin' the apartment above the bookstore and he's got quite a bit of information that he believes—"

"Hold that thought," Brantley said when his phone rang. "Walker."

Reese watched as Brantley's eyes widened.

"Seriously?" Brantley's smile grew. "That's fantastic. We're on our way, man. Y'all need us to bring anything?" There was a brief pause, followed by, "Then we'll head that way. See you in a few."

Brantley disconnected the call and shoved the rest of his second sandwich in his mouth, motioning for Reese to hurry it up.

Although he suspected he already knew, Reese asked, "Who was that?"

Brantley didn't answer right away, attempting to chew and swallow. "Baz."

Reese frowned. "Everything okay?"

Brantley nodded as he got to his feet. "The babies are comin'."

"Oh, shit." Reese hopped up and grabbed Tesha's leash. "Come on, girl."

He was halfway to the door when he realized Brantley wasn't behind him. He looked back to see him gathering up the food from the table. He tossed one bag and balanced two cups and a salad as he headed for the door.

If his head wasn't attached to his shoulders, Reese had to believe he would've left that behind, which was very much unlike him. He blamed Simon. For whatever reason, Reese was compelled to learn more about this supposed conspiracy. He was intrigued—perhaps borderline obsessed—and that was throwing him off his game.

Reese took the salad and his drink, then pushed open the door.

"Are the babies comin' now?" he asked.

"Not yet. On their way, though."

Reese had to wonder why he was so nervous. It wasn't like he was about to be a father, yet his stomach was doing flip-flops.

They weaved between the rows of cars waiting in the drive-thru lanes. Reese managed to open the back door so Tesha could hop in. He snuck her one of the nuggets from the salad as he buckled her in, then closed the door and climbed into the front passenger seat.

"We should probably tell everyone else, huh?" he asked, setting his salad on the dashboard.

"You do that. I'll drive."

Reese pulled up the group text thread he maintained with the team and shot one quick message.

> BABIES ARE ON THE WAY. WHAT'RE YOU WAITING FOR?

For the next few minutes, his phone chimed again and again with responses as people replied to say they were heading there as soon as they could.

"Let's hope Baz didn't jump the gun," Reese said, setting his phone in the cup holder.

"You message Z?"

"Damn it." He grabbed his phone and shot a quick message to his brother, letting him know he would keep him updated. He figured there was no sense in Z driving down until the babies were born.

"It's gonna be fine," Brantley said, taking his hand.

Reese didn't realize he was fidgeting until Brantley's strong fingers twined with his. As he'd been doing for the past couple of weeks, Brantley rubbed his finger on Reese's wedding ring. It was a simple gesture, likely not even something he thought about, but it made Reese remember how lucky he was.

"Why aren't you nervous?" he asked Brantley.

"Because JJ'd kick my ass. Plus, I owe it to her after all she did for the wedding. I figure Baz'll be enough for her to deal with."

"You think he'll freak?"

"I think he's been far too calm and collected through the whole process."

"I'm pretty sure that's what he wants us to see," Reese told him.

"Probably." Brantley grinned. "But Wes is there. Baz seems calmer when his dad's around."

"He leans on him a lot." It was something Reese admired about Baz. The relationship he had with his father. Having lost his own father, he didn't have that relationship anymore, and he missed it.

"Yeah, well. Wes is a good guy."

"Speakin' of fathers," Reese prompted. "You tell your parents?"

"Oh, shit. Can you do it? They'll wanna be there."

Reese grabbed his phone with his free hand and took care of that, then he sat back and enjoyed the silence for the rest of the drive. He figured he should savor it since it was all they were gonna get for a while.

Chapter Ten

"HOW'RE YOU DOING?" THE NURSE CALLED AS she strolled into the room like it was any other Tuesday.

All right, fine. Maybe Marybeth was having a good day, but JJ could not say the same.

Rather than use her words, JJ was being ornery, so she grunted. These people did not get to stand around all happy like while she was going through … *this*. Jesus. How in the hell was she going to do this? It wasn't possible to squeeze a watermelon through a straw hole. Maybe her vagina wasn't the size of a straw, but the mental image was still effective.

"Dr. Tinder's checking on a couple of patients, then he's heading this way. He'll check your cervix, and we'll have a better idea how long you've got."

JJ's gaze snapped to Baz. She noticed he was shaking his head very subtly. It was a warning for her not to go off on this nurse the way she had the other one who'd come in earlier. It took tremendous effort and might've cost her a little blood, but she managed to bite her tongue.

"We're watching the monitor so we can see when you have a contraction. They're consistent and getting closer together. That's a good sign."

JJ's eyes darted to the woman. "A good sign?" she snapped.

Baz was instantly at her side, taking her hand, squeezing more than gently. "Take a breath, baby."

"If I wasn't breathin', I'd be dead," she bit out.

Baz inhaled long and slow, a silent request for her to do the same. JJ glared up at him. "I know what you're doin'."

His response was a sexy smirk and she wanted to slap it right off his handsome face.

"Dr. Tinder will be in shortly," the nurse repeated as she headed for the door.

Before JJ could shout something obscene at the woman, Baz leaned down and kissed her.

"This is *not* a good sign," she hissed against his mouth. "It's not time yet."

"It's gonna be fine," he said, sounding far too confident.

JJ wanted to believe him. She wanted to think that her babies would be born and everything would be fine. She wanted to believe that, come tomorrow or the next day, they would get to go home. She'd read so many horror stories about premature babies, and it terrified her. She just wanted to cross her legs and keep them there for a few more weeks, just until she knew for certain.

Right.

Certain.

Like anyone could ever be absolutely positive about anything.

"Is Brantley here?" she asked.

"He's on his way."

"What about Iris and Frank?"

Baz smiled. "I texted Iris myself. She said they would break all the speed limits just to get here."

JJ exhaled, a modicum of relief inching out some of the panic. Iris and Frank had been the closest thing she had to parents since her own parents pretty much forgot about her. She wanted them to be there. No, she *needed* them to be there.

A soft knock sounded on the door.

"Come in," Baz called.

The door opened slowly and Wes's handsome face appeared. "Wanted to let y'all know we'll be down the hall if you need us."

"Don't go yet," JJ told him. "It's not time."

The door opened more and Wes held out his hand, urging Jules to come in. She had a beaming smile on her face, and her brown eyes didn't reflect an ounce of worry. The woman was far too kind to let JJ think she was worried.

"How far apart are the contractions?" Jules asked, moving to the side of the bed.

"Right about eighteen minutes," Baz answered. "And lasting close to forty-five seconds."

"You might have a ways to go," Jules acknowledged.

"They started about two hours ago. Almost an hour passed before we realized they were consistent," Baz told his mother.

"Well, we'll just let those babies take their time, and we'll all be here to take care of anything that comes up."

JJ fought the urge to cry when Jules brushed her hair back from her face.

"From here on out, your only job is to breathe," Jules said, her tone soft and soothing. "You let the rest of us worry about everything else. You breathe for yourself and for those beautiful babies who're ready to see their mama."

A tear trickled down her cheek, but JJ didn't wipe it away. It was pointless. She was flipping between white-hot rage and bone-chilling sadness for absolutely no reason whatsoever, all thanks to the hormones flooding her system.

Another knock sounded, this one louder and more authoritative. JJ didn't have to guess who it was, and apparently neither did Baz because he didn't call out. He didn't have to. Dr. Tinder strolled into the room, a smile on his face.

For a doctor, the guy really was attractive. JJ figured it was a damn good thing the man was gay; otherwise, she might've been too freaked out to let him see her girly parts—medical degree be damned.

"I won't ask how you're feeling," he said, holding her gaze. "I can see by the glare that it's the wrong thing to say."

He knew just how to make her smile.

"But I will tell you, I'm here and ready to go as soon as the little ones are. How about you?"

JJ nodded, although she definitely wasn't ready. It was easier to nod than to explain how freaked out she was. Plus, she didn't want Baz's parents to know. They might think she was a horrible person, and the last thing she needed was to piss off another set of parents to the point they wanted nothing to do with her.

"We'll start with an exam. Why don't we get a little privacy here?" Dr. Tinder said. "You're welcome to stay, but you'll probably want to move *that* way." He pointed toward the head of the bed.

"We'll step outside," Jules said, grabbing Wes's hand.

JJ didn't bother telling them they didn't need to.

"Let's get this show on the road, shall we?" Dr. Tinder said, grinning.

"Looks like they won't be makin' it today," Archer told Simon.

Rather than sit at the apartment, they had gone back to the B&B to wait for Brantley and Reese to arrive. Or rather, Archer had come back to the B&B and plopped his ass right on the couch to watch TV in the common room. Simon had snuck over to the bookstore to have lunch with Violet. He'd walked in a few minutes ago, his smile amped up a few million megawatts.

"Why not?"

Archer held up his phone. "If I'm gettin' it right, JJ's in labor."

At least, that was what he assumed the text from Reese meant. He'd been surprised to get it, but it appeared they'd added him to a group text they had for the team.

"Is that good news?"

Archer shrugged. He honestly didn't know. From the bits and pieces he'd picked up, she'd been in the hospital for a while, so he wasn't sure what the hold-up was.

"You gonna go to the hospital?"

Archer frowned. "I wasn't plannin' on it. I don't think one conversation with her makes us best buds. Why? Are you goin'?"

"Probably not." Simon pulled out his phone and began texting. "I'll let Violet know I'll meet her at the house if she wants to go up there, but I don't want to get in the way."

Yeah, that was kinda how Archer felt. Plus, he wasn't a fan of hospitals.

"If she doesn't go, you wanna grab dinner with us tonight?"

"Can't. Got a date."

"Oh, really?"

"Yup."

"With whom?"

Archer replied with a roll of his eyes because Simon already knew that Archer was interested in Violet's best friend. Hell, he was more than interested. He was intrigued. Now, it was a matter of getting to know the man on more than a primal level. That would come eventually if their kiss that morning was any indication. And when they did, it would be so fucking good.

But he had to take things slow with Spencer. If he was being fair, it was partly because of Spencer's revelation, but only a small part. He could still recall the conversation like it was just last night. But it wasn't. It had been a couple of weeks since the night Archer interfered, making it his business to come between Spencer and the woman he'd been arguing with at Moonshiners.

"Excuse me," the woman all but hissed. "I'd like to take my friend home if it's all right with you."

"It isn't," Archer told her.

"What?"

"I'll take him home."

The woman shook her head. "That's not necessary."

"I'll talk at you later," Archer called to Paige, hating to leave her but eager to figure out what the hell was going on between Spencer and the woman.

He urged Spencer forward and out into the humid September evening.

"I've got a room at the B and B," he informed the man attempting to walk a straight line but failing. "You think you can walk?"

Spencer nodded.

"Good then. It's a nice room. Not all that big, but it's got a bed. You can have it. I'm used to sleepin' on the floor."

"I can call an Uber."

"And risk that woman showin' up at your place?"

Spencer didn't respond.

Shortly thereafter, Spencer revealed the horrifying news that his ex-sister-in-law had raped him nearly a decade ago. Archer figured a revelation like that deserved a slow stroll rather than a sprint. He was sensitive to the situation to the point he would take his cues from Spencer, but he damn sure didn't feel obligated, as Spencer had assumed that morning.

Archer also had some selfish reasons for wanting to take things slow. He was hoping to build something, and he knew from experience that racing to the finish line would not provide the foundation he was looking for. Coyote Ridge was the first place he'd been where he felt like he fit. It was weird, but he felt a spiritual connection to the small town, and he was eager to discover who he could be there.

"I know they've got personal stuff to deal with," Simon said, pulling him out of his thoughts. "But I've got to get movin' on this. I've stalled as long as I can. I'll reach out to Brantley and Reese for a better time, but if they can't do it soon, I'm gonna meet with Max Adorite and get the ball rollin'."

Archer looked over at his friend. "You can't go alone."

"I know." Simon glanced his way. "I found out Reese has history with one of Max's sisters. I was hopin' he could get me an in there."

"That's probably not a good idea."

Archer and Simon both looked to the doorway to see Rex Sharpe standing there.

"Hey," Simon greeted Rafe's brother, the man responsible for remodeling this old farmhouse and turning it into a bed and breakfast.

"They have issues?" Archer asked, figuring it was best to get the bad news out of the way.

"It ain't pretty, I'll tell you that much."

"They dated," Simon said.

"Reese and Madison? Yeah. A while back. Before Reese met Brantley," Rex answered. "And a year ago, almost to the day, Reese met up with Madison to talk. Some guys came into the restaurant lookin' to kidnap Madison. Reese got in between them and ended up takin' a bullet for his troubles. Almost died."

Oh, shit.

"Turns out, Madison's brother had his henchman come to her rescue, but they both left Reese there to die. Brantley didn't take too kindly to it. Since then, the Adorites have been off limits."

"How do you know so much about it?"

"Small town."

"So it's all hearsay?"

"Steeped in fact, yeah."

Archer got the feeling there was more truth to that story than fiction. He knew it wouldn't stop Simon from using Brantley or Reese to get an in with Max. When it came to a story, there weren't too many roadblocks that Simon would heed.

"I'll be sure to mention it to Brantley and Reese before I do anything," Simon told Rex.

Rex held up his hands. "Hey. You do you. I'm just tellin' you what I know."

Yeah, but it sure did sound like a warning.

Archer got the feeling it wouldn't be the first they'd encounter before this mystery was unraveled.

"Usually, the father's the one pacing."

Brantley didn't bother slowing down, nor did he look at Reese. It had been over an hour since they were kicked out of JJ's room shortly after arriving to find that, yes, she was in labor, and the babies were well on their way to making their debut into the world. Only it could be an hour or perhaps ten before that happened. So they were stuck in wait mode.

"Do you wish you were in there?" Slade asked.

"No, I'm good out here," he said honestly.

While he was nervous for his best friend, the last place he wanted to be was in the delivery room. He had gladly told his mother she was welcome to stay as his proxy. For the few minutes he'd been in there, he could tell Iris and Jules were the ones who managed to calm her. That and the idea of an epidural that the doctor had promised her.

When he told JJ he would be hanging with the team in the waiting room, she told him that was the best option. After all, she didn't want to risk dealing with him passing out.

Not that he would.

Probably.

"Anyone know if they settled on names?" Holly asked.

"Last I heard, they narrowed it down to two lists," Charlie said, smiling from her spot beside her girlfriend, Autumn.

Reese's phone buzzed, drawing Brantley's attention.

"It's just my mother checkin' in," Reese said, reading the screen. "They're an hour out."

Brantley nodded and continued to pace.

He was glad Cindy was coming down. Between Jules, Cindy, and Iris, JJ would have all the motherly support she needed. He doubted it would take away the sting of not having her own mother there, but he only hoped she was too preoccupied to think about it. If it weren't for the fact she would castrate him, Brantley would've confronted JJ's parents a long time ago for how shitty they'd been. If and when JJ ever decided to do that herself, he vowed to be right by her side.

"I heard y'all hired a new guy," Bryn said from her spot beside Reese.

Brantley looked at his sister. "How the hell'd you hear that?"

"I have my ear to the ground, little brother. You should know that by now." She flashed a grin. "Any chance he's single?"

"He is," Brantley said, mirroring her self-satisfied grin. "He's also gay."

"Aw, man," she drawled dramatically. "But seriously. Who is he?"

"First off, we haven't hired him," Brantley corrected because he knew how quickly rumors spread. "We offered him a job. If and when he accepts, then we've hired him."

"Who is he?" Bryn repeated.

"Archer Halligan," Reese told her. "He works with Simon Jennings."

"The guy Violet's datin'?"

"Yep."

"Isn't he a podcaster or something?" Bryn looked around the room as though she wasn't sure who might answer.

"*Havoc Your Way*," Holly said. "Best true-crime podcast ever."

"I might have to give it a listen," Bryn said.

"You really should," Elana told her. "I started a few years ago…"

Brantley was grateful when they started chatting amongst themselves. He was too antsy to carry on a conversation, although he had no idea why. It wasn't like he was going to be a father. Then again, he was going to be an uncle again. Since he'd been OCONUS—outside the continental US—for the births of his nieces and nephew, he hadn't been able to be there. Now that he was firmly rooted in Coyote Ridge once again, he didn't have to worry about a mission interrupting his personal life.

He rubbed the ring on his finger and looked at Reese, something he'd found himself doing quite a bit since they tied the knot a couple of weeks ago. He was still wrapping his head around the fact he was married to the man. Of all the things he'd done in his life, that was the most satisfying accomplishment to date.

The doors leading to the rooms opened, and a woman walked out. The room went silent for a moment until they realized she wasn't coming to give them any information.

"It might be a while," Bryn told them. "Tori was in labor with Eric for thirteen hours."

"Fuck that," Atticus mumbled under his breath.

Brantley laughed.

The next several hours crept by at a snail's pace. Afternoon turned to evening and finally to dinnertime. People came and went from the waiting room. Some heading down for food, others taking a walk to wake up. Brantley ventured outside a couple of times, taking Tesha along with him so he'd have an excuse when he really just wanted some air.

As the minutes ticked by, his anxiety increased. There were plenty of reassurances going around, people sharing war stories about the births of people they knew. Evidently, a lengthy labor wasn't abnormal.

"You want coffee?" Cindy asked, standing up to stretch.

Brantley could feel Reese's gaze on him. "Nah. Thanks, though."

He didn't need the caffeine, and his husband liked to remind him of that. Stress and caffeine were the perfect combination to trigger a migraine, and that was the last thing he needed. Ever since the wedding, he'd suffered more than he had in a while. Enough that he'd gotten in to see his doctor last week. His bloodwork had come back fine, but the doctor suggested they start a once-a-month injection that should offer some relief. As for whether it would work for him, only time would tell. He had his fingers crossed.

"What about you?" Cindy asked Reese.

"No, but I'll walk down with you."

She beamed a smile at her son. "Perfect."

Brantley got up to move around when they left the waiting room. He took one of the bottles of water that Holly had brought with her. He was about to take a sip when the doors opened and Wes appeared.

"Any news?"

Wes shook his head. "No babies yet. She's only at six centimeters."

"Six centimeters? How big is that?" Atticus asked.

Slade held up his Dr. Pepper can. "About the width of this can."

"Oh, Jesus. Holy fuck. Her…" Atticus looked down at his lap, then back to Slade. "Her—" he waved a hand—"She's got a hole *that* big?" Atticus shook his head dramatically as he leaped to his feet. "Uh-uh. Nope."

Wes chuckled. "I came out to get Jules some water."

Brantley grabbed one of the unopened bottles and passed it to him. "How's JJ doin'?"

Wes grinned. "Good. The epidural is working, and Jules is distractin' her by makin' her talk. She's tellin' all kinds of stories about you."

"Oh, boy." Since most of her stories involved him and high school, Brantley could only imagine what she was saying.

"Your mama's lovin' it."

Oh, shit. Brantley forgot his mother was in that room. His father had opted to hang with everyone else in the waiting room, but Iris was in there holding JJ's hand and likely making the nurses crazy.

"Is it true that you and her brother streaked through town on a dare?"

"We did," he said, remembering that night like it was yesterday.

"Is it true you and her brother are the reason they removed the fountain in Walker Park because you opted to pee in it? Repeatedly."

"That was *you*?" Slade bellowed, laughing.

"I can neither confirm nor deny."

"I guess I better get back in there." Wes held up the bottle. "Thanks for this."

Brantley nodded and took a stroll around the room, glancing from face to face. The team was all there. Everyone looked content to ride this out for as long as it took because that was what you did for friends.

Then it dawned on him. They weren't just a team anymore. And they weren't merely friends.

They were family.

Chapter Eleven

ARCHER WAS STRADDLING HIS HARLEY, ABOUT TO start the engine, when his cell phone buzzed, vibrating in his back pocket. He pulled it free and glanced at the screen.

"Hey," he said, forcing more cheer into his tone than he felt. A call right before a date was never a good thing. Especially when it was a call *from* your date.

"I was thinkin'…" Spencer said.

"Were you now? I was, too. About how much I'm lookin' forward to dinner with you tonight."

There was silence for a moment, followed by, "Me, too."

"Yeah? So you're not callin' to cancel."

"Actually, yes."

"Well, I'm glad you changed your mind," Archer told him, hoping he would continue to veer in the direction of keeping the date.

He waited for Spencer to say something.

He didn't.

"We don't have to meet at the diner. If you're not comfortable with it. We could head into Pflugerville or Round Rock. Find a restaurant there."

"How about my place?"

That was a surprise. One Archer was usually quick to accept, but he wasn't sure that was a good idea where Spencer was concerned.

"I'll cook," Spencer added. "I'm not that bad in a kitchen."

Archer laughed at the man's tone. His *not that bad,* sounded like it was said with a scrunch of the nose.

"Why don't I grab somethin' to go from the diner," Archer suggested, because deep down, he knew he would be having dinner with Spencer, no matter the place. He'd been looking forward to this ever since Spencer agreed. No way was he going to miss the opportunity.

"Okay."

"Text me what you want, and I'll swing by there real quick. Then text me your address. You live in town?"

"Yeah."

"Perfect. I'm lookin' forward to seein' you, Spencer."

There was a slight pause, followed by, "Me, too."

Archer ended the call, tucked his phone in his pocket, and started the engine. He pulled on the half-shell helmet he wore when he was going short distances and buckled the chin strap. Had it not been for his grandmother's insistence that he always wear a helmet, Archer would've gone without one for this short of a distance simply to feel the wind in his hair. However, a deal was a deal. Even though his grandmother would likely never find out, it would weigh on his conscience.

He released the jiffy stand and started the engine, relishing the throaty rumble as he did every time he started the bike. Less than two minutes later, with traffic—which equated to passing three different cars—Archer was parking the bike in the diner's lot. He pulled off his helmet and hung it on the handlebars before heading into the restaurant. Armed with the text from Spencer, he placed a to-go order and waited patiently for them to prepare the food.

As he stood there, he could feel eyes on him. Some were curious who he was because they hadn't seen him yet. Others were likely wondering why he was still there.

The bells over the door jingled, and he stepped back to keep from blocking the path.

"Evenin', Sheriff," Archer greeted when Jeff Endsley walked in, an older, bearded man beside him.

"Archer," Jeff said, shaking his hand before glancing at the man beside him. "Have you met my husband?"

"Haven't had the pleasure," Archer responded.

"Mack, meet Archer Halligan. Archer, this is Mack Schwartz."

Archer shook Mack's hand. "Nice to meet you."

"Likewise. You're new in town?"

"Yes, sir," he answered easily. "Came to check somethin' out for a story. My buddy fell in love, so it looks like we're here to stay."

Mack's bushy eyebrows lowered as he peered over at Jeff. "That make any damn sense to you?"

Jeff laughed. "We're glad you're stayin'. I heard Simon and Violet are buyin' the Raikkonnen house."

"You heard correctly. They close on it on Halloween."

"Glad to hear it."

The hostess appeared, greeting both men by name.

"Good to see you again," the sheriff said.

"Nice to meet you," Mack said.

Archer stepped back, giving them room to pass. "Likewise. Enjoy your dinner."

Several minutes later, his food was brought out, packaged in a brown sack. Armed with dinner, Archer carried the food to his motorcycle, secured it, pulled on his helmet, then straddled the seat. He clicked to pull up Spencer's address on the map and put the phone in the mount on the handlebars.

It was about that time that he felt a trickle of first-date jitters.

He intended to enjoy that feeling.

Ten minutes later, he was pulling down a long, narrow dirt driveway lined with large trees on both sides. It wasn't until he reached concrete that a house came into view. A sprawling ranch-style with a metal roof and a wraparound porch secured by wrought iron fencing around the perimeter.

Archer followed the driveway around to the side-facing garage and stopped. He took it all in as he secured his helmet and pocketed his phone. He noticed the landscaping, which consisted of a variety of rocks and stones and a plethora of heat-resistant plants—cacti, sage trees, and yucca.

If he was being honest, it wasn't what he was expecting.

Then again, he hadn't been sure what to expect.

With food in hand, Archer headed for the gate that opened to the front of the house. His boots thudded on the wooden porch as he walked down the length of the house, passing clusters of windows on his way to the front door.

He was about to knock when the door opened and Spencer appeared.

Damn, he looked good.

Not to mention nervous.

"Hey."

"Hey back." Archer smiled. He couldn't help himself. Seeing Spencer did that. It made him feel weird things churning inside, and it just made him fucking happy. He couldn't remember the last time he'd even been on a date, much less the last time a man had lit him up without doing a thing.

"Let me help with that," Spencer offered, reaching for the food.

While he didn't need help, Archer passed it over and then strolled inside as Spencer headed in the direction of the kitchen.

He closed the door behind him, taking in the open space. He could see clean through to the swimming pool and outdoor kitchen in the backyard.

"This is beautiful," he told Spencer, and he meant it.

The walls were painted off-white, the floor was dark-stained concrete with several rugs tossed about. The vaulted ceilings were white with dark wood beams. There was a stone fireplace on the right. It stretched to the ceiling, accentuating the height. A set of glass doors beside it led to another part of the house. On the left was the kitchen, lined with white cabinets and stainless steel appliances. It was separated from the living space by a large white-quartz-topped island complete with several stools. Three pendant lights hung above it. The ceiling was lower in the kitchen, allowing for a handful of recessed lights to brighten the space.

At the back of the kitchen was a breakfast nook. The table had been set, and a bottle of wine was chilling in an ice bucket.

"You need help with that?" Archer asked when he noticed Spencer was staring at him.

Spencer shook his head.

"Somethin' wrong?" he asked, moving toward him.

Again, Spencer shook his head.

Archer closed the gap between them, walking around the island and stopping when he was mere inches away.

"Spencer?"

"Hmm?"

"Are you nervous?"

Spencer nodded his head as he said, "No."

Archer grinned. "Me neither."

Those pretty brown eyes glittered.

To his surprise, Spencer moved closer, eliminating every inch between them. They were chest to chest when Spencer tilted his head, their breaths mingling.

"I've spent the entire day thinkin' about that kiss," Spencer whispered.

"Yeah?"

"It's all I can do." Spencer's gaze shifted to Archer's mouth. "I think you broke me."

Archer chuckled. "Are you hungry?"

"Yes," Spencer said, his voice low.

Archer studied his face, admiring the gold in his eyes.

"But not for food."

"No?"

"No."

"What're you hungry for?"

Spencer swallowed hard. "Somethin' I've never had before."

As soon as those words registered, Archer's smile faded, and his chest clenched painfully tight.

Never?

As in never *ever?*

"Are you sayin'…?"

"That I've never had sex?"

It was Archer's turn to be speechless, but he managed a nod.

"I haven't." Spencer pulled back enough to meet his gaze. "Not willingly. And not with a man."

Archer wasn't sure what to say to that.

"I know. You probably think I'm lyin'. I'm thirty-one years old and I've never had sex with anyone I wanted to have sex with."

"I don't think you're lying, Spencer."

"It's weird. I get it." Spencer took a step back. "It's the very reason I'm practically a virgin. Because even the mention of it freaks people out."

"I'm not freaked." He took a step closer, but Spencer merely moved back again.

"I can see it on your face. You've never had sex with a virgin, and you're worried you'll break me."

"Actually…" Archer grabbed Spencer's arm before he could back up again. He pulled him close. "I'm tryin' to figure out how to stop my body's reaction to this conversation."

Spencer looked down, then back up quickly. "Seriously?"

"Oh, yeah. Hard as steel."

Spencer swallowed hard.

Had he been with any other man, Archer might've acted on the chemistry between them. However, he wasn't sure he was capable of taking what he wanted, knowing he would be Spencer's first in all the ways that mattered.

"Did I just scare you off?" There was a hint of frustration and embarrassment in Spencer's tone as he started to move back.

Archer stopped him with a hand on his back, holding him there, chest to chest, thigh to thigh.

"You didn't scare me," he told Spencer. He wasn't lying. He had some concerns, sure, but he wasn't scared.

"Then what is it?"

"Well, for starters, I'd like to get to know you a little before I take your virginity."

Spencer gasped.

"Not what you expected me to say?" Archer grinned when Spencer remained silent. "I don't think I've ever been anyone's first but I'm damn sure not opposed to the idea."

"No?"

"Not at all."

"So what're you waitin' for?"

"I enjoy sex. A lot. My desires run the gamut from sweet to rough and dirty and everywhere in between. I'm lookin' forward to exploring the spectrum with you. In time."

As soon as the last two words were out, Spencer attempted to back away again. Archer banded his arms tighter.

When Spencer stopped pulling away, Archer cupped his face with both hands. "Are you in a rush for a reason?"

Spencer held his stare. "Aside from the fact I've never been quite this turned on before?"

That made him smile. "Yeah. Aside from that."

"No."

"Good."

"Why's that good?"

"Because I'm gonna slow you down."

Spencer frowned.

Archer firmed his grip on Spencer's face, not allowing him to back up. "Baby, I've wanted to fuck you since the moment I saw you."

Spencer's eyes widened, the amber gold darkening with arousal.

"And God willing, that'll happen. But not until the time's right."

"What's wrong with right now?"

"I want to know you before I lose myself in you, Spencer." He skimmed Spencer's eyes for a reaction. "Because I get the feelin' I'm gonna get lost fast."

Spencer's sigh settled the all-too-familiar churning in his gut. The one that urged him to jump in with both feet. That was his MO, the very thing that ruined every potential relationship he'd ever had.

Yeah, Archer wanted to feel this man. Inside, outside. Every delectable inch.

But he wanted more than that.

Until he could give Spencer a reason to want the same, Archer intended to refrain. Even if it killed him.

Chapter Twelve

Very, very early on Wednesday, September 28, 2022

"It's time, JJ," Dr. Tinder said, his tone firm. "I need you to push."

Sweat dripped down her face, and she felt as though she'd run a marathon.

Twice.

Once in reverse.

Every part of her body ached.

"I've got you," Baz said softly, his hand gripped firmly in hers. "Our babies are ready to meet their mama."

That was the incentive she needed. The gentle reminder that she would soon see her sweet babies for the first time.

"Ready when you are, JJ," Dr. Tinder said from his perch between her legs.

Luckily, the discomfort was far more powerful than her modesty. Otherwise, JJ would've been embarrassed that he was staring at her most private parts. Or that something the size of a papaya was going to make its debut through there.

"Okay," JJ groaned, peering up at Baz. "Let's do this."

REESE WATCHED AS BRANTLEY CONTINUED TO PACE. The man couldn't seem to sit still. Every time he thought Brantley might relax, he would launch up from his chair and do a lap around the room or slip out into the hall. He was never gone for long. Just long enough to let everyone know he was worried.

The good news was they hadn't been given any reason to worry. According to Frank, who was receiving updates via text from Iris, the doctor and nurses were optimistic.

Granted, Reese knew better than to tell him there was nothing to worry about. He prayed this was an easy delivery for JJ. As easy as one could be after—he glanced at his watch to see it was just shy of zero-one-hundred—nearly twelve hours in labor, at least. She'd been through enough. Her and Baz. They deserved every ounce of happiness that could come their way.

So, rather than go after Brantley, Reese sent up a silent request to the man upstairs to send only good vibes down to that delivery room.

BAZ STARED DOWN AT JJ, OVERWHELMED BY a myriad of emotions. Love, fear, elation, stress. It churned inside him, but he refrained from showing it—he hoped—because he had the easy job here. Holding JJ's hand, letting her know she wasn't alone in this was the most he could offer.

"Uhhhhh!" JJ groaned, her face scrunched as she pushed when the doctor told her to.

"That's good, JJ. Real good. Don't stop. We've got a head and shoulders."

Dr. Tinder then said something to one of the nurses. It was too muffled to make out, but Baz didn't detect worry or concern. Or maybe that was his ears playing tricks on him.

"I want you to rest for a second, JJ. Take two deep breaths, then I want you to push as hard as you can."

Baz pressed a kiss to JJ's forehead and let her squeeze his hand, no longer worried that she might break his fingers. If she did, he'd get over it.

BRANTLEY FOCUSED ON BREATHING.

In. Out. In. Out.

Slow and steady was his goal. As he walked, he tried to relax his shoulders. He was tense, the stress more powerful than he expected.

Wes had just texted that JJ was beginning to push, and the babies would be coming along at any moment.

It should've been a relief. Instead, his heart was in his throat, and fear trickled into his bloodstream.

Please, God, let them be okay.

Did he want to be in that hospital room with his best friend? Absolutely not. It wouldn't help. Not her. Not him. He simply had to wait like everyone else.

He stepped out into the hallway, away from all those curious eyes. He stopped and put his hands on the wall, tilting his head down.

It was the not knowing that was killing him.

Not knowing that JJ was okay.

Not knowing that the babies were healthy and strong.

Not knowing, not knowing, not knowing.

"Hey."

Brantley didn't lift his head when Reese put a hand on his back. "Hey."

"We should hear somethin' soon."

He appreciated that Reese didn't try to placate him with promises. They knew from experience that saying good things would happen didn't make it true. Hell, they'd endured far more loss and devastation than anyone should have.

But they had survived.

Reese leaned in, resting his chin on Brantley's shoulder. "I love you."

"I love you, too."

They would survive this, too.

THE SOUND OF A BABY CRYING HAD tears flooding JJ's eyes.

"That's one," Dr. Tinder said. "A beautiful little boy, JJ. He gets the title of big brother. Now it's time to get his sister out."

"Come over here, Grandpa," the nurse said, clearly speaking to Wes. "You can help."

Wes, who had been standing near her left shoulder, behind Iris and Jules, walked around the machines toward the corner where incubators were waiting.

"You ready for this?" Dr. Tinder asked her.

JJ was tired. So very tired, but somehow she managed to nod.

"Good. I want you to relax for a moment, catch your breath. When you're ready, let's do this one more time."

JJ peered up at Baz, and her heart clenched. He was watching her, tears running down his face. He didn't pretend he wasn't crying, didn't try to hide it. She loved that about him. That and so much more.

"Ready?" she whispered to him.

He nodded and mouthed, "I love you."

"I love you, too," she whispered, then gritted her teeth and got ready for round two.

ATTICUS SKIMMED THE ROOM, TAKING IN ALL the faces. Everyone was there. Holly, Charlie, Becs, Jay, Darius, Luca, Elana, Evan, Slade. Reese's mom was there, along with her boyfriend, Hugh, and Hugh's friend Mark, who was … well, Atticus figured technically, Mark was also her boyfriend, though maybe it wasn't quite as serious?

Hell, he had no idea. And to be honest, he didn't care.

Brantley's sister, Bryn, was still hanging out alongside their father, Frank. Brantley's brother, Trey, was on the other side of the room, Ava asleep with her head on his shoulder, and Magnus conked out next to her, his head tilted back, resting on the wall.

Even Reese's brother, Z, who happened to be their boss, and his husband, RT, had made the trip down from Dallas. Z was staring at his phone screen while RT was busy on his laptop, which had been perched in his lap since the moment he sat down.

As he stared at these people, he wished he had taken a picture when they first got there. Hours and hours and hours ago. Back when there were conversations to be had, news to be shared, jokes to be laughed at.

Hours and hours of sitting around had drained the excitement from the room while at the same time causing backaches and the need for lots of stretching.

Although the energy might've been gone, and there was a little discomfort to be had, there was still a hum of anticipation that kept most eyes open despite the overwhelming exhaustion that was beginning to set in.

"Almost there, baby," Baz crooned to JJ, keeping his voice low.

He knew he was supposed to encourage her to breathe because he'd learned that during their Lamaze classes. Since JJ seemed to be doing a good job of doing exactly as they'd learned, he felt no need to overwhelm her with instruction. Or piss her off. It was a wonder she wasn't angry already. Then again, they'd waited what felt like a lifetime for this day, so perhaps her emotions were simply in chaos. Whatever the reason, he opted to remain silent, squeezing her hand gently to remind her that he was there.

"We're gonna do it this time, JJ," Dr. Tinder said, peering over the sheet that was draped over JJ's knees. "You ready?"

JJ said, "Yes," although she was shaking her head no.

Baz could see Dr. Tinder's eyes crinkle, the only sign that he was smiling since there was a mask covering his face.

"Good girl."

Taking a moment to brush her hair back from her face, Baz took a deep breath when she did and then held on one more time.

JJ LET OUT A CRY SO LOUD she figured for sure her throat would be raw.

But then Dr. Tinder was praising her and congratulating them on a little girl. He was mumbling other things, but she was too focused on listening for the baby's cry to pay attention.

"Breathe, honey," Jules urged, brushing JJ's hair back. "They've got her."

Every second she didn't hear it, her chest squeezed tighter and tighter and…

An irritated squall sounded, and everyone released a pent-up breath.

"There it is," Dr. Tinder said, his voice muffled because he was still between her legs, doing whatever doctors did after babies were born.

JJ exhaled on a rush of air so powerful, it was a wonder she didn't pass out.

"Baz, do you want to go over there?" Jules asked.

"You can go," he told her, his eyes never leaving JJ's face.

For a few minutes, JJ closed her eyes, grateful the hard part was over. At least for today. Once she was at home, attempting to take care of twins, she figured this would feel like a cakewalk.

She was grateful she didn't have to do this alone. So very grateful for the man she loved with all her heart.

"I think Mom should see these little angels." Wes's sturdy voice sounded from behind her.

"I think that's a good idea," the nurse told him.

The next thing she knew, Iris was stepping back and the nurse was settling a baby in a blue blanket in the crook of JJ's right arm. And then a bundle in pink was placed on her left side.

JJ glanced down at them. Back and forth, taking it all in as her heart swelled ten times its normal size. She made a vow right then and there that she would never, no matter what, let them go for a single minute without knowing that she loved them with all her heart. She would do what was necessary to ensure they never doubted it for a second.

Chapter Thirteen

"HOW BIG WERE THEY AGAIN?" BRANTLEY ASKED Reese as they sat across from one another at the diner.

When they'd arrived, just after six, the darkness of night was slowly being saturated by daylight even though the sun hadn't risen yet. It had been late enough for the diner to be open but too early for it to be occupied by anyone other than a couple of temporary ranch hands helping out somewhere in the vicinity. Now that it was closer to seven, people were beginning to trickle in as steadily as the sun was rising in the sky.

"Little boy was five pounds two ounces," Reese said, pushing his plate away. "Eighteen inches exact. And the little girl was four pounds fourteen ounces. Seventeen and a half inches."

"The numbers seem big to me, but they were so small."

"I think the doctors were impressed with their size."

Yeah, that's what Wes had told them.

After receiving the good news that JJ and the babies were doing well, they'd lingered at the hospital, waiting for a moment to slip in and see her. As soon as Brantley laid eyes on his best friend, he knew she was eager for some rest. Still, she managed to smile, reassuring him that everything was good. After a quick hug, they slipped out with everyone else who was heading home to get sleep, what little there was to be had. When they left, Wes, Jules, and Baz were the only ones still there and upright. He figured they would faceplant in a bed at some point, but probably not until some of the elation of the day wore off.

As for faceplanting into bed, it sounded like the best idea in the world, and Brantley intended to get right on that just as soon as they had breakfast. Afterward, they could catch a few hours of sleep and hopefully not lose an entire day.

"What're your thoughts on havin' kids now?" Brantley asked, taking a sip of his coffee.

"I'm good with the four-legged variety," Reese answered, sipping coffee. "They sure were cute, though."

Yes, they were. As cute as something that had spent the past eight or so months cramped in a tiny space full of fluid could be.

"Is it all the cryin' that puts you off?" Brantley probed. "Because I'm sure fathers and grandfathers don't do that all the time."

Reese huffed a laugh. "They were tears of relief."

"That's what Baz claims, but I have to wonder."

Brantley didn't feel guilty about picking on Wes or Baz, but that was likely because he'd shed a tear or two as well. The babies were as close to perfect as premature twins could be. At least, that was what the scuttlebutt was. Since the babies had been moved to the NICU, as Dr. Tinder had warned might happen, Brantley questioned the validity of the rumors. Something about Apgar scores not being where they would like them to be. According to Wes, the doctors and nurses were doing everything they could to ensure the babies got what they needed.

Since they were the ones with the training and know-how, he had to believe that was the truth. So they were taking it all as good until someone told them otherwise.

Which he hoped didn't happen.

"They are kind of adorable, huh?" Brantley asked Reese, watching his face.

"Considerin' who their parents are, they've hit the gene-pool lottery."

Brantley smiled. "True."

Reese lifted a hand and waved the server over.

"More coffee?" she asked.

"No, thank you," Reese told her while Brantley covered his cup to signal he didn't want any. "Can we get the check?"

"Sure thing." She pulled out her notepad and ripped off the top sheet. Reese didn't even look at it before passing her his credit card.

Brantley leaned back and fought the urge to rub his eyes. He felt like his eyeballs had been sandblasted, and he knew if he didn't get horizontal soon, that headache he'd managed to avoid was going to come on with a vengeance.

The server returned with the card and the receipt for Reese to sign. Before he even picked up the pen, Brantley was on his feet. Tesha followed suit, lumbering out from under the table where she'd been sleeping.

"It's naptime, girl," Brantley told her as they waited for Reese.

As they walked out of the diner, Brantley was already daydreaming about his pillow. But as soon as he stepped into the brilliant Texas sunshine, he got the feeling that faceplanting in his bed wasn't going to happen as soon as he would like.

"Is that—" Reese nodded in the direction of the woman strolling their way.

"Slade's mother? Yeah."

"She's up early, huh?"

"Real early," Brantley agreed.

"Do you think we're in trouble?" Reese whispered, a smile plastered on his face.

Since she was making a beeline for them, he had to think there was a good possibility.

"Heel," Reese said to Tesha, his way of keeping her close and letting her know everything was all right.

Rose Jameson-Elliott started speaking as she approached. "Oh, good. I'm glad I ran into you boys. I need a favor."

Standing up straight because he couldn't help himself, Brantley pasted on a smile. "Good mornin', Mrs. Elliott."

She chuckled, her expression softening. "First, let me apologize for my manners. Good morning." Rose swatted a hand in his direction. "And secondly, Mrs. Elliott was what you called me when I taught you in third grade. Since we're all grownups now, you can call me Rose."

Brantley wasn't sure he could do that, but he nodded his head and fought the urge to salute her and call her *ma'am*.

Rose looked a lot like her older sister, Lorrie. She had the same softness to her face, the same intelligent blue eyes. If Brantley recalled correctly, Rose was about a decade younger than Lorrie, but they both looked significantly younger than they probably should, considering they'd raised such rowdy boys. And yeah, Rose's sons—Kieran, Brad, Grady, Vince, Slade, and Spencer—could easily give him and his brothers a run for their money. Hell, they were quite possibly rowdier than Travis and his brothers back in the day.

"I'm here on behalf of my niece Callie." Rose pointed away from the diner, far off into the distance. "As you probably know, she's the principal of CRHS."

Was that what she was doing? Aiming in the direction of Coyote Ridge High School?

Perhaps she thought she was. It was actually a bit south of her position, but Brantley wasn't about to tell her that. He also didn't tell her he didn't know she was related to the principal. Or that he didn't even know the principal's name until two seconds ago. Since he wasn't around kids that fell in that age range, Brantley didn't keep up with the goings-on at the high school. Or any of the schools, for that matter, except for the rare occasions when his nieces or nephew had a Christmas pageant or something of the sort.

"Is everything all right?" Reese asked.

"No." Rose sighed heavily. "Someone stole the mustang."

Brantley frowned. "Are we talkin' a car or a horse?"

"Horse. Specifically, the bronze statue," Rose clarified. "From in front of the school."

It took a moment for that to sink in. When it did, Brantley wasn't sure whether he was worried or impressed. Considering the rearing horse sculpture probably weighed close to half a ton, he had to give props to whoever pulled off that prank. And since the principal wasn't aware of it being rehomed, he had to figure that was what this was. However, he tended not to leap to conclusions.

"Maybe someone sent it out to get repaired and didn't tell the boss?" he suggested.

"If only it were that easy."

Brantley waited for her to say more, but Rose simply stared back at them with what looked like expectation in her cool blue eyes.

It freaked him out that his first instinct was to fidget like he had back when he was in the third grade.

REESE FOUGHT THE URGE TO LAUGH.

In all the time he'd known Brantley, he wasn't sure he'd ever seen him quite so ... uncomfortable. Almost as though he was standing in the principal's office, about to be reprimanded. Not having a casual discussion in a parking lot with one of his former teachers.

Sure, she was now a school board member, but what did that matter? They didn't have kids in school. Didn't know anyone who did.

Well, that wasn't true. They knew people. People who had kids. In school. Not high school. Probably.

Regardless, Mrs. Elliott was harmless because they were grown men now, not kids.

So why was she looking at them like that? Like she was studying them, looking deep into their thoughts. Was that something they taught in teacher school? How to intimidate kids. Or grown men, as was the case here.

Okay, so maybe he understood a little of Brantley's discomfort. Mrs. Elliott had been one of Reese's favorite teachers, but coming face to face with her now was strange.

Since neither Rose nor Brantley appeared eager to speak up, Reese asked, "Is there somethin' you'd like us to do about the statue?"

Rose's gaze shifted to him. "Yes. Find it."

Reese's eyebrows hopped toward his hairline. "Find it?"

She flashed a smile at Tesha, reaching down to pet her head. "Yes."

Surely he wasn't understanding. "The bronze statue?"

She stood tall once more. "Correct."

Now it was his turn to stammer. "We ... umm ... that's not usually the ... uh ... the sort of case we handle."

"I'm aware." Rose looked back and forth between them. "And I know this isn't an urgent matter—well, it kinda is to Callie with homecoming and all that, but..." She waved her hand again. "But it's missing, and your team finds missing people, so I just figured if you could tackle finding the human element, you could easily do this."

He was still fighting the urge to laugh as he shot a confused glance at Brantley.

"She does kinda have a point," Brantley noted.

Reese's mouth fell open. Was he saying...?

Brantley's grin was that of a devilish man, but Reese suspected only he would notice.

"We'll get our best people on it, Mrs. Elliott," Brantley told her.

Reese harnessed every ounce of willpower to keep from asking Brantley if he'd lost his damn mind. Instead, he watched as Rose narrowed her eyes at Brantley, cocking one perfectly arched eyebrow.

Brantley cleared his throat. "I mean, Rose."

She smiled. "Thank you. And if you could keep it quiet, that would be wonderful. The last thing we need is for Brett to get word of it."

Brett? Reese let the name tumble around in his gray matter until it found something that made sense. He assumed she was referring to Brett Jameson, the superintendent of Coyote Ridge ISD, who also happened to be Callie's older brother. The only reason he knew of the man was because Trey had mentioned him when explaining that he was building an agricultural barn for the high school on their newly acquired property. Apparently, Brett had to sign off on it.

"We'll do our best," he promised when Brantley didn't respond.

"Okay then." Rose smiled. "I'll let you get to it."

With that, she strolled into the diner on her two-inch heels, as prim and proper as he remembered her when she was his teacher. As soon as she was inside, he hurried to catch up with Brantley, who'd made a beeline for the truck.

"I think you're sleep deprived," he accused, helping Tesha into the truck.

"Probably."

"You just had to tell her we'd do this." Reese shook his head, still baffled that Brantley would cave so easily.

"You do know I'm not huntin' down that horse, right?" Brantley muttered as he was getting behind the wheel.

"You're the one who took the case," he countered.

Brantley's eyes were wide when he looked over, his voice raspy. "I couldn't tell her no. It's like she had this"—he mimicked gripping someone around the throat—"hold on me. I had no choice."

Reese understood the feeling all too well, which was why he said, "Why don't we let Atticus run with it?"

Brantley barked a laugh. "Oh, that should be fun."

Reese thought so.

Chapter Fourteen

"How long did we sleep?" Brantley asked as he came awake slowly, drifting out of a deep, dreamless sleep.

"Almost five hours."

"So, it's what? Thirteen hundred?"

"Ten after."

Brantley breathed in deeply, enjoying the warmth of the man pressed up against his back. He could easily drift off for another hour, but it would accomplish nothing.

"If we get up now, we can get some shit done today," he grumbled.

"We could," Reese agreed from behind him.

Neither of them moved.

Brantley wasn't sure he wanted to. He was comfortable right where he was, Reese's arm draped over him, his hard body warm along his back.

"We could even meet up with Simon," Brantley suggested. "Find out if he knows anything worth lookin' into."

"We could," Reese said again, sounding as unenthusiastic as he had the first time.

Brantley sighed when Reese kissed the back of his neck. He tipped his head forward, encouraging more. Reese placed another kiss on his neck and another on his shoulder.

"Or we could stay right here," he mumbled, moaning softly when Reese's hand glided down his stomach, lower.

"Or we could stay right here," Reese echoed, his touch feather-light as he began stroking him.

"God, that feels good."

"It's meant to," Reese whispered.

When Reese shifted, Brantley took the opportunity to roll to his back. Before Reese could get any ideas of going anywhere, Brantley cupped the back of his head and pulled him in for a kiss.

"You brushed your teeth," he said, grinning against Reese's mouth. "You cheated."

"Mmm." Reese didn't respond, his tongue sliding into Brantley's mouth. He could feel the eagerness in Reese's kiss, in the way his hands moved over him. He wasn't rushing, he was savoring, and it was perfect.

He let Reese lead, his hands sliding over Reese's warm skin as he shifted until he was draped over Brantley. Banding his arms around Reese, he held him tight as their tongues glided in a heated mating of mouths. He would never get enough of this man.

He loved moments like this. When they could slow down enough to simply be together, neither of them in a hurry to finish. Sure, his blood was pumping faster, thickening as lust consumed him. He wanted to feel Reese. It was an addiction that had to be fed, a need that couldn't be ignored. Whenever he was with Reese, everything felt right.

"I want you inside me," he whispered against Reese's lips.

Reese didn't break the kiss, but he shifted, a clear sign that he'd heard him. Brantley moved with him, lifting his knee, making room for the man he loved. Long minutes passed, and the kiss continued as Brantley reached for the lubricant, prepared Reese's cock. When he was hanging by a frayed thread, Reese finally pushed inside him.

Brantley groaned, shifting, moving so Reese could slide in deeper.

"Fuck," he grunted, grabbing Reese's ass, pulling him closer, taking him to the hilt. "Yes. Just like that."

Reese continued to move inside him, his cock tunneling deep with slow, sensual strokes while their foreheads rested together, breaths mingling.

"I love you," Brantley told him because he'd promised himself he would always ensure Reese knew how he felt. Well, that and because it was so easy to say when it was true.

"God, Brantley," Reese hissed. "You feel..."

Brantley cut him off with a kiss, letting himself feel everything.

Seconds turned to minutes, and the slow and leisurely pace picked up speed, morphing into a frantic need for release. They chased it together, Reese fucking him with rough thrusts.

When he knew Reese was close, Brantley reached between them and stroked his cock, wanting to come when Reese did.

"Now, baby," Brantley urged. "Come inside me."

"Oh, fuck … oh, fuck…"

Reese grabbed Brantley's free hand, pinning it to the bed as he slammed into him one final time.

They came together in a cacophony of grunts and moans.

And when it was over, Brantley savored the lingering completion that allowed him to float for a little while. It was a feeling he'd only ever felt with Reese. It was a release so much more powerful than merely his body.

"I love you, too," Reese said as he dropped to his side of the bed, panting like he'd run five miles.

Brantley chuckled. "What do you say we get up, figure out what the team's up to, then grab some food. Maybe run by the hospital? We can check on JJ, and when we're done, we'll meet up with Simon and Holt."

"Need a shower first," Reese said, his breath still labored.

"Me, too. We'll do that first, then take care of the rest."

And maybe, if he were lucky, they'd linger in the shower for a little while. Just because they could.

The lingering didn't last nearly as long as Brantley would've liked. Two minutes. Maybe five.

That was the point when Reese turned to face him, sliding his hand over his head to push the water back. "You need to talk to Atticus about the missing statue. And you need to do it before he leaves for the day."

Brantley traded places, stepping beneath the water. "I thought you would've done that already."

"And when would I've had time?"

He shrugged. "You did brush your teeth without wakin' me up. You're a multi-tasker."

"Not this time. This is all you." Reese reached for a towel. "You told Rose we'd look into it. *You* get to deal with Atticus when he freaks the fuck out."

"If I recall correctly, it was *your* idea to assign him to it."

"Only because *you* took the case."

Brantley smiled. It was hard not to when he thought about how Atticus might react when he learned he was going to have to look into a missing statue. The kid hadn't been on the team long, and he was already going stir-crazy without any cases to work. Brantley figured they should pass some along, but he didn't want Atticus to get used to working alone. He'd done enough of that during his time as a bounty hunter. Luckily for him, they'd found him a partner—assuming Archer intended to accept the job. As soon as they could get Archer onboarded and acclimated, they'd start shoving bigger things their way.

Until then…

"Fine," he told Reese. "We'll tell him."

"*You'll* tell him."

Laughing, Brantley acquiesced. "*I'll* tell him."

"By yourself."

Brantley's eyebrows hopped toward his hairline. "Yeah? And what're you gonna do?"

With the towel wrapped around his hips, Reese crossed the bathroom toward the door. "First, I'll start by checking my email and ensuring we haven't missed anything."

"That'll take five minutes, tops," Brantley called after him.

"It'll take as long as it takes you to tell Atticus," Reese shouted back. "Good luck."

Ten minutes later, dressed and ready for the rest of the day, Brantley stepped out onto the back patio, a cup of coffee in his hands. Thankfully, his husband had been gracious enough to start a pot before he went upstairs to hide in his office. It was needed if he was expected to deal with Atticus first thing.

Because it was roughly lunchtime for most of the team, he took the time to check the parking area to see if Atticus's truck was there. He located the big gray Chevy, and his grin amped up a few watts at the thought of witnessing Atticus's reaction when he learned he was going to be the lead investigator for the first time since he started working for the task force.

Since he wasn't going to get out of it, he sucked it up and made his way to the barn. He was keying in his passcode when Tesha came racing out of the dog door, hauling ass across the yard to join him.

"Don't even act like you haven't been over here all day," he told her as he opened the door and she rushed inside.

"Afternoon, boss," Slade called from his desk. "Didn't think we were gonna see you today."

"Can't take a day off. Someone's gotta keep an eye on you and Atticus."

Atticus spoke as he hen-pecked the keyboard with his fingertips. "What did I do?"

"Nothin'. And that's the problem."

Atticus frowned at his computer screen. "Thanks."

"Since you look bored, I've got a case I need you to work on."

The way the man slowly lifted his head was comical. As though he was rerunning the words again and again, trying to ensure he heard correctly.

"I thought you wanted me to be partnered up before? Is Archer startin' already?"

Ignoring the man's questions, he said, "Do you want the case or not?"

Atticus eyed him suspiciously. "Maybe I should know what it is first."

"Not the deal. You either want it or you don't."

"Yeah," Atticus blurted. "Of course I do."

"Good. And no, Archer's not startin' yet, so I'll let you pick a partner this time around."

"Can you give me some of the details first?"

"It's local," Brantley told him. "Missing for about forty-eight hours or so."

That seemed to get his attention. "Who is it?"

"Not a who. A *what*."

Atticus frowned. Slade and Evan snickered.

"I change my mind. I don't want it."

"Too late. It's yours."

Atticus glared at him. "You play dirty, boss."

Brantley laughed. "I play to win."

"Fine. It's my case. *What* am I finding?"

"The bronze mustang statue at Coyote Ridge High School went missin' in the last coupla days. They want it back."

Atticus's lips parted, his eyes widening. It was obvious he was waiting for the punchline.

"Unless you can't handle it."

The laughter grew louder, with Luca and Jay chiming in.

"I can handle it," Atticus said firmly. "Just not sure I *want* to."

"Good thing you don't have a choice."

Slade doubled over, his laughter echoing in the barn.

Atticus's glare alternated with pinpoint accuracy, shifting from Brantley to Slade and then back.

Brantley had to give the kid credit. Back when he first came on board, Atticus would've lost his shit if he thought he was going to have to deal with something like this. He was holding it together pretty well.

Atticus stood. "Fine. I need to know who to talk to."

"I'll write it down for you," Brantley assured him. "You also need a partner."

"Slade," Atticus said without hesitation.

Slade looked up, his face red from his giggling spell. "Nuh-uh. Someone else can help with that."

"Sorry, man," Brantley told him. "He's the lead. He picks his team."

That earned more laughter, this time from Evan and Luca.

Slade was still smiling, but he didn't sound amused. "Seriously?"

"Yep." Brantley grabbed a Post-it note and a pen, then scribbled down the principal's name before passing it to Atticus. "Talk to her. She can give you details. I suggest you get over there sooner rather than later."

Atticus sputtered, but Brantley didn't wait around for him to say anything more. The kid could handle this. Brantley was sure of it.

"OKAY, CHUCKLES. YOU WANNA GRAB LUNCH?" ATTICUS asked Slade, frustrated that he'd been tricked into taking a case that made everyone else laugh their asses off.

Slade glanced over, dark eyebrows angled down. "Sure. Now?"

It was already well after Atticus's lunchtime, but due to the chaos of the morning, he'd forgotten all about eating. Now his stomach was rumbling, and the hunger mixed with the anxiety of taking on a case by himself was making him nauseous.

Okay, so maybe the interruptions weren't the only reason he'd been procrastinating for the past hour. Most of it had to do with Slade's attitude. Ever since their introduction to Archer Halligan on Monday, Slade had been ... well, for lack of a better word, he'd go with pissy. And that was saying something since Slade wasn't exactly a ray of sunshine on a good day. And since Atticus was all about keeping the peace—at least when it came to Slade—he'd ensured they hadn't gotten on the topic of his potential new partner. It was a self-preservation instinct. Avoid, and give the man some time.

Since Slade had been laughing for the better part of ten minutes, he figured now was as good a time as any.

"If you think you can stop laughing long enough to eat."

A nod was the man's only response. Maybe a smirk. Yeah. There was a smirk lurking there.

Asshole.

"We're gonna grab lunch," Atticus told Becs, who was skimming her finger over a file in front of her. "Then we're gonna swing by the high school. You want us to grab you anything? We can drop it back by on our way."

She looked up, smiled. "No, thank you. I brought some egg salad."

Atticus's nose scrunched. "If you change your mind…"

Becs's smile warmed, and he appreciated that she wasn't going to make fun of him.

Atticus headed straight for sunshine and humidity, both of which he got in spades when he walked out into the sticky September day. Officially, it was fall, but someone evidently forgot to tell Mother Nature because the afternoon temps were hovering in the nineties still.

Once they were in the truck, Atticus considered picking Slade's brain about Coyote Ridge High School. Mainly, where it was located and how he would get there. Since Coyote Ridge now provided him with a permanent address to put on his driver's license, he felt a little stupid that he hadn't already known. Then again, why should he? It wasn't like he had kids. Or knew any, for that matter. Well, unless you counted Carly Richter. He knew her. Becs's nine-year-old daughter was cool AF. He'd only been around her a few times, but she had this way of making him laugh whenever he was.

Atticus stared out the window, shaking his head.

Since Slade didn't bother to make small talk, Atticus didn't either. He wanted to. Sort of. He wanted to ask Slade if he'd heard from Carson today. He hadn't. Not yet. But that wasn't unusual. Even if they hadn't spent most of the night at the hospital, Carson was keeping his distance during the day, and Slade was being standoffish at night. Unless they were having sex. Then Slade was fully engaged. And since that seemed to be the only time Slade was in a relatively decent mood, Atticus was finding more time to get naked than he normally would have.

Okay, that was a lie. Given the choice, Atticus would have sex morning, noon, and night. Double that on weekends and holidays. Especially if he was given the choice between Slade and Carson. Or both. He'd never been turned on as much as he was when he was near them. He could only imagine how hot he would be once the three of them finally succumbed to some real threesome action. Which they hadn't done yet. Not really. There'd been some alternating action once. Plus, he'd watched the two of them that one time. And he'd suspected Carson had snuck a peek a time or two. But not the real deal. Not the way Atticus wanted.

Fuck.

Now he was thinking about both of them fucking him. At the same time.

"Somethin' wrong?" Slade asked.

"What?" Yeah, that was him sounding all guilty and shit.

Is something wrong with the air conditioner?

"Lemme guess." Slade cut his gaze toward him. "You're thinkin' about how hot your new partner is."

"Of course he's hot," Atticus said. "Although I'm not sure he wants to be my partner."

"Why the fuck wouldn't he?" Slade snapped, his tone irrationally defensive. "He'd be fuckin' lucky to be your partner."

Wait. What?

Feeling as though he was missing something, Atticus asked, "Who're we talkin' about again?"

"Archer."

Atticus snorted a laugh.

"What's so funny?"

"I thought we were talkin' about you."

"I'm not your partner."

"On this case you are," Atticus corrected. Which was why he'd thought it was witty banter they were engaging in. Otherwise, he wouldn't have said anything about anyone being hot.

Slade's eyes narrowed. "So you don't think he's hot?"

"Who?"

"Archer," Slade bit out.

"Jesus Christ. Why the fuck would I think he's hot?"

"Because he's hot."

Atticus couldn't help it; he laughed. Partly at the absurdity of this conversation. And partly because Slade just admitted to finding Archer Halligan hot.

"Well, it's good to know where you stand on the matter."

"I don't mean it like that," Slade said.

No, he probably didn't. However, the topic of this conversation explained why Slade's good mood had disappeared. Although Atticus wondered how it was possible, the man was nothing if not insecure. So, yeah, the presence of a new guy who happened to swing the same way they did would undoubtedly send him into a tizzy.

"Perhaps we could talk about somethin' else," Atticus suggested.

"Or maybe we shouldn't talk at all," Slade grumbled.

"Fuck." Atticus was ready to pull his hair out. Slade's mood swings were powerful enough to take out a town, and Atticus always seemed to be on the receiving end.

Slade shook his head, his fingers tightly wrapped around the steering wheel. "I'm sorry."

Atticus didn't respond. He wasn't sure what to say. He wanted to tell Slade he had nothing to be insecure about, but he'd tried that, and it didn't stick. It would. One day. He hoped. Maybe after he'd had time to prove to Slade that he was the man he wanted.

Well, him *and* Carson.

Okay, so maybe Atticus understood part of why Slade was insecure. The three of them were caught in this vicious cycle of want and need, and no one seemed to know how to get what they wanted without pissing someone else off.

To be honest, Atticus was ready to give up wanting anything for himself. He'd gladly resign himself to watching Slade and Carson together because *holy fuck*. He'd seen the chemistry between those two men firsthand the night Carson came over and apologized to Slade. Yeah, maybe he'd come over because Atticus set it up, but still. They'd worked it out. Naked. And Atticus had watched. He wasn't insecure about it.

And he knew Carson liked watching him with Slade. The man was a self-proclaimed voyeur.

Despite what Slade might say, Atticus knew Slade enjoyed watching, too. There hadn't been too much of that happening, but the one time it had, he'd seen the gleam in Slade's eyes.

So maybe he needed to push for more of that. Odd man out watching for a little while. Perhaps then Slade would see that they wanted him as much as they wanted each other.

And if that didn't work, Atticus would give some thought to how he could show Slade once and for all that this thing between the three of them was real.

Maybe if he could do that, they could settle into something that didn't result in uncomfortable situations like this. Otherwise, Atticus wasn't sure this type of relationship was sustainable.

Chapter Fifteen

RATHER THAN GETTING FOOD OR STOPPING BY to check on JJ and the babies, they adjusted the schedule to meet with Simon and Holt first. It wasn't ideal, but Simon had something he needed to do, so it was their only option if they wanted to talk today. Since Brantley was eager to get this out of the way so they knew whether they would be tackling a new case or moving on with their lives, he opted to forgo food for the time being.

Not that his stomach was happy about that.

With his stomach rumbling, Brantley steered the truck toward downtown Coyote Ridge. They were a few minutes early for their meeting, which was why he'd opted to call Baz, check in. The man sounded as though he hadn't slept for a month, but there was still a smile in his voice, so Brantley considered that a good thing.

"That's great to hear," Brantley told Baz. "I figure we'll stop by later this evening to check on y'all. If you need us to bring anything, just holler."

Baz chuckled. "You realize you're sounding more and more like Reese every day. Just holler." He laughed again. "But thanks. I'll talk to JJ once she's awake. I know when she wakes up, she'll want to go down to the NICU, but I'm hoping she'll sleep for a bit."

"You might want to grab some sleep yourself. From what I hear, there's not much to be had when you've got a newborn, much less two."

"One of these days I'll grab a minute or two with my eyes shut."

"Talk atcha later," Brantley told him, then ended the call.

"More and more like me, huh?" Reese asked, grinning from his spot in the passenger seat.

"That's what he tells me all the time."

"I guess I'm more redneck than you are."

"Well, that's for damn sure," Brantley agreed.

He turned off Main Street and headed for a lot a couple of blocks away. He preferred not to park on the street and risk being blocked in.

Once parked, Brantley got out and waited for Reese and Tesha. They walked the short distance to their destination, then slipped down the alley behind the buildings.

Reese and Tesha went up first, so Brantley followed. When Reese reached the apartment, he knocked on the open door.

"Come in," someone called from inside. "You can close the door behind you."

Brantley did after he stepped into the small apartment. The sun was shining in through the windows that lined the front wall, casting waves of light across the hardwood floor. He figured it would've been the living room had it been used appropriately. However, it appeared to be an office if the desk in the middle of the room was any indication.

"I use this space when I need to get away from the chaos," Holt said, walking in from an adjacent room.

"That explains why it's so clean."

"Yeah. I try to keep it that way." Holt gestured toward the room he'd come from. "I can't say the same for in there. Ignore the clutter on the left and the storyboards behind the desk."

Looked as though they were going to get right to it.

"Hey, girl," Archer greeted Tesha without touching her. "You can leave her with me if you'd like."

"Break," Reese told Tesha.

Tesha's tail—her whole butt, really—started wagging instantly as she moved closer to Archer, causing the man's face to split in a grin as he squatted down on his haunches to pet her.

"Go on. She's safe in here."

Brantley led Reese into the only other room in the apartment, except for the small bathroom just past the kitchen area. The door was open, and the light was on, so he stepped inside. On the left was the chaos Holt had mentioned. Colorful Post-it notes covered the desk and were pinned to the wall. Some had notes on them, others had arrows, and some others had doodles that, to Brantley's eye, looked as though they'd been drawn out of frustration.

A tap on his arm had him turning. Reese was pointing to the wall opposite the desk area. It took a moment for everything to register. There were photos and articles clipped from newspapers, along with more Post-its, most bigger and lined, with handwritten notes on them.

Brantley moved closer, skimmed the data. He recognized most of the information because it pertained to the cases they'd worked—Kate Walker's kidnapping, the hunt for Juliet Prince. There were clippings of images of him and Reese from an article on the task force back when they'd been hired by Governor Greenwood.

"They've gathered a lot of information," Reese noted.

Yeah. They had. Most of it wasn't news to Brantley because they'd worked alongside Travis's family from the very beginning, back a few years. What *was* new to him were the articles pertaining to the Southern Boy Mafia and the FBI task force hired to take them down.

"Believe it or not, there's a timeline depicted there," Simon said when he walked into the room. "Or the beginnings of one, anyway."

"It starts here? Twenty years ago?" Reese asked, gesturing to the farthest left, where there was an article about Samuel Adorite, Max's father.

"Roughly seventeen, yes." Simon pointed to the next article. "There's a gap, but I had a buddy of mine look into the FBI agent handling the case at the time."

Brantley looked at Simon. "And?"

"That's where things get weird." Simon lowered his hand and sighed. "I was skeptical about this whole thing at first." He glanced at Holt. "No offense."

"None taken."

"But after gathering only a few more details, I'm inclined to think Holt might be onto something."

"Something like what?" Brantley asked, not understanding the doublespeak.

"I think it's safe to say we've got what appears to be a deeply-rooted conspiracy to take down the Southern Boy Mafia."

Brantley looked at Reese, then at Holt, and then back at Simon. He was so fucking confused. "Conspiracy? I thought we were lookin' for a missing woman."

"She's key, yes," Simon noted.

"Okay. Correct me if I'm wrong, but the FBI creates task forces to take down criminal organizations all the time. Why's this different?"

"Because I don't believe in coincidence," Simon stated. "And Meredith Prescott's disappearance lines up too perfectly with the information Holt's uncovered about the task force."

Brantley directed his attention to Holt. "Do you have any facts to prove this? Or are you makin' shit up as you go?"

"I've done my best not to trip any flags," Holt stated.

"Meaning?" Reese asked.

"Meaning he hasn't started digging," Brantley answered.

Reese crossed his arms over his chest. "So what makes you think it's a conspiracy?"

Holt glanced from one person to the next and took a deep breath, exhaling slowly. "This is gonna sound strange."

"Try us," Reese stated.

"Something feels off."

Brantley waited for him to elaborate, but he didn't.

"Off?" Surely, he didn't hear the man right. "That's what you're goin' on? Somethin' feels off to you, so it must be a conspiracy?"

"Like I said, I was doing my best not to trip any flags, so I reached out to Simon to see if he thought it had merit. I figured if he thought there was a story there, he'd dig into it."

"Which you did. And you do," Reese stated, addressing Simon.

Simon nodded. "But I've been careful, too. Up to this point. Until I get my bearings, I don't want to draw the attention of someone who might end up on my radar."

"Like an FBI agent," Reese stated.

"Exactly."

Brantley wasn't sure if they were giving him the runaround on purpose or if they hadn't thought this through all the way. Whatever the reason, he was starting to think they were wasting his time.

"How do you think we can help?" Brantley asked because he wasn't sure what else to say.

"I was hoping we could all sit down and map out a timeline, including the most recent occurrences."

"What recent occurrences could possibly have anything to do with the Adorites?"

"Kylie Walker's death."

"What?" Brantley frowned. "What the hell're you talkin' about?"

"We think it might be related," Holt said.

Brantley stared at the man, almost positive he'd lost his damn mind. Kylie's death had nothing to do with the Southern Boy Mafia. It was the tragic result of an unhinged woman.

"Did you know about this?" Brantley asked Reese.

"Know what?"

"That they're lookin' into Kylie's death?"

"We're not," Holt said quickly.

Reese spoke over him, answering Brantley. "No. It didn't come up." Reese looked at Holt. "Related how?"

"We believe—" Holt looked at Simon and amended his statement. "*I* believe it's possible the FBI used Kylie's death as a way to draw her mother out."

Brantley couldn't hold in his frustration. "Did it work?"

"No."

"So why the fuck would you think that?"

"Because it was a convenient opportunity," Holt said.

"Convenient?" Brantley ground his molars together, expecting them to crumble into dust. There was absolutely nothing *convenient* about Kylie's death. Tragic? Absolutely. Catastrophic. Awful. Deplorable. Those were all words that made sense. Not *convenient*.

"It won't be an easy subject to broach," Holt started, as though he was oblivious to Brantley's internal rage.

"No. It'll be hell," Brantley snapped. "We've lived through it once. I'm not sure I've got it in me to..."

He let the sentence trail off rather than say what he wanted to. *I'm not sure I've got it in me to dredge up all my mistakes.*

"Why do you need to bring Kylie into it? Why would anyone?" Reese asked when Brantley spun on a heel and paced to the other side of the room.

"Because there's someone out there who wants to take down the Adorites that damn bad," Simon answered.

"Who?"

"That's a good question. And one we need to answer. Which is why we need your help. If anyone has half a chance of connecting the dots on this, I think it'll be your team," Simon said.

Figuring it was best to just launch right into it, Reese glanced between Simon and Holt. "Have you talked to Travis? I mean, after your conversation about..."

Holt filled in when Reese let the sentence fade. "About Kylie's mother and the Southern Boy Mafia?" Holt shook his head. "I haven't. Nothing more than pleasantries in passing. And by that, I mean he's no longer trying to kill me with his death ray glare, but we aren't exactly friends. Why?"

"You?" he asked Simon.

"I brought him here," Simon explained. "Showed him the work Holt had done. I needed to see if I'd be causin' more harm than good by followin' this story."

"And?"

"Since Travis's bid for my services was about to reach two mil, I figure I'm movin' in the right direction."

Reese frowned. "He's payin' you two million? For what?"

"He's not payin' me. I turned him down. I don't take payment for a story. When there's money involved, there are also expectations," Simon explained. "What about you? Y'all are tight with Travis, right?"

"We are." *Usually.* Reese cut his gaze to Brantley, then back to Simon as he explained. "He's been keepin' his distance. With the wedding and all, we didn't have time to catch up with him. We've tried since, but he's not makin' it easy. I think he's dodgin' us, to be honest."

"What did you tell Travis?" Brantley asked Simon, waving his hand at the stuff on the walls.

"I told him I would investigate the story how I see fit and that I'm not lookin' for payment. And I'm not. Not from the families. I earn my paycheck from the podcast. Anyway, he said he'd pay me to look into Meredith Prescott. I told him I wasn't that kind of investigator."

"We are," Brantley noted.

"I know. Which is why I've come to you. Regardless of whether Holt's theory is true, I think he's stumbled across something that needs to be looked at. I do think there's a story there."

Brantley gestured at the wall. "Based on what I see here, the story's already been told. The total sum of this is right where we are today, and to be honest, I'd prefer not to rehash the loss."

"I get that," Simon said, glancing between them. "I'm not here to stir anything up, but I would like to look into Meredith Prescott's disappearance. Based on what little information I've gathered, the woman no longer exists."

"And you think what? That she's in hiding?" Reese stated.

"Or dead?" Brantley added.

"Yes," Simon said simply.

"Which is it?"

"I won't know until I start looking." Simon gestured toward the door. "I was hoping to see if I could review any case notes you have."

"On?"

"Everything. I'm looking for a thread to pull. There'll be something somewhere that leads me to what happened to Meredith when she vanished from her life. It's my understanding her family believes she left for greener pastures. I want to start looking at where she went from the moment she walked away from them." Simon gestured toward the door. "And since you just took my investigator, I was thinking it's logical to look to you for help on this."

"I'm pretty sure you started lookin' into this before we offered Archer the job," Reese corrected.

"Perhaps." Simon grinned. "Still leaves me without an investigator."

Brantley stepped forward, pointed at Holt. "Tell me what you know."

"Me?"

"Yes, you. Keep it simple. Just the facts. I know you have them because you wouldn't've confronted Travis otherwise."

"The facts," Holt said, shifting his feet.

Reese could tell he was uncomfortable, but he waited patiently, willing the man to push past it.

Holt took a deep breath. "As you probably know by now, I'm using Coyote Ridge as the backdrop for my next book. Well, for a series of books now that my editor's on board."

Reese wasn't sure they were on the same page when it came to the facts they were seeking, but he didn't interrupt.

"Anyway," Holt continued. "The idea of a mystery unraveling in a small, tight-knit town that rarely sees any crime appeals to me in a big way."

"Of all the towns on the map, you just plucked Coyote Ridge right outta your ass, huh?"

From his tone, Brantley didn't buy it. Reese wasn't sure he did either.

"It wasn't a coincidence, no. When I learned about the small town Rafe grew up in, I researched it."

Ah. Reese recalled hearing some chatter about Rafe Sharpe having known Holt from the time he spent away from here.

"As for how I came to learn about Kylie… When I'm coming up with the story arc, I like to draw from real events. In order to do that, I read a lot of true crime stories, listen to a lot of podcasts."

Curious, Reese asked, "Is that how you met Simon?"

"Yeah. I contacted him to suss out some information on a book I was writing. He was helpful. We became friends." Holt stood tall, his eyes glittering with renewed energy. "Anyway. When I first started researching Coyote Ridge, I came across a news article about Kylie." Holt pointed directly at Brantley. "I've seen that look before. It's the same one Travis got when I told him the same thing. My book does not resemble Kylie's story in any way. Her story and the events that led up to her death have absolutely no bearing on my book."

"Go on," Brantley urged.

"When reading about Kylie, I came across a few things that didn't add up. Remember, unlike you and your team, I unravel a mystery backward, so there's a good chance I'm simply seeing things that aren't there."

"You think?" Brantley quipped.

Holt continued. "But that's the best way I've found to lay out the story. I need to know the ending, along with my character's motivation so I can fill in the rest. But it was the ending of Kylie's story that felt off to me."

"Meaning?" Reese prompted.

"If I were to write the story…" Holt took a deep breath and looked between Reese and Brantley. "The end of Kylie's story would've been the beginning."

"What the fuck does that mean?" Brantley asked, his exasperation evident.

"Just what I said earlier. I know it sounds crass, and I assure you, I don't mean it that way, but her death felt convenient. At least based on what I now know about Meredith and the Southern Boy Mafia."

"Makes sense," Reese said, although he wasn't sure it did.

Brantley's gaze slammed into him ."The fuck it does." He looked back at Holt. "You do realize that Kylie's death isn't a mystery, right? She was killed here. In downtown. In front of a few dozen witnesses."

Holt nodded. "I know that. I also know Juliet Prince is responsible. And because Juliet was a dedicated journal writer, we even have her motivations. In her own words."

Reese felt his chest tighten. Anytime he thought of Juliet Prince, he found it difficult to breathe.

"I'm not disputing that it happened the way everyone says it did. What I told Travis is that, based on what I came across, it felt to me like something was going to happen at that exact time. No matter what. Maybe even that exact place."

Reese frowned. "What do you mean?"

"It's hard to explain." He flashed a wan smile. "Doesn't bode well for a writer, huh? But it's true. It's like I can see the puzzle's picture, but some of the pieces are missing, so it doesn't completely add up. It's been bugging me. That's why I reached out to Simon. I asked him to look into it to see if he saw it the same way I did. At the very least, he'd tell me if I'm way off base."

"Not way off base," Simon noted, his expression serious. "But I did question his sanity at first."

Yeah. Reese talked to Simon, and yeah, he knew Simon was going to pursue the story. The problem was, Reese wasn't sure what story they intended to tell. Based on the information pinned to this wall, they were merely restating a story that had already been told.

Holt exhaled heavily, his tone serious when he spoke. "I definitely think there's more to this story."

"Which story?"

"The big one. The one that all these little pieces feed into." Holt glanced around before looking at Reese again. "Meredith Prescott's disappearance. The mob hit. The FBI agents sprinkled throughout this little town."

Brantley stood tall. "What FBI agents?"

"Trust me, they're here. Seems a little too coincidental that they're popping up now after they tried to strong-arm Meredith Prescott into testifying."

"Testifying? Because someone claims she saw Max Adorite kill a man?"

Holt's eyebrows dipped down. "At the time, the FBI boasted they had a star witness who would bring down the Southern Boy Mafia once and for all. But before she could testify, Meredith disappeared."

"How do you know Max didn't eliminate her?" Brantley asked.

"We don't know that," Simon admitted.

"It would've solved all his problems, would it not?"

"Sure. I don't think she's dead," Holt admitted. "If there were even a whiff of that, the FBI would've backed off."

Reese had to agree with Holt. He wasn't sure what Max Adorite was capable of, but someone would've noticed her absence. Meredith would've had to sign the divorce papers. And surely she'd sent birthday cards to her kids over the past decade and a half. If she had disappeared off the face of the earth, they would've realized it.

Which meant finding Meredith was key to understanding what did or did not happen all those years ago.

"Hey, Archer," Reese called.

"Yeah?" he replied a second before he appeared in the door.

"What're your thoughts on this? Story? No story?"

"I think it's a bit convoluted at the moment," he said, glancing at the walls. "Too much information. But if we can narrow the scope and outline some of the data, I think we'll find a pattern."

Reese looked at Brantley, silently putting the ball back in his court. As far as he was concerned, he was all in.

Chapter Sixteen

BRANTLEY TOOK IN THE INFORMATION RELAYED ON the wall and tried to see it from Archer's perspective. He had to agree that the man had a point. At the very least, they needed to weed out the information that didn't matter to see if there was a pattern. As much as it pained him to admit, he had a feeling Holt and Simon were on to something.

He wouldn't deny—at least not yet—that there was something here. What, he had no idea, but there was only one way to find out. And it wasn't by standing around arguing back and forth. Clearly, Holt and Simon had given serious thought to what they had uncovered. Perhaps it was only fair that Brantley do the same.

"Y'all really want our help?" he asked, turning to look at Simon.

"We really do."

Brantley fished his phone out of his pocket and pulled up his contacts. Once he found who he was looking for, he stabbed the screen to dial.

"Hey, Darius. I need you to get over to Shelf Help."

"I can do that. Do I need to bring anything?"

"Yeah. Somethin' to digitize a whole bunch of information. You might wanna bring Elana or Holly to help."

"Okay," Darius said hesitantly.

"Simon and Holt are lookin' into a case, and they need our help on it. Figure it'll be easier if we consolidate the information. Once we have it in electronic format, Simon will need access to it."

"Easy to do."

Brantley explained where the apartment was and how to access it, then informed Darius that they would leave the key with Violet, the bookshop owner, and asked him to stop in there to get it.

When he disconnected the call, he turned to Simon and Holt. "Let's grab some food and talk about next steps."

The two men shared a glance before Holt said, "I think I'm gonna sit this one out. Thanks for the invite, though."

"You sure?" Reese asked.

"As curious as I am, I can't let myself get too far off track." He smiled sheepishly. "As it is, I'm supposed to be holed up in the apartment working on a chapter."

"Writer's block?" Simon teased.

"It's a living, breathing thing. I shit you not."

Brantley chuckled, although he had no idea what writer's block was like. He'd never dealt with anything like it, and if he were lucky, he never would.

"You and Archer then," Brantley told Simon. "The diner."

"I'm game!" Archer shouted from the next room where he'd disappeared as soon as he was no longer needed. He got the feeling the guy really liked dogs.

"If they serve food, the guy'll come runnin'," Simon joked.

"He's not wrong!" Archer added, his voice booming.

Simon turned to leave. "I'll take the key down to Violet and meet y'all there."

Brantley nodded, then followed Reese out of the room.

Archer got to his feet as they approached. "Mind if I hitch a ride with y'all? I left my Harley at the B and B."

"Sure," Reese told him as they headed for the front door. "You've got a motorcycle?"

Brantley listened to Archer talk about his Harley as they stepped outside, making their way to the truck. Tesha had an extra spring in her step, although Brantley got the sense she was trying to hide it. Part of her training, he figured.

Their conversation finally died off a few feet from the truck, so he figured it was the perfect opportunity to pick their brains before Simon joined them.

"What're your honest thoughts about all that?" Brantley asked as he was climbing inside.

"You want my insight?" Archer said, buckling his seatbelt.

"Both of you, yeah."

"As an outsider who doesn't know the history, I think there's a story there," Archer answered. "I think it involves the Southern Boy Mafia and some corrupt FBI agents."

"What about Meredith Prescott?" Reese asked. "Where does she fit in all this?"

"That one I don't know. If she witnessed the hit, then I think it's as simple as they want her to testify."

"Isn't there a statute of limitations?" Reese asked.

"Not on murder," Brantley and Archer said at the same time.

Archer added, "But they'd have to want her pretty bad if they're still stalking her family. It's been fifteen years, and the Southern Boy Mafia hasn't lost its stronghold on the territory. Not that I can tell, anyway. Surely they could've come up with something else to take them down. I mean, seriously. Max Adorite isn't made of Teflon."

Brantley grinned. He liked that analogy.

Expecting a chuckle from Reese, he looked over at him.

The man was quiet. Too quiet.

He drove toward the diner, trying his patience on for size. They lasted relatively well. Right up until he was turning the truck into the diner parking lot.

"Reese?"

"Hmm?"

"Where'd you go?"

He swallowed, then shifted in his seat, facing Brantley more fully. "There's some stuff I haven't mentioned."

Brantley frowned. "About?"

"I honestly don't know. Just some stuff the team uncovered back when we went to New York."

He pulled the truck into a space, put it in *Park,* and turned it off. "What kinda stuff?"

"Little things. I specifically told the team to put it away until after the wedding. I knew if you got wind of it, you'd start lookin' into it, and we had too much goin' on at the time."

Brantley wasn't sure he liked where this was going. "Little things like what?"

"For starters, we found a connection between Decker Bromwell and Kylie. They went to the same high school."

He would admit that was interesting information, but Brantley wasn't sure it had much to do with anything they'd worked out.

"JJ's the one who found it," Reese continued. "I told her to put it away until after the wedding."

As much as he hated the idea of Reese—or anyone, for that matter—keeping things from him, Brantley understood. To a degree.

"And you were holdin' off until...?"

"I wasn't. Swear. We just hadn't gotten back to it yet. With JJ at the hospital, the babies, us creating a plan for the new hires…"

Brantley could feel Archer's gaze following the conversation. He appreciated that the guy didn't interrupt.

Reese continued. "Now that we've got all this new information, I think it might be worth mapping out a timeline, seeing where they intersect. If one has to do with another, there will be a nexus."

Brantley didn't disagree. Reese was correct. There would be an intersecting point.

"Is your brother still in town?" Brantley asked.

"Yeah."

"Good." Brantley tapped his fingers on the steering wheel. "Text him and let him know I want to meet with him later today if possible."

"You think his brother's somehow involved?" Archer asked.

"In a way, probably." Brantley chuckled. "But I'm invitin' him because he's our boss."

"Ah. Sniper 1 Security?"

"Yep. Stick around. I'll introduce you."

"I'd appreciate that."

Reese glanced over. "RT, too?"

"He's welcome to join us," Brantley told him. "If he doesn't know what's goin' on, it's probably time someone fills him in."

While Reese did that, Brantley pulled out his phone and shot another text to Darius.

GET THAT DATA DiGiTiZED ASAP. i NEED ACCESS TO iT iN A COUPLE OF HOURS.

WiLL DO, BOSS. i'LL SHOOT YOU A TEXT AS SOON AS WE'RE DONE.

FEELING LIKE AN ASS FOR NOT FILLING Brantley in before now, Reese got out of the truck and helped Tesha out. With her leash in hand, he started toward the diner. He intended to fall a few steps behind and let Brantley and Archer talk while they waited for a table, but Brantley had other plans.

"I know you're gonna kick yourself for not mentioning it to me beforehand, but don't."

Reese looked at Brantley. "I honestly was gonna tell you."

"I know."

His phone buzzed with a text. Reese pulled it out and checked the screen. "Z said they can meet us at the house later this evening."

"Perfect."

Brantley opened the door and waited for Archer and Reese to file inside. He followed.

"It's just kinda been a whirlwind since the wedding," Reese explained, picking up the original topic.

Brantley smiled, lightly touching his hand. "I know." He tipped his head toward the server moving toward them. "Let's get some food in us, and we'll talk about next steps, and you can fill me in on all the little details."

Reese nodded, feeling a little better. He knew Brantley wouldn't hold a grudge, but that didn't mean the man wasn't disappointed. He wouldn't show it, but Reese would know.

"Will this work?" the server asked, gesturing toward a four-top table.

"This really is the go-to place, huh?" Archer asked as they took their seats.

Reese grinned. "It's convenient, and you can get your variety if you need it. Plus, the service is pretty damn spectacular."

"They should hire you for their advertising team," Archer said with a smirk.

Brantley laughed, which Reese took as a good sign.

Once they were situated, the server returned to take their order. Reese opted for a salad while Brantley ordered a cheeseburger and fries. Archer ordered for himself and Simon—two burgers and *three* orders of fries, insisting that growing boys gotta eat. The restaurant was slow, but that would change in the next hour or so when the early dinner rush came.

"All right," Archer prompted. "I have to know how long you've had Tesha."

"It'll be two years in November," Reese answered.

"Where'd you get her?"

"It's a funny story," Brantley said with a laugh.

Reese listened while Brantley told the story about how Reese had rehomed her after finding her chained up in a backyard with no food or water in sight. Looking back now, perhaps it was somewhat amusing that he'd taken it upon himself to save her, not caring one fucking bit what her owners thought.

"Just walked right back there, unhooked her and carried her out," Brantley said with a grin.

"I'd do it again in a heartbeat."

"And her training? If her previous owners were neglecting her, I can't imagine they invested money in training."

"No. That's all Magnus. He owns Camp K-9, which is exactly what it sounds like. A daycare for dogs. But he also specializes in training search and rescue dogs."

"I've seen the signs somewhere."

"They're relocating to some land they bought across the street from us," Brantley explained. "Magnus, Ava, and my brother, Trey."

"Do they have any that might need a good home?" Archer asked hopefully.

"Tell you what," Reese said. "As soon as we get some time, I'll run you by there and introduce you."

Archer beamed. "That would be great."

They'd just gotten their drinks when Simon walked in.

To Reese's surprise, Z and RT strolled in right behind him.

"Z's here," Reese told Brantley.

Brantley looked up. "Maybe we can get this outta the way now."

"I ordered for you," Archer told Simon when the man took his seat.

"Thanks."

"Don't thank me yet. You don't know what I ordered."

Reese was laughing when Z and RT walked up to the table.

"Hey, man," Brantley greeted. "It's good to see you again."

"Feels like it was just yesterday," RT joked. "Or maybe that was today. It's all crowding together at this point."

Reese knew exactly what he meant.

"Z just told me y'all invited us to stay in town for an extra day or two."

"We did." Brantley nodded. "Got some things to talk about. Thought you should be here to hear it. Y'all wanna join us."

Z looked at RT, who nodded.

Brantley raised a hand, signaling their server. "You think we could take that table too? Maybe move 'em together."

"Of course."

When she started to lean forward to do it herself, Brantley and Archer took over. RT, Z, and Simon stepped back, waiting until they'd rearranged the chairs to accommodate.

"Let me introduce you," Reese said, gesturing as he spoke. "RT, Z, this is Simon Jennings and Archer Halligan. Simon, Archer, this is my brother, Zachariah Tavoularis."

Simon and Archer stood to shake hands.

"Call me that, and you're fired," Z stated, only partially joking.

Reese continued, "And this is Ryan Trexler. RT owns Sniper 1 Security."

RT snorted. "I'm *one* of many owners. This guy just likes to give me shit."

Reese smirked. It was true. "He's my brother-in-law. I'm allowed."

"Nice to meet you," RT told Simon as they all took their seats. "I'm a fan of the podcast."

"Thanks." Simon gestured to Z, then Reese, then Brantley. "Is it in the water down here?"

"The asshole thing?" Z quipped, causing everyone to laugh.

"I was referrin' to how big y'all seem to grow 'em down here."

"Since you brought the biggest one to town, maybe we should ask you that question," Brantley told him, grinning at Archer.

Reese listened but didn't contribute much. He was still kicking himself for not talking to Brantley about the information they'd uncovered. The conversation continued with random topics—weather, Formula 1, Dallas Cowboys—until the server delivered more drinks and their food.

Once they had everything situated, Brantley explained Holt's theory to RT and Z. Reese watched their expressions, namely his brother's. Neither seemed surprised by the news, which made Reese wonder whether they knew something he didn't. It would make sense that they did, considering Z had sent them on a wild goose chase in New York a few weeks ago.

"And you're gonna do a podcast on it?" RT prompted.

"I am," Simon confirmed.

"You have information that might tie it together?"

Reese noticed his brother wasn't contributing. In fact, the man looked as though he was willing the floor to open up and swallow him.

Not for the first time, Reese wanted to blast Z with questions. All of them pertaining to the case they'd taken in New York. The one that involved finding Decker Bromwell, although Reese was pretty damn certain Deck hadn't been lost.

As though sensing what Reese was thinking, Z looked up and met his gaze. He held it for a few seconds before giving a subtle shake of his head.

Z didn't want him asking those questions right now.

That acknowledgment only gave Reese many more.

Chapter Seventeen

"This does not look like the way to the high school," Atticus stated from his spot in the passenger seat of Slade's truck, his eyes cutting from side to side out the window.

Slade smiled. Nope, they were a few miles out for that.

And for good reason.

No sooner had they finished lunch than Atticus suggested they head over to the high school and talk to the principal. Slade would've preferred to talk a bit more, but he understood Atticus's desire not to. After all, Slade had acted like a world-class jackass bringing up Archer. It wasn't the first time he'd stuck his foot in his mouth, and he knew it wouldn't be the last. No matter what he told himself, no matter how many times he tried to convince himself that this would be different than every other relationship he'd had, Slade always managed to let his insecurities get the best of him.

While he knew Atticus would eventually forgive him and pretend that nothing happened—that seemed to be the trend—Slade knew of a faster way to get back in Atticus's good graces.

Hence the brief detour.

He didn't say a word, continuing to drive while Atticus pulled up the map on his phone. Slade fought the urge to laugh when Atticus held it up, turning it this way and that as though that might change the direction Slade was driving.

"The high school's the opposite direction," Atticus said, tapping the screen before shifting that glare Slade's way. "Where the hell are we goin'?"

"Detour."

"Where?"

Slade kept his eyes on the road, unwilling to share those details just yet. Sure, he was looking to make things right, but he wasn't above taking advantage of a situation. Especially not when it allowed him to have some alone time with the man he could not for the life of him stop thinking about. So, yeah, he wanted Atticus to sweat it a bit. After all, this was partly payback for Atticus choosing him to work this case. Seriously. A missing statue, for fuck's sake. Worse than that, the statue belonged to the high school. The last fucking place Slade cared to ever return to.

Yet, that was where they were going *after* Slade took care of something.

Not that Slade really minded partnering up with Atticus on this case. It was a break from the routine, one he needed in order to maintain his sanity. It wasn't easy uncovering every stone when looking into cold cases. They were cold for a reason. When every available lead had been exhausted and there were no other avenues to pursue, a case went cold. Some of those they had on their plates had been that way for years. And despite a desperate need to find closure for the families of the victims, they often worked themselves in circles, only to come up with nothing more than what the original detectives came up with. It was mentally and emotionally draining.

So yeah, looking for a statue was a nice break from the norm.

However, Slade figured it was the perfect opportunity to level the playing field before they got started.

"You know this is a dead end, right?" Atticus said, pointing toward a sign that depicted the road ending ahead.

"Yup."

"And isn't that…?" Atticus leaned closer to the passenger window. "Isn't that the lake?"

"Two for two."

Atticus sighed, his frustration clear.

When Slade reached the end of the road, he made a U-turn before putting the truck in *Park*. This way, he could see any oncoming vehicles, just in case.

He turned down the radio but left the truck running.

Atticus frowned at him. "What are you doin'?"

He unbuckled his seat belt.

"Slade…"

He pressed the button to move his seat all the way back.

"What the hell are you doin'? We've got work to do."

"Technically, *you've* got work to do," Slade told him as he lifted the steering wheel as high as it would go.

Relaxing in his seat, Slade turned his head to look at Atticus as he worked the button free on his jeans.

Atticus swallowed hard, jerking his chin toward Slade's lap. "You want me to…?"

Slade chuckled. "Baby, I *always* want you to…" He let the sentence trail off the same way Atticus had.

That seemed to settle the man somewhat. Plus, seeing the heat in Atticus's eyes relieved some of Slade's insecurities.

"This is payback for me picking you, isn't it?"

Slade flashed a grin. "This is me takin' charge. And while you might be the lead on the case, I make the rules when it comes to *other* things."

"What *other* things?" Atticus asked, his gaze locked on Slade's hands as he eased the zipper down.

"Do you really need to ask?"

He watched Atticus watch him as he pushed his jeans and underwear down just enough to reveal the thick, swollen head of his dick.

When Atticus licked his lips, Slade's cock kicked hard.

"Unbuckle your seat belt," Slade ordered Atticus as he pushed his jeans lower, freeing his straining erection.

"Are you happy now?" Atticus retorted as he unbuckled the belt.

"No. Lean over and put that sweet fuckin' mouth on my dick. *Then* I'll be happy."

Atticus did as he was told, shifting in his seat so he could lean over the center console.

That was one thing Slade had learned about Atticus. The man loved to be dominated. And the more forceful Slade was, the hotter Atticus got.

When Atticus leaned over the console, Slade slid his fingers into the cool, soft hair at the back of his head. But rather than guide him down so Atticus could deep-throat his dick, Slade tugged him until he was close enough that he could feel Atticus's breath on his lips.

"I'm sorry for how I acted earlier," he whispered.

"Don't apologize. It's not necessary," Atticus said, his eyes glazed.

Maybe not, but it made Slade feel a little better.

"I want your cock," Atticus mumbled against Slade's mouth.

Slade hissed when he felt the soft flutter of Atticus's fingers over his dick.

"How bad?"

"Real bad."

"Beg."

Atticus pulled back enough so their eyes locked. "Let me have your dick, Slade. Please."

Fuck, this man made him crazy.

"I want you to make me come. Usin' only your mouth."

Atticus swallowed hard.

"If you do it well, I'll reward you when we get home."

Atticus's lips parted, his eyes shimmering with heat. "How?"

"Suck me, and I'll tell you."

Although he hadn't phrased it as a question, Atticus nodded his head as much as Slade would allow. Using more force than was necessary—because he knew Atticus liked it—Slade guided his head down into his lap.

He felt the moist heat of Atticus's breath teasing the head of his dick. His stomach muscles tightened in anticipation. The soft flutter of Atticus's tongue came next, stealing his breath and more than a little of his sanity.

"I fuckin' love your mouth," Slade whispered, rubbing the back of Atticus's head. "I love when you worship my dick."

And that was the best way to describe what Atticus was doing. The way his lips and tongue worked up and down his shaft with such exquisite precision.

He was lost to the pleasure when his phone vibrated. He glanced at the navigation screen and saw Carson's name.

"Hello?" he answered, gripping the back of Atticus's head to hold him in place.

"Have you seen Atticus lately?" Carson's voice came through the truck's speakers.

"I have."

There was a brief pause, then Carson said, "Oh. I was tryin' to get a hold of him. I guess he's busy."

"He's definitely busy. Right now, he's got his mouth on my dick."

"Oh, fuck," Carson hissed, and Slade could hear how much that turned him on.

"Where are y'all?"

"Back road. In my truck."

Carson chuckled.

"That's it," Slade crooned, palming the back of Atticus's head. "Make me come while Carson listens."

"Maybe tonight y'all can give me a replay so I can … watch." Atticus hissed.

Slade knew Atticus was turned on by the idea of being watched. They'd experimented a few times in recent weeks. Probably not as much as Atticus or Carson would've liked, but Slade was easing himself into it. His fears still had a stranglehold on him and it usually resulted in him being an ass.

Not that he wanted to think about that now.

He tightened his grip on Atticus's hair, but he didn't shove his head down. He was hanging by a thread as it was. The fantasy of the three of them together was one Slade had been entertaining far more than he should have. He was ready to explore this. To see where it went. The animosity he'd harbored for Carson had dissipated—mostly—replaced by need and maybe a little confusion. It was hard for him to trust someone who'd hurt him so badly, but Slade knew he had to if he wanted to be with Atticus. And he did. He was trying to be patient, not wanting to push too hard. Patience wasn't his strong suit. And his need to push too hard and too fast was likely the reason he found himself still single.

"That's it, baby," Slade crooned softly. "Oh, God, Atticus. Suck me. Make me come so we can fuck you tonight."

The suction of Atticus's mouth intensified, pushing Slade right to the razor-sharp edge where he dangled precariously for painfully long seconds.

"Ah, fuck. Swallow," he bit out. "Swallow, Atticus."

Slade's cock jerked and pulsed as he came in the heated cavern of Atticus's mouth.

He was still panting when Atticus lifted his head. Slade used the grip on his hair to guide Atticus's mouth to his own. He kissed him. Softly at first, then indulging in the sweet surrender.

"Jesus," Carson groaned.

Slade smiled against Atticus's mouth as they separated. He hurried to fix his jeans while Atticus returned to his seat.

"Did you enjoy that?" Atticus asked Carson as he sat back in the passenger seat, adjusting himself before pulling the seatbelt across his body.

"Very much."

"Good. Where are you?"

"Sittin' in front of a client's house. Last appointment of the day. I thought I'd see if you wanted to grab dinner tonight."

"Sounds good," Atticus agreed. "The three of us can meet at the house and then go out somewhere."

Slade pretended that comment didn't do weird things to his insides, like turn them all fuzzy and warm. As easy as it was to ride along on the wave of hatred he'd felt for Carson, he would give just about anything to go back to where they'd once been.

"Works for me," Carson said.

"Me, too," Slade said when Atticus pinned those intense green eyes on him.

"Good. But first, we've got a case to work. I'll let you know if we're gonna be late."

"Lookin' forward to tonight. Later, Slade."

"Later," he said before Atticus ended the call by tapping the navigation screen.

Atticus stared at him. "If you're done playin', we do have a case to work."

"Anyone tell you you're hot when you're bossy?"

Atticus huffed a laugh. "Hot. Right."

"You are."

"I've been called a lot of things, but hot's not one of 'em," he said, popping a breath mint from the container Slade kept in the truck.

"Well, it's true, so stop fishin' for compliments."

"I'm not fish—"

Slade cut him off by grabbing him and jerking him over for a kiss. He lingered for a bit longer simply because he could.

He had no idea whether this was going to work—the three of them together—but he was past the point of pretending he didn't want to try. He only prayed Carson didn't rip his heart out of his chest and stomp all over it again. That was a real possibility.

And while he might survive that, Slade knew for a fact he wouldn't survive if Atticus did the same thing.

But he was willing to take the chance. If it meant moving forward.

"DAMN," ATTICUS MUTTERED WHEN HE WALKED THROUGH the doors of Coyote Ridge High School.

His high school hadn't looked anything like this.

Three sets of double doors allowed entry into a grand common area where kids could congregate. Or at least that was the impression he got as he watched several kids sitting on benches or the carpeted floor, talking, laughing. He did notice there was very little studying going on. Yeah, some had books open, but he figured that was to use as justification for being there. Others had earbuds in their ears. Several of them held bags of snack food, and he was pretty sure he smelled pizza, probably left over from lunch.

Along with kids scattered about, the common area also had a couple of map stands that looked like those you'd see at the mall. Directions, maybe, considering the size of this place. The entire space was surrounded by six feet of stained concrete that acted as a walkway toward the main offices.

"This way," Slade said, following the walkway that ran parallel to the common area.

Atticus fell into step, keeping pace but leaving a bit of distance between them so he could continue to take it all in.

"That's the gym."

Atticus glanced to the right, checking out the closed double doors that Slade was pointing at. Next to the doors were inset cases that held a wealth of different trophies and other awards the school and its students had acquired over the years.

"Over there's the auditorium."

He peered at the opposite wall, noticing the same sort of cases. From where they were, Atticus couldn't make out what was in them, but he figured the same, only showcasing artistic achievements versus sports. High above on that same wall was an enormous banner announcing the upcoming performances of *Romeo and Juliet,* which would take place in a couple of weeks on Friday, Saturday, and Sunday, October 14th through the 16th, in the auditorium.

Fun stuff.

Atticus followed Slade deeper into the school, pausing at the hallway that bisected the common area and a wall of glass that separated them from a handful of adults working on the other side. The banner taped to the window announced homecoming tickets were still on sale in the cafeteria, and the small placard on the single wooden door read: MAIN OFFICE.

Not sure what Slade was waiting for, Atticus watched kids and teachers as they walked back and forth, some disappearing through sets of double doors on each end of the glass wall. If he had to guess, that was the cafeteria since the smell of pizza was stronger there.

Slade confirmed it a moment later when he pointed and said, "Cafeteria's back there." His finger shifted toward the end of the hallway on the right. "Stairs on each end that lead to the second and third floors. The school forms a large square with the largest classrooms at the back. Behind the cafeteria is a courtyard."

"You went here?"

"Yep. Graduated 2008."

Atticus wondered what Slade's high school years were like, but didn't get a chance to ask because they were walking again. This time toward the main office door. Slade paused to open it, allowing him to walk in first. Before Atticus took a single step, two kids squeezed between them and into the office. They were laughing, but at what, Atticus didn't know.

Suddenly nervous, Atticus forgot why he was there.

Thankfully, Slade didn't have the same problem, walking inside and right up to the short counter that separated visitors from several people working at small wooden desks on the other side. An older woman stood at the counter, a book open in front of her, a slim finger skimming over the page. The finger paused when she looked up and smiled like she was happy to see strangers walking into the school during what looked to be a busy afternoon.

"Hey, Mama."

Wait. What now?

Atticus took a step, then another, not sure he'd heard correctly. Surely not. Mama? *As in* … the older woman wearing a CRHS sweatshirt and flashing a big grin was Slade's mother?

"What're you doin' here?" Slade asked.

"Just fillin' in this week." The woman who looked nothing like Slade pinned her blue eyes on him. "Who's your friend?"

"Mama, this is Atticus James. He's my partner."

Her eyes lit up like her son had just told her he was getting married. "Is that right?"

"Task force partner," Atticus clarified. "I mean…" His gaze snapped to Slade. *Help me.*

Slade chuckled. "Atticus, meet my mother. Rose Jameson-Elliott."

"Nice to meet you," Atticus said with a nod, rubbing his hands on his jeans since he wasn't sure what to do with them.

"The pleasure's mine. What brings you boys by?" Rose asked.

"We have an appointment with Callie," Slade answered when Atticus couldn't seem to find words.

"The statue," she said, her voice quiet. "Good. I'd hoped Brantley and Reese would get someone to look into it."

Slade's eyebrows dipped. "You're the one who brought this to Brantley?"

She shrugged one dainty shoulder. "I might've mentioned it when I saw them at the diner."

Well, that explained—sort of—why Brantley and Reese had taken on something drastically different than their usual.

"You know we don't look for missin' *things*," Slade told her.

"Usually," she corrected, grinning at Atticus.

Atticus didn't know what to do with his face. Was he supposed to smile? Remain stern to maintain professionalism? Not that it mattered. If she kept looking at him like that, there was a good chance he was going to run out of the office crying.

"Would it be possible to meet with Ms. Jameson?" Atticus asked, unable to think of anything else to say. Now, he wondered whether that was confusing. How many Ms. Jamesons worked there? One? A dozen? He knew it was a big family because he'd been in Coyote Ridge long enough to get the gist. Between the Walkers and the Jamesons, they made up probably half the town. Maybe more.

And to think, Atticus was dating one of each.

Enough of that, he mentally chastised. He was there to do a job, not to think about being sandwiched between a Walker and a Jameson.

Shit.

Rose's soft yet authoritative voice pulled him from his thoughts as she came around the counter.

"Let me show you to her office." She paused beside him, clearly expecting him to fall into step. "You're Slade's new roommate?"

"Uh…" Atticus swallowed hard. "Yeah. I … Yes, ma'am … uhm…"

"Leave him alone, Mama."

"What? I'm allowed to get to know my son's *friends*, am I not?"

"Mama," Slade drawled in warning.

They navigated a maze of hallways, and Atticus suspected Rose had taken the long way in order to chat him up.

"How long have you been working for the task force?"

"Since May, ma'am."

"Please, call me Rose."

Yeah, he wasn't sure he could do that because, for some reason, it sounded like *Mama* in his head. Weird.

"And how long have you been Slade's partner?"

He got the feeling her definition of partner leaned more toward the intimate interpretation, but he kept it professional. "Only for this case."

"Is that right?"

"Yes, ma'am."

She chuckled softly, then guided them down another hallway before pausing in front of a closed door with a placard that read CALLIE JAMESON, PRINCIPAL.

"Here we are," Rose said, opening the door. "Callie's takin' care of something, but she should be back in a few minutes. You boys can wait inside." She looked at him. "It was very nice to meet you, Atticus. I look forward to havin' you to the house for dinner."

What now?

"Mama," Slade hissed.

Her gaze slowly slid to Slade. "How about Friday night?"

Slade didn't answer, which caused his mother to look at Atticus again. He held his breath, not sure what to do or say. That whole running and crying thing was sounding better and better.

"Will that work for you?"

He found himself nodding, and he wasn't sure why.

"Perfect," she said sweetly, then stepped aside so they could walk into the principal's office.

When she was gone, Atticus turned to Slade. "What just happened?"

"It looks like you're havin' dinner with my folks on Friday night."

Atticus shook his head. "I ... how...?"

Slade chuckled. "She's cool. I promise." He leaned in and lowered his voice. "Now sit."

He tried to shake it off as he eased into one of the armless chairs facing the principal's desk. One minute, he'd been walking into the high school to talk about a missing bronze statue, only to find himself agreeing to dinner with Slade's parents.

How did that happen?

More importantly, what the fuck was he supposed to do now? He'd never met anyone's parents before. Hell, he'd never officially dated anyone. Not until ... well, *now*.

Voices sounded outside the office, and Atticus tried to pull himself together before Callie Jameson walked into the room.

When she came into view, he checked her out, curious whether she looked like Rose or not. He knew the family tree had many branches, but since he'd yet to ask Slade about it, he wasn't sure how they were related.

Callie looked nothing like Rose. She was younger. Probably early-to mid-forties if the lines around her eyes were anything to go by. She had long, board-straight, white-blonde hair and big blue eyes. Her makeup was applied with a light touch, and she wore a CRHS sweatshirt and jeans—not at all what he'd expected—making her look more like one of the students rather than the woman in charge of the place.

She must've noticed Atticus checking out her attire because she said, "It's spirit week."

"Homecoming already?" Slade asked.

"I know. Seems like school just started," she said, grinning widely. "It's good to see you, Slade."

"Likewise."

"And you must be Atticus," she said, holding out her hand.

Atticus shook it, surprised that his palm was dry despite the butterflies doing the jitterbug in his chest cavity.

Callie moved around behind the large desk, her gaze shifting between them as she took a seat. "What can I do for you?"

"We're here to talk about the statue," Atticus said, wondering why she sounded like she had no idea why they were there.

Her white-blonde eyebrows angled down, her big blue eyes shifting between them. "The statue?"

"The missing one," he clarified.

Her eyes darted to the door, then back to him. "How'd you hear about that?"

Slade barked a laugh. "You seriously think no one's noticed the infamous mustang statue missing from in front of the school?"

Infamous? Why did Slade use that adjective? What was up with this statue?

"I was hopin' they haven't."

Okay, so maybe this was something they kept in one of those trophy cases and not the large kind he'd been thinking.

Atticus's eyebrows lifted. "How big of a statue are we talkin' about?"

"Big," Slade stated. "Oh, wait. Hold on." He got to his feet and leaned over Callie's desk, grabbing a book off a shelf. "I bet it's in here."

Atticus waited while Slade flipped through the pages of a yearbook before stopping on one. He set the book down, pointing toward…

"Holy shi—*ishkabob*," he blurted, barely stopping the curse. "That's a *real* statue."

Callie nodded. "I know."

"And it's missing?"

She nodded again.

"How?"

"I think that's what you're here for, right?"

Right. But … how? Atticus couldn't wrap his head around how a bronze statue that weighed *at least*—

"How much does that thing weigh?"

"Fifteen hundred pounds, probably," Slade said.

—*fifteen hundred pounds* had simply disappeared from in front of the school.

"Do you think it's a prank?" Slade asked Callie.

"It seems a bit extreme, but I can't think of another reason. It's not like it's worth anything."

"It's bronze," Atticus stated. "That's worth somethin', right?"

"About two bucks per pound," Callie said. "But a statue that size is cast hollow. Only the exterior is bronze."

"Maybe the person who took it didn't know that?" Atticus wouldn't have known. Then again, he'd never considered hijacking a statue, bronze or otherwise.

"My guess is it's a prank. For homecoming," Callie supplied.

"Your students? Or the rival team?" Slade asked.

Atticus frowned. "Prank?"

"Believe it or not, this is mild compared to some of the things they've done," Callie answered. "My senior year, we relocated this entire office out to the middle of the baseball field. Constructed walls and everything."

Atticus glanced around the room, trying to imagine.

He couldn't.

However, the more he thought about it, the more it made sense that it was a prank. Regardless of why, whoever took it would have to be determined because it wouldn't be light enough to haul away unless someone had a tow truck or a trailer. Something to load it onto. Not to mention, something to move it with.

"To answer your question, if anyone took it, I'd say it was CRHS students."

"Who'd you think of first?" Slade asked Callie.

She frowned. "What?"

"When you first noticed it missing, what names came to mind?"

"Leif and Lance Walker," she said without hesitation.

"Are they here today?" Atticus asked. "Can we talk to them?"

Slade barked a laugh. "I'm pretty sure they're long past pullin' pranks at the high school."

Callie smiled. "I know. But there's no one better."

Atticus frowned.

"I think Braydon and Brendon pulled a few stellar ones back in their day."

Listening raptly to their back and forth, Atticus tried to take mental notes.

"True."

"But anyone now?"

She shook her head. "Not really, no."

Damn. They had zero suspects.

"How long's it been missing?" Atticus asked, trying not to get lost in the conversation.

"It was there on Monday when I left for the day," she said. "When I came in on Tuesday, it was gone."

"And you really think no one's noticed?"

"Of course they noticed," Callie said. "But I'm tryin' to keep it quiet. Like I said, it's Spirit Week, so there's a lot goin' on. I need this to stay quiet for as long as possible."

"And on Friday, when the football team goes out to take the annual picture with it…?" Slade grinned.

Callie frowned.

"What?" Atticus didn't understand.

Callie looked at him and exhaled. "As soon as people start talkin', word's gonna get back to the superintendent."

Atticus didn't understand. "You have a problem with … that person?"

"Only that he's my brother, and I really don't want him comin' down here to give me shit about a giant statue walkin' away on my watch."

"Understood." Atticus grinned. "You know we're gonna have to ask around, right? It's the only way to find it."

"I know," she said solemnly. "Just maybe do it quick so my brother doesn't have a chance to get on his high horse."

Slade shook his head. "Still with the puns, huh, Callie?"

SLADE FOLLOWED ATTICUS OUT OF THE SCHOOL, taking the route to show him where the statue usually stood.

"How hard would it be to steal somethin' like that?" Atticus asked as they stared at the empty concrete pad where the mustang had resided for as long as Slade could remember.

"Probably not as difficult as you might think."

"Really?"

Slade gestured toward the concrete pad. "If they have the equipment to lift it, it's really easy. Otherwise, the statue sits on a base, so as long as someone has something to jack it up with, they could push something beneath it with wheels. From there, it's a matter of pulling it onto a trailer. Would definitely take a wench to get it up there. I guess someone determined enough could probably pull it up onto a flatbed truck, provided the bed tilted."

At least, that was how Slade saw it playing out.

Atticus was frowning at him. "You've given this some thought."

Laughing, Slade shook his head. "Stealing it was one of the options for our senior prank. We just couldn't figure out where to put it. Since no one could come up with a way to get it into the courtyard or on top of the school, we went a different route."

"How were you plannin' on movin' it?"

"My cousins own Walker Demolition. They had the tools."

"Could they have done it?"

"No."

"Maybe their kids?"

"None of them are old enough."

"You sound certain."

"Trust me, if one of my cousins did this, I would know."

"It seems like a lot of work," Atticus mused as they turned to walk back to the truck.

"Probably, but it's about the shock value."

"If nobody notices it's gone, where's the shock in it?" Atticus asked.

Slade opened the driver's door, climbed in. "That'll come when it reappears."

"Someone's just gonna put it back?"

"Of course they are." Slade grinned. "Just won't be where it's supposed to be."

"You sound like you've done this before."

"Not with the mustang," Slade told him as he started the truck and put it in *drive*. "My senior year, we relocated the goats from the Ag building."

"Goats?"

"Yep."

"Where'd you put them?"

"In the common area." Slade laughed. "Then we opened the doors so they could come in and roam the halls. It took them hours to find where they'd all gone."

"Interesting."

"What about you? What did you do for your senior prank?"

Atticus glanced his way, then looked down. "I didn't go to a traditional high school."

"Where'd you go?"

When Atticus looked back at him, Slade knew the answer wasn't easy for Atticus to say.

"Mental hospital."

"Oh."

"Yeah." Atticus gestured toward the empty space. "Got any ideas on where to look first?"

"I say we start by checking to see if any students have parents who own or work at a heavy equipment company. Or maybe someone who has access to a tow truck."

"Good idea. Know anyone who might have that information?"

Slade glanced back at the school and grinned. "I think I do."

"Who?"

He chuckled. "I call her Mama."

Chapter Eighteen

JJ SAT IN THE ROCKING CHAIR, CUDDLING her daughter, unable to stop smiling.

They had allowed her and Baz to visit the babies in the NICU for short periods. This was her third visit of the day and unfortunately the last until tomorrow morning. If it were up to her, she would live in there with them until they were strong enough to go home. On a positive note, the doctors informed her they'd seen a marked improvement in such a short time.

A soft tap had her looking up. There, on the other side of the glass, were Brantley and Reese.

"Uncle B and Uncle Reese are here," she whispered. "I promise, one of these days you'll get to meet them. Aside from your daddy, they're the best men I know. Oh, and Tesha. You'll love her and she'll love you. You get stronger, and you'll get to hang out with them sometime."

Offering a small wave so Brantley and Reese knew she saw them, JJ turned her attention back to her daughter. Her time was quickly running out, and she wanted to cherish every single second. In a week, maybe two—she hoped—they would be strong enough to go home. According to the doctor, they would stay for the better part of ten days—based on their current assessment—but they were already getting stronger. The fact that they were eating well went a long way toward proving they were thriving. JJ took that as a good sign. As much as she wanted them home, she wanted them healthy more, so she would be patient.

Ten minutes passed in the blink of an eye. Because they were sticking to a schedule, JJ didn't want to disrupt that, so she passed her daughter over when the nurse came by. She stopped by her son's bed, peered down at the sleeping baby. He was hooked up to a bilirubin light due to his jaundice, and tiny goggles protected his eyes. JJ bent down and pressed a gentle kiss to his head before rubbing his little fingers.

"Good night, peanuts," she said, the same as she'd said every night.

With a heavy but hopeful heart, she made her way out into the hall where Brantley and Reese were waiting.

"Hey, Mama," Brantley greeted. "How are they?"

"Good." She couldn't stop smiling. "They're perfect."

"I bet they are. You want me to get you some wheels?" he offered, pointing toward a wheelchair.

"I'd rather walk, but we're takin' it slow."

Brantley linked her arm to his and moved at her pace. It took some time, but it allowed them to give her an update on their day.

"Do you think there's any truth to it?" she asked when Brantley finished. "A conspiracy? Really?"

"It's got merit," he admitted.

"What about you?" she asked Reese.

"I think it's worth lookin' into."

"So that's what we do now? Chase conspiracy theories?"

JJ felt Brantley's mood shift as he slid his arm back and opened her hospital room door.

"You tell me." His tone had an edge. "The information you held back seems to plug right into this one."

JJ shot a look at Reese.

"We had to keep it from you," she told Brantley. "It was too close to the wedding."

"That's what I hear," he said, his jaw ticking.

"Come on, B. You know we wouldn't've kept it from you otherwise. At the time, we didn't know whether the information meant anything." She looked at Reese again. "We still don't. Do we?"

"Not yet. We need to map it out first."

JJ eased into bed, watching Brantley pace in frustration.

"What're the next steps?" she asked.

Brantley didn't respond, but Reese finally did.

"Darius is digitizing the information Holt has. Once we have a chance to review it, we'll map it out on a timeline, see what it tells us."

"Okay, good." JJ felt a flutter of excitement. She liked the idea of something to dig into. "How can I help?"

Brantley stopped pacing. "We need to bring the team in first. Get their input. See if they want to take on something like this."

She watched her best friend, admiring how much he'd grown in the past couple of years. Back in high school, he was so gung-ho, plowing ahead without considering the consequences. Time, maturity, and likely the structure of the military had changed him. He was a strategic thinker now, and she found it fascinating.

"And if they do?"

"Then we'll go from there."

JJ patted her lap. "Well, you know where to find me when you're ready."

"How long did the doc say you'll be here?" Reese asked.

Watching Brantley, JJ felt his frustration and, yeah, a hint of betrayal, too. She got it. She did. They'd kept some information from him. At the time, she hadn't wanted to, but Reese and Baz had convinced her. And they were right. If they had shared that information, there was a good chance the wedding never would've taken place.

"At least another day," she told him.

"And the babies?"

"Ten to fourteen days. They'll assess them every day, so that could change."

"Hopefully, you can get some sleep during that time. You're gonna have your hands full."

Yes, she was. And she was looking forward to it.

"We should go," Brantley said, looking at her, his expression masked once again. "Let you get some rest."

"Don't be mad, B."

"I'll get over it," he told her, and she knew he meant it. Brantley didn't hold a grudge, and he didn't let things fester. He addressed it and then moved on. She appreciated that about him.

"When you meet with the team, I'd like to be there," she said, smoothing the blanket in her lap. "Even if it's a video conference."

Brantley moved closer, leaned down, and kissed her forehead. "We wouldn't do it any other way. Get some rest."

JJ watched as they walked out of the room, letting the information they'd shared sink in a bit. She knew without a doubt that they were going to pursue this. Secretly, she was excited about the prospect. She was also nervous, but she wasn't sure why. She got the feeling they'd left something out. Something big.

Relaxing against the pillow, she sighed. Then again, there was a good chance she was the one looking for something that wasn't there. These next few days were going to crawl by, and she wanted something to keep her busy until the twins were strong enough to come home.

At that point, there was a good chance she wouldn't care one iota what case the team was working on. Her heart would be too full to worry about anything except for her sweet babies and the wonderful man who'd been by her side through it all.

ARCHER SAT ON HIS HARLEY, STARING OUT at the land that seemed to go on for miles. To his left, there was a small brick house, and straight back, a few hundred yards in front of him, what appeared to be the beginning of a barn. Directly in front of him was a closed gate that held a sign that read: CAMP K-9 / STORME SHELTER COMING SOON.

Reese had called a few minutes ago, asking if he wanted that introduction to the owner of Camp K-9. Rather than sit on his ass at the B&B, Archer had eagerly jumped at the opportunity.

Now, as he waited for Brantley and Reese to arrive, he took it all in, wondering what the owners intended to do with so much space. The idea of building a sanctuary for animals was one that Archer had given considerable thought to. When he was a kid, back when he'd lived with his grandmother, he'd shared his big dreams of owning a lot of land and taking in all the injured and abandoned animals. Every time he saw a dog or cat in a cage, their eyes wide and pleading, his heart had clenched, and he'd wanted nothing more than to steal them away and let them run free in a space made just for them.

Of course, taking on a venture such as that required far more money and resources than he had, so the dream had been just that. He contributed by donating money to local no-kill shelters to help in whatever small way he could. He wondered whether Camp K-9 would take on an endeavor like that. Perhaps he could also donate his time, as well as money, if they did.

The sound of an engine had him peering back to see a black Chevy heading his way, bumping along the uneven dirt path. It came to a stop a few feet away. A moment later, a man got out. He was tall and broad, with long hair that was tied back with a leather strap. He was wearing boots, jeans, and a dark blue T-shirt that hugged what looked to be a rather muscular body.

"You must be Archer," the man greeted. "Reese just called. Said they were a few minutes out."

Archer climbed off his motorcycle so he could greet the man. He walked toward him, holding out his hand when the man did the same. They shook.

"I'm Trey. Brantley's brother."

"Nice to meet you."

"Magnus and Ava should be here in a few minutes. We're supposed to be reviewing the blueprints for the new facility. Construction starts in two days." Trey pointed to what looked to be a barn that was being erected. "We started the Ag barn for the high school first. They tell me it'll only take a couple of weeks to complete it, so we were hopin' to get it done before the rest of the construction begins."

Trey stepped up to the gate, unhooking the chain that was holding it closed.

"How much land are you working with?"

"We bought ninety-five acres," he said, then pointed to the east. "And we're gonna close on another two hundred in the next couple of weeks. It's more than we anticipated when we started lookin'. We'll be relocating the current Camp K-9 from Embers Ridge to here once it's complete."

"The sign says Storme Shelter. Is that something different?"

Trey nodded, pulling a set of keys from his pocket and unlocking the door of the small construction trailer.

"It's a rescue sanctuary," he explained. "The shelters in the area are so overcrowded, and there aren't many options for large farm animals—horses and whatnot. Ava talked us into expanding."

Archer smiled. Trey sounded put out, but his tone didn't quite match the smile on his face.

"Here's the blueprint," Trey said, walking over to a large wooden table. "We finalized it last week."

Archer skimmed the drawing, noticing there was a house and several other structures on the plan.

"We've got an aggressive timeline," Trey explained. "We're hopin' to have it completed by March."

"Six months?"

"Like I said. Aggressive."

"Doable?" Archer asked, chuckling.

"With Ava driving, I'd say so. She managed to get all the permits before we even signed the papers." Trey looked up, his grin growing wide. "Speak of the devil and she will appear."

Archer glanced out the window to see a man and a woman heading toward them at a jog. No. Not a jog. They were running full out and not in a straight line.

"Is he … chasing her?"

Trey laughed. "He is. And if I'm right, he'll paddle her ass when he catches her."

A moment later, the door swung open and the woman barreled inside, giggling and squealing.

The man wasn't far behind, growling softly.

Trey cleared his throat. "Magnus. Ava."

They stopped instantly, clearly just realizing they weren't alone.

"Hi," Ava said, waving as she gasped for air.

Magnus looked at Trey, then at Archer. "Hey."

"Archer, this is Magnus Storme and Ava March. My soon-to-be husband and wife."

"Husband *and* wife. Interesting." Archer shook their hands.

"Best of both worlds," Magnus said, gripping his hand firmly. "You're the investigator the task force just hired, huh?"

Archer nodded. It wasn't official, but he figured it probably should be. There was no reason for him to pretend otherwise. "And you must be the Storme in Storme Shelter."

"In my defense, I didn't come up with the name." Magnus's eyes were a bit dreamy as he looked at Ava.

"What do you think of the plans?" Ava asked, glancing from him to the blueprints on the table.

"It's impressive."

"We hope it will be," she said. "For the animals, anyway."

"I think it's commendable what you do."

"Thank you. It's not just us, though," Magnus said. "We've got a great team, and if we're lucky, we'll have some volunteers."

"Well, you can count me in if you're looking for someone to sign up."

"Animal lover," Trey muttered with a smirk.

"That I am."

"We'll gladly take whatever help you're willing to offer," Magnus said. "If all goes well, we'll be up and running by May or June."

"March," Ava corrected. "We'll be open for business in March."

Magnus grinned, mouthed, "May," and subtly shook his head. Evidently, he was a bit more pragmatic.

"In the meantime, you can swing by Camp K-9 in Embers Ridge. Check out the search and rescue operations. Reese mentioned you've bonded with Tesha."

Archer chuckled. "Like you said. Animal lover."

A knock interrupted them a moment before the door opened, and Reese and Tesha strolled into the cramped space.

Tesha's hind end started wagging before Magnus could crouch down to pet her.

"Hey, beautiful. What's shakin'?"

Tesha lifted her paw to shake.

Archer watched the interaction, noticing how easily Magnus communicated with Tesha.

"Where's Brantley?" Trey asked.

"We dropped him at the house."

Archer heard something in Reese's tone, but he didn't know the man well enough to identify what it was.

Obviously, Trey noticed too. "Problem?"

"It's all good." Reese stepped over to the table. "This looks great. Construction startin' soon?"

Archer crouched down when Tesha came over. He rubbed her head and her back, listening while Trey and Ava outlined what was what, noting the construction timelines.

"If you need anything, just holler. I'll stop in whenever we've got a few minutes to help out."

"We're gonna put Archer to work, too," Ava told him.

Standing tall, Archer smiled. "Whenever you need me."

"As long as we don't need him first," Reese corrected.

"What he said."

Reese cocked an eyebrow, clearly anticipating an answer. Archer managed to sidestep the conversation for a few minutes, chatting with Trey, Magnus, and Ava about the accommodations they were working on. But when they were back at their vehicles, Archer waited until the trio had left before giving Reese the answer he was waiting for.

"You already know I'm all in," he said sincerely. "Just like everyone else on your team."

"Then I guess I should welcome you." Reese held out his hand. "We know you'll be an asset to the team."

Archer would agree with him there. But only because he consistently gave 150% to everything he did.

Chapter Nineteen

"I MEANT TO ASK EARLIER. HOW'D ATTICUS take the news?" Reese asked when he walked into the house after his quick trip to Camp K-9.

"He did a little dance. It was interesting," Brantley answered, grabbing a beer from the refrigerator. It had been one of those days.

"A dance?" Reese's skepticism bled into the words.

"Yeah. There was music."

"You're fuckin' with me."

"Of course I am. The kid took the job because that's what he's supposed to do. I did let him choose a partner."

"Who'd he pick?"

Brantley grinned. "Slade."

Reese barked a laugh. "I bet that went over well."

"Like a fart in church." Brantly took a swig. "How'd it go with Archer?"

"He offered to volunteer at Camp K-9."

"Really?" Then again, Brantley wasn't sure why he was surprised. Archer seemed like that kind of guy.

"It got me thinkin'," Reese began. "If he's up for it, I thought maybe we'd get another dog for the team. Train him or her to be their partner."

Brantley studied Reese. "Does that mean Archer accepted the offer?"

Reese's smile was slow and proud. "He did."

Thank fuck for that. The team needed another strong leader. They had Evan and Baz, both former detectives and capable of leading a team, who were skilled at what they did. Evan worked well with Slade, and he knew they would succeed together, as partners, but not as a driving force behind the entire team. And Baz ... he had a knack for leading, but not from the front like Brantley would've preferred.

No, for some reason, he saw Atticus in that role. More so with someone as strong as Archer at his side. He could honestly see them leading a task force of their own one day.

Granted, he could be completely off base, but he didn't think so.

"Did y'all talk about a start date?"

"ASAP."

"Even better." Brantley looked at his watch. "I need to make a couple of calls, then we'll meet up on the couch and watch a movie."

"I'm gonna take Tesha out to play ball for a bit, so yeah. That works for me."

As soon as she heard the word *ball*, Tesha began pouncing around Reese's feet like a puppy.

While they headed out the back door, Brantley made his way upstairs to his office. He took a seat in his chair and keyed in his password to unlock his laptop. He had a couple dozen emails that needed his attention, but he decided to put them off until tomorrow.

His first order of business was to call Baz, see how the new father was doing. He wasn't thrilled with the way he'd left things with JJ, but he also didn't want to disturb her if she happened to be resting.

Baz answered on the first ring, his voice soft and low.

"How're things?" Brantley asked.

"Better than expected," Baz said, a smile in his voice. "Give me just a sec to get out into the hall."

Brantley waited, picturing JJ asleep in that king-size hospital bed—which they'd returned after the delivery—all those pillows propped up around her.

"Okay," Baz said a moment later, voice clearer. "Sorry about that."

"We stopped by a little while ago, but you weren't there," he said, leaning back in his chair.

"I'd gone down to get JJ some food from the cafeteria for when she was finished with her visit. My mom and dad caught me on my way back up."

"We saw those little ones. Cute as a bug. They have names yet?"

Baz chuckled. "JJ can't decide, so no."

Brantley considered asking what names they were tossing around, but he'd done that once already, and it hadn't gone over well. Apparently—at least to JJ—choosing names was a sentimental process and required a lot of thought. Brantley was fairly certain that wasn't true for everyone since he was named after a small town in Alabama. To hear his mother tell the story, they'd been passing through there on one of their earlier vacations, and she loved how small and quaint it was. Since Brantley considered himself pretty much anything but small and quaint, he didn't see the sentimentality. But to each his own.

"JJ mentioned ten to fourteen days in the NICU."

"Yeah. If we're lucky. The doctors are optimistic. It all depends on how they progress."

"Is there anything we can do in the meantime? We can run to the store, pick stuff up, and take it back to the house."

"My mother's got that covered. But thanks for the offer."

Brantley smiled. Of course she did.

"How're things there? Did you talk to Simon?"

Brantley relayed the conversation they'd had, giving Baz the high-level details.

"Wow. That's … wow."

"My thoughts exactly. I'm gonna talk to the team tomorrow, get their input. I want their buy-in before we venture down this road." That was only partially true. Brantley had every intention of seeing this through to the end, but he wasn't going to force the team to go along if they didn't want to.

"Would you mind if I came by when you talk to them?"

"Why don't you call me in the mornin', let me know a good time. We'll plan it around you."

"I don't want you to have to do that."

"I don't have to do anything," Brantley said with a gruff chuckle. "I want to."

"Thanks. I know JJ's gonna want to know all the details."

That was an understatement, but Brantley didn't bother telling Baz as much.

"Well, give JJ a hug for us, and we'll see you at some point tomorrow."

"Will do."

Brantley set his phone on the desk and stared at it while he mentally replayed all the information back as best he could. He kept getting stuck on the photograph of Jessie and Kate at the funeral. It was one of the pictures that had been featured in the newspaper shortly after. The first time he saw it, he thought of his cousin Travis.

Before he realized he was dialing, the phone started ringing. Brantley figured it would go to voicemail since Travis hadn't answered any of his calls as of late.

"Yeah?"

"Well, I'll be damned," Brantley grunted, sitting up. "I thought you'd blocked my number."

"It hadn't crossed my mind, but I won't argue it's a good idea," Travis said in that infamous monotone of his.

Brantley took a deep breath, exhaled slowly, buying time to gather his thoughts. He hadn't anticipated Travis answering.

"What's up?" Travis asked. "Why'd you call?"

Had he always been that blunt and to the point, Brantley wondered. Or was this the new Travis? The *after* Travis?

Because there was no easy way to broach the subject, he decided to jump right in. "You've had a conversation with Simon Jennings recently?"

There was a brief pause before Travis said, "I have."

"He gave you details of the podcast he wants to do?"

"He did."

"And you're okay with it?"

"Why're you asking?"

"Simon came to us," he said quickly. "Lookin' for more information."

"On what?"

"Our investigation."

"Into?"

Brantley hated this conversation already, and they hadn't gotten to the difficult part yet.

"I don't have time for this, Brantley. Spit it out."

"Fine," he huffed. "Simon's lookin' for the task force to help him nail down the truth about Meredith Prescott's disappearance."

"And?"

"Do you have a problem with that?"

"With what? You and Reese helpin' him?"

"Yeah."

"No."

Brantley waited for him to elaborate. He didn't.

"No?"

"Did you not hear me the first time?"

Brantley ignored Travis's frustration. "Did he happen to lay out the conspiracy?"

"Conspiracy? No. He mentioned Kylie's mother was the sole witness to a mob hit."

"And you don't have a problem with him diggin' into this?"

"Why would I?"

"Well, for starters, you'll likely end up on Max Adorite's bad side."

"Provided Simon ferrets out the truth, then so be it."

Brantley knew what would happen if he explained the hell that could potentially rain down on them if they ended up on the wrong side of a mob boss, so he left it at that.

"Are you plannin' on helpin' him out?"

"Yes," Brantley answered honestly. "There are a lot of missing pieces at the moment, but we intend to get them nailed down so we can see what direction we're headed."

"Good."

"And you're sure you're all right with this?"

"I don't see as I really have a choice."

"That's why Simon came to you," Brantley answered defensively. "If you didn't want him doin' this, you should've told him."

"I didn't say I didn't want him doin' it," Travis growled roughly. "I want the truth. Whatever that might be. Plus, what've I got to lose, Brantley? Huh? My wife's dead. That's not gonna change."

Brantley swallowed the knot that formed in his throat. Although Travis had never come out and said so, Brantley got the feeling his cousin blamed him for Kylie's death. He didn't blame him. Hell, he felt responsible. If they'd found Juliet Prince before she made her way back to Coyote Ridge, they could've stopped it from happening.

Not that hindsight did anything more than add heaping amounts of guilt to the already exhaustive pile.

"I would appreciate one thing, though," Travis stated.

"Sure. Name it."

"You keep me apprised of what's goin' on."

Nodding, Brantley said, "Yeah. Sure. I can do that."

"Good. Anything else?"

"No."

"I'll talk to you later, then."

Travis didn't even give him a chance to say goodbye. The call ended, and Brantley was left wondering whether they would be better off letting this one go unsolved.

REESE LOOKED UP WHEN HE HEARD BRANTLEY'S footsteps on the stairs. He noticed the crease in his forehead, the one that appeared when he had something on his mind. As soon as Brantley noticed him watching, the crease disappeared.

Hmm. Reese wondered how often the man masked his expression for his benefit.

Brantley nudged his chin in Tesha's direction. "You wear her out already?"

"She gave up first," he said, smiling over at the dog now curled up asleep on her bed.

"Yeah, well. I can attest it takes effort to keep up with you."

Reese grinned. "I thought it was the other way around."

"Did you decide on a movie?"

Definitely something on Brantley's mind if he was changing the subject so quickly. Especially with an opening like that.

"I was thinkin' *Wrath of Man.*"

"Jason Statham." Brantley smiled. "You know how much I like him."

He did know.

"Popcorn?"

"Maybe later," Reese answered, patting the couch cushion. "Sit."

"Let me grab some water."

Reese shifted on the couch so he could watch Brantley in the kitchen. "What's wrong?"

"Nothin'."

"Brantley."

With a bottle of water in hand, Brantley stood tall and sighed. "I talked to Travis."

Well, that pretty much said it all. "And?"

"And he wants us to work with Simon to find Meredith Prescott."

"I assume you didn't tell him about their conspiracy theory."

"No. And I'd like to keep that under wraps until there's even an ounce of truth to it."

"I agree." Reese turned around as Brantley joined him. "I emailed the team, told them we'd meet at HQ tomorrow afternoon to discuss a case. I asked them all to be there."

"Good. I'd like to get their input." Brantley took a swallow of water. "I talked to Baz. JJ's sleepin' and the babies are doin' good. No names yet."

"I'm sure she'll come up with something soon enough."

"If not, we'll just call 'em Baz and JJ junior."

"I'm sure that'll go over well." Reese grabbed the remote and turned on the television. "I talked to Z and got Archer's paperwork started. He said he'd fast-track it."

"You also tell Z that we can't afford for Archer to spend a month in Dallas?"

"I did. Considering his background, Z agreed it wasn't necessary. I'll be interested in watchin' him in the simulations, though."

"We got another trainin' session comin' up soon, huh?"

"End of next week if all goes well."

Reese waited when Brantley went silent. He could tell there was still something on his mind.

Unfortunately, Brantley being Brantley, he didn't cough it up easily.

"All right. Let's hear it. We talked about JJ and the babies, Travis, the case, and Archer comin' on board. I can tell somethin' else is botherin' you. What is it?"

"Besides me lookin' forward to watchin' Jason Statham kick some serious ass?"

"Yes." Reese chuckled. "Besides that."

"Besides me wantin' to get you naked so I can do dirty things to you?"

A chill—the good kind—danced down Reese's spine. "Besides that."

Brantley passed the water bottle over. Reese set it on the end table.

"I'd like to find a way to keep Simon close while this all plays out."

Reese frowned. "Why?"

"For starters, I'd like to control the information he gets."

"That defeats the purpose of his podcast."

"Ask me if I care," Brantley grumbled. "This is my family we're talkin' about. Travis is my cousin. So is Braydon. The last damn thing I wanna do is dig up somethin' that might cause them more pain. Remember, Jessie's gonna have to go through it all again if Simon chooses to rehash what happened."

Reese considered those words carefully. Brantley wasn't wrong. And Reese understood the need to protect family. They were, after all, Reese's family now, too.

"Okay," he told Brantley. "Let's come up with a way to talk to Simon without puttin' him on the defensive. Maybe it's as simple as askin' him to work as a member of the task force for the duration of the case."

"Not a bad idea."

"That might have to come with a paycheck," Reese noted, watching Brantley.

"I'm not sure that's exactly a bad thing."

Reese got comfortable, resting his shoulder against Brantley's. "No?"

"We can always use another set of eyes."

"True."

"Now, would you mind startin' that movie?"

"Eager to watch Jason Statham?"

Brantley shifted closer. "Eager to do dirty things to you in the dark."

Reese felt his cheeks warm even as his cock thickened with anticipation. He lifted the remote to turn on the movie, but before he could, Brantley grabbed it from his hand. He tossed it aside, and in one swift move, Reese was flat on his back, Brantley's comforting weight on top of him.

"I know you would never keep somethin' from me unless you had a good reason."

Reese's breath caught as he stared up into Brantley's face. His expression was hard, cold almost.

"Never."

"Don't do it again, Reese."

He heard the pain in Brantley's voice. He wouldn't admit it, but he clearly felt betrayed.

"I expect you to trust me."

"I do trust you," Reese declared.

"Trust me to do the right thing. I wouldn't've let anything delay our wedding."

Reese nodded. He knew that. Deep down, he knew that was true. At the time, he'd been overwhelmed with so much going on. It hadn't been Brantley he didn't trust, but rather JJ. The woman was fiercely headstrong, and when she wanted something, she dug in her heels. And she had the ability to derail the best of intentions. Not on purpose, of course.

Brantley gripped Reese's jaw firmly. "Trust me, Reese."

A tidal wave of emotion swept through him. Reese grabbed Brantley as he lifted his head, seeking his lips. Their mouths crashed together, hard and demanding.

As he hoped, that triggered Brantley's desire to dominate. Sex—hard, punishing sex—was a surefire way for Brantley to burn off the residual frustration. Reese needed that. Needed to submit to this man, his husband. Needed to atone for his lapse in judgment.

"Fuck," Brantley hissed when Reese bit his bottom lip.

"You can have what you want from me, Brantley," Reese growled. "But I won't make it easy."

Brantley's grin was fierce. "That's why I love you."

When Brantley attempted to flip him, Reese wrestled out from under him, falling to the floor. They rolled together, tongues and teeth clashing as they drove the need higher and higher.

Fighting for air, Reese managed to get to his feet, stumbling down the hall with Brantley right behind him. He barely made it into the bedroom when Brantley was on him, knocking him onto the bed before climbing on top of him.

Reese used every ounce of strength he had to buck Brantley off so he could flip over. As soon as he was on his back, Brantley was on him again, straddling his thighs and pinning him to the bed. They were both panting, their breaths labored, bodies primed.

Brantley managed to shackle his wrists with one hand. The other began jerking the button on his jeans, yanking down the zipper. When his husband fisted his cock, Reese cried out, the pleasure so intense, it blinded him momentarily.

"Fuck my hand," Brantley commanded, his voice raspy with desire. "Now, Reese."

His body had a mind of its own, his hips lifting as he began thrusting into Brantley's fist. It wasn't enough, but he chased the pleasure because it felt so damn good.

But as quickly as it came, it disappeared when Brantley released him, jumping to his feet. The next thing Reese knew, Brantley was manhandling him, yanking his boots off, then his socks, jeans, boxer briefs. He helped by discarding his shirt, crying out in surprise when Brantley deep-throated his cock without warning.

"Oh, fuck ... oh, fuck. Brantley ... don't ... not yet."

He tried to fight the man bringing him to the brink of orgasm, but it was no use. Brantley was on a mission, clearly intent on sending Reese into hyperspace with his exquisite mouth.

His cock jerked and he was seconds from detonating when Brantley released him. Rough hands grabbed behind his knees, shoving his legs toward his chest. Reese had mere seconds to brace for what was coming, but it didn't matter. Brantley tongue-fucked his hole with brutal accuracy, driving him to the brink once again.

"Fuck me, Brantley," he pleaded, jerking his cock in time with the rhythmic thrust of Brantley's tongue. "Oh, fuck ... yes!"

He came with a roar, sensation assaulting every nerve ending.

When he came back to himself a few minutes later, Brantley had stripped his clothes off and was crawling onto the bed with him.

The ferocity was still glowing hot on Brantley's face as he straddled Reese's chest. "My turn."

Yes, it most definitely was.

Reese stared up at Brantley's thick, heavy cock, admiring the way he stroked himself, firmly, almost roughly.

He opened his mouth, eager to taste him, desperate to give him the same pleasure. But most importantly, eager to surrender, to let Brantley use him. He couldn't explain why he loved that so much, but he did.

"Wider," Brantley growled, the thick head pressing against Reese's bottom lip.

He relaxed his jaw, opening as wide as he could. Watching Brantley's face, he saw the relief that passed over his features when he began thrusting into his mouth.

"God, yes. I love that fuckin' mouth."

Brantley planted both hands on the bed and began fucking Reese's face. Slow and deep.

It took effort and focus to breathe through his nose, but Reese managed. He let Brantley use him for long minutes.

"I'm gonna come," Brantley warned. "Oh ... fuck ... Reese ... baby."

Reese lifted his head, meeting Brantley's thrust and was rewarded by the pulse against tongue, the spray against the back of his throat. He swallowed, taking everything Brantley had to give him.

When Brantley flopped down on him, Reese wrapped his arms around him. Words weren't necessary as they both dragged air into overtaxed lungs. He knew without a doubt that Brantley had forgiven him for not sharing the information when he should have. That was the way Brantley worked. He got it out of his system, and then they moved on.

"I love you," he whispered, pressing his lips to Brantley's shoulder. "So much."

"I love you, too." Brantley lifted his head. "But don't hold out on me again."

Reese met his gaze and willed him to see his sincerity as he said, "Never. Promise."

Brantley smirked. "How about that movie now?"

Reese agreed, knowing that there would be a round two before the night was over. And he looked forward to it as much as Brantley looked forward to watching Jason Statham kick bad-guy ass.

Chapter Twenty

Thursday, September 29, 2022

"Mornin'."

Nope. Not morning. Had to be a joke.

Atticus tugged his pillow from under his head and smashed it against his face. "No way is it morning yet."

"What did you say?"

He lifted the pillow enough to let his words become clear as he repeated the sentiment with an additional curse word, but then smashed it down again.

Slade's warm body moved up close to him. "I'm sorry, but it is."

"What time *is* it?" he asked, lifting the pillow enough to be understood.

"Six thirty."

Atticus sighed and yanked the pillow away from his face. "That's only morning in your world. The one where overachievers live. In my world, I've still got two hours of night left."

He was already running on far too little sleep. It was what? Only two days ago that they'd spent the entire night at the hospital?

Maybe once he'd slept for eighteen hours straight, he'd feel like himself again. Unfortunately, Atticus didn't have the discipline to go to bed at a decent hour. If he had, he wouldn't be so damn tired. Last night, rather than coming home and face-planting to catch up on the sleep he'd missed, Atticus had spent far too much time outlining the missing statue case. He felt kind of stupid treating it as they would a missing person's case, but since this was technically his first case with the task force, he wanted to show Brantley and Reese that he was serious. Regardless of what he was looking for.

The next thing he knew, it was midnight, and he was once again shorting himself on sleep. Especially since Slade felt it was necessary to get up at the ass-crack of day.

"You talk to Carson?" Atticus asked.

"I texted him last night. He was still at his parents' house. It was their anniversary. All the kids got together to throw them a party."

"I guess that's a good enough reason to back out on dinner," Atticus mumbled. He'd been looking forward to spending the evening with Slade and Carson. Especially since that was the plan. Then Carson came by, but only to tell them he needed a raincheck on dinner. Unfortunately, that raincheck had extended to sex as well because Atticus ended up going to bed alone.

"How many people were there?" he asked, though he didn't expect Slade to have the answer.

Slade rested his head on the pillow. "I guess if you count his brothers, Wade and Jaxson, and his sisters, Piper, Renee, and Cara, that would be six. Then there's Piper's son, and if any of them have significant others."

"Do they?"

"I honestly don't know."

"He's got a big family, too, huh?"

"He does. And they're close."

For whatever reason, Atticus liked that Carson was close to his family. He knew the same couldn't be said for Slade. While he seemed to have a good relationship with his mother, a decent one with his father, Atticus had heard stories about Slade's relationship with his brothers. Although he understood Slade's reason for hating Spencer—the guy screwed his wife—he didn't know the full story behind his animosity toward the others.

"Shouldn't surprise you." Slade rolled to his back. "Carson's a damn good son. Even a good friend. He's just a really shitty boyfriend."

Atticus wasn't in the mood to listen to Slade dis Carson this morning. "I should get ready to head in."

He tried to sit up but was flung back when Slade grabbed his arm.

"I didn't mean it like that," Slade said quickly. "He's tryin' now. I'll give him that."

Too tired to fight, Atticus relaxed against the pillow. What he needed to do was get his tired ass out of bed and into the shower. Since Reese had texted about a potential new case for the entire team, Atticus wanted to get an answer for the missing statue as soon as possible. He hated the case already, and he'd only been working it for one day. But he would be damned if he was going to give up or skirt his responsibilities. It might've been a shitty assignment, but Brantley and Reese wouldn't have given it to him if they didn't trust him to get it resolved.

That or they hated him.

"What's the plan for today?" Slade asked, his hand wandering beneath the blanket, shifting over Atticus's stomach.

"I was plannin' on taking a ... oh, fuck," he hissed when Slade's fingers curled around his cock, soft and gentle.

"I'll take one with you."

"Take one what?" he asked, his train of thought completely obliterated by the pleasure of Slade's hand.

Slade chuckled, his voice pitched low. "A shower."

Shower. Right. *Fuck that feels good.*

He gritted his teeth when Slade's fingers firmed around his shaft, stroking leisurely. The man knew exactly how to touch him to make his head spin.

"We'll save water and time," Slade whispered, the heat of his gaze searing him.

Atticus rolled his hips, fucking Slade's fist. "I've been in the shower with you before. We damn sure don't save water."

Slade's voice lowered. "But it's worth it, right?"

"So worth it," Atticus whispered, closing his eyes as the pleasure of Slade's touch moved through his entire body.

Slade tugged the blanket, pulling it down. Atticus peered down, watching his cock tunnel in and out of Slade's fist.

"I love watchin' you like this," Slade groaned, his thumb gliding through the pre-cum pooling on the tip of Atticus's dick.

Yeah, well, Atticus liked when Slade watched. And touched. Sometimes, he wondered whether Slade had taken a class on exactly how to touch a man to make him lose his mind. No one had ever touched him the way Slade did. No one had ever made him feel like he was burning up from the inside out. Not even Carson and that man knew how to fuck. But there was no denying Slade was extremely attentive in the bedroom.

Or on the couch.

In the kitchen.

In the truck.

"Slade ... oh, fuck," Atticus moaned softly, reaching up, running his fingers through Slade's hair, pumping his hips, fucking Slade's fist. "Put ... your ... mouth ... on ... me."

The bed shifted beside him, causing Atticus to open his eyes. Slade propped himself on one elbow before scooting down the bed. Atticus stared down his body, watching as Slade once again began his smooth, rhythmic stroke. He dared a glance at Slade's face, saw the man watching him with a smile.

Feeling self-conscious, Atticus said, "What?"

"Nothin'. I like watchin' you, is all."

He knew that was true because Slade was always watching him.

Atticus's breath hitched when Slade leaned forward, his mouth hovering dangerously close to the sensitive head of his dick. He felt warm breath seconds before the soft rasp of Slade's tongue nearly sent him into hyperspace.

And then Slade was sucking him, drawing him in deep, teasing with his lips and tongue. It was all Atticus could do to hang on, letting the pleasure carry him to new heights.

Clearly Slade knew what he was doing because he never sent Atticus careening over the edge despite his eagerness to do so. He wanted to come, but every time he thought he would, Slade would pull back just enough to move that cliff a little further away.

His hand found its way into Slade's hair, his fingers twining in the silky, dark strands. He didn't dominate, didn't urge Slade's head down, he merely touched him because he could. He enjoyed being grounded in the moment, reminded of who he was with and where they were. Being with Slade differed from being with the men from his past. Slade and Carson were the first men in his life who'd made him feel like something more than a nameless indulgence.

"Slade ... more ... I need more."

To his regret, Slade didn't give him more. Instead, he pulled off, shifting so that he was blanketing Atticus's body, his knees cradling Atticus's hips.

"Let's shower," Slade whispered, trailing his lips along Atticus's jaw.

Atticus was nearly boneless from the pleasure, but he managed a nod. He got to his feet and stumbled along after Slade.

When Slade bypassed his bathroom, Atticus said, "Give me a sec. I'll join you."

He took the opportunity to brush his teeth, running through multiplication tables in an effort to get his aching dick to settle long enough for him to take a piss. Once he was done, he wandered naked through the house toward Slade's bedroom. He found Slade in the shower, his naked body on display through the glass that was steaming up.

The man was devastatingly gorgeous. With all that muscle and sinew, he would've made one hell of a cover for *Muscle & Fitness* magazine. Slade was actually the one who had inspired Atticus to want to get into shape when he went to training a few weeks ago.

Slade tipped his head back, closing his eyes and letting the water pour down on his head. Atticus took the opportunity to join him, admiring the way the water glazed all that smooth, bronzed skin.

As he stood there, staring like it was his job, Atticus realized he had new reasons to get up in the morning. Reasons that didn't include a job or trying to make a living. Reasons that made him believe he was actually living instead of trudging through day by day.

He grinned, realizing something else, too. Having the opportunity to see Slade Elliott in all his bare glory meant somewhere along the way, he'd won the fucking lottery.

SLADE FELT COOL AIR WAFT OVER HIM when Atticus stepped into the shower. The heated caress of the man's eyes raking across his skin caused warmth to churn through his veins. He liked the approval he saw in Atticus's gaze, the lust.

"You wanna touch?" Slade taunted.

Atticus's eyes slowly lifted. "Hmm?"

"Touch me, Atticus. Now."

Slade chuckled, then moaned when Atticus's hands moved over his stomach, then inched higher. He rubbed him from chest to hip, teasing him with the smoothness of his palm. For long minutes, Slade continued to wash, and Atticus continued to tease. It didn't take much for Slade's dick to return to the iron-hard state it had been in when he'd been sucking Atticus's cock a short time ago.

When the water was rinsing the soap away, Slade grabbed Atticus, jerking him against him so he could band his arms around the man. He kissed him, losing himself in the determined thrash of Atticus's tongue against his own. He could've kissed him for days and never tired of it.

Unfortunately, they had things to take care of, which meant keeping to the agenda.

Slade managed to pull back, staring down at Atticus as he reached for the bottle of body wash. They did the little dance that allowed Atticus to switch places, moving beneath the water while Slade stepped out of the stream. Without a word being spoken, Slade took the liberty of soaping Atticus from neck to toes, working the lather into every crook and crevice. He did some teasing of his own, using his soapy hand to stroke Atticus until his cock was pulsing in his fist.

"You wanna come?"

Atticus grunted and groaned.

"I'll let you, but before we get out of this shower, I'm gonna bend you over and slide my dick in your ass. Your choice. You wanna come before, during, or after?"

"Oh, fuck." Atticus snapped his hand around Slade's wrist, stopping him from sending him over the edge. "Fuck me."

Before Slade could stand tall, Atticus had turned away, spreading his feet wide and pushing his ass out. Slade would've used the water as a lubricant, but it wasn't quite enough for his liking, so he grabbed the small bottle of lube he kept on the shelf. He greased his cock and stroked as he stepped up behind Atticus. Some shifting ensued, but then Slade's cock was tunneling deep inside Atticus while his arm banded across his middle, keeping him in place.

"Yes," Atticus sighed, tipping his head back as Slade pushed in to the hilt.

"You are so fucking tight." Slade retreated slowly, pushed in again, one hand planted on the wall to keep him from falling over.

He fucked Atticus like that, slow and deep, the heat of the water causing steam to billow around them. His pace naturally progressed, faster and harder. And when Atticus began jerking his dick, Slade began pounding into him, chasing his own release.

"Oh, fuck, baby," he growled near Atticus's ear. "I can't stop. I ... oh, fuck ... I'm gonna come."

He did, groaning low in his throat as his cock pulsed inside the heat of Atticus's body. He had enough presence of mind to reach around, taking over for Atticus, stroking his cock hard and fast until Atticus's asshole locked down on him as he came with a breathless groan.

Twenty minutes later, Slade found Atticus in the kitchen, pouring Cheerios into a bowl.

"Want some?"

Slade chuckled. "Nah. Thanks, though."

"Let me guess, two hard-boiled eggs and orange juice."

"It'll tide me over for a couple of hours," Slade told him as he opened the refrigerator.

"I got the names of some tow services last night," Atticus said, slipping the milk carton into the refrigerator. "Thought we'd go by each one, see if they know anything that might help."

Slade closed the door. "Okay."

"Since we've got a meeting this afternoon, I thought we'd split up the list. You take half. I'll take the other."

"Uh … okay."

"Is that a problem?"

"No."

Atticus frowned. "What is it?"

Slade shook off the thoughts flooding his brain, refusing to give in to the insecurity eating away at him.

"It's nothing. I'll take half, you take half. We'll meet at HQ when we're done."

"You sure?"

"Yup. It's a good place to start."

"I thought so." Atticus nodded toward his phone. "I sent Becs a list and asked her to identify any kids whose parents either own or work at a place that would have the equipment to move a statue of that size. Or access to one. Figured we'd talk to them, see if one of their trucks disappeared for a little while."

"Good idea." Slade took a sip of juice. "Maybe we could grab lunch before we head into HQ for the meeting?"

"I'm actually meeting Carson for lunch. You wanna join us?"

As though he were an afterthought? No, thank you. "I'm good. Y'all enjoy."

Forgetting breakfast, Slade spun on his heel and left the kitchen.

"Slade!"

"Shoot me the list. I'll do my part."

With that, Slade walked out of the house, hating himself for letting his insecurity ruin what started as a damn fine morning.

Chapter Twenty-One

BRANTLEY LEANED AGAINST THE KITCHEN COUNTER, SIPPING coffee and trying to work through the day in his head. They were meeting with the team to discuss the case, and he wanted to be ahead of the game. As it was, he was still mentally sifting through the information they received yesterday and making no progress.

Which meant he needed to get ahead of this, and there was only one way to do that.

"Did you get a chance to look at the information Darius digitized?"

Reese closed the dishwasher and pressed the button to start it. "Not in depth, no. I glanced at what Becs sorted. She won't be able to map it out until she understands the objective."

"Did she ask what it was all about?"

Reese shook his head. "I could tell she wanted to, though."

He appreciated that about her. Becs was very professional and, for the most part, she stayed in her lane until she needed something to accomplish her task. He wasn't sure how he was going to relay this to the team just yet, so he was grateful that she wasn't asking questions. It was one thing to ask them to locate Meredith Prescott. That was their job. They were a missing persons task force. It was something entirely different to go down the road of a conspiracy theory.

Only one case had they taken that required them to understand the why, and that was when Dante Greenwood, JJ's ex-boyfriend, staged his kidnapping and dragged JJ into the plot. They generally left the why of it to the police.

But a conspiracy theory … that was a whole other beast.

Regardless of how he presented it, Brantley wasn't sure any of them were going to be professional once they sprang this on them. Maybe that was the issue. Perhaps they shouldn't be bringing the team in on this. They could deal with it on their own until they had more information. Since he wasn't prone to conspiracy theories, it made sense. He could look for actual proof that there was a case before wasting their time with something that might be nothing.

He exhaled heavily, remembering what Reese had said about information they'd obtained but held back because they didn't want to disrupt the wedding. They'd kept information from him because they didn't trust he could handle it at the time. No, holding back from the team wasn't an option. He hated that Reese had done that to him, and while he understood—at least on some level—he didn't care for the feeling of being coddled like he wasn't capable of handling the information during a stressful time.

Brantley snorted. "If only." Shaking off the thought, he turned to face Reese. "Before we meet with the team, I want you to walk me through everything you found."

"It wasn't so much what I found," Reese said, his tone somewhat defensive. "Luca found the information, although he didn't put it together at the time. JJ did."

"Put what together?"

"I honestly don't know. Not yet. I can show you the folders and files, and you can see the anomalies that JJ identified. But that's all they are at this point. We didn't dig into it."

"You're sure she didn't?"

"She promised me she wouldn't until after the wedding. Baz wanted her to wait until after the babies were born. There was a lot goin' on."

"You don't have to defend your decision," he told Reese. "I get it."

"Are you sure? Honest to God, I wasn't tryin' to cut you out of the loop."

"I know." And he did. It hurt a bit, but he trusted Reese would never betray him like that.

Reese still didn't appear convinced.

"I get it," Brantley continued. "There was a lot goin' on. And I know you. If you'd found a legitimate lead, you would've dealt with it then. So where's the information?"

Reese pointed toward the ceiling. "I've got it on my computer. I can send it to you."

"No need to do that. Just show me what you've got."

SLADE COULD FEEL THE CURIOUS GLANCES BEFORE he ever reached the door to Hank's Towing.

The place was small. Little more than an old converted gas station with the pump still in place, although listing a little to the left. The white awning overhead had seen better days. One good windstorm like they'd seen back in 2018, and the thing would be in their neighbor's lot along with half a dozen beat-up old junkers Hank had lining the perimeter.

Before he could reach the main door with the little plastic sign that said they would be back in fifteen minutes, a man wandered out from the single-bay garage, a red rag in his hands.

"What can I do you for?" The man's voice was rough, likely from the Marlboro Reds he pulled out of the bib of his overalls.

"Are you Hank?"

The man adjusted his grease-stained trucker cap. "Could be. Depends."

Slade fought the urge to roll his eyes. As amusing as this could be, he wasn't really in the mood.

"Any chance one of your tow trucks went missing on Monday night?"

The guy looked around like he was expecting someone to jump out and tell him he was being punked.

"Seriously, boy?"

"Slade," he corrected the guy. "And yes, I'm serious. The statue at Coyote Ridge High School went missing on Monday night, and we're lookin' to see if someone might've relocated it with one of your tow trucks."

The guy's thick, dark eyebrows angled down. "Naw. My boys run calls on Monday and Friday nights. We didn't have any trucks left on the lot."

Although he couldn't be positive Could-Be-Hank wasn't blowing smoke up his ass, the man sounded honest.

"That's all I needed to know. Thanks for your time."

Slade headed back to his truck. He climbed in and turned on the A/C before checking off another shop on his list to visit. This was the third one he'd been to, none of which had been any more helpful than Could-Be-Hank.

Now he was wondering whether this was a waste of time. What if they hadn't used a tow truck? But how else would they move it?

As he stared out the windshield, he tried to envision various scenarios. A flatbed with a wench? That seemed like the most logical way. Unless they had access to a crane. That would've done the job in no time at all. But who had a crane besides Walker Demo? And if they got a crane, who would operate it? It wasn't as simple as it looked, he was sure.

Did they do it alone? Were there adults around to help?

And that was assuming some of the kids had done it as a prank.

Or hell, maybe his cousin Callie was pranking him. It didn't seem like something she would do, but who knows anymore?

When Slade didn't come up with an answer to any of the questions, he decided to drive over to the high school. Maybe he would see things from a different perspective if he went back to the scene of the crime one more time.

Ten minutes later, he was walking toward the empty space where the statue once stood. Once he reached it, he did a three-sixty, noting the neighbors across the street on three sides and the school behind him. Whoever took the statue had brass stones; that much was for sure. There wasn't an inch of space that wasn't visible from at least one of those houses. Which meant there was likely a witness. Or perhaps one of those homeowners was responsible. How else could you haul off a half-ton brass statue and no one be the wiser?

Slade had considered heading over to Walker Demo to talk to his cousins, see if they could help make sense of how someone could move the statue, but paying a visit to each of those residents was probably a better place to start. He could canvass the area, talk to people, and see if anyone saw anything out of the ordinary. Surely if there'd been any heavy equipment used, someone would've heard something.

As he headed for the sidewalk and the row of neatly kept houses opposite the school, he found himself wishing someone would run out and say, "Oops. We forgot. We sold the stupid statue. Our bad."

Unfortunately, no one came out, so he kept going.

He started from the end and worked his way down. Eighteen houses total faced the school directly. Fourteen of those houses had no answer. Made sense. Mid-morning on a Thursday. They were likely at work. That, or they ignored the doorbell because they thought their *no solicitation* sign spoke for itself.

At house number three, he was greeted by a grumpy old man who had no comment. That was what he said. Verbatim.

At house number six, he was greeted by a teenage girl who claimed she was just home to grab homework for third period and was going right back. And no, she had no idea who might've taken the statue.

At house number eleven, Slade thought he hit pay dirt when the elderly woman wandered outside, claiming she knew exactly who took the statue. His hope dwindled when she insisted it was one of the sheriff's deputies because he was secretly an alien in disguise. Slade thought he smelled whiskey on her breath.

Last but not least, at house number seventeen, the one directly across from where the mustang usually stood proudly, he spoke to a man who looked to be in his late twenties, maybe early thirties, and tired from a strenuous workout. "Sorry, man. I honestly thought it was still there."

Yeah, yeah, yeah. Story of his life.

"Thanks," he told the guy as he started back down the driveway.

"Hey! Are you related to Spencer?"

Slade stopped and turned. "Yeah," he admitted grudgingly.

The guy smiled. "Cool. I haven't seen him since high school." His grin widened. "We kinda had a thing back then."

A thing? Slade was about to tell him he was likely one of a few dozen, but he refrained.

"If you see him, tell him I said hello."

"Will do," Slade lied, waving a hand and continuing toward his truck.

The morning had been bad enough, the last thing he wanted to do was think about his backstabbing asshole of a brother.

NOW THAT THE TASK FORCE HAD CLEANED out all the articles and photographs from the apartment, Archer didn't have any reason to go over there. Since he wasn't quite an official member of the task force—paperwork and all that—he didn't have a reason to go there, either. But he was tired of sitting around the B&B waiting for something to do.

Okay, so that was only partially true. He didn't mind it so much since he'd spent the better part of the morning listening to Bailey tell the story of how she ended up with Rafe and Holt. It was interesting, he'd give her that much.

Now that she was finished, he didn't want to sit idly anymore, so he decided to make the most of a morning off.

At least that was what he told himself as he strolled across Walker Park toward the downtown businesses on the other side. He pretended he didn't have a destination in mind, but that only lasted so long. As soon as he crossed Main Street, he was forced to make a decision. Go into the bookstore and strike up a conversation with Violet, or slip between the buildings and head up to the second floor.

Right. As if it were really a choice. Sure, he liked Violet and all, but choosing between seeing her or seeing Spencer … kind of a no-brainer.

Archer didn't miss a beat, aiming for the metal staircase. He took the stairs two at a time, not bothering to pause at the top. He strolled right up to the real estate office, knocked on the door and then turned the knob to let himself in.

Spencer was on the phone, holding up a finger without bothering to look over.

"Yes. This afternoon. Three o'clock," Spencer said into the phone. "On paper, the house has everything they're looking for. They need a quick close. Is that something your clients could accommodate?"

Archer remained where he was, watching Spencer work. As had been the case since the first time he saw Spencer in the bookstore, his body responded to the man's presence. It was an instant attraction on his part, and it hadn't decreased even a fraction since that day. In fact, it was growing significantly more intense with every passing minute. That was likely due to him taking things slow, which caused the intense lust to simply build inside him. He figured at some point—probably in the very near future—it was going to burst, and his hard-earned self-control would be put to the test.

Kinda like it was right now. Just thinking about the guy made his dick hard. Those moments when he recalled kissing the man … yeah, it was going to be painful to walk in a few minutes.

Spencer's dark brown hair was styled as though it had been cut just that morning, and for some reason, that made Archer want to run his fingers through it to muss it up a bit. And while he was at it, he wanted to tip Spencer's head back so he could—

"That's fantastic. They'll be happy to know that," Spencer continued.

Jesus.

Not helping.

Archer took a cleansing breath and collected himself. Good thing he had patience in spades. Uncle Sam had ingrained that in him when he joined the Marines. As a sniper, he'd spent his fair share of time tucked into a blind, unable to move for hours, sometimes days, on end.

The thought made him smile. Maybe this was what he'd trained for.

"Perfect," Spencer said. "We'll be by at three and I'll send you feedback once I have it."

Archer stood taller, waiting for Spencer to look his way. When he did, he saw surprise mixed with a little bit of … was that heat glittering in Spencer's brown eyes?

"Hey," Spencer greeted.

"Hey back."

"What're you doing here?"

Archer waved him back before he could stand up. "Don't get up on my account. Just thought I'd stop by. See you before I head over to Brantley's this afternoon."

"Is it your first day?"

"Not officially, no. They've submitted the paperwork." Archer moved toward him, scanning the room. "Once the background check comes back, I'll be good to go. You here alone?"

Spencer nodded, watching him.

He continued moving toward Spencer. "You expecting anyone to come in that door in the next few minutes?"

"No. Why?"

"Because I really need to do this," he said, leaning down, planting his hands on the armrests of Spencer's chair. He held Spencer's gaze for a few seconds before he leaned in for a kiss.

The heat from the other night exploded when Spencer kissed him back, his hands cupping the sides of his neck. When he attempted to back up, not wanting to overwhelm the man, Spencer didn't let him, holding on tight. The next thing he knew, Spencer was on his feet and Archer had him pinned against the wall.

"Don't stop," Spencer whispered. "Just kiss me."

So he did.

And he did some more.

Archer wasn't sure Uncle Sam had trained him for the likes of Spencer Elliott. The man could so easily fray his good intentions along with his patience with little effort.

When Spencer's hand slid beneath his T-shirt, Archer sucked in a breath and prayed his self-control remained intact.

"I don't wanna go slow," Spencer said, biting Archer's lower lip.

"I can see that." Archer focused on his breathing as those smooth hands moved higher. It would've been so easy to let Spencer have his way, but Archer couldn't help but wonder about tomorrow. He got the feeling that once with Spencer wouldn't be nearly enough. But he wasn't sure Spencer would feel the same way about him. Archer wasn't willing to risk that. Not until he'd given Spencer a reason to want to be with him. A reason that didn't involve the two of them naked and sweaty.

"Fuck," he groaned, gripping Spencer's forearms when he began tweaking his nipples. "You're playin' a dangerous game."

Spencer pulled back enough to meet his gaze. "Am I?"

"No more of that or I might give in," Archer told him as he maneuvered Spencer's hands from under his shirt. He clutched both wrists in one hand and lifted them above Spencer's head. "I assure you, when I do give in, we won't be in this office."

"Where will we be?" Spencer asked, his breath labored.

"Has anyone ever told you you're cute when you're eager?" Archer kissed him softly.

"Dinner tonight?" Spencer asked. "My place."

"Yes to dinner. No to your place."

Spencer frowned.

"You're a temptation I'm havin' a difficult time resisting."

"Then don't."

"No sex on the second date."

"The third?"

Archer smirked. "Doubtful, but not impossible."

"Fourth?"

"You'll have to wait and find out."

"Not sure I can."

"You can. And you will." Archer kissed him again before releasing his wrists. "I might be working late tonight, but I'll call you when we're finished."

Spencer nodded, but there was disappointment shimmering in his eyes.

Archer leaned in, this time pressing his entire body against Spencer's. "Would it help to know that I've jacked off five times a day since I met you?"

Spencer's eyes widened.

Archer lowered his voice, letting his lips hover over Spencer's. "And it's still not enough."

And it wouldn't be, but Archer believed that Spencer was definitely worth waiting for.

Chapter Twenty-Two

ATTICUS HAD CHECKED OFF EVERY BUSINESS ON his list, and he was no closer to identifying how someone could've moved a fifteen-hundred-pound bronze statue, much less who was responsible.

And somehow his search had led him here, to Batter & Bliss for his mid-morning pick-me-up.

"Let me guess?" Ramona said with a smile. "Red Bull and a donut."

To be fair, he wanted neither, but he needed something to do while his thoughts tumbled around in his head. "Yes, ma'am."

She lifted a small sack already prepared. "Grab your drink and I'll ring you up."

Atticus completed the transaction, said goodbye to Ramona, and headed out into the mid-morning sunshine. Rather than eat in his truck, he headed for one of the benches in Walker Park. Perhaps it would give him a better perspective if he viewed things from there.

How fucking hard could it be to figure this out? Surely *finding* the person responsible was easier than actually moving the damn statue.

What Atticus didn't understand was who the fuck wanted to move it? Sure, he understood a prank. But if taking it was a practical joke, wouldn't they have simply relocated it somewhere else on school grounds? Like on the front steps or the football field. Why take it? And where did they take it to? Someone would notice if their neighbor suddenly acquired a giant statue in their yard, wouldn't they?

"Atticus?"

Dragged out of his thoughts, he looked up to see Archer coming his way.

"Hey," Atticus greeted, watching as Archer approached.

Archer nodded toward the paper sack. "Whatcha got there?"

Atticus lifted the small white sack in one hand and the open can of Red Bull in the other. "Energy."

"Interesting." Archer glanced at the bench. "Mind if I sit?" Atticus scooted to the left, giving Archer room beside him.

"What brings you out here?"

"I'm tryin' to find a statue."

"What kind of statue?"

"Bronze. Life-size. School mascot. It's a horse. Or a mustang, I guess they call it."

"Ah. Gotcha. I assume someone stole it?"

He was grateful Archer wasn't laughing his ass off. "Looks like it. Although I think it was more of a prank."

"That makes sense. Where was it last?"

"Coyote Ridge High School. In the front."

"High school. I saw signs for the homecoming game and dance," Archer mused. "I could definitely see someone relocating it as a prank. When did it go missing?"

"Monday night or sometime early Tuesday."

"Has anyone stolen it before?"

Atticus looked at Archer. "That's a damn good question. Based on Callie's reaction—she's the high school principal—I'd say no. At least not on her watch."

"Okay, then."

"Wouldn't it be difficult to steal?" Atticus asked, still genuinely confused about how someone would've rehomed the damn thing.

"Not exactly. If you can figure out what they used, then you could check places that have that equipment. And that should lead to who," Archer told Atticus.

"Do you think it's that simple?" For whatever reason, Atticus didn't want to let the school down. More importantly, he didn't want to be known as the asshole who let the school down.

"I can tell you that moving it isn't as hard as you'd think," Archer said, staring out at the park. "A forklift and a trailer would be all you'd really need."

Atticus tried to play it out in his head, but couldn't. "A forklift? I seriously don't see someone drivin' away with it on a forklift."

"That's what the trailer's for."

"How would you get under it to hoist it up?"

Archer leaned back. "If it were me, I'd use heavy-duty straps. Wrap them under and around the statue, loop them over the forks"—he used hand motions to explain—"then use the lift to raise it high enough to get a trailer under. Once it's there, lower it. Then drive it away."

Well, shit. That was simple. And would be relatively unobtrusive in the dark. No wonder no one saw them take it.

"Would they need a heavy-duty forklift?"

"Not necessarily. A good one, sure. A lot of 'em will lift up to five thousand pounds easily."

"And you know so much about forklifts, why?"

"I worked a missing statue case before. Art gallery, though. Not as big, but more delicate. The thief used air sleds to get it to the loading dock, then hoisted it up with a forklift and moved it right into the back of a truck."

"So we're lookin' for someone who owns or has access to a forklift?" Atticus asked.

"Sounds like it." Archer glanced his way.

"Know anyone who's got one?"

"There's a heavy equipment company in town. Walker Demolition, I think. They probably have several." Archer chuckled. "And probably every warehouse in a one-thousand-mile radius."

Well, that didn't narrow it down much.

"Say you've got a forklift and those heavy-duty straps. You drive the forklift out there?"

"If you're close, sure. Otherwise, you'd trailer it, I imagine."

"They get it out there," Atticus stated, not sure it mattered how it got there. "Then they do all that shit and hoist it up, put it on a trailer, drive it away. What then? Where do they take it?" He looked at Archer. "More importantly, why?"

"A prank, like you said. You want my opinion?"

"I'll take anything at this point."

"All right. You've got high school kids, right?"

"Assuming so, sure."

"They've come up with a mischievous plan."

"If we're lucky," Atticus said.

"If they just wanted to be destructive, they could've left it where it was. I think they want to make a statement. The home team or the rival. Either way."

"Callie and Slade think CRHS students took it."

"I'd say that's a good bet. If it's not on the property, then they wouldn't go far. Someone's house. Their parents' business. Maybe they're gonna paint it. Is there a body shop around here? With a paint booth?"

Atticus grabbed his phone and pulled up the list Becs had given him.

"There's one," he noted. "Gary's Auto Body."

"I'd look there. You could find out if Gary has kids who attend the high school. If he does, then go by there. Even if it's just a drive-by. Scope it out."

With Red Bull in hand, Atticus shot to his feet. "Man, thanks."

"Anytime."

Atticus started toward his truck but stopped, looking back at Archer. "I can get Becs to check out the kid thing, but do you wanna head over there with me? Unless you've got somethin' else to do."

"No. I'm kinda in wait mode," he said, standing tall. "I wouldn't mind checkin' it out."

Atticus jerked his head toward his truck. "Come on then. Maybe we can solve this one today so I can get on with my life."

"CAN YOU READ THAT?" ATTICUS ASKED, PASSING his phone over when it buzzed.

Archer took it, glancing at the screen. "It's from Becs. She says Gary's is owned by Dave Costello and his wife, Julie."

"So not Gary?"

Laughing, Archer said, "Doesn't look like it, no."

"Then why call it Gary's?"

"That's a question you'll have to ask Dave and Julie."

Atticus shook his head, grinning. "Okay. What else?"

"They've got two kids. A little girl, six. And a son, sixteen."

"Sixteen's old enough for high school," Atticus said.

"Yeah. Definitely worth a look." Archer continued reading. "Also says here that Gary's owns a flatbed tow truck."

"What are the chances a sixteen-year-old decides to hijack a bronze statue just to take it to his parents' body shop and paint it?"

"Likely slim to none, but as good a chance as any we've got so far, right?"

"True. Maybe the parents are in on it. Or maybe they're out of town."

While Atticus continued to think out loud, Archer discreetly checked out his truck as they drove. It was almost compulsively clean. No trash in the cup holders, no old bottles on the floor. Even the dash looked like it had been polished to a shine recently.

"So are you comin' to work for the task force or not?"

He huffed a laugh, surprised by the question. "I accepted the job yesterday."

Atticus's gaze shot over. "Why didn't you lead with that?"

"It didn't come up."

"Fuck, that's great, man. I am so ready to get to work."

"Aren't you working this case?"

"Yeah. Because Brantley and Reese like to fuck with me."

Archer laughed.

"Seriously. It's the first case they've given me. Not once has the team taken on a case of a missing item, but they don't hesitate to throw it my way."

"You mentioned you were a bounty hunter before."

"Yep."

"Solo job, right?"

"Pretty much, yeah."

"That's likely why. They don't want you workin' alone."

"I get it, but I swear they've turned down a few dozen people just because they know it irritates me to look at resumes all day."

"Did you look at mine?"

Atticus peered over quickly. "No. I would have, but they didn't even mention it."

"Well, if it helps any, I grew up in Franklin, Tennessee, about thirty minutes outside of Nashville. I was raised by my grandmother after my parents died in a car accident. I joined the Marines right out of high school. Spent eight years in. Since then, I've been working for Simon as an investigator. To supplement my income, I've done some one-offs for local PDs. I'm single, never been married. No kids. I'd like to get a dog."

"You live around here?"

"I'm staying at the B and B for now. Violet and Simon bought a house. I'm moving in with them at the end of next month."

"Cool."

"What about you?"

"Where do I live?"

Archer laughed. "Or you could give me key points. Up to you."

"Grew up in Garland, north of here. My mom overdosed, dad's MIA. My grandmother tried to raise me. Died. I went into the foster care system at fourteen, ran away at seventeen. Met a guy who made bounty hunting look like a glamorous job. Did that until Reese's mom Louisville Slugger'd me when I was huntin' her ex-boyfriend. Reese and Brantley felt sorry for me, hired me on. Not married, no kids. In a semi-relationship, but it's complicated. And by that, I mean it's straight up fucked-up and I can't really explain it."

Archer laughed. "You said it with a smile, so I'll assume fucked-up's your kinda jam."

Atticus barked a laugh. "Never thought of it that way, but maybe."

"You'll have to tell me the full story about the baseball bat and Reese's mom sometime," Archer told him before pointing at a sign. "Gary's is up here on the right."

Atticus pulled into the lot, parking in one of the four available spaces near the front door.

"Well, I guess we should see what Dave and Julie have to say. Since we're here and all," Atticus said, shutting off the truck.

When Atticus got out of the truck, Archer followed, meeting him at the front door of the small office. No sooner did he pull open the door than Slade walked out, a frown marring his features.

"What're you doin' here?" Slade asked Atticus, his tone biting.

"We were followin' a lead."

"We?" Slade glared at Archer. "Since when did y'all become a *we*?"

Uh-oh. Archer wasn't sure what was happening, but he got the feeling that Atticus's complicated relationship involved a very pissed off Slade Elliott.

"Since he accepted the job yesterday," Atticus told him. "Come out here and shut the door."

Archer backed up, giving Slade space to join them rather than share their business with everyone in the office.

"You could've called," Slade said when the door closed. "Told me you were working with him."

"When would I've done that, Slade? We saw each other in the park, I picked his brain about the case, and I asked him to come with me to talk to the owners."

"Why were you in the park?"

Realizing this conversation had a personal undercurrent, Archer walked around to the back of the truck, giving them space. He kept walking until he could no longer make out what they were saying. It was, however, impossible to mistake Slade's tone. He was clearly unhappy with the fact Archer was along for the ride.

"Oh, for fuck's sake, Slade! He's my goddamn partner."

Archer tried to recall the drive in, wondering how long it would take him to walk back to the B&B. An hour. Two? Probably less time than it would take Slade to get over being pissed.

"No, Slade. Dammit." Atticus appeared at the side of the truck. "Archer! Let's go."

While he wasn't used to being ordered around by people he just met, Archer figured now wasn't a good time to argue. Atticus obviously got enough of that with Slade.

Doing his best to look contrite, Archer headed back over, got in the truck. He didn't look at Slade or Atticus, didn't say a word.

It wasn't until they were nearing the B&B fifteen minutes later that Atticus finally spoke up.

"I'm sorry about that."

"Don't apologize. And you don't have to explain."

"Good. Like I said earlier, it's fucked-up." Atticus sighed. "You'll be at the meeting, right?"

"I was summoned, so yeah."

"Well, I guess I'll see you there in a bit."

Not sure what to say, Archer nodded and got out of the truck.

He wasn't surprised when Atticus put his foot to the floor and laid a band of rubber on the road.

Complicated didn't seem to be working all that well for Atticus. Not from what he could tell anyway.

Chapter Twenty-Three

AFTER REESE PROVIDED HIM WITH INFORMATION HE'D originally withheld—which turned out to be not much at all—Brantley went to his office and buried himself in busy work. For the first time in possibly ever, his inbox was almost at zero. Granted, his trash bin was full, but he still deserved kudos for the effort.

It was all he could do to keep his mind occupied because it would've been so easy to start digging into Holt's theories. He wanted to, but Brantley knew it was crucial to bring the team in, get their input before he proceeded. They deserved that much.

Brantley's phone buzzed with a text from Holly.

"Holly said Simon and Archer are here," he informed Reese.

Reese appeared in the doorway of his office, looking at his phone. "RT and Z aren't far behind."

"You ready to do this?"

Reese looked up. "Not sure I'm ready, but it needs to be done."

Brantley understood Reese's reluctance. They were heading down a road they hadn't ventured before. Finding Meredith Prescott would likely be the easy part. Provided she wasn't dead. If that were the case, he doubted anyone would ever find the body. Not if the Adorites were the reason for her disappearance.

"Come on, girl," Reese called to Tesha, who was in the midst of her afternoon nap on her bed between their offices. "Let's go see the gang."

The word *gang* was one of her trigger words, causing her to jump to her feet, tail wagging ninety miles a minute.

Brantley followed Reese and Tesha down the stairs. He started for the refrigerator to get an energy drink, then decided against it at the last second. He didn't need more caffeine. He could already feel his heart pumping faster than it probably should. He settled on a bottle of water instead.

Reese opened the back door, letting Tesha dart out before following. Brantley pulled up the rear, taking a deep breath and preparing for the upcoming conversation.

He would admit he was looking forward to getting fresh eyes on the details they'd uncovered. All of them. The ones Reese had held back, and everything Holt and Simon had identified. Between the lot of them, he was certain they could make sense of it all. And if they couldn't, that was because there wasn't any sense to be had. Which meant Simon would understand there wasn't a story there.

"Hey, boss," Slade called out when they walked into the barn.

"Everyone here?" he replied, mentally doing a roll call as he glanced around the room.

Simon and Archer were standing near the conference room, clearly waiting for an invitation to sit. Evan, Slade, and Becs were sitting at their desks, noses buried in their computers. Luca and Darius were getting the electronic board set up. Jay, Atticus, and Elana were pushing some of the desks out of the way to make room.

"I'm here," Baz noted as he came out of the kitchen, bringing two stainless steel pots of coffee.

"Me, too," Charlie said as she came in behind him with a stack of disposable cups, sugar, and creamer.

"RT and Z will be here in a minute," he informed the team.

"Were y'all able to talk to the principal?" Reese asked Atticus.

"We did." Atticus glanced at Slade, then back at Reese. "Nothing helpful, really. According to her, the statue was there one day, gone the next morning. But we're still workin' on it."

"A statue?" Charlie asked.

"The bronze mustang in front of CRHS," Becs explained.

"It's *missing*?" Charlie's expression shifted between amusement and confusion. "Like it disappeared?"

"Seems that way," Atticus answered.

"Is it a big statue?"

"Yeah. Life-size."

"Really?" Charlie laughed. "How does that happen?"

"That's what they're tryin' to figure out," Reese told her.

"You two workin' it?" She pointed between Atticus and Slade.

"We are," Atticus grumbled.

Charlie's laughter was enough to make Brantley grin. While he sympathized with Atticus, this case couldn't have come at a better time. It gave them something to focus on. Something that wasn't mission-critical since they had important things to tend to at the moment.

"I need everyone down here. Including you, Holly," Brantley said, directing his voice toward the loft.

"Coming!" she called back.

A moment later, she rushed down the stairs carrying an armful of notepads and some pens.

"I know it's the digital age," she said as she dumped her loot on one of the desks. "But personally, I like to jot things down."

"I thought maybe we could record this," Simon said, stepping up beside Brantley. "Unless you've got a problem with it."

Brantley looked at Reese. "You cool with that?"

Reese's response was a curt nod.

"We're working on this together, remember?" Simon stated.

"We are?" Evan asked.

"Who's *we*?" Becs questioned.

Brantley addressed the team. "Archer has officially accepted the offer and will be joining the task force immediately. Simon will be working alongside us on the case we're about to discuss." Brantley glanced at Simon briefly. "Meaning he'll likely be here with us assisting while doing what he does."

"So you'll be recording us?" Elana asked.

"It's part of the process, but I promise, you'll have first listen of everything I do."

That made Brantley feel slightly better.

"Will some of it make it into the podcast?" Becs questioned.

"More than likely," Simon told her before looking at Brantley. "But again, you'll have first listen."

Brantley didn't know what it meant for the recording to make it into the podcast, nor did he care for a lesson on it. Not right now, anyway.

"If everyone could settle, we can get started," Brantley told the team.

Once everyone was sitting, Brantley gestured to Baz.

"Let's start by going through the data we collected when we were looking for—"

His sentence was cut off when the door opened.

Ryan Trexler, a.k.a. RT, walked in. "Sorry we're late. We had to wait for someone."

Z came in behind him.

Brantley was about to ask who they were referring to, but then Z stepped aside, and Decker Bromwell stepped forward.

It took effort, but Brantley managed to avoid grinding his molars to dust as he kept his mouth closed. He had a few things he wanted to say to the man who'd clearly been keeping things from them. But now was not the time or place. Had he not been privy to the information Reese uncovered—the fact Decker went to the same high school as Kylie—he would've wondered why the man bothered to show up now. He only hoped the guy had something to contribute other than excuses.

"Thanks for comin'," Reese said to RT.

"Glad we could be here." He gestured to Decker. "Y'all remember Deck."

A few grumbled greetings sounded from the team.

RT continued with an official introduction. "Deck, this is Archer Halligan. He's the newest member of the team. Archer, meet Decker Bromwell. He's a tenured agent of Sniper 1 Security and a former member of the task force."

"I've heard quite a bit about you," Decker told Archer, shaking his hand.

"All good, I hope."

"So far," Z retorted, reaching out to shake Archer's hand after Decker. "Glad to have you on the team."

"Glad to be here." Archer gestured toward Simon. "This is Simon Jennings."

Z stepped aside so Decker and Simon could shake hands and exchange pleasantries.

Brantley waited patiently. Once they were finished, he motioned for Baz to continue. "It's your show."

"Have a seat. There's coffee if you want it." Baz pointed toward the stainless steel pots on the desk. "We're just getting started."

There was some shifting as people moved around, making room for the newcomers.

"Is JJ gonna join us?" Elana asked Baz.

"Yeah. Could you text her?"

"No need," JJ's voice sounded a second before her face appeared on the big screen. "I'm here."

The team launched into greetings. Brantley found himself smiling as he peered at his best friend. She looked good. A little tired but perhaps a bit less stressed than she had been.

"How're the babies doin'?" Z asked.

Brantley leaned against the wall, watching the interaction. He figured they deserved a few minutes before they were launched headlong into this.

"They're perfect," she answered with a sweet smile. "They're doin' well."

"Will y'all be goin' home soon?"

Her smile widened. "They're optimistic."

All eyes cut to Baz.

"You two breed strong stock, huh?" Z asked Baz.

That resulted in some laughter.

"We do. And while I'd love to flash all the pictures I've got on my phone, I think we should get started."

"Coffee, boss?" Holly asked, her voice low.

Brantley shook his head. He didn't need more caffeine. He had enough adrenaline flooding his system.

Baz tapped the screen on the large board, bringing it to life. Several folders appeared, all containing the information he and Reese had discussed earlier, along with the data that Darius had digitized. Becs had neatly organized it into various folders, all labeled.

"Are we expectin' more company, boss?" Slade asked, drawing everyone's attention to the monitor that reflected the exterior camera views.

"Not that I know of."

"That's Holt," Simon noted. "I told him where we'd be."

"I knew he couldn't resist," Archer said with a chuckle.

They wasted another five minutes introducing Holt to the team and vice versa before finally getting down to the nitty-gritty. By the time Baz started talking again, Brantley could feel his anxiety level soaring. While this seemed like a good idea in theory, he wasn't so sure anymore. At the first mention of Kylie's name, the team got quiet. There was no doubt they were reliving the horrific events as they'd played out not so long ago. Some of them, anyway. A few of the team members were new to both the team and the town, so they weren't there when it all went down. Several others had been born and raised in Coyote Ridge and were up to speed on the details.

"Where should we start?" Baz asked after he provided a high-level overview of the various folders and their contents.

All eyes shifted to him. Brantley wasn't sure why he was the one at the wheel, but he figured it was time they steered this thing in the right direction.

"Meredith Prescott," he told the team. "From all accounts, she seems to be the root of this. She's the reason Holt came up with his theory."

"Who is she?" Atticus asked, his full attention on the screen.

Baz tapped a folder labeled M. PRESCOTT.

"Meredith Aileen Prescott, born February 7, 1962," Baz read. "Mother of Kylie Marie Prescott and Jessica Renee Prescott. Formerly married to Joseph Edgar Prescott from 1983 to 2006. Meredith left in 2005, as soon as Jessie turned 18. The assumption has always been that she left for greener pastures. At least that's what I've been told."

"That's the consensus," Simon agreed.

"Holt's uncovered some information that makes him believe otherwise," Reese said, looking at Holt. "Care to walk us through that?"

Holt nodded.

"You want to drive?" Baz asked, gesturing toward the screen.

Shaking his head, Holt said, "You can."

Brantley listened with half an ear as Holt walked them through his spiel about how he researched things before starting a story and how he ultimately came across Coyote Ridge as the basis—though fictional—of a new series he was writing.

On the screen, Baz pulled up various articles as Holt referred to them.

"Are we lookin' into a real case?" Luca questioned. "Or is this somethin' we're doin' to help Holt with his story?"

"This has nothing to do with what I'm writing," Holt assured him. "There's one article in particular that I came across that piqued my interest. Once I started looking into it, I realized something seemed off about it."

"Which article is that?"

Baz tapped the screen, and an article appeared. The photograph was of the Adorite family. It looked to be one they likely displayed over their mantel, with a smaller photograph overlaying it, this one of Max.

"Is that real?" Atticus asked. "It reads like fiction."

"The article's real, yes," Holt confirmed. "As to the legitimacy of the information, that's yet to be determined."

"It states that Meredith Prescott witnessed Max Adorite kill a man and cites the source as…" Luca looked over at Holt. "The FBI."

"Correct."

"Do we have a timeline set up yet?" Evan asked.

"I've started one," Becs answered.

Baz pulled it up. The data was sparse. They hadn't yet tied together the information in a manner that made sense, and rather than having a significant amount of insignificant data, they usually started small.

"Okay, so that article refers to the Southern Boy Mafia," Z noted. "I guess for the sake of full transparency, it should be noted that Max Adorite's wife, Courtney, is as much a sister to RT as his biological sister, Marissa. Marissa and Courtney have been best friends since they were kids. The Kogans and Trexlers started Sniper 1 Security, and Courtney still plays a part in the everyday business dealings."

"The wife of a mob boss works for a personal protection agency?" Atticus snorted. "Isn't that an oxymoron?"

"You're an oxymoron," Luca teased.

"It's irrelevant," Brantley said before they could get off topic. "Whatever Meredith Prescott did or did not see wouldn't pertain to Courtney at all. She wasn't married to Max at the time."

"It would if it meant bringing down a mafia boss," Slade stated. "If this ends up being true and this woman did see the head of the Southern Boy Mafia kill someone—"

"She didn't," Decker barked, getting to his feet.

Brantley stared at the man, watching Decker's fists clench and unclench at his sides.

The room went quiet, the only movement from Tesha as she stood quickly, moving directly in front of Reese.

"It's cool, girl," Brantley told her, reaching down to pet her head.

She relaxed somewhat, but all eyes, including hers, remained on Decker.

"Didn't what?" Reese inquired.

Decker's nostrils flared as he breathed slowly. "Meredith Prescott did not see anyone kill anyone."

Watching him closely, Reese asked, "And you know this how?"

"Because I know," he seethed.

Something had tripped the man's trigger. One second he was sitting there bored, the next he looked as though fire was going to flame out through his nostrils.

"Elaborate," Brantley instructed, eager to hear what the man had to say.

"No," Decker stated firmly. "Not in front of..." He gestured toward the room.

Perhaps he was already on a hair trigger, but Decker's belligerence and blatant disrespect set Brantley off.

Before he even knew he was reacting, he stood tall, bracing himself for a fight. "Bullshit. You had your chance to tell the fucking truth without an audience. You didn't. So it's high time you tell us everything." He took a step toward Decker. "And if you don't, I'm gonna drag your ass outside and beat it outta you."

Fuck.

Reese started to put a hand on Brantley's arm but stopped himself. Had the team not borne witness to the standoff, he might have. The last thing they needed was a fight, but he wasn't about to stand in Brantley's way. Especially since he understood the man's frustration. They'd been sent to New York City on a wild fucking goose chase and came up empty, and still no one had given them any answers. Hell, Reese hadn't even gotten excuses out of his brother.

"The truth this time, Bromwell," Brantley snapped, his attention jerking to Z. "That goes for you, too."

Z started to get to his feet, but RT held him back with a rigid arm across his chest.

"You brought them into this when you sent them to New York," RT told Z. "They deserve to know the truth."

"What truth?" Baz asked, moving around the room to stand beside Brantley, as though facing off with Decker and Z.

Shit. Shit. Shit.

Standing tall, Reese positioned himself between them. "Obviously, there are details we don't have. Which is the whole reason for this meeting." He looked at Decker. "If you've got something pertinent to this case, we need to know what it is." He looked at Brantley. "We're gonna keep this civil. We have to."

Brantley's eyes narrowed, but a moment later, he nodded, his shoulders relaxing.

Reese exhaled his relief. The last thing he wanted was a knock-down, drag-out. Sure, it might be warranted, but the team did not need to be witnesses to it.

"Tell them," Z hissed, relaxing in his chair.

Decker slowly sat down. He was silent for several beats before finally speaking, his tone cooler than before. "Kylie's mother did not witness a mob hit."

"You sound certain," Evan said, resting his elbows on the desk.

"I am."

"How do you know this?" Reese probed.

Another lengthy pause filled the room with the loudest silence Reese had heard in a long damn time.

"Because Eddie was with me the night she supposedly saw it."

Son of a bitch.

Reese recognized the name. He looked over at Brantley and saw the same recognition in his husband's eyes. Eddie was the name of the person Decker had been talking to when they found him in New York outside of the brownstone.

"Eddie? I thought we were talking about Meredith. Who the—"

Charlie cut Atticus off. "Eddie's a nickname for Meredith."

"Oh." Atticus's eyes widened. "Wait. You were *with* her?"

Decker glared at Atticus, not confirming or denying.

Slade sat up, his bored expression sliding away. "Like y'all were hangin' out? Or y'all were…?"

"We're talkin' about the same person, right?" Reese asked. "Meredith Prescott. Kylie's mother."

"Yes," Decker said through clenched teeth.

"For fuck's sake. Tell them the fuckin' story," Z bellowed, elbowing Decker.

"Kylie and I went to school together from the third grade until graduation," Decker explained. "Her mom was a teacher. Ninth grade English. That's when I met her."

"Met who? Kylie? Or her mom?" JJ asked.

"Eddie," Decker clarified.

"Were you and Kylie friends?" Reese asked.

"Not so much friends. Acquaintances, I guess you could say."

"You hooked up with the teacher," Darius stated. Not a question.

"Yeah. I started … *seeing* her when I was in ninth grade. We continued to see each other even after I graduated."

"I assume *seeing* is a euphemism for *fucking*," Luca noted, looking downright disgusted by the idea.

"You were dating your teacher?" Evan asked, his tone lacking any judgment. That was the detective in him, seeking answers without formulating an opinion.

"I was in love with her," Decker countered. "And she was in love with me."

Reese was grateful the peanut gallery kept their opinions to themselves that time.

"Were you and Kylie the same age?" Baz asked.

"Yes."

It was obvious everyone was doing the math, but Reese had already figured it out for himself. Decker would've been roughly fourteen when he started having a sexual relationship with his thirty-six-year-old teacher.

Brantley spoke up. "What did Kylie think about you fucking her thirty-six-year-old married mother?"

"She didn't know. We kept it on the DL."

"How's that even possible?" Atticus asked. "You're tellin' us no one ever saw the two of you together?"

"No."

"Where were these *dates* taking place?" Evan asked, sounding like the detective he was.

"I'm not on trial here," Decker countered hotly.

Evan replied easily. "Maybe not, but if you expect us to believe you were having a sexual relationship with a married teacher for four plus years and no one knew about it, we're gonna need more to go on."

Reese appreciated Evan's candor, as well as his professional demeanor.

"My dad was an alcoholic," Decker said, his tone laced with fury. "When he wasn't on the road and he wasn't beating on me, he was out getting drunk. Most of the time, he was too fucked up to find his way to the house."

"Meredith Pres—*Eddie*," Evan corrected. "Was coming over to your house and having sex with you in your childhood bedroom."

"It wasn't like I had Superman posters on my fucking walls," Decker snapped. "You try living with an alcoholic asshole and you'll see how fucking fast you grow up."

Reese could see Decker unraveling, knew they needed to pull this back some.

"So you and Eddie had a relationship for several years. You mentioned she did not witness a mob hit. I assume you're her alibi for the night in question," Reese mused.

"You could say that," Decker said, looking at him for the first time. "Or you could say that I'm the reason the asshat FBI got their hooks in Eddie in the first place."

"Blackmail," Brantley said softly.

"Yeah." Decker exhaled heavily. "There is no night in question. To my knowledge, Max didn't kill anyone. At the time, his father, Samuel, was the head of the Adorite Crime Family. Max would've been nineteen years old."

"Doesn't mean he wasn't capable of killing someone," Baz noted.

"Sure he was," Decker acknowledged. "But on the night in question, Eddie wasn't strolling by some warehouse downtown. She didn't happen upon a hit." He swallowed hard, his eyes locked on the wall. "She was in bed with me. At my apartment, roughly twenty miles away."

"Is this before or after she walked out on her husband and kids?" Brantley asked, and there was no disguising his disgust for Decker.

"Before. Eddie wanted to wait until Jessie graduated from high school before divorcing Joe. She didn't love him but was trying to do right by her kids."

"By fucking you on the side." Brantley snorted. "Keep tellin' yourself that."

Decker narrowed his eyes on Brantley. "I don't have to explain my actions to you, asshole."

"The hell you don't," Brantley bit out, stepping forward. "If there's even a remote chance you're responsible for this..."

All eyes were on Brantley as he trailed off, making his way to the door.

"What?" Decker shouted. "If there's a chance, then *what?*"

Reese watched Brantley walk out the door without looking back.

"Give us a minute," he told Baz before following.

Chapter Twenty-Four

"SOMEONE WANNA TELL ME WHAT WE'RE MISSIN' here?" Atticus asked when Reese tore out the door after Brantley.

"That could've gone better," RT noted, glaring at Z.

"Hey. Don't look at me. I'm just the messenger."

"Seriously. What're we missin'?" Atticus repeated, looking around the room.

Surely, he wasn't the only one surprised by Brantley's reaction. The man was always cool and calm in situations such as this. Yet, it was like he'd been in a pressure cooker for hours and was about to blow. Or maybe a teakettle and the whistle was getting louder and louder and...

Whatever it was, Atticus wanted to know what the hell set their boss off like that.

"Give them a minute to talk," Baz said to the room, his expression as bewildered as Atticus felt.

"Do *you* know what's goin' on here?" Atticus asked Slade.

"Not a clue."

"I feel like we're watchin' two different movies and only seeing clips of each one," Becs said, eyes wide as she stared at Decker Bromwell.

Yeah. That was a good way to put it.

"The objective of this meeting is to bring the team up to speed," Baz stated. "Since Brantley and Reese know the basics, I'd like to continue."

The room quieted, and all attention shifted to Baz.

"I have a question," Atticus said, raising his hand, then putting it down. "You said Meredith couldn't have been at the scene because she was with you. Did someone mistake her for someone else?"

Everyone looked to Decker for an answer.

"No. Someone made up the whole thing," Decker said, sounding defeated.

"Hold up," Baz said. "We *do* need to wait for Brantley and Reese to return to hear *this*."

"I'll text them," Holly offered.

"No," several people shouted at once.

Holly's eyes widened. "Okay."

"Give them a few minutes," RT told the room. "Everyone, take a break. Let's reconvene in fifteen."

Atticus stood. "Come on, Tesha. Let's stretch our legs. Wanna play ball?"

She was up on all fours in an instant, her tail snapping happily.

He led the way outside, making his way to the small bucket that held half a dozen tennis balls. He grabbed one, waited for Tesha to pay attention, then lobbed it as far as he could, giving her a chance to run.

"You avoiding me?"

Turning, he saw Slade walking his way.

"What? You just watched me come outside."

"Doesn't mean you're not avoidin' me."

Atticus remained calm, reminded himself that Slade was simply being Slade.

"Why would I?"

Slade shrugged one shoulder. "Don't know."

"You worry too much."

"Do I?"

Atticus smiled when Tesha came charging back, ball in her mouth. "Sit," he instructed.

She sat.

"Drop it."

She dropped the ball.

"Good girl." He gave her head a rub before reaching for the ball and throwing it again.

"It just seems—"

"It doesn't," Atticus interrupted, turning to face Slade. "It doesn't seem like anything. I'm not ignoring you. I'm not upset. I'm not anything. We're at work. We've got things to focus on. I assure you, if I were mad at you, I'd let you know."

"Would you?"

Clamping his teeth together, Atticus turned back to Tesha. They went through the motions again until she was darting after the ball.

"I—"

"Slade," Atticus said slowly. "I can't do this right now."

"Can't do what?"

"The insecurity. If you can't trust me for a day, I'm not sure why we're even tryin' this."

Slade's mouth opened, then closed again. Atticus could see the pain in his eyes, the fear. Whoever hurt him did a serious number on the guy. But as much as he wanted to heal him, to prove to him that not everyone was out to cause him pain, Atticus wasn't sure how. And he certainly wasn't sure how to do that and work with the guy at the same time.

"Right now, let's focus. Once this"—he gestured toward the barn—"is done, we need to keep followin' leads and find that statue so we can move on with our lives."

"Move on? Is that—"

"Stop," he snapped under his breath. "Just. Stop."

Taking a deep breath, he turned toward Tesha, smiling as she jogged toward him.

"Come on, girl. Let's get you some water so we can get back to work."

"YOU READY TO HEAD BACK OVER THERE?"

Brantley stared blankly at the wall. "I'm not sure what I want right now."

He wasn't sure whether he should feel bad that Reese was perched on the back of the couch, shoulders slightly hunched, looking utterly defeated, but he did. Guilty was probably a better word for it. He wasn't one to lose his cool often—or liked to think he wasn't—but he was definitely dangerously close to the edge today. And Reese obviously knew because Brantley could feel the concern wafting off him. The man was watching him like he was a caged animal whose door was about to be opened. He wasn't too far off because that was exactly what he felt like. Only thing was, he wasn't sure why.

"I know you're pissed at Deck. I get it. He kept information from us."

"Vital information," Brantley pointed out.

"Yes. What we don't know is why he did. I'm sure he has a valid reason."

"You really think so?" Brantley pivoted, dropping his arms to his sides. "The guy was in New York talking to the woman he'd been screwing since he was a kid." A shudder ran through him at the thought. "A woman who everyone claims is missing. You think Z and Decker wanted us chasing our asses in New York for a reason other than that?"

"I'm not sure Z—"

"Don't," Brantley bit out. "Do not defend your brother right now."

"I'm not."

Brantley grunted. "He obviously knew Decker was up to something when he sent us up there."

"I'm not arguing with you."

No, he wasn't. And that was the problem. Brantley was itching for a fight.

"He was with her," Brantley stated.

Reese's forehead creased. "Who?"

"Deck. With Meredith. *Eddie*. Whatever the fuck you wanna call her. She was in New York. Right under our noses."

"We didn't know about her at the time."

"Maybe we should have. For fuck's sake, maybe we *could* have if Z hadn't kept us in the dark. At some point, your brother needs to be upfront with us about his agenda. He's got one. The man doesn't do much without a plan."

"I agree."

"So what is it? What the fuck is Z up to? Did he hope we'd stumble upon Deck and Meredith? Did he expect us to tow her back here, though we didn't even know who she was? Or was that supposed to be a field trip to help us with this moment? Maybe your brother's fucking psychic."

Brantley grabbed his head, tipping it forward as he paced. He didn't expect answers to those questions, and he didn't get any. They remained in silence for a moment while Brantley tried to cool the fire in his veins.

He stopped and turned to look at Reese. "Why? Why does this piss me off so much?"

"Because it dredges up painful memories."

It did that. Really painful memories. Losing Kylie had been … he couldn't even put it into words.

"It would be so much easier to just pass this off to someone else. To ignore it. To pretend Holt didn't find anything. How is finding her gonna benefit us? How is taking down some corrupt FBI agents—alleged—gonna help us?"

"It might not. But that's not who we are. We have to see this through, no matter the outcome. Like it or not, Meredith Prescott is family. She's your cousin's wife's mother."

"His dead wife," Brantley grumbled, choking the emotion that clogged his throat whenever he thought about it.

"We'll work this the same way we do all the others. With an open mind."

He didn't bother telling Reese that he could not be open-minded about a woman who'd taken advantage of a fourteen-year-old boy. That was disgusting, and he wasn't sure he'd ever get past it. However, he could find her, bring her home, and figure out what kept her running all these years.

Brantley nodded. "All right. Let's get this over with."

He followed Reese back to the barn. As soon as they walked in, the team took their seats. Brantley could feel their concern, knew they were wondering when he was going to flip his lid.

"Let's pick up where we left off," Baz said, taking control of the meeting. "Decker, you mentioned someone made up the story of Meredith seeing Max."

Brantley looked from face to face, wondering if they'd continued the conversation while he was gone.

"Yeah." Decker held a cup of coffee. "As I said, Eddie was with me that night. At my apartment."

"You're saying there wasn't a witness to a hit?" Simon asked, driving the back-and-forth between him and Decker.

"Since we were told Eddie would testify exactly as instructed, I'm fairly sure there wasn't a hit at all."

"Told by who?"

"The FBI."

"What's the agent's name?"

"Martin Calloway."

"He approached you?"

"No. Eddie said he cornered her when she was leaving school." Decker's gaze dropped to his coffee cup. "Told her she had two choices: testify that she saw Max kill someone or go to prison, and the world would find out she had sex with a minor."

"You were over eighteen at the time, correct?" Evan asked.

"There's no statute of limitations on statutory rape," JJ noted.

Decker ignored her. "Yeah. I'd graduated already. I was an adult."

"But not for the four years you were in high school," Brantley stated, distraught by the thought. "And we all know sex with a minor is illegal."

Decker shot him a glare. "Her career would've been over if it got out."

"Did she really give a shit?" Brantley snapped. "Or was she scared her ass would've been put in jail for having sex with a child?"

"It wasn't like that," Decker argued.

"The fuck it wasn't. You were fourteen. The same fucking age as her daughter, for Christ's sake. She was in her goddamn thirties, Decker. That's a fucking felony."

Decker's jaw bunched, and Brantley could tell he was holding back his rage. Barely.

"Worst case, it was indecency with a child," Decker said through clenched teeth.

Oh for fuck's sake. It made Brantley's stomach turn that the guy had already looked up the penalties for it.

"You mean *best* case," Evan corrected.

Reese cleared his throat. "Let's move on."

"We were gonna get married," Decker said when the room remained silent.

Brantley snorted. "She was already married, you asshole. She had kids. Did you ever think about them? Fuck no. Because you were a kid."

He did not like that Decker didn't seem concerned about Kylie's family at all.

"Her marriage was over already."

Brantley bit his tongue. His comments were getting them nowhere. It didn't matter what Decker said; Brantley would never be okay with this. Never. Meredith Prescott should be in prison for her actions.

Simon sat up straight, his full attention on Decker. "Did Martin Calloway have anything to back up his threat?"

"Pictures."

"Of you and Eddie," Simon clarified.

"Yeah."

"I assume these were compromising photos."

"They were. When we first got together, I took pictures of her ... of us *together*. There might be a video or two."

Jesus. Brantley didn't know Meredith Prescott, but he knew for a fact he didn't like her.

"Where'd he get them?" Simon continued.

Decker glared at the man. "From me."

"How's that possible?"

"Because I took them."

"So you said. But how'd he get them?"

"My father. He found them in my bedroom." Decker sighed. "Martin Calloway is an equal opportunity blackmailer. Eddie wasn't the only person this asshole had by the short and curlies."

"Do you know where he is? The agent?" Archer asked.

"Probably sittin' on his fat ass in his office in Dallas."

"What was he blackmailing your dad for?" Evan asked.

"Trafficking narcotics."

Brantley stood up straight. "That's a serious offense."

"Yeah. And an easy one to pin on a long-haul truck driver with a record of alcohol abuse and child neglect," Decker stated, disdain weaving through every word. "I'll admit, he was a shitty father. No doubt about that. But he was not trafficking narcotics."

"I pulled up Special Agent Martin Calloway," Luca told the team, gesturing toward the large screen. "Looks like he was part of a task force working a RICO case involving the Adorites in the late nineties. Nothing ever came of it, though."

JJ picked up where he stopped. "He's currently assigned to the Dallas field office, assistant special agent in charge, handling transnational organized crime."

Luca continued to type, his fingers flying across his keyboard. "Oh, shit, boss."

"What?"

"It looks like Martin Calloway's a member of Censorious."

"Really?" JJ asked, sounding intrigued. "I didn't think they existed anymore."

A moment later, more data came on the screen.

"What's Censorious?" Atticus asked before Brantley could.

Simon got to his feet, moving closer to the screen as he spoke. "It's a group of vigilante LEOs who believe they're above the law. They see themselves as judge, jury, and executioner. But they disbanded back in 2007."

"What's a LEO again?" Holly inquired.

"Law enforcement officer," several people replied.

"They didn't dissolve completely," Luca said. "From this, it looks like they scattered for a bit but came back together with new leadership in 2014. And guess who's at the top of their leadership roster?"

"I assume that's rhetorical," Z said.

"It'll take some time," Luca continued, "but I can get more information."

"Do that," Brantley told him.

"On it, boss."

"Where's Meredith now?" Simon asked Decker.

"She's working as a caretaker in New York."

Brantley hoped like hell there wasn't a teenage kid in the house.

Irritated at Decker and Meredith Prescott, Brantley went for the jugular. "If Eddie's alive and well, then she was what? Too busy to come to her daughter's funeral?"

Decker's head snapped over, eyes blazing fire. "Fuck no. She wanted to be here."

"Why wasn't she?"

"Calloway's still looking for her."

"So?" Brantley shrugged. "She's no longer teaching. What does it matter if they out her for screwing teenagers?"

The muscles in Decker's jaw flexed and bunched. He was harnessing his anger, but Brantley suspected it wouldn't take much to push him over the edge at this point. Brantley knew he was getting under the man's skin. Since that was his goal, he considered it progress.

When Decker didn't speak, Brantley looked at Simon. "I guess there's not a story here after all."

"I have a question," Baz said, once again standing at the screen, tapping away. "Luca, back when the team was in New York, you created this folder."

Luca looked up. "I did, yeah. I can't remember right off how I came across her. I made a note because something seemed off. Can't remember what, though."

"Across who?" Becs asked.

Baz pointed at a Post-it note icon with the initials AB. He tapped it, and a photograph of a woman appeared.

"Allison Bogart," Luca answered.

"Who is she?" Atticus asked.

"She was one of our new hires," Reese explained. "She worked one case with us, then disappeared."

"You hired an FBI agent?" Decker asked.

"She's not FBI," Brantley stated. "She worked with the Dallas Police Department. Special Victims Unit."

"The hell she did," Decker argued. "She's a surveillance specialist with the FBI."

Brantley looked at Reese. What the fuck?

Chapter Twenty-Five

"HOW DO YOU KNOW SHE'S FBI?" REESE asked Decker, confused by the turn of events.

"Because she told me."

"Did you know about this?" Brantley asked.

"That Luca had tied her to this?" Reese nodded. "But I had no idea she was FBI."

He felt the familiar itch of guilt on the back of his neck. He hated that they'd kept that information from Brantley. At the time, he hadn't seen another way. The man he loved was headstrong and fierce, and he didn't doubt for one second that Brantley would've put the wedding on hold in order to chase a lead.

"I thought you said she was a new hire," Atticus noted, looking at Reese before his gaze moved to Decker. "Weren't you a new hire, too?"

"Decker didn't come on board until a month after everyone else," Reese explained. "He was finishing up an assignment."

"Was that intentional?" Brantley asked, spitting the words at Z. "Did you hold him back so their paths didn't cross?"

Z was about to answer, but RT shook his head, silencing him.

"Apparently, he pleads the fifth." Atticus pursed his lips. "Still doesn't make sense, but okay."

"Tell us how you know Bogart," Brantley commanded.

Decker glanced around, then got a nod to continue from RT.

"I met her while I was in Dallas. She told me she was FBI, working on a special assignment." Decker rolled his eyes. "A case against Max Adorite. She wanted to know if I knew Eddie's whereabouts because they had some questions for her."

Reese was beginning to think Holt's theory about a conspiracy wasn't all that far off. Or perhaps it was spot on because something was clearly not right.

"When was this?" Simon inquired.

"I don't know. Before Z assigned me to work for the task force."

Archer got to his feet, his gaze locked on the screen. "I've seen that woman before."

"Where?" Reese asked.

Archer made his way across the room. "May I?" he asked Baz, gesturing toward the screen.

"Go ahead."

Reese watched, along with the rest of the team, as Archer flipped through images. He stopped on one and enlarged it before stepping aside. "She was at the funeral."

"Where'd you get those photos?" Brantley asked.

"They come from various people. We skimmed through social media accounts, gathered up the ones we could find. It's how we usually identify players," Simon explained.

Impressive. That was precisely what they would've done, but they had programs to do that for them. Which was another reason Reese thought it would be a good idea for Simon to become an official member of the task force. He would have access to the same tools they did.

"There's another one," Archer noted. "She's wearing a hat and glasses. I assume it was a disguise if she wasn't expected at the funeral."

Definitely a disguise. Reese didn't recall seeing her, and considering how she'd disappeared, he would have.

"We saw her, too," Baz said, his gaze shifting between him and Brantley. "At the diner a few days before the wedding."

Brantley looked his way, accusation in his eyes.

"This is the first I'm hearing of it," he told him.

Brantley's attention returned to Baz. "Who was she with?"

"No one."

"Did you confront her?"

"JJ wanted to, but I asked her to leave it alone until after the wedding." His gaze shifted to the monitor where JJ's face was filling the screen. "Want to add anything to that?"

She shook her head. "I'm takin' notes. I've got a ton of questions, but I figure now's not the time."

"If it's pertinent, ask," Brantley told her.

"I will." She gestured toward the screen. "We did see her, and yeah, I wanted to confront her, but Baz convinced me not to. I disagreed, but he was right. We had too much going on at the time."

Brantley stood. "I need someone to create a timeline of events, starting with Meredith Prescott being approached by the FBI. Fill in everything we have from Holt's research. Use dates from articles if they're related. We'll meet back up tomorrow to continue this. If you've got anything that's hot, keep on it. Otherwise, help Becs and Darius with this."

Reese wasn't surprised that Brantley ended the meeting abruptly. They'd received a lot of information. Probably too much to actually do anything with until they had time to sort it out.

"I'll be at the house," Brantley said before walking out, not saying anything to anyone else.

Reese sighed.

"He okay?" RT asked, his expression reflecting his concern.

"It's a lot."

"It is."

"When are y'all goin' back?" Reese asked his brother-in-law.

"Not until we've got this situation sorted."

"You have a place to stay?"

"We're staying at the B and B." RT grinned. "I think your brother wants to buy a farmhouse."

Reese laughed. "Does he now?"

"He mentioned it last night. Said we should invest in a farmhouse and adopt a few dozen kids."

"Sounds like my brother."

"Look," RT said softly, his tone serious. "I apologize for what went down. I had no idea Z was sending your team to New York. And I damn sure didn't know it was to find Decker. He kept that part from me."

"I take it Decker wasn't missing?"

"Not so much missing, I don't think. More like off the grid. Your brother was worried, and I think he suspected something was up."

"How?"

"We've got quite a bit of information about Decker's past. More than you do. We knew about the connection to Kylie. Same high school and all that. But I figured it was purely coincidence."

Reese would've assumed that as well, but as Brantley would say, there's no such thing as a coincidence.

"Again," RT said. "I'm sorry."

"Don't apologize." Reese met his gaze. "But I would appreciate you and Z helping us to figure this out."

"We're here until you don't need us anymore."

"Thanks." He gestured toward the door. "I should go check on Brantley."

RT nodded. "Let me know if I can help."

Without a word to the team, Reese slipped out with Tesha, leaving them to discuss details. He knew that once they put their heads together, they would likely make sense of it all. He wasn't sure it would result in a story for Simon to tell, but they would figure that out soon enough.

He hoped.

RATHER THAN SPEND THE NEXT TWO HOURS fretting over shit they couldn't control, Brantley suggested they visit JJ. He needed some time to cool his heels, and this was the perfect way to do that. And because he wanted to spend some alone time with Reese, they left Tesha at home to rest.

"I'll bet you a blowjob that there are at least a dozen vases in that room," Brantley told Reese as they walked through the hospital toward JJ's room.

Reese coughed.

"Your face is red. Does that embarrass you?"

"Behave," Reese whispered as they passed one of the nurse's stations.

"I am behaving. I haven't dragged you into one of these storage closets yet, have I?"

A nurse looked up, grinning.

"Brantley," Reese drawled.

Laughing, Brantley kept his mouth shut until they reached the door to JJ's room. He knocked softly, not sure what state she would be in. After he left the meeting, he shot her a text to let her know they would be coming up to see her unless she didn't want them to. Her response had been: **Come. And bring a chocolate shake.**

They'd brought both chocolate and strawberry in case she changed her mind before they got there.

"Come in," JJ called from inside.

Brantley opened the door and gestured Reese in first.

As soon as he saw the forest of flowers, all sitting pretty in their giant glass vases, Brantley cleared his throat and nudged Reese.

"Stop it," Reese muttered.

"Is it hot outside?" JJ asked, shifting so that she was sitting up.

"Not unusually. Why?" Brantley asked.

JJ pointed at Reese. "Your face is red."

Brantley choked on a laugh.

"Chocolate *and* strawberry," Reese said, lifting the bag, clearly wanting to change the subject.

"You know me so well." She smiled, and it reached her eyes.

"You're in a good mood," Brantley acknowledged, making his way to her bedside.

"I have two beautiful, strong babies. Of course I'm in a good mood." She took the sack from Reese, opened it. "What did you think of that meeting?"

Brantley shook his head. He honestly didn't want to discuss it. He needed time to process.

"I don't really know what to think right now," Reese told her.

"I think I'm glad I wasn't there." Her nose scrunched. "Decker was fourteen?"

If he didn't want to discuss the meeting, Brantley damn sure didn't want to think about *that*, so he changed the subject. "The team's workin' on getting the information together. I think we'll know which direction to go tomorrow."

Her green gaze was inquisitive. "I didn't realize there was a direction."

"This is Simon's deal. If there's a story, I don't think it's the one he started out thinking it was."

"Finding Meredith Prescott?" JJ put the straw in her mouth, sucked on it as she shook her head. "No. I don't think so, either. But there's something."

"Did Baz make it back yet?" he asked, looking around, changing the subject again.

"Yeah. He's with Wes. They're checking on the babies."

"Any updates from the doctor?"

JJ's eyes glittered, and Brantley was positive that was hope he saw reflected there.

"They're doin' better than expected. The doctor said they might change the minimum from ten days to seven."

"Well, that's good news."

"I know, right?" Her eyes teared up. "I can't wait to get them home."

"Do these babies have names yet?" Reese asked, dropping into a chair near the bed.

JJ sighed. "I can't decide."

"What are you working with?" Brantley perched on the corner of the bed.

Laughing, she said, "Too much and not enough."

"Why not name the boy after Baz?"

"Uh … no," she said emphatically. "Sebastian's too long."

"What's his middle name?"

"Wayne," she said, scrunching her nose again. "So that's a definite no."

Brantley chuckled. "Does Baz have any suggestions?"

"He likes Naomi and Noah."

Brantley considered those for a moment. "Very nice names."

"They are, but…" JJ shrugged. "I really like Naomi." Her face took on a dreamy expression. "But I'm not so sure about Noah."

"What are you leaning toward?"

"Nothing."

"Naomi and Nothing," Brantley mused. "Not sure it works."

JJ laughed, setting her cup on the table. "Shut it."

"Help us out here, Reese," Brantley told him. "Pull up some names."

"That start with the letter N," JJ instructed.

Reese pulled out his phone and tapped the screen a few times. "How about … Neil?"

"Nope," JJ said instantly.

"Norton?"

JJ shook her head.

"Northrop?"

Her head tilted. "Be serious."

Reese laughed. "What about Nolan?"

"I've considered it, but I'm not sold."

"Nicolas?"

"Too common."

"Newton? Neville?"

JJ stuck out her tongue.

"Ned?"

"No."

Reese continued to look at the screen. A moment later, he looked up and said, "Nathan."

JJ opened her mouth but closed it before a sound came out.

"Naomi and Nathan," Brantley said, getting a feel for the sound. "I think that works."

"It kinda does," JJ agreed, but he could tell she wasn't ready to pen them on the birth certificates.

"You've got a little time." He patted her knee. "You and Baz can toss them around."

She reached for her milkshake. "We will, I'm sure."

The door opened behind him, so Brantley got to his feet.

"Hey, Wes," he greeted Baz's father, shaking his hand when he walked in. "How's it goin'?"

"I've got two beautiful grandbabies. How do you think it's goin'?"

Brantley smiled. He'd gotten a text from Iris earlier saying pretty much the same thing. Granted, JJ wasn't her biological daughter, but he knew she thought of her as family. Which meant she got to be the surrogate grandmother.

"I think I'm gonna head home," Wes said as he walked over to JJ. He leaned down and hugged her. "You need anything at all, just holler."

"I will," she said, her cheeks pink. "Thank you."

Brantley stood back until Wes slipped out of the room.

"Have they said when you get to go home?"

"Tomorrow," JJ answered. "I could probably go today, but I'm milking it to be close to the babies."

"Don't blame you there."

"But we aren't going home exactly," JJ noted. "We've booked a room at the hotel behind the hospital. Nothing fancy, but it allows me to be here until the babies are released."

He looked at Baz. "Well, that's good, right?"

"It is. It allows me to work a few more days, too. Once they come home, I'll want to be there."

"Of course you will," Reese told him. "Just remember, you can always work remotely. Not that you should," he tacked on quickly. "But it's an option."

"I know."

"We should probably get going, too," Brantley said, wanting to give them some time alone. He doubted they got much with the nurses coming in and out.

"Wait," JJ said as Reese got to his feet. "We wanted to ask you somethin'."

Baz moved closer to JJ, taking her hand when she reached for it.

Brantley waited patiently as they traded glances and smiles.

"You ask them," JJ told Baz.

Baz looked up, met Brantley's gaze. "We wanted to know if you'd be the babies' godfather." Baz looked at Reese. "Both of you."

Brantley grinned. "I'm in for sure."

"Of course we will," Reese said, moving to stand beside Brantley. "We'd be honored."

"Yeah. What he said."

"Perfect." JJ clapped softly. "Now you can go."

"Wow. You're in a rush to get us outta here, huh?"

"It's the first time all day that I've had the chance to have this man all to myself. I'd like to take advantage of that."

"Eww." Brantley grimaced dramatically.

"Shut up." JJ laughed.

"Talk to him about the names," Brantley ordered, pointing between them as he made his way to the door. "They'll need them to get outta here."

With that, he jerked his chin toward the door, smiling at Reese.

And for that brief moment, he forgot about all the other shit they were dealing with and simply enjoyed a few moments with his husband.

It wasn't until they neared the elevator that Brantley grabbed Reese's hand and tugged him down the narrow corridor.

"What are you doing?" Reese rasped.

"Taking advantage of the situation."

"There is no situation," Reese hissed, attempting to pull free from his grasp.

Brantley tried the knob on the first door they came to and found it locked. He tried the next and grinned when it turned.

Slowly opening the door, he peeked inside to find what appeared to be a cleaning supply storage area. It was neatly organized and exactly the sort of spot he was looking for.

He manhandled Reese into the room and closed the door.

"Brantley, we can't—"

"You should stand here," Brantley told him, pushing Reese against the door.

"Why?"

"In case someone needs in here."

"Brantley," Reese drawled. "We can't d—"

"We can and we are," he insisted.

He effectively silenced his husband by crushing his mouth to his. There was a moment of surprise, but then Reese was kissing him back, hard and hungry. Within seconds, Brantley unbuttoned his jeans and lowered the zipper, eager and desperate to get his cock into Reese's mouth.

Gripping Reese's jaw, he pulled back, met his stare. He let the emotions of the day free, driving his need for a distraction. He channeled the frustration and disappointment into a hot, desperate hunger. The only thing that would sate him was this man.

"I want to fuck this beautiful mouth," he growled softly, swiping Reese's bottom lip with his thumb. "I *need* to fuck this beautiful mouth."

Reese's golden eyes glazed over.

"Now, Reese. Get on your knees and suck me."

He watched as his husband slid down the door, their gazes locked the entire time. Brantley backed up only enough to give Reese room to position himself. Then, fisting Reese's hair tightly, he guided his cock past those plump lips and into the heated cavern of his mouth.

"Oh, fuck, yes," he hissed when Reese sucked him in deep. "Suck me, baby. Make me crazy."

Reese took over from there, fisting the base of Brantley's dick, stroking in tandem with the heated pulls on the sensitive head. Inundated with pleasure, Brantley let it consume him, wiping away the stress, eliminating the worry. He got lost in the man he loved.

"Damn, I love that mouth," he mumbled under his breath as he stared down at Reese. "It feels so fucking good. Ah, yeah. Suck me deep, Reese."

He pumped his hips, pushing in deeper. Reese seemed to know what he needed because his hand fell away, allowing Brantley to push into his throat.

"Can you take more of me?" he groaned, overwhelmed.

Reese's answer was in the glittering gold of his eyes and the surrender he saw there.

Holding Reese's head with both hands, Brantley shifted so that he could fuck Reese's face. He took what the man offered, letting the intense pleasure overtake every nerve ending until he was precariously hovering at the brink. He remained there for several seconds, grunting as he drove his cock into Reese's mouth again and again.

"Oh, fuck, baby. I'm gonna come." He growled softly, trying to be quiet but too far gone to give a shit who might hear them. "Swallow!"

Reese's throat closed around him, triggering a mind-blowing orgasm. It was all Brantley could do to remain on his feet as his cock pulsed and spurted.

He stumbled back, catching himself before he crashed into a metal shelf. Reese was on his feet, grabbing his shirt and jerking him forward. The man's mouth sealed over his, and he tasted himself on Reese's tongue. It spurred more desire, but he refrained. He knew without asking that Reese would balk at the idea of fucking him in that closet, although Brantley would've gladly bent over just to feel his husband inside him.

"Let's get home," Reese said when some of the intensity waned.

"Only if you promise to fuck me as soon as we get there."

Reese smirked. "You'll be lucky if we even make it inside."

Chapter Twenty-Six

SLADE WAS LYING IN BED, STARING UP at the dark ceiling, when he heard the front door open.

After their meeting, he'd helped Becs with a few things, but found that there were too many hands in the pot after a while. Rather than start another fight, he'd slipped out while Atticus was talking to Archer. He knew it wasn't rational, but the jealousy had been eating a hole through him all afternoon.

On top of that, he felt like an ass.

Then again, he kinda was an ass. Or he had been to Atticus earlier when he'd harped on the man about avoiding him. It hadn't taken Atticus five seconds to get fed up with it, and honestly, Slade couldn't blame him. He was doing it again. Being too needy, too clingy. It wouldn't be long before Atticus decided it was too much for him.

And it wasn't the first time in the past couple of days that Slade had fucked up. He'd practically accused Atticus of thinking Archer Halligan was hot. It was more of a kick in the pants that Atticus hadn't even been thinking about their newest addition to the team. The guy was Atticus's partner, for fuck's sake. That didn't mean they were going to have a secret rendezvous. Yet, for some fucked up reason, Slade's insecurity got the best of him and when he looked at the two of them together, that was all he could think about.

Well, that and how he was going to make it up to Atticus.

Unfortunately, he didn't think that would happen tonight.

It wasn't until he was home that Atticus sent him a text to let him know he was having dinner with Carson. There was no invite, but Slade hadn't expected one. He'd really fucked up this time.

Now, as he lay there, he wondered whether Atticus had come back alone or if Carson was with him. He didn't care enough to get up to look.

Okay, that was a lie. He cared enough. But he wasn't a glutton for punishment. Not tonight, anyway. If Atticus was leading Carson to his bedroom, he didn't want to know about it. Best to go to sleep and find out tomorrow.

But he wasn't perfect, so he listened intently, trying to capture the sound of footsteps that might tell him how many feet were moving down the hallway. He heard nothing except for the rapid beat of his heart as anxiety flooded his system.

Slade wasn't sure how much longer he could do this. Every single day, he found himself balancing on pins and needles, waiting to find out which way the wind was going to blow so he'd know which direction to move. He was in this vicious cycle, waiting to find out what Atticus did or did not want from him. When they were together, he didn't wonder; he simply savored every second. When they were apart, he felt as though he was seconds from being pulled in two.

He'd considered confronting Atticus, asking him point-blank where he saw this going. But what if he was the only one who cared? What if Atticus saw him as the pain in the ass who needed more than a good fuck to feel like he was worth a shit? Slade didn't want to be that guy. He was trying to go with the flow, to ignore his feelings, even as they intensified.

Truth was, he was pathetic. A sap who wasn't built to sustain casual sexual encounters. It was the reason he'd never been able to maintain a real relationship. He was too needy, too—

A sharp knock sounded on his bedroom door a second before the knob turned. He didn't even have time to call out before the door swung open.

"For fuck's sake," Slade hissed, sitting up straight, eyes locked on the two men stepping into the bedroom. The light was on in the hallway, so he saw mostly a silhouette, but enough to tell that Carson was fully dressed while Atticus didn't have a stitch on.

"He's not allowed to talk," Carson explained, his tone casual.

Likely to prove his point, he was standing behind Atticus, one hand covering his mouth, the other wrapped firmly around Atticus's cock.

"Turn on the lamp," Carson instructed.

Slade didn't look away even as he fumbled for the lamp on the nightstand. He was mesmerized by the rapid rise and fall of Atticus's chest as Carson stroked his dick.

The lamp came on, bathing the room in soft white light, highlighting the ridges and valleys of Atticus's muscular torso. Slade was still getting used to how much the man had changed during his time in Dallas. Atticus was on the small side as far as stature went. Probably around five-eight, maybe five-nine, with a slim build and small bone structure. Although Slade clocked in at six-two, two twenty-five, for some strange reason, he was fascinated by his smaller size.

When they met, Atticus had been rail-thin and slightly underweight, but that was no longer the case. During his time in training, he'd started working out, lifting weights, and eating healthy. It had allowed him to pack on some pounds—all muscle—and filled him out. And he'd stuck to the regimen of healthy eating—most of the time—and consistent workouts, which Slade found insanely hot.

"Move to the end of the bed," Carson insisted as he urged Atticus forward.

Slade threw off the blankets and scooted to the end of the bed. He usually slept naked, but tonight, he'd kept his boxers on, unsure whether he would confront Atticus when he returned. Not that they did a damn thing to conceal the erection now fighting to get free.

"Stroke his dick," Carson said. "Go easy. He doesn't have permission to come."

"Where are you goin'?" Slade asked when Carson released Atticus's cock.

"To get a chair. I'll be right back." He pressed his mouth to Atticus's cheek. "No talkin'."

Slade saw the way Atticus's Adam's apple bobbed slowly in his throat. He noticed the glitter in his eyes. He liked to be dominated.

Since Atticus was instructed not to speak, Slade didn't bother asking questions. He knew Atticus was obedient when it came to their instruction. He'd noticed it more than once. Instead, he watched his hand move up and down Atticus's shaft, admired the pearly drop of precum lingering at the tip.

Carson returned with a chair from the kitchen, setting it at the end of the bed before walking around to admire Atticus from all angles.

"How's our boy doin'?"

"His cock's weeping with anticipation," Slade answered, surprised by how much he liked that Carson had called Atticus theirs. Despite the tension, it still felt right. The three of them together.

"How would you like to play this?" Carson asked.

Slade wasn't able to hide his surprise, his head snapping around, eyes slamming into Carson. "You're askin' for my input?"

"I'm askin' if you want to have a say."

Slade's cock pulsed and thickened. That hard, dominating tone always got him. It was one of the things he'd loved most about Carson. The way he could turn him into putty without even trying.

Slade looked up to see Atticus watching him closely, waiting for his response.

"What do you think?"

"He doesn't get a say," Carson snapped. "He doesn't get to speak."

Slade was still watching Atticus, still had his hand around the man's dick, so he felt and saw how much that turned him on.

"Decide," Carson said firmly.

He turned his head slowly, meeting Carson's gaze once again. "No. I don't want a say."

"Good boy."

Jesus fuck. Those words said in that dark baritone were nearly enough to make him come. He hadn't heard them in so damn long he'd forgotten just how powerful they were.

Carson moved closer, gripping Slade's wrist and stilling it.

"You take over," he instructed Atticus as he pulled Slade to his feet.

Slade stood, his own breaths labored as anticipation coursed through his veins.

"Undress me," Carson commanded, his eyes fixed on Atticus's hand moving up and down his shaft.

With so much heat churning in his veins, it was a wonder Slade was capable of performing such a simple task. Yet, he got to work doing exactly that.

CARSON WATCHED ATTICUS WATCHING SLADE REMOVE HIS clothes, piece by piece. The more he took off, the hotter the gleam in Atticus's eyes became. It was a heady feeling to know the man was turned on as much as he was. Especially like this. Carson got off on instructing, on watching a scene play out. But being part of the action only added to the intensity.

Admittedly, he used to keep himself detached from the action. It was easier that way. Back when he'd been with Slade, Carson had kept it that way, choosing to watch Slade with other men. On occasion, he would participate, but for the most part, he would revel in the debauchery and then simply take what he wanted from Slade after the fact.

With Atticus and Slade, Carson didn't want to be on the periphery. He wanted to be with them. Both of them. With every passing day, his need for both of them was intensifying. Almost to a point that it scared him. He knew Slade still hated him for what he'd done, for how he'd mishandled their relationship. He didn't blame him. It was the least Carson deserved.

Still, he wanted more, but he wasn't exactly sure how to express that. When it came to sex, he was a pro at taking control, pushing boundaries, fulfilling fantasies. When it came to feelings, he was a novice.

"Atticus, get on the bed. All fours, facing that wall, not the headboard," Carson told him. "Put your chest on the mattress and spread your cheeks." Carson looked down at Slade. "You can stand up now."

Slade got to his feet and moved to Carson's side, watching as Atticus crawled up on the bed and did as instructed. He was breathing hard, his chest rising and falling as he got into position. When he reached back to reveal his puckered hole, he hesitated for only a moment, but it was enough to give Carson a reason to swat his ass, which he did.

Atticus moaned.

"Grab the lube," Carson told Slade as he grazed Atticus's hole with the tip of his finger. "Gotta prepare you for my dick."

Another moan.

"You want my big dick to fill this tight little ass, huh?"

Atticus didn't respond, which made Carson's cock thicken even more. He loved how submissive the man was, how he obeyed as though it were his only job.

Slade returned from the bathroom with a pump bottle.

"You can finger his ass. Start with one. End with three." Carson walked to the side of the bed and fisted Atticus's hair, lifting his head. "And you, sweet boy, are gonna suck my dick while he stretches you wide so you can take all of me."

Atticus moaned, fumbling to put his hands under him so he could lift himself up as Carson guided him with his hand still fisted in his hair.

Carson pushed his cock past those soft lips, deep into Atticus's eager mouth.

"Oh, fuck, yes. That mouth."

Atticus hummed when Slade pushed one slick finger into his ass. Carson watched the digit slide in and out. Easily, gently, Slade fingerfucked him.

"When you're ready, I'm gonna sit in that chair while you sit on my dick," Carson told Atticus, but his eyes were on Slade. "While you ride my dick, Slade's gonna fuck your face."

Slade's eyes snapped up, meeting Carson's. His approval glittered in the dark brown depths.

"You get both of us. At the same time."

Atticus began rocking forward and back, impaling himself on Slade's fingers and Carson's cock with each sway. Carson remained in control, holding his hair, not allowing Atticus to get himself off before it was time.

"Look at that. Three fingers buried deep in your ass. You ready for my cock?"

Atticus nodded but didn't make a sound.

"You wanna slide that tight little ass down my dick and let me fill you up." It wasn't a question.

That earned him a moan.

"One more minute," Carson said, watching as Slade gripped his own dick while he continued to finger Atticus's ass.

Watching Slade was a pleasure unlike anything Carson had ever known. The man was an absolute masterpiece; like that, he was a walking wet dream.

Aware of his own limitations, Carson tightened his hold, stopping Atticus's momentum before he exploded. He moved to the chair and sat down, then pointed toward his cock.

"Lube my dick first," he told Slade.

It was torture, but Carson endured because he knew they liked him like this. Slade was a contradiction in that he loved to be dominated, but he also got off on dominating. Carson liked seeing both sides of the man, especially when he was dominating someone else.

"Come here," Carson growled, holding out a hand in Atticus's direction. "Sit on my dick."

Atticus got to his feet and joined them, waiting for Slade to step back before he got into position, facing away from Carson.

Gripping Atticus's hip with one hand, he held his cock with the other, guiding the man right where he wanted him. He shifted in the chair to provide a better angle, allowing Atticus to impale himself, his tight, hot hole stretching around him.

"Oh, fuck," Carson whispered. "You feel so fuckin' good."

Better than good. This was heaven.

He shifted on the chair, getting more comfortable, allowing Atticus to take more. Seconds felt like years as his cock pushed deeper, inch by inch, into Atticus. He held his breath, the pleasure bordering on pain. It felt so damn good.

"All of me," he rasped, guiding Atticus down until he was balls deep inside the man.

Oh, yeah. So damn good.

"Fuck me, Atticus. However you need to."

To prove he was giving Atticus free rein, Carson gripped the edges of the chair, remaining as still as possible. He watched Slade move in front of Atticus, spreading his legs to accommodate Carson's legs.

Carson moaned when Slade fisted Atticus's hair and pulled him forward, guiding his cock into his mouth while Atticus lifted, sliding off his dick before sinking back down.

"That's it, boy," Carson said, trying to hold on to some semblance of control. "Fuck us both."

Slade groaned, his head tipping back, eyes closing. "Oh, yeah. Suck me. God, baby. Suck me."

Chills danced down Carson's arms, ignited by the reverence he heard in Slade's voice. This was more than the three of them were pretending it was. So much more. He wished someone would speak up because when they were together like this, Carson couldn't imagine anything more perfect. He knew as soon as it was over, the tension would return, and they'd go back to tiptoeing around one another until the next time.

That was the part he was tired of. He wanted more. He wanted to look forward to seeing them every chance he got, not fearing that each time might be his last.

He just wasn't sure how to broach the subject. Not without pissing Slade off and ultimately ruining whatever chance he might have.

THIS.

This was what Atticus had been looking forward to since the first time the three of them were together.

He breathed through his nose, savoring the feeling of them both at the same time. This was what he craved, what he fantasized about. Both of them fucking him.

Yeah, Carson gave the illusion that Atticus had the power, but they all knew the truth. He didn't want it. He wanted to be dominated, to be taken, to be manhandled for their pleasure. It turned him on like nothing else ever had.

The best part?

Here in this room, no one was thinking about past transgressions or irrational jealousy. No one was arguing about what might or might not happen in the future. They were giving in to their baser instincts, and that was the only thing that mattered.

"Atticus … fuck … oh, yeah. Ride me, boy."

His legs were cramping, his thighs on fire, his asshole stretched to the point of pain, but he didn't stop. He lifted and lowered, impaling himself on Carson's dick while Slade fucked his face rough and deep.

It wasn't until Carson reached around, grabbing his cock and stroking firmly, that Atticus knew he was dangerously close to orgasm. It was inevitable. He could feel the electrical current through every fiber of his being. That was what happened when the three of them were together.

He gasped, causing Slade's cock to slide out of his mouth. Closing his eyes, he let the pleasure roll through him.

This was what he wanted.

What he needed.

To fuck. To be fucked.

And he realized, it was all it would ever be. There was too much history, too much insecurity for it to evolve into something more. Surprisingly, he was okay with that. He had too much going on for anything more than this, anyway.

Atticus opened his mouth, but before he could take Slade's cock inside again, Carson pushed to his feet. Atticus fell forward, causing Slade to fall back. Slade's ass landed on the bed.

"Suck him," Carson bit out. "Make him come."

Atticus was about to say something, but words failed him when Carson pulled out and slammed into him. Hard. Deep. It was all he could do to wrap his lips around Slade's cock. Then they were fucking him again. Slade fisted his hair, holding him in place while pumping his hips, driving up into Atticus's throat. Carson rammed into him from behind, deeper than Atticus thought possible.

And it was *goooood*.

God, it was good.

"You better come when we do," Carson bellowed, both hands firmly on Atticus's hips.

He took that as permission, fisting his cock and stroking roughly, bringing himself right to the brink. He panted, breathing through his nose because Slade's big cock was cutting off his airway. He figured he was seconds from hyperventilating or passing out when Carson drove into him one last time, roaring as his cock pulsed inside him.

It was enough to trigger him, his cock spurting in his fist while Slade shouted, cum spurting against the back of Atticus's throat.

And then it was over.

The three of them fell into a heap on the bed, huffing and panting. Atticus somehow ended up between them, content to be crushed beneath their arms and legs as the sweat on his skin cooled.

"This is good, huh?" he said, breathing hard.

"Damn good," Carson agreed.

"I think we should do more of this."

Carson lifted up, propping himself on one arm. "Yeah?"

"Definitely. Let's just keep it casual from here on out. Just fucking."

No one said anything for several beats.

Atticus turned his head, looking at Slade. "You good with that?"

"I guess I'll have to be."

Atticus noticed Slade's gaze shifted to Carson when he said it, and he could sense the man's vulnerability.

Only time would heal those wounds, but it wouldn't be easy. Chances of these two getting back to where they'd once been were slim. Maybe they could, but Atticus realized he didn't want to be in the middle anymore.

Complicated wasn't something he was interested in, and truth be told, this was about as complicated as it got.

Chapter Twenty-Seven

As soon as the meeting let out, Archer spent another hour talking to Atticus, discussing some of the data as well as next steps for the statue case. He'd been relieved that Atticus was already letting him become part of the process, rather than seeing him as the enemy.

After that, he gave more time to Simon, listening as the man tried to wrap his head around Decker Bromwell's revelation. When it became obvious Simon wasn't sure how to proceed, Archer told him they'd pick it up tomorrow, then hopped on his Harley and headed to Spencer's house. Since there was an hour to spare before their date, he was hoping Spencer would be home.

So what if he told the man he preferred a public place for their date? It wasn't like he couldn't control himself around the guy. And right now, he wasn't interested in sitting at a table, making polite small talk, while a server hovered nearby to ensure they didn't need anything. He wanted some privacy and somewhere quiet so they could talk.

Or hell, they didn't even have to talk. He was all for watching a movie or whatever. He just wanted time with Spencer. Time to learn every nuance about him. He wanted to hear stories of growing up in a small town, learn what made him happy, sad. He wanted to know everything there was to know about Spencer Elliott, and the only way to make that happen was to spend time with him.

A little while later, Archer pulled up to the house, admiring it the same as he had last time. The green of the plants in the well-maintained flowerbeds, the sprinkle of color throughout. The large boulder propping up an old wagon wheel in the center of the circular driveway. It was a beautiful place, there was no doubt about that.

There were no cars in the driveway, but he knew Spencer parked his car in the garage, so if he were lucky, that was the case now.

After securing his helmet, he walked around the house to the front door. He was halfway across the porch when he heard music. Loud music. "Old Time Rock and Roll" was coming from inside the house.

He slowed when he saw movement through the large glass windows. A smile crept up on his face as he watched Spencer dance across the living room, wearing white socks and a button-down shirt. He couldn't see what he had on beneath, but Archer had a damn good imagination.

It was quite a good rendition of the iconic scene from *Risky Business*, but rather than holding a microphone, Spencer was holding a white tapered candle. And rather than lip sync, he was belting out the words along with Bob Seger.

After a few more creative leg moves, Spencer set the candle on the mantel, then popped the collar on his shirt as he continued to dance across the room.

Oddly enough, it was one of the sexiest things Archer had ever seen.

Because he didn't want Spencer to catch him watching, he went to the door and knocked, adding some power behind the move to be heard over the music. A moment later, the music cut off, followed by silence. He was almost positive he saw a shadow behind the security hole, figuring Spencer was checking to see who it was.

The door opened a crack, and Spencer peeked out. "Hey. I ... uh ... thought we were meetin' somewhere."

"We were. But I decided eating in works for me. Thought we could order a pizza."

Spencer didn't open the door as he glanced down, then back up. "I need to ... um ... get dressed."

"What you're wearin's fine," Archer said, his grin growing. "I got a peek of your performance through the window."

Instantly, Spencer's face turned a rosy pink.

"It was hot," Archer told him. Keeping his cadence smooth, he lowered his tone an octave and leaned forward. "Seriously fucking hot."

Spencer continued to stand there, holding the door.

Archer made no move to go inside, but he did say, "You wanna get dressed so maybe I could come in?"

"Shit." Spencer swung the door open wide. Before Archer could step inside, the man was racing across the room, sliding on his socked feet through a doorway, then disappearing down a hallway.

Chuckling, Archer came in, shutting the door behind him.

The house smelled good. Something citrusy. It could've been a lemon-scented cleaner, or perhaps one of those plug-in air fresheners discreetly hidden somewhere.

Not wanting to appear too comfortable, Archer remained near the front door, admiring the house until Spencer reappeared a few minutes later. Gone was the button-down shirt and white socks, replaced with a heather-gray long-sleeved cotton shirt and a pair of loose-fitting gray cotton shorts. His feet were bare.

"I can order the pizza," Spencer said, making a beeline toward the kitchen island without making eye contact. "What would you like on it?"

Archer could tell he was nervous, which was endearing. It warmed something inside him.

"I'm pretty easy when it comes to pizza," he admitted.

Spencer chuckled, but it sounded forced.

Wanting to ease his nerves, he came over, standing beside Spencer and leaning an elbow on the kitchen island, trying to get him to look his way.

When Spencer finally did, Archer grinned. "Hi."

That seemed to ease his tension because he gave a soft "Hi" in return.

From this proximity, Archer could smell Spencer's cologne. He smelled as good as he looked.

Archer tipped his head forward, still smiling. "Don't be nervous."

"I'm not." The subtle vibration belied his words.

"Well, I am."

Spencer rolled his eyes. "Whatever."

Archer chuckled. "Don't believe me?"

"No."

"It's true."

Spencer's gaze remained unsteady, moving from Archer's face to the phone, then back.

When Spencer held his stare, Archer said, "I thought about you today."

"You did?"

"I did. All day."

"Oh."

Smiling, Archer stood tall and took a step closer. He reached up, pressing his finger beneath Spencer's chin, tipping his head up so Archer could kiss him.

That was all it took for Spencer's nervous energy to disappear, replaced by a sensual hum that Archer felt in his veins whenever he was near this man. He wasn't sure what it was, or whether he'd ever felt anything like it before. Whatever it was, he wanted more. He hadn't had nearly enough of Spencer Elliott, and he was already addicted.

Spencer turned to face him, their lips locked as their tongues mated. Gently at first, then more urgently when Spencer's hands started to roam.

"I thought about you, too," Spencer whispered.

Archer pulled back, cupping Spencer's head to hold him still so he could meet his gaze. "Yeah?"

"Yeah."

"And what, pray tell, did you think about?"

Spencer's amber-gold eyes shimmered.

"Tell me," Archer urged, wanting to hear his voice, to understand what he was feeling.

"What do you mean?"

"Tell me," he repeated, gently tapping Spencer's temples. "I want to know what goes on in this beautiful head of yours."

"I promise, you don't."

Frowning, Archer studied him. "Why would you say that?"

"Because you're not wearin' clothes in my thoughts."

Smirking, he stepped closer, pinning Spencer between his body and the quartz-topped island. He eliminated the space between them, feeling the hard ridge of Spencer's dick pressed against his thigh and letting Spencer feel exactly what he did to him.

"I want to hear it all."

"I thought you said no sex." Spencer's voice was gravel-rough, his eyes glazed.

That wasn't what he meant, but he decided to play along. "I said not on the first date."

"Or the second," Spencer noted.

"So what number is this?"

"Fifteen."

Archer barked a laugh. "That many, huh?"

"I've lost count," Spencer said with a smile. "I think it's number three."

"Is it?" Archer canted his head. "Feels like there've been more."

He leaned in again, holding Spencer's head still so he could own the kiss. He licked his way into Spencer's mouth, relishing the taste of him. Archer liked the way Spencer submitted under his dominance. Since Archer enjoyed control, it was satisfying to feel Spencer become pliant and eager.

"One of these days I'm gonna lay you out like a feast," he mumbled, against Spencer's mouth.

"One of these days?" Spencer huffed.

Archer released Spencer when he pulled back.

"But not today?" The disappointment in Spencer's voice was like a sword, cutting deep.

"I'm not sayin' that," Archer told him, meaning it.

"I think you are."

Feeling the moment slip away, Archer backed up a step. "Why don't we take it slow for a bit. Cool?"

He was relieved when Spencer took a deep breath, exhaled. "Slow. Yeah. Okay. What do you want on your pizza?"

"Whatever you want's fine with me."

Turning, he headed for the couch, trying to adjust the steel bat in his jeans. The man made him so fucking hard he hurt. And while he wanted nothing more than to bend Spencer over and lodge himself deep within his body, something told him he had to go slow. Not because Spencer was damaged or fragile. Not entirely, at least. The man was no victim, of that he was certain.

No, Archer wanted to go slow because he didn't want Spencer to kick him to the curb.

He had no desire to be this man's one-and-done like he'd been for so many others.

Spencer stood with his back to Archer, pulling up the app for the pizza place on his phone. He skimmed through the menu, taking his time, needing a minute to calm down.

He appreciated Archer's desire to take things slow, but it wasn't necessary. Hell, it was an inconvenience if he were being honest. He was thirty-one years old for fuck's sake. He was tired of waiting.

Granted, he hadn't spent the past decade waiting. Quite the opposite, really. No, he'd spent that time doing his best to piss off any potential romantic interest because the desire hadn't been there. Initially, it was due to the fact he'd been raped. Waking up to find out he'd been roofied, force-fed Viagra, and sexually assaulted by his brother's wife was a hell he never wanted to relive.

Almost as bad was the fact that his sister-in-law had set it up so that Slade found them. Of course, his brother believed the worst of him, and to this day, Spencer hadn't bothered to correct him. Why should he?

Spencer had steered clear of pretty much anyone for the first few years after that. Trying to wrap his head around how something like that could happen wasn't easy. But several years later, he'd gotten past the denial and realized it wasn't his fault. Of course, therapy would've fast-tracked that, but he'd fought the idea of opening up to anyone about the event. It was just easier to pretend it never happened. For the most part, that worked, since he didn't remember the actual incident, only the lingering effects of the drugs afterward. If it weren't for Jennifer's boasting about how good it was for her, he could've put the whole thing behind him.

Probably.

Okay, probably not, but Spencer liked to believe that. He didn't remember what happened, but now and then, there would be a flash of something that niggled at his brain. He suspected it was remnants of that night, so he always forced them back. As far as he was concerned, the repressed memories were better off buried.

These days, as had been the case every day since, Spencer was doing the one day at a time thing. It wasn't until Archer that he'd felt that flame come to life, burning hot inside him.

Did he want a relationship with Archer? The correct answer should be yes, but he couldn't help thinking, probably not. Sure, he realized that sounded crass, but it was the truth. Spencer figured he needed to get a few rolls in the hay under his belt before he decided to settle down. He was pretty sure Archer was looking for something a bit more serious, and since Spencer didn't want to scare him off, he was willing to oblige.

At the same time, he was getting irritated by Archer's stalling tactic. The man claimed he wanted to take things slow, but he was throwing some serious mixed signals—a steady yellow light, never green, never red. Spencer was looking for the green light. He saw no reason why they couldn't indulge for a while. Sex for the sake of pleasure had to be a good thing. No strings, no complications.

Hitting the button to place the pizza order on his phone, he took a deep breath and set his phone down.

"So what do we do while we wait?" he asked, turning to see Archer sitting on the couch.

The man was enormous. And hot as a Texas summer. Fuck. Just looking at him made Spencer's dick hard and that wasn't something that happened often.

"We could talk," Archer suggested.

"Talk?" Yeah, he knew he sounded disappointed. He was.

"It's what people do on dates."

"They also fuck," he said, trying to sound like he was teasing. He wasn't.

Archer's brow furrowed. He opened his mouth as though to speak, but then closed it.

"What?" Spencer took a step toward him. "You've never had casual sex before?"

"Plenty," Archer said, watching him.

He joined Archer on the couch, keeping some space between them. "Then what's the problem?"

"I'm not looking for casual."

This time, Spencer frowned. "Then what are you lookin' for?" Before Archer could respond, Spencer shook his head. "And don't tell me you're lookin' for a relationship."

"And what if I am?"

"Bullshit."

Archer's frown deepened.

"Look," Spencer told him. "I get that I probably freaked you out and all that, but I'm good. I swear it. I don't have a problem with casual. In fact, I prefer it."

Right before his eyes, Archer's entire countenance shifted. He closed down the same as if someone had shut a door behind his eyes. A second later, Archer looked at his watch.

"I should probably be goin'."

"Pizza's on the way, remember?"

"I'm not all that hungry."

As soon as Archer got to his feet, Spencer did too. "So what? Are you a dick tease? Is that what gets you off?"

Archer continued toward the door, not looking back, and not responding.

"Fuck you, then," Spencer bit out. "I'm sorry if I'm not lookin' to pledge my love just to get fucked."

When Archer did look back as he opened the front door, Spencer saw a wealth of disappointment in his gaze.

As soon as the sexy man stepped outside, Spencer was slammed with guilt and regret.

Funny that. He'd managed to push away plenty of guys over the years, but this was the first time he felt bad about it.

Probably for the best. Spencer doubted he could give anyone what Archer was looking for. Though he would never admit it, there was a piece of him that was broken and likely always would be. There was nothing he could do to change that.

Chapter Twenty-Eight

BRANTLEY LET REESE GO INTO THE HOUSE first while he walked back and forth in front of the house to cool down a bit. They'd tackled five miles in record time, and he was feeling it.

Of course, Reese looked as though he'd only run a mile. Walking. Clearly that eating healthy thing had some merit.

"I'm gonna shower," Reese called, leaving the front door open.

Taking that as an invitation, Brantley got with the program. He made his way down the hallway to their bedroom, discarding clothing as he went. By the time he reached the bathroom, he was naked, and the room was filling with steam while Reese stood beneath the spray.

"I thought you needed a minute," Reese said, grinning as Brantley stepped in with him.

"When my husband's in the shower, eager to do me, I always feel instantly better."

Reese huffed a laugh. "Is that what I'm eager for? To do you?"

Brantley pushed Reese back so they were both beneath the spray. He reached around and turned down the heat, figuring they would be generating plenty of their own soon enough.

"I want you inside me," Brantley told him, sliding his hands up Reese's back.

Reese's hands began to roam, causing goosebumps to form on Brantley's flesh. He loved when Reese touched him.

"How do you want it?" Reese asked, his voice rougher than before.

"Slow," he said, dragging out the word. He lowered his voice and spoke right in Reese's ear. "I want you to slide your dick inside me nice and slow, then I want you to take your time."

Reese shuddered in his arms, causing Brantley to grin.

"Do you think you can do that?"

Reese's response came with a gentle push against Brantley's chest.

Laughing, Brantley turned away from him, planting both palms on the tiled wall. He glanced over his shoulder, watching as Reese fumbled with the lube. He could tell that Reese's cheeks were pink, and he figured it had more to do with his dirty talk than the water temperature.

"Slow, you say?" Reese asked, stepping up behind him.

Brantley took a few steps back so he could bend over more, offering himself up to his husband. He moaned softly when Reese teased his hole with his fingers.

"Fuck," he hissed, shifting his hips, pushing against those fingers penetrating him.

"Relax," Reese urged, scissoring his fingers inside him. "Let me in."

He did, accepting the intrusion, eager for Reese to drive his cock inside him.

"Fuck me, Reese," Brantley pleaded, dropping his head, savoring the pleasure.

Without a word, Reese drove two fingers in deep and hard seconds before he pulled out and pushed his cock inside him. Air rushed out of his lungs as pleasure consumed him. His knees went weak, but he managed to shore them up when Reese began sliding out.

In. Out.

Slow.

"Is this what you want?" Reese's voice was thready.

"Fucking perfect," he hissed, loving the way Reese's fingertips dug into his hips as though he was trying to hold himself back.

Their grunts and moans echoed alongside the water raining down.

"I love when you're inside me, Reese," he said, closing his eyes, his body humming with the electricity that arced whenever Reese was fucking him.

Reese's hand shifted from his hip to his shoulder. He rocked into him, a little faster, just as deep. When his pace quickened even more, Brantley reached down, stroked his cock, preparing to come at the same time Reese did.

"Oh, yeah," he urged. "Harder, baby. Fuck me like you mean it."

That triggered Reese's urgency because he began fucking him deep and hard, his grunts louder, his grip on Brantley's shoulder firmer.

Brantley grunted, trying to form words, but the pleasure was too intense. He gave himself over, holding off for as long as he could.

"Reese … fuck … baby … coming!"

Reese slammed into him hard, a throaty roar bouncing off the tile as he came deep inside him.

Brantley sighed, content and sated. He dropped his head, smiling.

Damn fine way to start the day.

Twenty minutes later, Brantley strolled into the kitchen to find Reese working at the stove, the smell of bacon permeating the entire room.

"Why do you have a smile on your face?" Reese asked, sparing a quick glance his way.

Unable to stop the grin from amping up a wattage or two, Brantley continued toward his husband.

"Why wouldn't I have a smile on my face?" he countered. "We're finally back to our routine."

For the first time in what felt like years, they were able to wake up, go for a run, shower together, and now they were about to have breakfast together. Toss in the mind-blowing sex under the spray of the water, and Brantley couldn't help but smile.

"I guess we are, huh?"

"Finally."

Reese chuckled. "This comin' from the man who used to boycott routine."

"That was before you," he told Reese as he stepped up behind him and kissed the back of his neck.

Reese leaned into him briefly before continuing to fry bacon in the pan.

"What're you makin' with that bacon?" He chuckled when he realized it rhymed.

"Thought we'd do bacon and egg sandwiches."

"As long as you don't put avocado on mine." The one time Reese had snuck some on his sandwich, it had taken Brantley forever to wash that taste out of his mouth.

"I won't. Promise."

Brantley poured two cups of coffee and brought them to the island. He took a seat and watched Reese work.

"I got a text from Baz this mornin'," Reese said, not looking back.

"And?"

"The team wants to meet with us this mornin'."

Shit. Brantley had feared they would. In fact, he'd feared an all-out boycott after yesterday's meeting. He could only imagine what they were thinking.

"They're not all gonna quit, are they?"

This time Reese peered back at him, his eyebrows lowered. "Of course not. Why would they?"

"We dumped a lot on them yesterday."

"We did, but they're a tough bunch."

Brantley didn't disagree. And he didn't doubt they would be on board. He needed to give some thought to how they should lay it out. He wanted to utilize the entire team as best he could in order to get this resolved quickly. He didn't know how long Simon's process took, but Brantley wanted to get this done and over as soon as possible.

He let his thoughts wander to how he would present the information while Reese continued to cook. It wasn't until a plate was set in front of him that he brought his thoughts back to the moment.

"Where were you just now?" Reese asked, settling onto the stool beside him.

Exhaling a sigh, Brantley resigned himself to having this discussion. "I need to give Travis an update. I promised him I would."

"What exactly can you tell him? We don't have any leads. Hell, we're not even sure Meredith Prescott is where Decker left her. There's a good chance she ran after they talked. If she thought someone might be on to her, it would make sense."

Brantley had thought the same thing. It was why he wasn't on a plane to New York to bring her back. Until they had a confirmation that she was there, he wasn't going to put too much effort into it. If he had to guess, Decker had already warned her that they knew where she was.

He glanced at the sandwich on his plate and, for the first time, he ignored it. He was suddenly not hungry.

Reese shifted closer. "We're gonna figure this out. One way or the other. We'll outline what we need to do to find Meredith Prescott, and I have to believe that everything else will work out the way it's meant to."

"What about the FBI agents that are in town? Who was Decker referring to?"

"I honestly don't know."

Brantley took a deep breath. "Okay. We'll meet with the team, get their input. From there, we'll decide how to approach Travis and Gage. And we *have* to keep them updated."

"Sounds like a plan," Reese said as his phone chimed on the counter. He pulled it over, peered down at the screen. "That's Atticus. He's headin' over to Walker Demo to talk to Ethan."

Brantley frowned. "About?"

"They're tryin' to figure out what type of equipment would be needed to move a bronze statue."

"It weighs what? About a thousand pounds?"

Reese shrugged one shoulder. "Roughly fifteen hundred."

"You sound certain about that. Did you research it?"

Another shrug. "I might've spent a few minutes lookin' into it."

"Leave it to Atticus. Sounds like he's on the right track. I do need him to close that case ASAP, though. As much as I want to help Callie and Rose, we're gonna need Atticus and Slade front and center on this."

"I'll let Darius know so he can stay on top of it."

Brantley nodded, reminding himself that Darius was in charge because Baz was on paternity leave. He hated that he was down two of their top people, but it was for the best possible reason, so he wouldn't bring it up. Baz and JJ deserved this time, and he would not interfere, no matter how much their expertise would be missed.

"What time are we meeting with the team?" he asked before downing what was left of his coffee.

Reese stood, grabbing their plates. "I'll find out. I'd say ten should be good. I'll talk to Z, see if they can be here."

"Decker, too."

"You sure that's a good idea?"

He understood Reese's reluctance, and Brantley couldn't blame him for asking. After all, Brantley could hardly be in the same room with Decker and not want to put his fist through the man's face. Everything about this situation was fucked up, the least of which was the fact Meredith Prescott took advantage of a kid. Just the thought of her and fourteen-year-old Decker together made his stomach churn violently.

However, Brantley knew he had to put that aside if they were going to find out what happened to Meredith. More importantly, if they were going to identify this so-called collusion that Holt was convinced was taking place.

"We have to be at HQ by ten," Atticus told Slade as he steered the truck toward Walker Demolition. "Darius just texted."

Slade flipped on the blinker. "I'm sure someone'll catch us up if we can't get there in time."

While he'd said yes to Slade's suggestion that they focus on the case while the team worked out the logistics of Simon's story, Atticus was now regretting it. He wanted to be in the thick of things, not out here trying to figure out what equipment was necessary to hoist and move a bronze statue. Who really cared? It was a damn statue. They could buy another one if it was that big of a deal, right?

At the same time, he wanted to figure out where the damn statue was, get it back to the high school where it belonged—provided it hadn't been sold on the black market, melted down for cash, or whatever the hell someone would do with a giant bronze horse—and put this case in his rear view so he could focus on other things. He was just torn between how much effort to put into it. It was a statue for fuck's sake. Surely it was insured.

"This should be quick," Slade said as they turned down a dirt driveway. "Ethan'll know what equipment they would've used."

Atticus nodded. He was content to go with Archer's theory that someone could've used a forklift, but when he tried to tell Slade that, anger had flashed in the man's eyes. So when Slade argued that they needed an expert, not some podcast investigator—Slade's words—Atticus didn't argue.

And here they were.

"My guess is they hoisted it onto a flatbed, drove away with it." He left off the forklift part.

"Had to've been something that didn't draw attention," Slade noted. "Not a single one of the people I talked to saw or heard anything."

"Not that they're tellin' you, anyway. What's to say one of those people didn't take it?"

"For what purpose?"

"Hell, I don't know. What purpose would *anyone* have for stealing a life-size bronze statue of a horse?"

"You want my honest opinion?"

Atticus glanced over. "Of course."

"I think it was the rival team. The homecoming game is this weekend. It's tradition for the football team to take a photo with the statue before the game. Without the statue, there is no picture."

In some warped and twisted, teenage-brain way, that made sense. As an adult, Atticus didn't get it, but that wasn't to say he wouldn't've done the same thing if he'd gone to a regular high school like these people.

Whatever the reason, they were up against a real clock if there was supposed to be a picture before tonight's game. In order for Coyote Ridge High School to uphold its tradition, the statue needed to be located and put back in place … in a few hours. Jesus. What were the odds they'd stumble across it by then? Even small towns had a lot of people. No way could they talk to everyone. And who was the rival team? An equally small town?

Slade pulled the truck up close to a large metal building, effectively cutting off Atticus's mental rant.

"Let's see what Ethan has to say. Then we'll go from there."

Nodding, Atticus got out, then walked around to meet Slade at the single door with the small glass window. Slade turned the knob and the door opened.

When they stepped inside, Atticus heard the echoes of metal tools clanging. The place was bigger than it appeared from the outside. Tall ceilings, tons of equipment, and tools. There was a small office to his right with what appeared to be a cluttered desk and computer. Next to that what looked like a breakroom.

He didn't see anyone in the brightly lit space, but it was easy to follow the sound.

"Ethan?" Slade called as they made their way toward the back wall.

A disembodied voice echoed with, "Who's askin'?"

Slade chuckled. "Slade and Atticus."

A man appeared—presumably Ethan—slowly rising from where he'd been working under the hood of a Walker Demo truck.

Atticus was convinced there was something in the water down here. Something that made all the men extremely large. Not to mention devastatingly good-looking. Ethan Walker wasn't quite as broad as his cousin Brantley, but he wasn't small by any means. He easily had a few inches on Slade's six-foot-two and many on Atticus's five-foot-ten. Like Brantley, Ethan was a good-looking man with dark hair, steel-blue eyes, and a chiseled jawline.

"What's up, cuz?" Ethan grinned, wiping his hands on a red towel before fist-bumping Slade in greeting.

"I'm not sure you two've met," Slade said, gesturing between them. "Ethan, this is Atticus James. Atticus, this is my cousin, Ethan Walker."

"Nice to meet you," Atticus said, doing his best not to fidget.

"Likewise. What brings y'all by?"

Atticus listened while Slade laid out the story of the missing statue, a story that seemed to amuse Ethan if the gleam in his eyes was anything to go by.

"And you've checked the football field?" Ethan chuckled.

"Would it be there?" Atticus asked, seriously.

"Tonight it might," Slade noted.

"But how would they move it? Wherever they moved it to."

"My guess is forklift and a flatbed."

Atticus didn't look at Slade, not wanting to remind him that was exactly what Archer said.

"How do you use a forklift to pick something like that up?" Slade asked.

"Like a hoist," Ethan explained. "Tie the straps around the forks and the statue, then raise it. From there, you could move the flatbed under it, haul it off."

Exactly like Archer said.

Again, he wasn't bringing it up.

"That's what I'd do, anyway," Ethan added with a grin.

"Any chance you stole a life-size mustang from the high school?" Atticus questioned.

"Not this time. Wish I'd thought of it, though."

He seemed genuinely amused by the prospect.

"Know anyone who might?" Slade prompted. "Or heard anything? Rumors?"

"Nope. Whoever did it's keepin' it on the DL. That or it was the rival team and they towed that bad boy out of town."

"Know anyone who's missing a forklift?"

"Can't say that I do. But you can get one pretty much anywhere."
Also what Archer said.

Atticus glanced between Ethan and Slade, hoping one of them
would add more. Something that would solve this case here and now
so he could get on with his life.

When nothing else came from either man, Atticus cleared his
throat. "Well, thanks for your help." He looked at Slade. "I guess we'll
be knockin' on doors."

"Lemme talk to Braydon," Ethan said. "See if he has any ideas. I'm
sure he thought of it back in the day, so he might know a way to get
one on the DL."

It wasn't a resolution, but it was more than they had. Atticus would
take it.

"Perfect," Slade said. "Thanks."

"Nice to meet you," Atticus said before following Slade to the
door. "Who's Braydon?"

"One of Ethan's brothers. He's a job foreman for Walker Demo."

Atticus wasn't sure how that benefited them, but he was at a loss,
so he figured it couldn't hurt.

Chapter Twenty-Nine

ARCHER ARRIVED AT HQ AN HOUR EARLY for the meeting. Not because he was an overachiever or wanted to impress the bosses—although that certainly wouldn't hurt. No, it wasn't so much eagerness as it was a text from Darius letting him know he had some paperwork that needed to be taken care of so they could get him on the payroll immediately.

For a brief moment after reading that text, he considered telling Darius he had changed his mind. He hadn't changed his mind, but his mood had deteriorated after the incident at Spencer's last night. While he wasn't one to dwell on things for long, Archer had spent a good portion of the night thinking about where he went wrong.

It wasn't until the light of day that he realized he wasn't at fault for that debacle. It was Spencer who was putting up the roadblocks. And last night, Archer realized that Spencer wasn't on the same page as he was when it came to what they were looking for in a romantic encounter. Hell, he wasn't sure they were even reading from the same book.

At twenty-nine, Archer wasn't interested in playing games, and he damn sure wasn't looking to be manipulated. He was ready to settle down. He wanted to find what Simon had found with Violet, what Brantley and Reese had found with each other. He was no longer interested in the casual routine.

Sure, he was all for some sweaty, naked fun with a hot guy. Who wasn't? But he wasn't interested in being shown the door afterward. After last night, he was convinced that was the path Spencer was on. He wasn't sure they'd had a single conversation that didn't involve Spencer bringing up sex. Or the lack thereof.

For fucks sake, they'd only been on three dates.

Well, two and a half since last night's was a bust.

So, after his momentary pity party, Archer decided he would keep putting one foot in front of the other. Sooner or later, he would find the guy he was meant to spend his life with. The one who would open up about himself and let Archer in. Or perhaps he was looking for something impossible, and he would be back on the casual sex bandwagon in a few months. Either way, he wasn't interested in having another mental debate.

Now, as he stood at the door of HQ and waited for someone to let him in, he shoved all thoughts of his romantic life—or lack thereof—to the back of his mind.

Finally, the door panel chirped, and the lock disengaged.

Not sure what to expect, he pulled the door open and stepped inside.

Archer was surprised to see people sitting at their desks, heads down, fingers flying over keyboards. The couple of times he'd been there, he'd found more personal interactions taking place. For some reason, he liked the idea of them having enough work to keep them busy like this, while at the same time, they could take a break to chat. Having worked for Simon for so long, Archer spent most of his time on the road, rolling solo. He was looking forward to having a team.

"Mornin'," someone muttered.

"Look who it is," another said.

Archer plastered on a smile. "Morning. Is Darius around?"

"He's upstairs," the redhead—he could not remember her name—said as she approached. "But I can help."

Archer tried to flip through his memories for a tiny clue, but he couldn't find one.

"Rebecca," she said as though reading his mind. "Everyone calls me Becs."

That's right. Becs.

"Good morning, Becs," he said, repeating her name in his head as he looked at her pretty features.

She pointed up to the loft. "Darius is workin' on something, but he told me what paperwork he needed. It's waiting for you at your desk."

"My desk?" He had a desk? Awesome.

"Don't sound surprised." She pivoted on her heel and led the way to the back of the barn. "You weren't planning to sit on the floor, were you?"

"Only if I had to." He grinned, realizing the entire space had been restructured since he was there yesterday. As in all the desks had been rearranged, and now there seemed to be more room. How that was possible, he wasn't sure because it looked like they had more stuff. He noticed a few additional screens mounted on the long side wall, a few chairs clustered around a small round table, and a dark blue loveseat tucked under the stairs, ready and available should someone want to sit on it.

The big question was: when did they have time to do this? Last night? This morning?

"This is us," Becs said, gesturing to a cluster of desks neatly arranged in the back corner.

There were five desks arranged in the shape of an I, with two on each end and one in the middle.

"Slade and Evan sit there," she explained, pointing to the two desks they were passing before swinging her arm to the other side. "You and Atticus there. And I'm in the middle so I can support all four of you when needed."

"Support?"

"I'm your research analyst. When you're out in the field and need things, you'll contact me. I can get you pretty much any information you need from here."

He liked the idea since he'd spent most of his career doing the legwork himself. He was sure he still would do a good portion of it, but having support would help tremendously.

"Check it out," Becs urged.

Because he saw no reason not to, Archer went to the empty desk and pulled out the large ergonomic chair. He eased into it and found it was far more comfortable than it looked. Plus, it was made for him—from the big and tall office supply store, he was sure.

"I don't see the paperwork," he told her as he wheeled himself forward, resting his elbows on his desk.

"That's because it's right here," she said, hefting a box from beside her desk. "MacBook Pro. All set up and ready for you. Just log in."

Amused, Archer opened the box and pulled out the laptop computer and the related accessories. When he flipped the lid up, the screen came on, asking for an email and password.

"It's in the top drawer," Becs told him from where she was sitting at her desk.

Within a minute, Archer was logged in and looking at the various applications on his home screen. He clicked the one for email, and there he found more instructions in the form of an email from Rebecca Richter, including details on how to set up a passcode for the door lock.

Glancing around to see that everyone was still working away, Archer decided there was no time like the present to get it taken care of. Half an hour later, he had submitted every required form and was considering going through the case board instructions when the door opened and Brantley and Reese walked in with Tesha in tow.

As though it were routine, Tesha wound her way through, getting attention from everyone while Brantley and Reese said their good mornings, making their way to the back. When Tesha approached his desk, Archer fought the urge to drop onto the floor and cuddle with her, choosing instead to give her head a scratch. He was a dog lover, and he'd already fallen head over heels for her.

"Archer."

Looking up from Tesha, he said "Brantley" in the same tone.

That earned him a smile.

"They get you all set up?"

"I'm an official team member now," he said, gesturing toward the computer.

"Fucking fantastic," Brantley muttered as though he hadn't expected him to say that.

"Guess it's a good day to start, huh?"

"You have no idea," Brantley responded, glancing back at Reese, who was coming out of the kitchen with two cups of coffee.

"Morning," Archer greeted Reese.

"Mornin'. You get a chance to talk to Simon about…" Reese waved a hand behind him.

"The meeting yesterday?" Archer shook his head. "We chatted for a while, but he was still tossing it around when I left. It wouldn't surprise me if he stayed up all night and hashed it out with Holt, though."

"I hope he did," Brantley said. "We're gonna need some direction, and if the team decides to take this case, I don't want to waste a minute."

Archer was about to ask him which part he was referring to when the door opened again. Ryan Trexler and Zachariah Tavoularis strolled in, Decker Bromwell right behind them, looking like a man walking into the chamber for his lethal injection.

At that point, talk about the case was put on hold as they waited for everyone to arrive. Jay Rodriguez came over with Charlotte Miller, aka Charlie, so that Archer could be formally introduced to her. He appreciated Jay doing the introduction since he'd forgotten the man's name already. Luca Switzer took a minute to say good morning, and shortly after that, Elana and Darius came downstairs, both greeting him with smiles.

More introductions—or rather re-introductions took place as people trickled in. Archer was grateful as it gave him another chance to put faces with names.

Holly appeared from somewhere, looking both dreamy-eyed and nervous, though Archer wasn't sure why. He attempted to put her at ease by asking how she liked working with her brother. Evidently, at least according to Holly, Luca was a pain in the backside. Based on the smirk he saw Luca flash, the man was well aware of his reputation.

Evan walked in, and Archer noticed his gaze shot directly to Becs, but he quickly rerouted his attention when she looked up at him. Interesting. The former detective recovered nicely when he plastered on a neutral expression and walked over.

"You on board full time yet?"

"I am," Archer confirmed, shaking the man's hand. "Starting today."

"That's really good news. We've got a great team. I think you'll enjoy it."

Archer did, too, but he merely nodded, letting Evan get on with his day.

"Is Baz comin'?" Brantley asked, his question directed at Darius.

"He is. Said he might be a couple minutes late. JJ's also gonna join via phone."

"We'll wait for him," Brantley decided, then addressed the room. "If you want coffee or whatever, get it. I don't want any interruptions."

Some muttering ensued, and then people were on their feet, heading for the kitchen.

Movement on one of the wall monitors drew Archer's attention. He saw Atticus and Slade walking in, and Simon's car was pulling down the long driveway.

When the doors opened, Archer turned his attention to his new partner. Atticus stopped abruptly, eyes wide.

"Are y'all serious right now?" he asked, looking around. "You rearranged? Again?"

Becs laughed. "You'll get over it."

"Maybe. Wanna tell me where I'm supposed to sit?"

She pointed at the desk beside Archer.

"And Slade, you're here," she said, aiming a finger at the desk beside Evan, directly across from Atticus.

As he watched the interactions, Archer felt Slade's gaze slam into him directly. He could feel a cold hatred coming off the guy, but he had no idea why. From what little he knew about Slade's relationship with his brother, he didn't think the man's anger stemmed from Archer going out with Spencer a couple of times. Then again, what did he know?

"Hey, man." Atticus dropped into his seat.

"What's up?"

"I swear I've sat in every spot you can sit in this barn. And yet, they always find a way to put me somewhere else."

"But at least you don't have a television at your back," Becs noted.

Atticus spun in his chair. When he came back around, there was a smile on his face.

"You got somethin' against televisions?" Archer asked.

"Only when giant heads pop out of them and scare the shit outta you."

"It happened once," came a voice from a speaker.

"Once was more than enough, JJ," Atticus replied, then pointed toward a wall-mounted monitor. A moment later, Jessica James's face appeared.

"That's the big head that scared me," Atticus said loud enough for JJ to hear.

"Hey, now. Careful, or I'll drain your bank accounts."

"Then the joke would be on you," Atticus said, barking a laugh. "I ain't got no money." Atticus looked his way. "In case you do, I suggest you don't get on her bad side. She can do that."

Archer smiled. "Consider me warned."

"All right. Baz is walkin' in now," Brantley announced. "Let's get seated so we can start."

Archer relaxed in his chair and glanced around. He realized for the first time since he left the Marines that he actually felt like he belonged somewhere. He couldn't explain why, but he could feel it. And he'd be damned if he wasn't looking forward to what was to come.

"I KNOW WE DUMPED A LOT OF information on you yesterday," Brantley began. "And I'm sure Becs and Holly already have a notebook full of questions."

Reese smiled, watching the two women glow with approval. It was funny what a little recognition from the guy they admired so much did. It was something Reese knew all too well. He might've married Brantley and had the pleasure of waking up next to him every single day, but when it came to their careers, he held a different sort of respect for the retired Navy SEAL. No, he didn't usually mention it because Brantley wasn't the sort who wanted praise in that regard. But it was true nonetheless.

"I don't intend for this to be a lengthy meeting," Brantley continued, "but I do want to know whether you are on board with taking this case. Not so much the search for Meredith Prescott, since we know where she is." Brantley turned and looked at Decker. "We know where she is, right?"

Decker nodded.

"Good." Brantley scanned the faces again. "So not the search for her, but the conspiracy Holt eluded to yesterday. Plus whatever else that search dredges up. If you prefer to sit this one out, I will not hold it against you, but I need you to speak up."

Reese looked from one person to the next, waiting. He knew they had questions and likely a boatload of concerns, but those were things they could work through on the case board. This meeting was to determine who didn't want to proceed. He already knew the answer, and not because he'd talked to anyone about it. They'd put together a strong team. A diverse team. They worked well together, and they had each other's backs. They would come together to do what was necessary.

"No one?" Brantley asked, obviously not as convinced as Reese.

"I'm in, boss," Slade said, and his agreement had a domino effect.

"I'll do whatever you need," Luca stated.

"Me, too," Holly added.

"We're in," Charlie said, gesturing toward Jay, who nodded once. "And we'll bring the new hires up to speed as they come on board."

"Whatever you need," Evan said.

"I'll help however I can," JJ noted.

"I'm in," Becs said.

"We got your back, boss," Atticus added.

"Okay, then." Brantley sighed and took a few steps before looking up. "As you know from my outburst yesterday, this isn't an easy case for me. For any of us, I'm sure. Whether Holt is right or simply creating fiction in the real world, I'll admit there's enough information to warrant taking proper steps to address.

"With that said, I'm too close to this. Many of us are. By all accounts, we're lookin' for my cousin's mother-in-law. His wife's mother. That makes her family, and regardless of what she's done or how I feel about that, I owe it to my family. If she's been on the run all these years because someone in authority was blackmailing her, I owe it to her to help her get home. The hardest part is knowing that her daughter will never know what happened. Kylie died believing her mother ran off. I hope we prove otherwise."

Reese hadn't expected that, but he continued to watch Brantley.

"Because of that, I've decided to assign an impartial team to lead this investigation."

Everyone started looking around, evidently as surprised by that revelation as Reese was.

"Atticus and Archer," Brantley stated, looking directly at them. "You two are the lead investigators. You will coordinate and direct every step. If anyone has a problem—"

"Why them?" Decker asked, his tone barely disguising his anger.

The room seemed to hold its breath, anticipating another volcanic eruption from Brantley. To Reese's surprise, Brantley remained calm as he looked at Decker.

"Because they weren't here when Kylie died. Neither of them knew her. They can and will remain unbiased and do what needs to be done."

"That's bullshit. I should be in charge of this," Decker bit out, glaring at Z. "This is your fucking team. You make this decision."

Z frowned. "This isn't my team," he snapped back. "This is Brantley and Reese's team. I provide some direction when needed, but they run the show here."

"They work for Sniper 1," Decker argued.

Z's mouth opened, but RT put his hand on Z's arm and interjected. "Technically, yes. That doesn't change anything. And we're not here to debate that. If you don't like the direction Brantley's taking this, you can go back to Dallas and keep a desk chair warm."

Every ounce of attention was focused on Decker.

"No."

"Then shut up about it," Z hissed.

All eyes shifted back to Brantley despite the tension thickening the air.

"Do either of you have a problem leading this investigation?" Brantley asked Atticus and Archer.

Reese watched as the two men looked at each other briefly before both shaking their heads at the same time. They hadn't worked a single case together yet, but for some reason, the pairing felt right to him. Being a former bounty hunter, Atticus had the skills necessary to find things. And due to his military career, Archer understood the need for control and discipline. Plus, he could and would see things through to completion. There wasn't a doubt in his mind that Brantley made the right decision there.

"Good." Brantley scanned the room. "As I was saying a moment ago, if anyone has a problem, you can talk to me or Reese privately. If at any time you feel the need to step back from the case, be sure to let Atticus or Archer know. Just don't let it be at the eleventh hour."

"When do we start?" Atticus asked.

"We already have."

Chapter Thirty

"ARCHER. ATTICUS." BRANTLEY CURLED TWO FINGERS, A silent gesture for them to join him. He turned to Reese. "Let's talk to them for a minute."

Reese nodded, following him into the conference room.

"I hope I didn't blindside you," Brantley told him while they waited.

"A little. But it makes sense. I understand your reasoning."

Brantley wasn't sure anything made sense, but he figured the only fair way to handle this was to take the emotion out of it. As much as possible, anyway. And since he wouldn't have hired Atticus or Archer unless he had faith in their ability to get the job done, he figured it was as good a time as any to put them to work.

Too antsy to sit, Brantley leaned against the wall, instructing Atticus to close the door behind him.

"I know I put you both on the spot out there, so if you have a problem with the direction I'm headed, now's the time to say so."

Atticus glanced at Archer, then back at him. "I don't."

"It was a smart decision," Archer said, his expression lacking his usual amusement. "Being that I've got some insight and can bring Atticus up to speed quickly, and Atticus understands the way the team works as a whole and can keep me in line when needed, I think we're a couple steps ahead at this point."

Those were damn good points. Ones that Brantley hadn't even considered.

"I need you to be one hundred percent focused on this. Nothing else. No cold cases, no helping anyone with their cases. This is the absolute only thing you work on."

"What about the missing statue?" Atticus asked.

"You haven't closed that yet?"

Atticus's eyebrow quirked. "Seriously?"

Brantley couldn't hold back the smile. "No. Where are you at with it?"

"We haven't figured out who, but we think we know how after talking to Ethan this morning. He's gonna talk to his brother, see if he's heard anything. Evidently, that statue's important for the homecoming game. Football picture or somethin'. If we don't find it today, it likely won't matter."

"Let Slade finish that up. He's got far more insight into the town dynamics anyway." Brantley looked at Reese. "If he doesn't find it today, we'll have to tell Rose we can't focus on it right now."

"*You* will have to tell Rose," Reese corrected. "But understood."

Brantley laughed. "Fine. Whatever." He turned back to Atticus and Archer and gestured around the room. "Set this up as your command center. Bring in whatever equipment you need." He looked at Archer. "We use electronic case boards, so all that shit from Holt's apartment has been digitized."

"Got it."

He glanced between them. "I'm serious when I say you are not to be derailed. Put Simon to work, too. If he intends to handle this story, he can contribute to the legwork."

Archer nodded.

"But keep in mind, this is now our case. I don't expect it to be simple, but I want the answers. Whatever those may be." Brantley glanced over at Reese. "Anything you'd like to add?"

"Brantley chose you because you can do this objectively. Do not let anyone influence you. Not Decker. Not Z. We follow this where it goes, and you will direct the team accordingly."

"Understood," Archer and Atticus said at the same time.

"You've got the rest of today to get up to speed on this. Keep in mind, JJ and Baz are unavailable unless absolutely necessary. Otherwise, divide and conquer. Utilize every member of this team. Including Z and Decker. We will be working weekends. Whatever it takes." He looked at Reese. "We need to cancel the team training next week, but a trip to Dallas for a few days may still be in order." He shifted his focus back to Atticus and Archer. "Depending on what you determine."

"Got it," Archer said.

Brantley looked at Atticus. "I'll let Slade know about the statue. He can wrangle Becs in if he needs help. I'm sure she'd be open to working in the field." He started for the door. "We'll be around if you need us."

When he stepped out of the conference room, he scanned the room. When he saw Slade, he waited for the man to look up. As soon as he did, Brantley gestured for him to come over.

"What's up, boss?"

"I need you to take the lead on the statue case. But today's all we have left to give. If you can't find it, apologize to your mother but let her know we've got something that needs our full attention."

Slade frowned. "What about Atticus?"

"He's busy. Won't have time for it. Can you handle it?"

Although he looked none too pleased, Slade said, "Of course."

Because he could feel Decker's eyes on him and he had no interest in getting into it with the man, Brantley opted to head for the door. Reese whistled for Tesha, who came trotting out with him, eagerly anticipating their next move.

"Where to?" Reese asked.

"I'd like to give Travis a heads up."

Reese tapped his arm. "I think we should wait on that. I know you promised to keep him updated, but let's give Archer and Atticus time to outline what we have. Once they've got a direction in mind, we'll determine what information, if any, we need to pass along."

Brantley wasn't sure he was comfortable with that idea. Or rather, he wasn't sure how Travis would react if he knew they were holding back. However, he understood, and it did make sense to let the team come up with a plan before he ended up getting a barrage of questions he couldn't answer.

Brantley nodded, reluctantly. "All right."

They started toward the house.

"You up for visiting JJ and the babies?" he asked, needing something to do that didn't involve stalking Archer and Atticus, waiting for information that would likely take a couple of days to compile.

"Great idea."

Yes, it was.

SLADE DID NOT LIKE THE FACT THAT he was assigned the fucking statue case.

More than that, he did not like the fact that Atticus was currently closed up in a room with Archer. Sure, he could see them through the glass, but were they even talking about the case? Or were they chatting it up like new partners do? Getting to know each other, sharing war stories.

Shaking his head, Slade tried to dislodge the insane jealousy. It wasn't warranted. Atticus hadn't done anything that would make him think the guy was cheating.

So why the fuck couldn't he stop obsessing?

Thankfully, his phone rang, distracting him, if only for a moment. He glanced at the screen, saw it was Ethan.

"Hey, man," Slade greeted.

"I talked to Braydon. He said he might have some information for you."

"Why didn't he call me himself?"

"He's on a job, can't get away. Said to meet him at the diner at one. That's the earliest he can get away."

Slade glanced at his watch. It was noon.

"Will do."

"Talk atcha later," Ethan said before hanging up.

He had an hour to sit there and obsess over Atticus looking all chummy with his new partner, or he could get out of the building for a little while. It really was a no-brainer.

An hour later, Slade was standing by his truck in the diner parking lot, keeping an eye out for Braydon's truck. The guy was already five minutes late, and Slade had to wonder whether he was being stood up.

To be fair, he couldn't care less about the damn statue. So what if someone stole the fucking thing? They could get a new one if it mattered that much to them.

He pulled out his phone and glanced at the screen to once again check the time. The next thing he knew, he was pulling up the text thread he had with Carson and Atticus, looking to see if there was anything new. There wasn't. He knew that. But he looked anyway and that pissed him off.

His thoughts instantly went back to last night when the three of them had collapsed in his bed after one of the best orgasms Slade had ever had in his life. He could still hear Atticus's and Carson's voices in his head, ruining what he thought was the start of something incredible.

This is good, huh?

Damn good.

I think we should do more of this.

Yeah?

Definitely. Let's just keep it casual from here on out. Just fucking.

Then the guy had the audacity to ask him if he was okay with that. What was Slade supposed to say? *No, I'm not. I'd prefer we run down to the courthouse and get married.* He'd wanted to say that, but instead, he had agreed because what else could he say?

Casual sex with Atticus and Carson. He was *not* okay with that, dammit.

A honk sounded, snapping his attention up from his phone. Slade saw Braydon's big black Ford pulling in and appreciated the guy pulling his mind out of the gutter.

Slade waited for Braydon to park, then walked over.

"Hey, man," Braydon greeted, hopping out of his truck. "Thanks for meetin' me. I'm just runnin' in to grab a to-go order."

Slade fist-bumped his cousin when Braydon reached him.

"Ethan said you found somethin'."

Braydon's face split into a shit-eating grin. "You're not gonna like it."

"Then why're you smilin'?"

"Because it's kinda genius."

Frowning, Slade waited for Braydon to continue.

"It's definitely a prank. A good one. I'm just glad your mama got Brantley involved and not the police."

"Why's that?"

"Yeah, the kids stole the statue, but they didn't deface it. From what I hear, it's in the exact same shape as when they took it."

"So why take it?"

"They're plannin' to relocate it."

"To?"

Braydon paused, his grin huge. "I really think you should just go to the homecoming game tonight to see it for yourself."

Frowning, Slade stared at his cousin.

"Look. I agree, it was overkill to take the statue," Braydon explained. "I don't think they'd thought it through when they did. Call it spur-of-the-moment stupidity, or simply opportunity. They took it and they plan to bring it back unharmed."

"Who?"

Braydon canted his head. "Now you know I can't tell you that."

"Seriously?"

"Seriously, man." Braydon's expression sobered. "Just go to the game tonight. See for yourself."

Clearly he wasn't getting anywhere with Braydon. He should've known one of the reigning high-school-prank-kings would protect whoever took the statue.

Again, not that Slade really gave a damn.

"So, will we see you tonight?" Braydon asked, backing away.

Slade nodded. "We're havin' dinner with my folks before the game, so yeah, probably."

"Cool." Braydon offered a clipped salute before spinning on his heel and hurrying toward the diner.

Slade stood there, watching him go, trying to figure out what prank could possibly need them to steal the damn horse statue.

He came up with nothing.

Chapter Thirty-One

ATTICUS STOOD BACK AND STARED AT ONE of the electronic boards they'd relocated to the conference room. It'd taken almost two hours for them to get everything they needed transferred in with help from the team. Not that they'd required a whole lot. Two case boards, their laptops, a couple of notepads, some pens, their desk chairs—because they were more comfortable—and chargers for phones and computers.

Becs had assisted in ensuring they had all the files allocated to this particular case, rearranging per his request so that they made more sense. At the moment, there were a dozen folders on the screen, all containing bits and pieces of information that were supposed to lead them to answers.

Atticus feared they had a long road ahead of them.

"Where do we start?" he asked his partner when Archer got to his feet and walked around the table to join him.

"I think a timeline is key," Archer answered, staring at the screen. "And let's identify the key players. We know we've got a couple of FBI agents, plus now there's Decker. If we can start from the beginning and work forward, we'll know what questions to start asking."

"Works for me."

With that, they started going through the data, rearranging even more as they went along. Their starting point was with Meredith Prescott and Decker Bromwell in 1998. Atticus wasn't sure how, but Luca had managed to find some of the incriminating photos that were in the FBI's clutches. As soon as Atticus realized what they were, he made a mental note to never open that file again.

In 2003, the FBI opened a RICO case, looking to take down the Southern Boy Mafia. Archer had noted who the agents assigned to the case were, as well as some details that, again, Luca had uncovered.

As for Meredith Prescott supposedly witnessing Max Adorite kill a man in August of 2004, the only thing they had to go on was Decker's statement and the newspaper article that had been published about it. Oddly enough, the article hadn't been published by a reputable newspaper such as the *Dallas Morning News* or the *Fort Worth Star-Telegram,* or even in the *Dallas Observer.* That made the information suspect in Atticus's mind, which he figured was what prompted Holt to lean toward conspiracy.

In 2005, Meredith Prescott walked away from her life, leaving her children and husband behind. JJ had found a list of credit cards and bank accounts she had at the time and noted that a withdrawal of $10,000 was made just before she left, which made sense because none of the credit cards were ever used after that point. She clearly wanted to be off the grid.

Atticus noticed that as they worked, more data was coming in from Luca and JJ. They seemed to be following the same timeline, confirming the information and providing detailed backup.

The following ten years were pretty scarce on data, but in July 2015, Samuel Adorite, the head of the Southern Boy Mafia, was killed. There was some information speculating that Max killed his father to take over, and spottier information that claimed Samuel's wife, Genevieve, killed him. At that time, Maximillian Adorite stepped in as the acting boss of the Adorite Crime Family.

While they outlined, Archer started adding questions on the second board. Atticus skimmed over them, thinking of his own. When he had one, he asked so that Archer would add it to the list.

By the time they reached 2018, when notes from Luca stated that Meredith Prescott was suspected of living in Massachusetts, it was after five.

Taking a break, Atticus walked out of the conference room to find that everyone else had left for the day. He figured Luca had to be working from home since he was still pushing data their way.

After a quick trip to the restroom and a pass back through the kitchen to get two bottles of water, Atticus made his way back to the conference room, leaving the door open since they had the barn to themselves.

"You game to push through?" Atticus asked, setting one of the water bottles in front of Archer, who was sitting at the table, typing on his computer.

"Absolutely." He looked up. "What time is it?"

"About that time," Atticus joked. "A little after five."

Archer stretched his arms over his head, then cracked his neck. "Why don't we order dinner?"

"I'm game," he told him, pulling out his phone.

"I've got it," Archer said. "What sounds good?"

"Anything." And that much was true. He was starving. After the day they'd had … hell, after the past few days, Atticus felt like he was running on empty. The thought of sitting down and hashing out some of this case work sounded about perfect.

They agreed on Chinese, which Archer ordered through one of the food delivery apps. While they waited, they walked through the timeline again, discussing what little bit of information they had.

"I'm tellin' you, if I never see pictures of two people naked again, it'll be too soon," Atticus said, shuddering at the thought of the images of a teenage Decker and his teacher.

Archer laughed. "I'm with you there. But now there's proof that it happened."

"I would've gladly taken Decker's word for it," Atticus said with a laugh.

Someone cleared their throat from behind him. Atticus turned to see Slade standing in the doorway, glaring at them.

"Hey. I thought you left for the day," he told Slade, stepping away from the case board.

"We're supposed to be at my parents' house havin' dinner," Slade said, his tone harsh.

"Shit." Atticus set his water bottle on the table. "Sorry, man. I totally forgot."

"Forgot? Or just didn't give a shit?" Slade accused, his gaze shifting to Archer. "Too busy laughin' it up with him?"

"Don't be like that," Atticus said, his good mood turning sour quickly.

"Be like what?" Slade snapped.

Before he could embarrass him more, Atticus pushed Slade back, out of the conference room. "Outside. Now."

"What? You don't want him to hear that—"

Atticus cut him off with another shove toward the door.

"Seriously, Slade? This is where we work."

"Where we're *supposed* to work," Slade argued. "Looks to me like—
"

"The fuck it does," Atticus bit out, cutting him off. "You've got to stop this shit. You know good and damn well that I'm workin'. Nothin' else. Archer is my partner."

"Maybe he shouldn't be," Slade said, eyes narrowed. "Maybe you should ask Reese to reassign you."

Atticus flinched back, surprised. "What?"

"Ask Reese to reassign you," Slade repeated.

"What the fuck for?"

"Let Archer work with Evan. You can partner with me."

"Slade, be serious."

"What? You don't want to partner with me?"

"No, I don't," he told him.

If he'd slapped Slade across the face, he probably wouldn't have looked as pained as he did right then.

Figuring it was a good time to explain, Atticus toned down his anger and took a step closer. "Look. We live together and work together. I think it's safe to say that partnering would be pushin' it a bit."

"Brantley and Reese do it, why can't we?" Slade countered.

While Atticus didn't agree that the partner thing worked like that all the time, he couldn't argue because Slade had a point.

"It obviously works for some people. But not everyone. And I happen to like comin' home and listening to you talk about your day. If we were partners, I wouldn't get that."

Slade's eyebrows unknotted, his expression losing some of the harsh lines. "For real?"

"Yes." Atticus took a breath, let it out, grateful they'd avoided a nuclear meltdown.

"Do you mean that?"

Atticus wished he knew what set Slade down this path of intense insecurity. Someone had done a number on him at some point.

"Of course I do."

At least he wanted to. At the moment, Atticus was having serious doubts about where this was going. He thought Slade was on the same page with the casual thing. He'd said he was. But here, now... That little explosion said otherwise. He wished he could say this was out of character for Slade, but the guy was prone to intense highs and devastating lows. And the jealousy ... it seemed to manifest, growing in intensity with each encounter.

Taking a deep breath, Atticus stood tall. "I'm sorry about dinner. I honestly forgot."

"I get it. We can head over there now."

Atticus glanced back at the barn. "I can't. Archer and I need to keep pushing on this. Brantley's waiting for a timeline. We're making real progress."

"I'll help."

"Not yet," he said, realizing he'd said it too quickly. "And it has nothin' to do with Archer. Brantley wants us fully focused, and while I appreciate your offer, it would be … too distracting."

Yeah, he might've tacked on a little glimmer in those words.

Slade's gaze perused his face. "Distracting how?"

"If I have to spell it out for you, then maybe you weren't there last night."

That worked. A spark of heat flashed in Slade's eyes.

"Oh, I was there all right."

Atticus couldn't deny that thinking about it was all it took to cause his cock to twitch and swell. Last night had been incredible.

"Maybe we'll get to round two when I get home," Atticus offered.

Slade nodded, more of the tension easing from his shoulder. "All right." He looked down. "I'll tell my folks you got hung up with work."

"Raincheck, for sure."

Slade took a step back. "Yeah."

"I'll see you when I get home," Atticus told him.

"Okay." He started to turn, then turned back. "I'm gonna go to the homecoming game. My mother'll want to be there. Plus, my cousin told me the statue will turn up before the game. I want to make sure it does."

Atticus exhaled his relief. "That's fantastic. A prank?"

"That's what he claims."

"You'll have to tell me about it when I get home."

Slade nodded, shoving his hands in his pockets. He looked disappointed, and Atticus couldn't really blame him. While he didn't particularly want to have dinner with Slade's parents—he wasn't sure they were at that point yet—he had committed, and this felt a lot like backing out on purpose.

Atticus waited until Slade turned away. He continued to wait, watching until Slade's truck pulled out of the lot. When he tapped in his code to get back in the barn, he figured he should come up with something to explain. Unfortunately, he wasn't sure how, since this wasn't the first time Archer had witnessed Slade's inexplicable reaction to Atticus talking to another guy. A co-worker at that.

Then again, Atticus didn't really understand it himself.

WHEN ATTICUS RETURNED, ARCHER TURNED TO LOOK at him, purposely shifting focus to what they were working on. He understood all too well that feeling of being put on the spot to come up with excuses. He preferred to bypass that part of the evening. For both their sakes.

"Luca provided some information on Allison Bogart."

Atticus looked surprised and relieved to have a topic other than whatever had just happened between him and Slade, so he kept going.

"He did a deep dive on her." Archer tapped the screen, pulling up the full dossier. "She was born and raised in Dallas. Graduated halfway through her senior year, went straight to Texas State University in pursuit of a degree in criminal justice. She was twenty-four and armed with a master's degree and two years of experience interning with the FBI Forensic Science Research Lab when she went to work full time for the FBI."

Atticus moved closer. "Looks like she was a real go-getter."

"You'd think that, right? More like Martin Calloway moved her up the ladder because he had another agenda."

"Why would he do that? Why her?"

"I assume because of this." Archer zoomed in on a section outlining Allison's upbringing. "Her mother is the illegitimate daughter of Stewart Crawford, the big oil tycoon."

"I've heard of him," Atticus said. "Up in Dallas."

"Correct. Back in 2012, Stewart's legitimate son, Stephen, was arrested for blackmailing government officials in order to protect his father's company. They were racking up a lot of violations for illegal drilling and whatnot."

"What'd he blackmail them with?"

"There's not much to go on, but I found this." He tapped the screen to bring up an article written by McKenna Thorne. "Allegedly, he had a list of people who were members of a private fetish club. They called it The Club at Club Destiny."

"Not very creative."

Archer laughed.

"Was there a list?"

"Not that I can find. Coincidentally—or maybe not—Luke McCoy, the owner of the club, shut it down right around that time."

"Sounds suspicious, but okay. How does Allison play into this?"

"Like Decker said, Martin's an equal-opportunity blackmailer. It looks like he threatened to prove that Allison's mother and father played a part in Stephen's crimes."

"I thought you said Big Oil Daddy didn't claim her."

"He didn't. But he set her up financially. My guess is, Martin followed the money and latched onto the opportunity."

"I thought Martin was responsible for organized crime. How'd he go down this path?"

"Unknown at this time."

Atticus nodded, staring at the screen. Archer gave him a moment to let it all sink in.

"What about this?" Atticus pointed to a name on the screen. "It says Allison's father worked in construction. Why do you have a star by this?"

"That just happens to be owned by one of many shell companies tied to the Adorites."

"So her dad worked for the Adorites?"

"I don't think that was how it started. I figure Calloway forced him into the business. Another way to get dirt on the Adorites."

"Ah. Okay. But if he's got his claws in her dad, why bring her in? Was it a convenient career path?"

"Not exactly." Archer turned to face Atticus. "Allison Bogart was on a path to Juilliard."

"That's the music school, right?"

"Performing arts, yes."

He walked over to his computer and pressed play. Music came from the speakers, filling the room.

"Is that her?" Atticus asked, coming to stand beside him.

Archer turned the laptop so Atticus had a better view of the young girl sitting at the piano, her fingers working magic on the keys. "From what I've read, she was a child prodigy."

"Wow. She's impressive. I mean, I don't know the first damn thing about the piano, but it sounds like she knows what she's doing.."

Archer chuckled.

Atticus's eyebrows darted down as he stared up at the case board. "How does a pianist go from that"—he pointed at the computer, still playing one of her performances—"to criminal justice?"

"With the help of one Martin Calloway. It's all speculation at this point, but it looks like he wasn't satisfied with simply getting his hands on the mom and dad."

"That's a serious new low for this asshole. He took a young girl with a gift and turned her into what? His personal chess piece?"

Archer liked the analogy. "I think that's exactly what he did."

Atticus propped a hip on the table. "I guess the question I have is, why didn't Martin Calloway take down the Southern Boy Mafia already? With so many chess pieces, it should've been a ringer for him, no?"

That was a damn good question. One Archer didn't have an answer for.

"Decker said Allison was a…" Atticus snapped his fingers. "Some kind of specialist."

"Surveillance," Archer supplied.

"Right. That means she watches people?"

"Looks that way."

"Decker said she reached out to him. Do we have the timeframe on that?"

"Not yet." Archer went back to the case board and pulled up the timeline. "Based on everything else, I'm going to assume it was sometime between when she started with the FBI in 2015 and September 2021, when the task force hired her."

Atticus walked up to the board, pointed to a date. "You have pictures of her at the funeral in January 2021, so she was surveilling them at that point. It probably wasn't a coincidence that she applied to join the task force."

"Doubtful. I figured that was the next step when Meredith didn't show at the funeral. Baz has notes stating Allison worked with them on one case as a probationary member, but she disappeared before they solved it."

"Clearly not invested," Atticus muttered, staring at the screen.

Archer's phone buzzed. "That's the food. I'll walk out and get it. Be back in a sec."

When he returned, he found Atticus sitting at the table, staring at his phone.

"Everything okay?"

"Probably not," he muttered before looking up and shaking his head. "It's all good."

Not wanting to pry, Archer proceeded to pass the food out before taking his seat. They ate in silence for a few minutes when Archer felt the need to clear the air.

"I just want you to know, I won't pry. Your business is your business. I'm sure you'll see plenty of my business the longer we work together."

Atticus chewed and nodded.

"But if you ever wanna bounce shit off me, I've been accused of bein' a good listener."

Atticus grinned. "It's a fucking mess, that's all I know."

"Relationships aren't easy," he said, keeping his eyes on his food so Atticus didn't feel the need to keep talking.

"It's a new thing. Me and Slade. And Carson." Atticus grabbed his water. "Three of us tryin' to make somethin' work. And those two ... they've got history. Not the good kind. And now I'm in the middle. By choice. I thought it'd be fun, but it's getting complicated fast."

Archer couldn't hide his reaction. He lifted his head, surprised by the information.

"It doesn't help that I live with Slade. Roommates. That became a thing after we ... you know." Atticus waved a hand. "Now I'm kinda stuck. I think Slade'll get over himself. Or maybe he won't. Fuck, I don't know. But I don't have time for it right now."

Still staring, Archer noticed the instant Atticus realized he'd been on a rant.

"Oh, shit." Atticus shot up from his seat. "I can't ... Fuck me. I'm sorry. I don't know what the hell I was thinking."

"I'll say it again." Archer kept his tone even. "Relationships aren't easy."

Atticus stared at him. A slow smile began to creep across his face. "Shit. I really am sorry."

"Don't apologize. If we're partners, we'll pick on things in each other's lives. It's natural."

"Yeah?"

Archer nodded.

Atticus sat down. "Okay then."

They continued to eat for a few minutes. Again, Atticus spoke up first.

"What about you? In a relationship?"

Archer thought about Spencer and the argument they'd had last night. "Can't say that I am."

"Well, when you are, I'll listen if you pop your cork and spew all your shit all over the table."

Archer barked a laugh, nearly snorting water out of his nose. "That's a deal."

It took a few minutes in complete silence for them to finish eating.

"You want coffee? Or there's some Ghost energy drinks," Atticus asked, gathering up the empty containers.

"I wouldn't say no to a Ghost."

When Atticus slipped out, Archer walked around the table and perched on the edge, staring at the timeline they'd developed. It wasn't all-inclusive (not yet), but it had enough information that it seemed wise to consider that Holt was on to something. There were definitely signs of a conspiracy.

Atticus returned a minute later with two cans. He passed one over as he stood beside Archer, also staring at the screen.

Gesturing forward with his drink, Atticus said, "Luca mentioned Censorious or somethin' like that."

"Yup." Archer stood, tapped the back button on the screen, and located the folder Atticus referred to. He opened it and clicked on the first file.

"Censorious," Atticus read, "is a group of vigilantes, consisting of civilians and law enforcement who see themselves as upholders of justice. First operational in ... holy shit. 1957. Really?"

"They split several times over the years, but they always seem to come back together."

"How many members?"

"Close to two thousand at last count," Archer answered.

"All working for the greater good."

Archer snorted. "The problem with groups like that is it's perceived justice. They often pervert the law in order to get the result they want."

"Not to mention, it morphs, right?" Atticus asked. "They can lose sight of what they intended to stand for because the power they wield becomes an addiction."

"They can, yes."

"I watch TV," Atticus said with a chuckle. "So my view is based on fiction."

"Fiction or otherwise, it's all the same. They have an end goal, and they bastardize their original beliefs to obtain their objective."

"Do we have a list of members?"

Archer flipped back to the folder, scanned the list of documents. "I don't see one yet."

Atticus set down his can and grabbed the notepad with their running list. "I'll make a note to get that."

Chapter Thirty-Two

SLADE SAT AT HIS PARENTS' DINING ROOM table, picking at the food in front of him. He'd been looking forward to his mother's meatloaf all afternoon, but his appetite had disappeared about the time he saw Atticus laughing it up with Archer. More so when Atticus backed out of dinner at the last minute.

He should've expected it. That was the way things went for him. Every time he found someone he was interested in, they turned out to be more interested in someone else. His ex-wife had turned her attention to plenty of other men, including Slade's own brother. Carson had latched on to every guy he wanted Slade to fuck. And it looked as though Atticus was doing the same.

"You goin' to the game tonight?" his mother asked, pulling him from his thoughts.

Grateful for the distraction, Slade pushed his plate away. "Yeah. I think I'll head over there now, in fact."

She frowned as she glanced at the clock on the wall. "It's not for another hour and a half."

"I know. I heard a rumor that the statue's gonna end up there." He placed his napkin on the table and pushed his chair back. "Thanks for dinner."

When he reached for his plate to take it to the sink, his mother put a hand on his arm to stop him. "I've got it."

"You sure?"

She nodded. "Go on. Tell Atticus I'm sorry he couldn't make it."

"I will," he lied. "Later, Dad."

His father waved him off, his full attention on shoving food in his face.

Fifteen minutes later, Slade pulled into the school's parking lot. It was halfway full already. Cars and trucks of players and staff were scattered throughout. It wouldn't be long before the buses from the rival school joined them, along with families and friends.

To keep from thinking about Atticus and what the man was doing with Archer, Slade got out of his truck and made his way toward the football field. They hadn't set up to take tickets yet, so he managed to slip inside, making his way around the bleachers on the home team's side.

That was as far as he made it when he came up short, a smile sliding into place.

"Holy shit."

There was the life-size bronze statue dressed like an orchestra conductor, complete with black pants, a white shirt, a bowtie, and a blonde wig, facing a makeshift stage that had been set up between the two sets of bleachers. He had to give the kids credit, they hadn't done any damage to the statue—that he could tell—nor had they interfered with the team's ability to play the game tonight.

He moved closer, taking in what looked to be dozens of smaller statues positioned in a semicircle, each sporting a small bowtie and posed with a miniature version of an instrument. When he was close enough, Slade noticed the small statues weren't bronze, but rather 3D printed. As were the instruments.

Behind the miniature orchestra, a banner had been strung up, hooked to the bleachers. It read: HAPPY RETIREMENT! WE'RE GONNA MISS YOU, MRS. TANNENBAUM.

If he recalled correctly, Mrs. Tannenbaum was the band teacher.

"A lot of effort just to say goodbye, huh?"

Slade glanced back, saw his cousin Braydon walking toward him. "That's an understatement."

"Did you know she's been the CRHS band teacher for thirty years?"

He hadn't known that. But he had known that she was a favorite of many of the students, past and present.

Braydon stopped beside him. "If it were me, I would've added a bunch of chocolate bars—with almonds—and scattered them around on the ground." He looked over, smiled. "Horse shit."

Slade shook his head. "Of course you would." He took it all in again, pausing for a moment before he said, "Or maybe Tootsie Rolls."

Braydon stared at him for a second before he barked a laugh. "Or Tootsie Rolls."

Smiling, Slade admired the bronze statue, the tailored clothing that the kids had clearly spent time on. "They could've done this in front of the school. Then they wouldn't've had to move the statue."

Braydon chuckled. "Too easy."

"Exactly my point."

"And that's why you're not the reigning king of pranks at this school."

"But you are."

Braydon grinned.

Slade studied his cousin, meeting his gaze. That was when he saw it. "This was your doing."

His cousin huffed a laugh. "I can't take all the credit. The kids came up with it. We just helped to make it happen."

"We? Did Brendon help?"

Braydon shrugged.

"What about Ethan?"

"I'll never tell."

He didn't have to. That wicked grin said it all.

WHILE SLADE, ALONG WITH A LARGE PORTION of Coyote Ridge, watched the CRHS football team go on to beat their rivals in the homecoming game, Archer spent several more hours going over the data with Atticus. They compiled the information that continued to trickle in from Luca, JJ, and Becs, who'd started researching as soon as her daughter went to bed. Or so Atticus informed him.

Archer ignored several texts from Simon. He knew the man wanted to know where they stood. He fully intended to tell him and to ensure he received all the data they had, but for the moment, he was working for the task force. As an official team member, he had to put them first. Simon would understand. Hopefully.

It wasn't until he was rubbing his eyes and heard Atticus yawning that he looked at the time.

"It's almost two." A heavy yawn escaped him. "How'd that happen?"

Atticus looked at his watch as he leaned back, stretching. "Time flies when you're havin' fun."

Before Archer could suggest they call it a night, his gaze snagged on some information on his computer screen. He'd been going through Holt's notes, trying to decipher fact from fiction, so he wasn't exactly sure what he was looking at. He leaned forward and read it again.

"Hey, uh … Atticus?"

"Hmm?"

Archer leaned back, pointed at his screen. "You should look at this."

Atticus got up, stretching his arms across his chest as he walked over. When he stopped, he leaned over Archer's shoulder to read the screen.

As Archer expected, he heard Atticus gasp.

A second later, he clamped a hand on Archer's shoulder. "Is that real?"

"I have no idea."

"Holy shit. That's … holy shit."

Yeah. Archer was thinking along those lines.

When Atticus stepped back, Archer peered over. "What should we do with that?"

"Take it to Brantley and Reese," he blurted.

"It's almost two in the mornin'," he reminded Atticus, who again looked at his watch.

"Maybe we … um … wait until morning? They get up early."

"How early?"

"Dawn."

Well, that was definitely early. And only a few hours away. Plus, Archer got the feeling Brantley and Reese would want this information ASAP. Hell, he wasn't sure how Holt had managed to keep this to himself. No way had he forgotten about it.

He glanced at the screen again, wondering if Simon knew. Surely he did. He'd been through the data ad nauseam. Or so he'd said.

Atticus stepped back. "Until then, I say we catch a nap."

"You headin' home?" Archer asked, forcing himself to look away from the computer. He got to his feet and felt the impact of the past few hours in the twinges of his muscles.

Atticus looked out into the main area of the barn. "No. If I do, I'm sure I'll oversleep. I think I'll grab a couple of hours on the couch."

"Since there aren't two and not one long enough for me to fit on, I guess I'll—"

"There's a leather one in the loft. Full sofa. I think it's even got a fold-out bed. I know JJ's slept on it before. So has Baz. He's not as tall as you, but…"

"I could do a full-size couch," he said, not sure if that was true, but willing to find out if it meant not having to leave. He knew the information they'd uncovered was something Brantley would want immediately. If it were before midnight, he would've walked over and knocked on the door. At this point, it would just be rude.

"Cool." Atticus returned to his computer, leaned over, and typed something.

"I'll set an alarm. Three hours. No more, no less."

Atticus nodded curtly, smiled, then walked out of the room. Before Archer reached the stairs up to the loft a few minutes later, he heard the guy snoring.

Three hours.

That was more than enough time to recharge.

Chapter Thirty-Three

Saturday, October 1, 2022

Brantley woke to Reese nudging his shoulder.

"Hmm?"

"Atticus just called," Reese's voice was low and deep, thick with sleep. "He wants us to meet them at the barn."

He didn't bother opening his eyes. "What time is it?"

"Not quite morning."

Not sure what that meant, Brantley grabbed his phone from the nightstand. He squinted at the screen. 04:41.

No, not quite morning.

"They found something," Reese added.

That was enough to pique Brantley's interest. "What?"

"Didn't say. But they worked almost all night."

He knew he'd picked the right two for this case.

"I told him to give us a few minutes."

"Can we get coffee first?" he asked, sitting up and swinging his legs over the side of the bed.

"Atticus already started a pot."

"He's a good kid," Brantley noted, smiling.

Fifteen minutes later, armed with coffee, Brantley stood in the conference room and skimmed the timeline on the case board. He had to admit, they did good work. Quickly, at that. It didn't quite tell a compelling story, but it tied the information they had together so that it made a modicum of sense.

"Where do you go from here?" Reese asked, addressing Archer and Atticus.

Brantley turned in time to see the two men share a look.

"What was that?" He gestured between them.

"We … um … found something we think you should see."

"Something more than that?" He nodded toward the case board.

"Yeah," Atticus drawled as Archer turned his computer screen toward them.

"What am I lookin' at?" he prompted, leaning forward and squinting to read the tiny print.

"That's the question of the hour," Atticus said.

Brantley frowned.

"What is this?" Reese asked, sounding as shocked as Brantley felt.

"We don't know exactly," Archer explained. "We were going through more of Holt's notes and saw it. Figured you'd want that information before we started digging further."

Brantley stood tall, looked at Reese. He felt his blood pressure rise, anger simmering in his bloodstream.

"Holt needs to explain," Reese said quickly, clearly detecting that Brantley was dangerously close to detonation.

"He's on the way," Archer added. "I called Simon at the same time Atticus called you. Told him to get Holt and head over."

As though it was planned, the monitor beeped, signaling motion detected on one of the cameras.

"They're here," Atticus told them. "I'll open the door."

Brantley set his coffee mug down, no longer needing the caffeine jolt. He felt as though he was attached to a live wire as it was.

It wasn't until Reese put a firm hand on his arm that Brantley realized he was seething.

"Give them a chance to explain."

Brantley stared at him as though he'd grown another head. "For fuck's sake. What is there to explain?"

"We don't know what it means. It could be fictional crap for his book."

He could tell Reese didn't truly believe that.

"Breathe," Reese said firmly, giving his arm a squeeze. "Let him explain."

Brantley inhaled slow and deep, forcing himself to calm down enough to have a civil conversation. How long that would last was anyone's guess. It was enough to stop him from slamming Holt up against the wall the moment he stepped into the barn.

"We've got some questions about information we found," Archer explained, speaking directly to Holt as soon as he stepped into the barn.

He had to give the guy credit. He wasn't smiling, so either Archer forewarned him, or Holt had been expecting this. Either way, Brantley wanted fucking answers.

"Is it true?" Reese asked, his tone far calmer than Brantley felt. "Do you really believe that crap about…?"

Evidently, Reese wasn't holding it together as well as Brantley thought. The man's sentence trailed off, disbelief glittering in his eyes.

It said something that Holt didn't even have to ask what they were referring to.

"I do," Holt said, his tone reflecting his conviction.

"That's fictional bullshit," Brantley accused, moving closer, facing off with Holt directly.

"But it's not." Holt took a deep breath. "I honestly believe there's a good possibility—"

Simon slapped a palm on Holt's chest, effectively shutting him up. He shook his head once, holding Holt's gaze.

"What?" Brantley asked.

Neither man spoke.

"Goddammit. Either you tell me what the fuck you were—"

"I'm not comfortable going there," Simon stated firmly, his gaze narrowed on Holt. "Yet."

"There?" Brantley stared between them. "Where's *there*?" He pointed toward Archer's computer screen. "Is that shit real?"

Holt blurted, "There's a possibility, yeah."

"God*damm*it, Holt," Simon bellowed.

Brantley's breath caught in his throat.

What.

The.

Fuck.

Before he knew what he was doing, he lunged at Holt, grabbing him by the shirt and slamming him against the wall.

Holt grunted, and Brantley's heartbeat thundered in his ears.

"I swear to God, if you start talkin' bullshit like that, my cousin's gonna bury you in the dirt himself."

Holt didn't attempt to shake him off, didn't even appear surprised.

"I know how it sounds." Holt's tone was quiet, even. "Trust me, I'm not grasping at straws."

Brantley shook him, then shoved back. "There's no fuckin' way."

"I didn't want to go this direction," Simon interjected. "Not yet, anyway. But when you look at it from a different perspective, I think you'll see what Holt's referring to." He held up a hand to stop Brantley from launching a tirade at him. "Doesn't mean he's right. But it wasn't until he shared this information with me that I realized just how big this story is."

Releasing Holt, Brantley took a step back. Then another and another until he had room to pace. He grabbed his head and walked, moving in the open area between desks.

It took a minute, but he managed to pull himself together. "There's a big fucking difference between a story and a life-changing revelation, Simon."

"I get it." Simon was placating him. "I honestly do. But trust me, I don't think it's something Holt pulled out of his ass."

"Thanks for that," Holt muttered.

"You're welcome."

"You said Holt told you. When?" Reese asked Simon. "When did he tell you this?"

Brantley spun around. "Tell me you didn't mention this to Travis. Fuck."

"I didn't," Simon stated. "Even if I'd known at the time, I wouldn't've said anything. Not without real evidence."

Brantley glanced over his shoulder, glaring at Holt. "I'll just wish you well now because once my cousin hears about it, you're as good as dead."

"Don't be dramatic," Holt said.

Brantley's grin was slow and menacing. If Holt thought he was kidding, he knew absolutely nothing about Travis Walker.

He could feel all eyes tracking him, and he could guess what they were thinking. That he was being dramatic. That he was overreacting. They were wrong.

This … information…

Jesus, God.

How the fuck was he supposed to spring this on Travis without risking losing a limb? Or at the very least, walking away with a black eye.

"I have to talk to Travis," Brantley told Reese. "We said we'd bring him up to speed if and when we had something. *This*"—he pointed at Archer's computer—"is something."

"I agree. We can call him, see if he can meet us somewhere."

Brantley shook his head. "I need to do this alone."

He could see the disappointment in Reese's gaze, but he also saw understanding.

"We'll hang here, then. Wait for you to get back."

Nodding, Brantley started for the door. When he reached it, he put his hand on it to open, but paused, not bothering to look back.

"I sincerely hope that you're certain about this. If I pass this along and I'm made to look like an idiot, there's gonna be hell to pay."

With that, he walked out the door.

TRAVIS SAT AT A BOOTH IN THE far back of the diner, watching the goings-on in front of him. This was the same booth he'd sat in when Holt revealed to him that he'd uncovered something about Kylie's mother. He'd been pissed at the time. Angry that someone would have the gall to interfere in his personal life. He'd thought the man was out of his mind.

That was a month ago, and he was still convinced that was the case.

Yet, here he was, gearing up to meet with Brantley to discuss something along those same lines.

According to the phone call he received from his cousin a short time ago, there was an update that couldn't wait. Travis doubted that was true. As far as he was concerned, it could all wait. Kylie was dead. There wasn't much that mattered in Travis's life anymore. His husband, his children. Family. That was all he had left and he no longer took them for granted.

Now here he was waiting for his cousin to show and spill whatever bullshit he'd learned about a woman no one fucking cared about. Kylie had detested her mother for what she'd done. Abandoning the family the way she had. Walking away without looking back. Hell, Meredith hadn't even shown up for her own daughter's funeral. What did it fucking matter that she might've been sent into hiding because she crossed a mob boss? No one gave a shit.

Should they? Maybe.

It was that doubt that had convinced him to let Simon Jennings look into the case. Or rather, why he'd given the man his blessing when he mentioned it. Truth was, Travis didn't care how it turned out.

At least that was what he told himself right up until he saw Brantley's face when he walked into the restaurant. The man looked … *spooked* was the first thought that came to mind. It was strange to see his cousin like that. The man was always so confident, so direct.

"Hey," Brantley greeted as he approached the table. "Thanks for meeting me."

"You said it was important."

Brantley exhaled as he sat across from him.

"Where's Reese?"

"At home. I told him I needed to do this alone."

Travis frowned. That was new. He thought Brantley and Reese were attached at the hip for as much time as they spent together. Newlyweds and all that.

The waitress swung by, but before she could say a word, Brantley waved her off.

"What did you need to tell me?" Travis prompted when Brantley sat there, staring at the table. "I've got things to do today."

Brantley's gaze lifted, blue-gray eyes clear. "As you know, we're lookin' into the circumstances of Meredith's disappearance. I've assigned Archer and Atticus to lead the investigation."

When Brantley paused, Travis fought the urge to get up and walk out the door. He didn't give a shit about any of this.

"They worked all night to put together a timeline that will allow us to start pursuing leads."

Again, he waited, his patience quickly dwindling.

"When they were going through Holt's notes, they found something. Something that … well, it sounds insane. So insane that I confronted Holt and Simon about it this morning. They assure me it's real."

Frowning, Travis leaned in. "What the hell are you tellin' me this for?"

Brantley took a deep breath, exhaled slowly. "I know you're not gonna believe this any more than I do, but…"

"Goddammit, Brant—"

"They've uncovered evidence—" Brantley shook his head, still holding his stare. "I honestly don't know how to say it."

"Just spit it out so we can move on with our lives."

"That's the thing. I don't think we can."

Confused, Travis pinned Brantley with a hard look. "Tell. Me."

The pause that ensued felt like it went on for years, but then Brantley opened his mouth and words began spilling out.

"They've uncovered evidence that leads them to believe Kylie's alive."

Words that didn't make a lick of sense.

Words that caused the Earth to stop spinning.

As those words sank in, Travis's entire existence tilted.

It. Fucking. Tilted.

Sending him off his axis for the second time in as many years.

Stay Tuned

Don't be mad. I know what I just did, and I'm sure you'd like to throttle me about now. I'll ask that you refrain. There is more to come for Brantley and Reese, JJ and Baz, Atticus, Archer, and yes, Travis and Gage.

A lot more.

Each book in this series is a full-length novel involving a new case and the continuation of the relationship between these two men. I promise not to keep you waiting long for each installment.

If you enjoyed *Missing Pieces*, please consider leaving a review.

—— ACKNOWLEDGMENTS ——

While writing is a solitary task, it's not a completely solo project. Because of that, I'd like to thank those who've assisted in one way or another.

As a side note, I received no compensation for these acknowledgments, so they are in no particular order.

Steven: The past couple of years have been a rollercoaster, but your patience and understanding have been my safety net. I also appreciate you whipping up my dinner and brewing my coffee. But let's be real, the coffee is the real MVP here!

Hennessy and Moscato (a.k.a. the high-maintenance golden retrievers who tell me what to do every day): How I got so lucky to have the two cutest dogs in the entire world, I do not know, but I am so incredibly grateful.

Chancy: I know you've got a lot going on right now, but I'm thankful you made time to read this book. And yes, I promise not to leave you hanging for too much longer.

Jenna: I'm really glad you didn't break your phone after reading this book. I know how much you love cliffhangers.

You, the reader: Thank you for your patience and understanding. It took me some time to get this book completed, and yes, I know it's not quite as complete as you would probably like. I intend to rectify that very, very soon. Oh, and thank you for reading, thank you for writing a review, and thank you for hopping on social media and telling your friends about the book. You're remarkable like that.

The Walker Family Tree

You can find the **Walker family tree** on Nicole's website.

www.NicoleEdwards.me

ABOUT NICOLE EDWARDS

New York Times and *USA Today* bestselling author Nicole Edwards spends her days stringing words together to make complete sentences. Sometimes not. Her best friend is coffee, and she has a love/hate relationship with sarcasm. She's been accused of having a filthy imagination, which she admits is true.

Nicole lives in the suburbs of Austin, Texas. She proudly claims one husband, three grown children, and two bosses (better known as the dogs). When she isn't writing, watching football or hockey, or keeping her bosses happy, you can probably find her with a book in hand.

Before you go!

Now that you've read one of my books, I'd like to think we can consider ourselves friends. And since friends usually hang out, I want to let you know where you can find me.

NIC NEWS: If you haven't signed up for my newsletter and want notifications regarding preorders, new releases, giveaways, sales, etc., then you'll want to sign up. I promise not to spam your email, just get you the most important updates.

RAMBLINGS OF A WRITER BLOG: My blog is used for writer ramblings, which I am known to do from time to time.

NICOLE NATION: Visit my website to get exclusive content you won't find anywhere else, including sneak peeks, A Day in the Life character stories, exclusive giveaways, cards from Nicole, or join Nicole's review team.

NICOLE NATION ON FACEBOOK: Join my reader group to interact with other readers, ask me questions, play fun weekly games, celebrate during release week, and enter exclusive giveaways!

INSTAGRAM: Basically, Instagram is where I post pictures of my dogs, so if you want to see epic cuteness, you should follow me.

NAUGHTY & NICE SHOP: Not only does the shop have signed books, but there's fun merchandise, too—plenty of naughty and nice options to go around. Find the shop on my website.

WEBSITE:	www.NicoleEdwards.me
FACEBOOK:	/Author.Nicole.Edwards
INSTAGRAM:	/NicoleEdwardsAuthor
TIKTOK:	/@nicoleedwardsauthor
BOOKBUB:	/NicoleEdwardsAuthor
GOODREADS:	/nicole_edwards

The Jamesons Of Coyote Ridge
Hot Chocolate Wishes
Rough & Dirty

Austin Arrows
Rush
Kaufman

Club Destiny
Conviction
Temptation
Addicted
Seduction
Infatuation
Captivated
Devotion
Perception
Entrusted
Adored
Distraction
Forevermore

Dead Heat Ranch
Boots Optional
Betting on Grace
Overnight Love
Jared (a crossover novel)

Devil's Bend
Chasing Dreams
Vanishing Dreams

Misplaced Halos
Protected in Darkness
Salvation in Darkness
Bound in Darkness

OFFICE INTRIGUE

Office Intrigue
Intrigued Out of The Office
Their Rebellious Submissive
Their Famous Dominant
Their Ruthless Sadist
Their Naughty Student
Their Fairy Princess
Owned

PIER 70

Reckless
Fearless
Speechless
Harmless
Clueless

PRIMAL INSTINCTS

Chase (Volume 1-3)
Capture (Volume 4-6)
Claim (Volume 7-9)

SNIPER 1 SECURITY

Wait for Morning
Never Say Never
Tomorrow's Too Late

SOUTHERN BOY MAFIA/DEVIL'S PLAYGROUND

Beautifully Brutal
Without Regret
Beautifully Loyal
Without Restraint

STANDALONE NOVELS
Unhinged Trilogy
A Million Tiny Pieces
Inked on Paper
Bad Reputation
Bad Business
Filthy Hot Billionaire

NAUGHTY HOLIDAY EDITIONS
2015
2016
2021